PRAISE FOR

MYSTERIA L[...]

"Fabulous paranormal tales of things that go bump in the night."
—*Romance Reviews Today*

"This super quartet of talent brings an off-kilter and humorous viewpoint to magic, romance, and daily life. Much fun."
—*Romantic Times*

MYSTERIA

"Splitting the difference between *Desperate Housewives* and *The X-Files*, this paranormal romance brings magic and monsters to the steamy suburbs in four satisfying novellas about the town of Mysteria. There's magic, heat, and lots of laughs."
—*Publishers Weekly*

"Charming, funny, and quite offbeat, this collection highlights the vast talents of these authors. The perfect escape read!" —*Romantic Times*

"Four enchanting paranormal romantic novellas."
—*Midwest Book Review*

"This [anthology] has all of the elements that I just love to read about. I had such fun reading this book. I really didn't want these stories to end. I loved the town of Mysteria and hope these authors see fit to visit the townspeople . . . again!"
—*The Best Reviews*

"*Desperate Housewives* meets *Charmed*, this collection of novellas is as varied in its content as the authors who've written them. From sweet and passionate to dark and sexy, the werewolves, vampires, demons, witches, fairies, and humans of *Mysteria* are as engaging and fun as they are diverse and compelling."
—*Fresh Fiction*

MYSTERIA NIGHTS

P. C. Cast
MaryJanice Davidson
Susan Grant
Gena Showalter

BERKLEY SENSATION, NEW YORK

THE BERKLEY PUBLISHING GROUP
Published by the Penguin Group
Penguin Group (USA) Inc.
375 Hudson Street, New York, New York 10014, USA
Penguin Group (Canada), 90 Eglinton Avenue East, Suite 700, Toronto, Ontario M4P 2Y3, Canada
(a division of Pearson Penguin Canada Inc.)
Penguin Books Ltd., 80 Strand, London WC2R 0RL, England
Penguin Group Ireland, 25 St. Stephen's Green, Dublin 2, Ireland (a division of Penguin Books Ltd.)
Penguin Group (Australia), 250 Camberwell Road, Camberwell, Victoria 3124, Australia
(a division of Pearson Australia Group Pty. Ltd.)
Penguin Books India Pvt. Ltd., 11 Community Centre, Panchsheel Park, New Delhi—110 017, India
Penguin Group (NZ), 67 Apollo Drive, Rosedale, Auckland 0632, New Zealand
(a division of Pearson New Zealand Ltd.)
Penguin Books (South Africa) (Pty.) Ltd., 24 Sturdee Avenue, Rosebank, Johannesburg 2196,
South Africa

Penguin Books Ltd., Registered Offices: 80 Strand, London WC2R 0RL, England

This is a work of fiction. Names, characters, places, and incidents either are the product of the authors' imagination or are used fictitiously, and any resemblance to actual persons, living or dead, business establishments, events, or locales is entirely coincidental. The publisher does not have any control over and does not assume any responsibility for author or third-party websites or their content.

PRINTING HISTORY
Berkley Sensation trade paperback edition / July 2011

Library of Congress Cataloging-in-Publication Data

Mysteria nights / P. C. Cast . . . [et al.].—Berkley Sensation trade pbk. ed.
    p. cm.
  ISBN 978-0-425-24173-8 (trade pbk.)
  1. Erotic stories, American.   2. Occult fiction, American.   I. Cast, P. C.
  PS648.E7M97 2011
  813'.087660806—dc22   2011013832

PRINTED IN THE UNITED STATES OF AMERICA

10 9 8 7 6 5 4 3 2 1

CONTENTS

Introduction

Once upon a time in a land closer than anyone might be comfortable with, a demon high lord was sent to destroy a small, starving (and, let's face it, weird) band of settlers who were fleeing the last town they'd tried to settle in (a place eventually known as Kansas City, Missouri, the Show Me State, which did indeed show them tar and feathers and the road west). The group was composed of magical misfits and outcasts: a bloodaphobic vampire, a black-magic witch and her white-magic husband, a pack of amorous (translation: hump-happy) werewolves, and a man named John, who had gotten confused and joined the wrong wagon train. When the demon spied this ragged, rejected bunch, he (for a reason known only to himself but which had to do with uncontrollable random acts of kindness) decided not just to spare them but to create a magical haven for them.

And so, nestled in a beautiful valley in the Rocky Mountains, the town of Mysteria was founded. Over the years, it became a refuge for creatures of the night and those unwanted by traditional society. No one—or thing—was turned away. Magic thrived, aphrodisiacs laced the pollen, and fairy tales came true.

The first settlers eventually died (those that weren't already dead or undead, that is), but they left pieces of themselves behind. The vampire invented a powerful blood-appetite suppressant for any other vampires with a fear of blood. The witch and the warlock created a wishing well—a wishing well that swirled and churned with both white and black magic, a dangerous combination. The hump-happy werewolves left the essence of perpetual springtime and love (translation: they peed all around the boundary of the city, so that everyone—

or thing—that entered or left Mysteria was, well, marked). John, the only nonmagical being in the group, left his confused but mundane genes, founding a family that would ultimately spawn more humans of nonmagical abilities who remained in Mysteria because finding their way out was just too much like geometry.

Each of the settlers thought, as their spirits floated to the heavens— all right, some of them went straight to hell, the naughty sinners—that their best contribution to the fantastical town of Mysteria was a happily-ever-after for their descendants. If only they could have known the events that would one day unfold . . .

MORTAL IN MYSTERIA

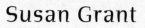

Susan Grant

For my three children:
Connor and Courtney (the human ones)
and Tala (the furry one).
All my love.

One

The dirty, sweat-soaked demon dropped to his knees. His hands, bound at the wrists with chains, rested awkwardly at the small of his back. Nevertheless, he formed his mouth into a smile he hoped appeared as contrite as his posture. *'Tis better if you do not infuriate the boss any more than you have already*, he thought. "I am prepared to pay for my transgressions, Master."

"And pay for them, you shall!" The Devil's forked tongue darted out to moisten thin, malice-curved lips. "I have thought long and hard about your crimes," he hissed with the very faintest of lisps. "Now, prepare to receive your sentence, Demon."

"Aye, Master." All the demons were named "Demon" down here in Hell. To their master they were all but indistinguishable. Only Lucifer stood apart, with his trademark black goatee, the horns, the pitchfork, and the crimson suit. Proof that the whimsies of fashion in Hell had been at a standstill since the birth of time.

Fashion? Hell's bells, didn't he have more important things to worry about? Like losing his head, or some other body part of which he'd grown fond? The demon winced. His concentration simply wasn't what it used to be after the century of torture he'd endured for his crimes. Or had it been two or three centuries that he'd been paying for his terrible deeds? It had become difficult to keep track. Ah, but what was an extra century or two in the grand scheme of things? He'd existed for more than ten thousand years, tasked to bring the worst sort of doubt into the miserable, pitifully abbreviated lives of human beings. Far from being just any demon, he was a demon lord, and one of the most ancient of them all: the Demon High Lord of Self-Doubt and Second Thoughts, the bane of many a human failure, simpering creatures all too eager to listen to the fears that he could so easily plant in their weak minds. *You can't,* he'd whisper until they believed it. *You won't. Try, and you will surely fail.*

Countless men who could have ruled the world had never stepped beyond their front doors because he'd made them doubt their abilities, made them afraid to take chances, to risk failure. Nor were women any safer from his dark murmurings through the eons. He'd frightened countless wenches, silencing their voices by playing up their fears of sounding too shrill, too stupid, too . . . different.

Humanity's failures—he'd been the force behind so many of them. Until that fateful day when he'd glimpsed true courage and couldn't bring himself to destroy it, giving the Will-to-Go-On to a small, starving band of settlers wandering in the snowy woods of the Rocky Mountains. He wasn't sure exactly why he'd spared them, why he'd given them the inner strength to push themselves until they reached warmth and shelter, but he had—and it had felt damned good, too. In fact, it had felt so damned good being good to the damned that he repeated the deed all around the globe, losing himself for years in a virtual frenzy of beneficence. That is, until he was finally caught redhanded in the midst of one of those random acts of kindness, a crime considered so heinous that Lucifer himself had marched upstairs and dragged him back down to Hell.

On the positive side, he'd come out the other side with all his body parts intact, the important body parts, at any rate. It could have gone much worse for him. And perhaps it still would. The devil, as always, was in the details.

The demon bowed his head. "Tell me what I must do to appease you, Master."

"There will be no appeasement! None! There is but one fitting punishment for such atrocities. Banishment!"

The demon's head jerked up. "Banishment?"

"Yes." The fiery red orbs that passed for Lucifer's eyes narrowed to pulsing slits. "I hereby banish you from Hell."

It cannot be! The demon had expected a reduction in rank, the loss of freedom to come and go as he pleased, perhaps, but permanent eviction? His salary, his benefits—*phoosh,* gone! Just like that. Hell's bells, he'd slaved ten thousand years—for nothing! Done the Devil's deeds only to end up like this: out of date, out of use, and without a transferable retirement plan!

"Is this truly to be forevermore?" the demon almost croaked, knowing how the Devil so enjoyed toying with his minions.

Lucifer chuckled. "Not really. I have made you mortal, as well."

"*Mortal . . .*" The mere word tangled around the demon's tongue like a serving of snake entrails.

"Never fear. Because of your newly finite life, you won't have many years to fret your fate. Consider it a favor for your years of service to the Dark Empire." Lucifer waved a clawed hand. "No need to thank me."

A growl rumbled in the demon's throat. Of all the many things he'd like to give Lucifer at that moment, thanks was not one of them. Yet, something told him it wasn't mortality itself he needed to fear as much as the locale in which he would suffer it. "Where am I to be sent?"

"Why, to the very epicenter of your initial act of kindness." Lucifer spat out that last word. Literally. A glob of moisture sizzled in one of the many fires burning deep within the bowels of the earth. "Mysteria. I trust you remember the place."

He remembered it, all right. Remembered it all too well. The settlers he'd helped had founded the village.

The demon shifted his weight on aching knees as he mulled over his options, which were near zero, as far as he could tell. Time was running out to reverse course, so he did what he did best and sowed the seeds of self-doubt. "Are you certain this is the best plan for me, Master? The best punishment? Are you absolutely sure?"

The Devil's voice turned deadly. "What do you mean?"

"What if it doesn't work out? What if they don't want me amongst them?" *You can't . . . you won't. Try, and you will surely fail. . . .* "Imagine it, the Demon High Lord of Self-Doubt and Second Thoughts living across the street, mowing the lawn. Coaching Little League?" The demon curved his lips into a between-us smile. "Absurd, is it not?"

Lucifer shrieked in incredulity. The sound of a thousand screams filled the chamber. Goblins and gargoyles somersaulted through the shadows, fleeing the chamber as a rumbling began under the cold stone slab of a floor. "Your dark magic does not work with me!"

"I'm merely suggesting that you look at all sides of the equation—"

But Lucifer continued to roar. Somewhere far above them, on the surface, the ground also shook. The demon half-wondered how many casualties there would be this time. But that was no longer his job. He'd been fired. He would no longer be tasked with planting defeat in the survivors' minds, riddling their psyches with despair. At that, something close to relief filtered through him. *Doing good has taken the fun out of doing evil.*

Aye, it had. The demon sensed he'd never be 100 percent good. Yet, neither could he ever return to being 100 percent bad.

Lucifer grew in size until he towered above the demon, his clothing splitting and hissing as muscled flesh bulged and tore it apart. Horns sprouted from a ridged skull, curling upward, until they, too, were lost in the swirling mist of the chamber. Finally, he spoke. "I do not doubt, fallen one. I do not err. I do not have *second thoughts*!"

That much was obvious. Couldn't Lucifer have made the point without all the needless death and destruction? Without the unneeded suffering? A growl vibrated deep in the demon's throat. He'd witnessed such showy outbursts many times during his long existence, but this time, for the first time, a reaction to the master's wrath formed inside the demon, as if he had a temper of his very own.

He made fists. It caused the manacles to bite into his wrists, pain he welcomed as a ball of heat swelled and exploded in his chest, a conflagration he couldn't recognize or explain, for he didn't have feelings. Never had. He couldn't have performed his duties if he'd been created any other way. And yet, he felt something now, aye, something too wonderful and terrible to absorb, a sensation too new and yet inexplicably ancient at the same time. The pressure built and built until something finally gave.

The demon gasped in shock. It was as if his very core had wrenched open, releasing all he carried within him. The vileness, the blackness, he realized. The evil.

For half a breath he was so frighteningly hollow, he wondered if he were about to implode; then into the vacuum rushed something so sweet, so indescribably wonderful, that he nearly sobbed. What was happening to him?

"I'm sorry," the demon whispered on a ragged breath. It was the only way to express what had boiled up inside him. "I am so very sorry. . . ."

"You don't look sorry," Lucifer hissed from high above.

The demon glared up at him. "Ah, but I am. Sorry for all the centuries of sowing doubt, of turning back those beings better than I. I am sorry for the evil I accomplished in your name. In fact, I hereby repent!" *Aye, take* that, *you gutless stinking mountain of dragon offal.*

"You . . . re-*what*?"

"I repent. R-e-p-e-n-t." Was that not an Aretha Franklin song? Or was he confusing his tunes? The demon gave his head a shake. There they went again, his thoughts wandering. One thing was certain, something had happened—*was* happening—inside him, and he was helpless to stop it.

To stop the emotion, sharp and pure, filling him with anger, resentment, shame at his past. And hope—hope despite the completely overwhelming odds against him. *Now you are just like the humans,* he thought.

"I ask forgiveness for all the deeds I ever did in the Dark One's name," he said quietly. "Aye, I truly do."

Lucifer's voice was deadly. "I never forgive. You should know this, my minion. You of all the demon high lords should know."

"It wasn't of you that I made my plea."

Lucifer's molten eyes pulsed and glowed, his fangs glinting in the cast-off light. "What?"

"You heard me." Angry now, the demon flicked his gaze upward—*heaven*ward—to make his point clear.

Only the fretful twittering of goblins interrupted the shocked, appalled silence. Then, a strange noise stuttered past Lucifer's parted lips. The demon marveled at that. It was the first time in all of history that he could remember hearing the Great Satan sputter.

Then, all hell broke loose.

Two jets of searing red lava shot out from the Devil's eyes and hit the slab where the demon crouched. Rocks exploded, pummeling him as he fell backward. The air was on fire, something that the demon should have been used to—Lucifer lost his temper often; they'd all been charred now and again—but this was different.

This was worse.

The demon spun in the center of a tornado, wrenched and torn in every direction, inside and out. He could no longer see or hear. And, after a blessed while, he could no longer feel the pain that wracked him.

Bathed in white light, he floated. *Is this what it feels like to die?* If so, perhaps he would not mind. But he knew, even as he tumbled into oblivion—or, rather, into the forested slopes of Colorado—that Lucifer would never let him get away as easily as that.

Two

In a clear, sweet voice, Harmony Faithfull concluded her Sunday service: "Now, go in peace and enjoy this beautiful day the Lord has given us."

The sound of her six-month-old puppy's tail thumping on the hardwood floor was all that broke the perfect silence.

"Thanks, Bubba." Harmony looked up from her handwritten sermon, which had taken all of ten minutes to read to the six rows of pews. Six rows of *empty* pews, lined up like abandoned soldiers on the pristine, knotty pine floor.

There should be scuffs marring those planks, she thought longingly, lost buttons in the corners, and crushed Cheerios. And under the pews, wadded-up Kleenex, handbags, and colorful hats . . .

Harmony sighed and neatened the lectern. "It's nice to know someone appreciated the homily today."

You're talking to the dog again.

"Yep. And when you're not talking to the dog, you're talking to yourself." Crossing her eyes, Harmony shut off the halogen reading lamp and the microphone. Sometimes, she wondered what she possibly could have been thinking—her, a city girl, relocating to Mysteria, a tiny hamlet in the Rockies, assuming she'd make churchgoers out of the locals here, who, um, weren't like any people she'd ever met anyplace else. There were supernatural happenings in the town, you couldn't miss them, really, and she had her suspicions that more than a few of the townsfolk had supernatural abilities. But God loved all creatures: great or small, good or bad, moral or immoral. Mortal or . . . ?

Harmony stopped that train of thought before it jumped the track. She was here because after two tours as an air force chaplain, she'd been looking for a new challenge. *It looks like you found it, girl. In spades.*

Six months ago, the church had been a tumbledown farmhouse with a barn on five overgrown acres. With the help of her father and brothers, she'd renovated the house, which now did double duty as a public place of worship and her personal living quarters, a cozy little home located in the back. She'd even stitched the white eyelet curtains herself in a spurt of delirious domesticity. Then her family had returned to Oakland, leaving her to grow her flock. Except that, aside from a few curious townspeople, no one had showed up.

Have some faith. Give it time.

Time . . . she had plenty of that lately.

Well, she'd simply have to drum up a little of the faith in herself that she'd always seemed to be able to drum up in everyone else. After all, she was Harmony Faithfull, the daughter of Jacob Jethro Faithfull IV, Oakland's most famous, and often infamous, but always ebullient, pastor of South Avenue Church. Daddy was a man who could fill football stadiums and concert halls with worshippers, who often traveled hundreds of miles to hear him speak. Charisma and the good word, it was a potent combination.

Harmony thumped her fist on the podium, and the puppy jumped. "It's in my genes," she said out loud. "I can't forget that. God sent me here because I have a job to do."

Bubba seemed to agree, a long pink puppy tongue draped over one side of his open mouth.

Harmony crumpled one of the sheets of lined paper she'd used for her sermon, crushed it in her fist, and aimed the ball of paper at the wastebasket across from the pulpit. It clipped the rim and spun inside. "Two points!"

She tapped a finger against her chin. "Maybe we can start an after-school basketball team. What do you think of that, Bubba-licious?" The puppy wagged his long black tail.

The idea of an after-school basketball team had worked for her father and some inner-city kids when he was fresh out of divinity school. The hoops had brought the children, and then the mothers, who'd dragged the fathers and the boyfriends, and within the year there was an entire community with Sunday potlucks and a fifty-two-member choir. Not that she could picture any of the O'Cleary great-grandkids shooting hoops, but it'd be a start. It was all about getting people through the door.

MYSTERIA COMMUNITY CHURCH. ALL FAITHS WELCOME. That last part she'd painted onto the sign as an afterthought when weeks had gone by and nary a lost soul tromped through the door. Well, save Jeanie Tortellini, the town sheriff, and sometimes Candice, the high school English teacher. They'd drop by to see how she was settling in, staying for chitchat and coffee but not the good word. But then, Harmony firmly believed everyone was welcome here, for whatever reasons they chose to come. If they preferred their so-called magic, fine, but Harmony's calling was to let them know God watched over them as well. As a child, her parents had taught her that a true heart excluded no one, and that the church was the heart of the village.

Except in Mysteria, where that honor was held by Knight Caps, the local bar.

Harmony sighed. How could she convince the townspeople to congregate here instead? At least on Sundays. What did she have that they couldn't find anywhere else? Well, besides the obvious, she thought with a vertical glance.

"God, I need your help. Show me how to fill up this church, and I'll do the rest. Please." Harmony squeezed her eyes shut and prayed. Prayed until her head throbbed and her eyes hurt. Prayed until she was all prayed out. And then she started wishing, plain old wishing, like you would on a four-leaf clover, or a star, because sometimes, even in matters of the spirit, and maybe *especially* in matters of the spirit, you just had to stack the deck. "Show me how to bring the townspeople here," she whispered. "Give me a sign." *I'm waiting, watching, eyes wide open, Lord.*

The floor rumbled. Was that the old furnace kicking on? No, it was warm today, too warm for the heater.

The earth moved again. Harmony frowned at her drinking glass still sitting on the podium. The water was rippling like San Francisco Bay on a windy day. No, the rumbling definitely wasn't from the furnace. It was coming from somewhere outside. Strange. Everyone knew a major fault line ran through Missouri. But Colorado?

One good jolt almost threw her to her knees. Then it was quiet.

Bubba started barking. In an instant, he'd transformed from drowsy puppy to barking, fur-covered projectile. Zero to sixty in 2.8 seconds, nails scrabbling for purchase on the hardwood, he flew out the front door.

"Bubba!" Grabbing the gauzy cotton of her skirt, Harmony hurried after the dog to the flower garden she'd planted near an ancient, gnarled apple tree. THE GARDEN OF EDEN, according to the ornamental iron garden sign that her sister Hope had mailed her as a housewarming gift. "Bubba! Bubba, come here!"

Three women jogged past on the road fronting the church. They were feminine confections coated in spandex, bling jingling, ponytails bouncing. One woman carried a broomstick gripped in her hand. Hmm, that was a little different, but maybe it was good for the arms. They waved, and Harmony, smiled, waving back. Now she remembered them—the Tawdry sisters. They had the most brilliant hazel eyes that almost seemed to glow. There was something else unusual about them, too, but Harmony couldn't place her finger on exactly what. But they, like the rest of the women in town, were always nice, if a little racy.

Black lace bra types, Harmony had dubbed them in private. Not meaning any disrespect. Her own sisters were black lace bra types. Not that Harmony had anything against a woman knowing her own charms or being confident about sex. God had never dissed procreation. In fact,

He encouraged it—within the context of a committed, monogamous relationship, of course. *Nothing you need to worry about, given your current state of isolation.*

"Ain't that the truth?" Harmony followed the puppy across the lawn. Birds chirped; bees buzzed. The sky was a pure, clear blue. And the sunshine, the scent of pine, she could almost taste it. Face lifted to the sun, she inhaled deeply and became so carried away by her appreciation of the outdoors that she swept right past the naked man who was the target of Bubba's frantic barking.

The naked . . .

. . . man?

Harmony froze, the skirt falling out of her hands. There was no naked man.

Oh, yeah? Then how do you explain the afterimage that just seared itself onto your retinas?

Heart thumping, Harmony whirled around. Yep, there was a man there, and he was most definitely naked, sprawled on his side among the flowers, one thick, muscled thigh thrown forward, the sunshine bouncing off his butt.

Three

Wow. Eyes wide, Harmony stood there, staring, rooted to the ground, as if her foot were locked in cement. She'd asked God to send her a sign. But she'd never expected anything like this! The best naked man she'd ever seen, she decided with no small amount of half-crazed, hormone-driven, lust-fueled objectivity. And she'd seen her share of naked men.

Hmm. That didn't sound right. But it was true, naked men in her life had been a buck a dozen. Only she just hadn't slept with them. Her one affair, in college, was a pleasant but distant memory, and since then she'd spied naked men, fairly frequently, glimpses here and there, in and out of locker rooms, military field hospitals, and in the desert, where there hadn't been much privacy when she'd served as a pastor in Iraq. . . .

Focus, Harmony. There is an unclothed hunk-a-love lying in your flower bed.

Right. And what in the name of heaven was he doing there? Men didn't just fall out of the sky. *Ask and ye shall receive.*

"Harmony," she warned herself.

She dropped to her knees, her fingers going to the unconscious man's corded neck to feel for a pulse. His skin was tanned, perfectly smooth. Midnight black hair curled long and loose around his neck. Taking a closer look, she saw he appeared flushed, as if he were sunburned or had stood too close to a fire. More likely, he'd collapsed after a night of carousing. He was going to be pretty embarrassed once he realized he'd left wherever he'd been hanging out without his clothes.

Bubba growled, low and deep. "Shush, boy," Harmony soothed. "It's okay. I know martial arts, and you have sharp teeth. If he turns out to be the town serial killer/rapist, we'll team up and put him away. Until then, Bubba, you behave."

Harmony pressed her fingers to the man's neck. There . . . she felt a heartbeat . . . slow, distant, almost forlorn. It was if he'd grown tired of living.

She sat up straight. Gosh, that was a weird thought. Tired of living? Where did that come from? If anyone was a mind reader, it was her great-grandmother Eudora, who was said to be a "seer." But as a child growing up in the Faithfull clan, the mere mention of Eudora's psychic talents would have earned Harmony the threat of having her mouth washed out with soap, if not the real thing. Yet, as Harmony studied the stranger's face, the resignation there, the weariness, she could almost believe it true that he was ready to surrender.

Well, she'd fix that. No one was giving up the ghost on her watch, especially not dressed in his birthday suit and crushing her best zinnias!

"Hello? Sir? Are you okay?" Bubba's brown eyes were wary and huge as Harmony tapped the man on the shoulder. "Come on, up and at 'em. You can't sleep here all day. People will talk."

Not even an eyelash twitched. She took hold of his solid shoulder and shoved. "Okay, Sleeping Beauty, time to rise and shine. I'll even brew you a pot of coffee to help things along. I make a mean pot of java, too."

No response, not even a snore. He was dead to the world. As a last resort, she switched to her air-force-officer voice. "Wake up, soldier! *Now*. Move, move, move!"

The man cracked open one eye, and then the other. At first she thought she saw a red glow, but it seemed to be a trick of the sun, because his eyes were beautiful, reminding her of the mellow gold of good scotch, the kind her father would reverently pour out in a glass once each week, late on Sunday night. "Now that God's work is done, Harmony," he used to tell her.

"Hell's bells." Sleeping Beauty frowned, squinting as if the bright sunshine hurt his eyes.

"It lives," she teased.

He peered at the Garden of Eden sign, his parched lips forming whispered words. "I'm dead."

"You're not dead. Not even close."

He turned toward her voice and his confused eyes filled with curiosity, maybe even wonder. "But . . . ye are an angel."

"Thanks for the compliment, but no. I'm a flesh-and-blood woman."

His head fell back to the dirt with a soft thud. "Dragon offal . . . goblin scum, he is." His accent was strong, a cross between a Scots burr and a bad Captain Hook parody. "The bastard did it, he really did, and now I'm here. Aye, and mortal, too. Mortal in Mysteria."

"Is that kind of like sleepless in Seattle?"

Groaning at her joke, he flung his arms wide and rolled onto his back.

Glory be. Her mouth went dry as she looked him over. For injuries, yes, that was it. Before she administered emergency caffeine, she'd better make darn sure he wasn't wounded.

Anywhere.

She gave him a thorough inspection. After all, it was her citizen's responsibility. Her pastor's duty.

He was built . . . incredibly, amazingly, *enormously*, and that's all she'd let herself think on *that* subject, dragging her eyes away from where she shouldn't have been looking in the first place. There wasn't an ounce of fat on him. Or a single scar. He was as sculpted as a statue of a Roman warrior, except with body hair, the perfect amount, too, short and coarse and dark.

Something drew her eyes back to his face, where she discovered he was watching her with something close to amusement. "You seem, uh, to be all in one piece," she quickly explained.

He flashed a blinding grin. "You like what you see, then."

She stopped her blush before the heat of it could reach her cheeks. She'd grown up with four brothers, two older, two younger. Like heck, she'd let the fact that a man was sprawled naked in her garden in all his admittedly very magnificent glory distract her.

"As a matter of fact, I don't like what I see." Was that the hurt of a wounded ego that flashed in his eyes? Certainly it was surprise. "I don't care for the sight of a man facedown drunk in my flowers on a Sunday morning—butt naked. But considering that I just got done praying for a sign, I suppose I shouldn't complain, because I didn't spell out the specifications!"

She tugged off the butter yellow sweater she'd been wearing over a matching shell and thrust it at him. "Here, put this on."

Sinew and muscle corded his arm from wrist to shoulder as he peered curiously at the sweater dangling from his fingers. It looked tiny grasped in his hand. Clearly, he didn't know what do to with the thing.

She waved her hand. "Cover up." *Your huge wing-dinger*, she almost shouted. "For modesty's sake." Although modesty was way more her issue than his, it seemed.

He pushed upright, clods of dry dirt sprinkling down as he sat up. Tight, defined stomach muscles brought new meaning to six-pack abs. She almost sobbed with relief when he spread the sweater over his private parts.

"I am not drunk," he argued.

True, his eyes were clear, not bloodshot, as he swept his gaze around the garden, lawn, and church. And he was in top physical form, too, gifted with the well-hewn body of an NFL running back—powerfully muscled, without a linebacker's bulk. Carving a body like that took time. Alcoholism didn't lend itself to keeping regular workouts.

"What happened to you?" She folded her arms over her chest. "It usually doesn't rain naked men. At least not in the six months since I've lived here. Unless it's a seasonal thing."

His lips twitched, his gold-brown eyes sparkling, as he sized her up in an approving way. "If it is seasonal, lass, then we had better take shelter."

"Clothes first. Where'd you leave them?" she asked as calmly as she could as he didn't seem to care that he wore none.

He glanced around. "They took everything. Left me with nothing."

"You were robbed?"

"Aye, you could say that." His expression grew bleak all over again. "Robbed and abandoned."

"Oh, no. I don't like hearing that. Everyone's so nice around here, law-abiding folks. I can't see anyone doing something like this. It makes me sick to find out it may be otherwise."

"Nay, lass. They were not from here. They were from . . . the south. Aye, that's it."

"Oh, you mean Colorado Springs?"

He shook his head.

"Pueblo?"

"Nay. Far, far to the south. Farther south than you have ever been, lass."

Mexico, she thought, nodding. "That's okay. We'll get them. Just because they skipped out over the border doesn't mean they're home free. You can use my phone to call Jeanie—Jeanie Tortellini," she added at his blank look. "She's our town sheriff. And a good one, too. She'll file a report."

He frowned. "Nay. No reports. Will do no good."

"If you don't let her know, the thugs who did this to you will do it to someone else next time they cross the border."

Tiredly but firmly, he said no. "'Tis over. 'Tis done."

"Wow," she said in a quiet voice. "Just wow."

He glanced at her strangely. "Wow?"

"You were robbed, beaten, stripped, and unceremoniously dumped in a pastor's flower bed. You have every right to be angry."

"I *am* angry."

"Yet, you haven't uttered one grumble of vengeance or head bashing."

"'Tis no use, truly, to wish for such things." He seemed to be ready to say more but stopped himself. "None of it would do any good. 'Tis done."

"That's exactly what I mean by wow. It's not easy to forgive and forget. A true man of mercy; that's what you are."

A look of pain crossed his face. "Aye, and 'twas my downfall, too," he muttered.

"Mercy is never wrong! Never. In fact, showing mercy is good for you. And not only for your body—" She threw her hand over her heart. "Forgiving is good for your soul."

He choked as alarm lit up his face. "Can you tell if a man has one—a soul?" All at once cynical and wistful, his expression revealed nothing of the reason behind the odd question.

She explained gently, as if to a child. Perhaps, spiritually, he was still very young. "Some people have rotten souls, and some have beautiful, generous souls, but no matter what, they have one. You, me. No exceptions to that rule. Everyone has a soul."

He made a skeptical sound, but the longing in his face was clear as he rubbed his cleft chin. "How do you know so much about souls?"

"It's my job. See that church? I'm the pastor." As much as she loved her chosen calling in life, she deflated a little. Once men found out she was a pastor, they stopped thinking of her as a woman. From then on, they only wanted one of three things: absolution, friendship, or free counseling.

"A woman of God," he said with dawning surprise. "You are a nun."

A laugh burst out of her. "It seems like that sometimes, but no, I'm not a nun. I can marry, have a family, just like anyone else." *I can have hot, feverish sexual fantasies about well-built naked men. I can feel so horny I can't see straight. I sometimes think of "celibacy" as a four-letter word.*

She thrust out her hand. "I guess I should introduce myself since you obviously don't know who I am. I'm Harmony—Harmony Faithfull." He grasped the tips of her fingers with a cool, dry hand. There was gentleness cloaked in that strength, softness that he seemed to want to hide, but that she recognized anyway, putting her at ease when common sense told her she should be feeling the opposite. *Just like when you sensed he'd grown tired of living.* "And you are . . . ?" Ironic how she could know what every pore on his body looked like but not his name. "You have a name, right?" she teased when he didn't immediately answer.

His dark brows drew together in concentration. She was about to suggest he see a doctor for shock or a possible concussion when he blurted out sheepishly, "I am called Demon."

"Oh. That's a favorite of mine. My nephew's name is Damon, too."

"Demon—*Damon.*" He looked up, brightening. "Yes, I am Damon."

She smiled encouragingly. "Damon what?"

Again he concentrated.

Boy, he sure did seem rattled. But after all he'd been through, it was understandable. "Damon, you really need to see a doctor."

"Nay."

"But—"

"I am Damon," he announced. "Damon of Mysteria."

"Damon of Mysteria. It doesn't sound familiar. Or maybe I just don't recognize you without your clothes."

A devilish glint sparked in his eyes, sending shivers from her neck downward, flipping the "on" switch attached to all the neglected places in between as the sensation plunged to her toes. "Well, lass," he said, winking, "I dinna think you can say that any longer."

Four

Do not blush, Harmony. Do not. She stood up so fast that she got light-headed, her rational side praying that she didn't faint, while at the same time the wanton tart she was fast becoming argued that there were far worse fates than landing in that incredible lap. "No, I guess I can't say that any longer. Next time I see you around town, naked, I'll know it's you," she retorted. Turning on her heel, she took a couple of steps and stopped. "Coming? I have some clothes inside I think will fit. I'll brew a pot of coffee, too. You look like you could use it."

"Nay," he winced, "nothing hot. Water."

I'm with you all the way on the water, bud. Only, I'll take mine ice cold and in the form of a shower!

Damon pushed to his feet, her sweater pressed between his massive thighs. Harmony was five-nine, but he towered over her, taller than all her brothers, even Jake Jr. He had to be six-foot-five at least.

That long shadow fell over Bubba, who until now had been hanging close to Harmony. The puppy growled and backed up, teeth bared, fur rising in a ridge along his spine. "Hey, boy. It's okay," Harmony soothed, but the puppy started snarling and wouldn't quit.

Damon turned one hand palm up as he focused on the dog. His gold-brown eyes were arresting as it was, but now they grew so intense that they appeared to glow. It was a much different heat from what she'd seen when he'd caught her staring at his, uh, equipment. Not quite human, Damon's gaze was animal-like in its intensity and focus, almost as if he were communicating with her dog, wolf to wolf, so much so that she half-expected them to start howling any minute as something went back and forth between dog and man. Then, spell broken, Bubba wriggled over to Damon to lick his hand, that cute little tail wagging furiously.

"Wow. He likes you."

"He trusts me," Damon corrected. "The like will come in time."

Mmm. The guy had a way with women *and* dogs, she thought. An interspecies charmer.

They started walking toward the house. The road on the other side of the picket fence was empty of cars and joggers. Thank goodness. If anyone saw the new pastor going inside her house with a naked man . . . well, she'd never be able to get anyone to believe the *real* story.

Even *she* didn't believe the real story.

Bubba pranced alongside them as they walked up the porch steps leading to the door at the back of the chapel where Harmony's living quarters were located. Stepping into her small, cozy living room, Damon looked painfully out of place: a towering, hard-featured, rugged man in the midst of everything small and soft. Or, it could be just that he was naked.

In five seconds flat, she'd found him some work clothes that belonged to her largest brother. When Damon returned to the kitchen after changing into a pair of Jake Jr.'s faded Levi's and a gray, oil-stained, long-sleeved Henley T-shirt, her hunch was confirmed: everything was too tight and too short. At least the buttons and zippers weren't popping. Yet.

"Have a seat, Damon. I'll fix you something to eat and drink."

Looking a little lost, Damon sat at her small table, smoothing large hands over the lace cloth. It was as if everything were new to him, everything a wonder. Even her, she realized with a tiny twist of her heart when his gold-brown eyes found hers for a moment before focusing on the glass of water she nearly spilled in his lap. It was more than her current state of isolation—or intuition; this man did things to her, plain and simple, with his ancient eyes and surprisingly young soul.

She reached into the fridge for a leftover apple pie, a baked ham, rolls, mayo, and mustard. Big men ate big; that, she already knew from the five super-sized men in her family. Grabbing utensils and napkins, she dropped a slice of ham in Bubba's bowl on her way back to the table, where she cut Damon a huge slab of pie and slid the plate next to the overloaded one that held a lumberjack-sized ham sandwich. After she made herself a much smaller sandwich, she carried her plate to the table to sit across from Damon as he downed his water with thirsty gulps. She poured him some more. "Feeling better?" she asked after he finished the second glass.

"Aye." He winked, pressing the back of his hand to his mouth, in a truly medieval way, to dab at the droplets of water left behind. "How can a man not feel better, taken in with kindness, tended by such a beautiful wench?"

She lifted a brow. "Wench. Is that Scottish for strong, capable, intelligent woman, I hope?

"Nay. 'Tis old English. Old, *old* English."

"But you're Scottish, aren't you? The brogue."

"I do have a brogue, don't I? You can thank my ex-employer for that, lass. His sense of humor knew no bounds." He winked at her and lifted the ham sandwich, sniffing it, his eyes closing. His pleasure in the scent was so palpable, his anticipation so sharp, that by the time the breathless second had passed and he'd dived in with a hearty bite, her throat was dry and she was left wondering what she'd just witnessed.

Did he approach all activities with the same explosive, all-consuming passion?

Harmony . . . behave.

Damon was thorough, but neat. Hardly a crumb escaped him. In short order, the massive sandwich was gone. Next, he turned to the slice of pie, hesitating for a moment as if he'd remembered at the last minute that he'd better use a utensil in her presence. In no more than four shovels of the fork, the pie was gone, too.

"More?" Strangely drained, she shoveled another slice onto his plate, and he started on that, too, without taking a breath. She might as well fix him another sandwich, because he was still going strong. "Something must appeal about my cooking, or you haven't eaten in about a thousand years."

"Ten thousand," he said, wiping his mouth and hunting around for more food. She slid the pie plate toward him and let him serve himself, which he did with as much grace as speedy efficiency. When the first bite of pie reached his mouth, he closed his eyes, savoring the taste, and was that a shudder that ran through him?

Fascinated, she balanced her chin on her hand, smiling as she watched him. "I don't know what to make of you, Mr. Damon of Mysteria."

"Make of me whatever you wish, fair maiden."

"Fair maiden. I like that better than wench."

His gaze went soft again. "It fits ye better, too."

She swallowed against the feelings his gentle, sexy tone fired up inside her. Sitting straighter, she tried to gather the scattered shreds of her professionalism. "Maybe you'd better call your family to let them know you're okay."

He shook his head. "There is no one."

"No one at all? You're not married?" She immediately bit her lip.

But he'd turned thoughtful. "Nay . . . never thought of it. My livelihood would have made such a pairing difficult. Impossible, rather. But, perhaps now that has changed. . . ." When he returned his attention to her face, it was with such bold intensity, such raw consideration, that this time she did blush.

Harmony got up too quickly, sloshing water out of the pitcher. She grabbed a dish towel and started mopping at the puddle. Damon grabbed her wrist.

All at once, his thoughts burst inside her skull. His experiences, his emotions, too. They spun in a blur too fast for her to interpret, like subtitles set on fast-forward, but in those few heartbeats, she was able to gain a sense of the man: his confusion, his lack of guile, and his genuine fear—something she sensed he was not used to feeling.

Harmony, you're not Great-grandmother Eudora. You're insane. Your overactive hormones are finally taking their toll. You should have stuck to talking to the dog.

She studied his big hand and then his face. She didn't know how to explain what had just happened—nor did she want to. Her brain felt like a snow globe that had been shaken too hard. If he let go, maybe everything would settle down. "I'm a third-degree black belt," she said softly. "And my dog will rip your throat out if you try anything stupid."

Bubba protested with a little whimper, looking from her to Damon and back again. Harmony had the sudden feeling that she might not want to test the puppy's loyalties.

Damon let go. "I did not mean to frighten you."

Harmony sat back down, her heart thumping. What had just happened? Somehow, she regained her composure. "I'd like to help you. But to do that, you're going to have to tell me how you came to be under my apple tree." She left out the naked part. Those were details he could fill in. "I'll keep in confidence what you tell me."

Damon leaned forward. The maple café chair creaked under the shift in weight. "The true story?"

She leaned forward, too. "No," she whispered. "I want you to lie to me."

He took a deep breath, and then spilled. "I am the ten-thousand-year-old Demon High Lord of Self-Doubt and Second Thoughts, or I was until I was kicked out of Hell by Lucifer for committing random acts of kindness. After centuries of torture, I forget how many now, I was made mortal and banished to live out my days here, in Mysteria, the site of my original crime of beneficence."

Harmony stared at him. Damon stared back, as serious as they came. "I was just kidding about the lying," she said.

He opened his mouth to say something then seemed to change his mind. He drummed blunt-tipped fingers, glanced out the window as if seeking inspiration before returning his gaze to her. "I worked for a corrupt employer for many years. I carried out my orders until I learned what it was to be good. I learned that I liked being good over being bad. My employer punished me for it—for changing—and then he . . . he did *this* to me. He let me go. And so now I'm here, in Mysteria. With no home, no job, and"—he cleared his throat—"no clothes."

"You've been through hell, haven't you?" With a bit of an alarmed expression, he agreed. She shook her head sympathetically. He was a strapping, healthy guy down on his luck; admitting he was jobless and homeless couldn't have been easy.

Jobless. Homeless. *Here.*

Inspiration hit like a thunderbolt straight from heaven. "I have an idea." She opened her hands so Damon could see the calluses, cuts, and paint stains. "I've been looking for someone to hire—a handyman and groundskeeper. It'd be a huge help to have someone here for the heavier work, so I can concentrate on the church. The fields haven't been planted, the fence needs repair, and the barn needs fixing. I'd like to make it into a social hall, eventually, maybe a school, or even a gym, and I thought if I had some help, it'd leave me more time for recruiting more parishioners. In fact, any parishioners." She sighed.

"No one comes?"

She shook her head. "Just this morning I asked God to help me. To show me how to bring people here. I asked for a sign. And what do I find in my yard? A naked Demon. Oh! I meant Damon. Sorry!" She threw her face into her hands to muffle the giggles bubbling up.

Through her fingers, she heard Damon assuring her, "'Tis an understandable mistake," in a surprisingly earnest tone.

She peeked between her hands and saw that his expression matched his dead-serious tone of voice. Her giggles turned to laughter. Something must have struck Damon as funny because he, too, fell into genuine laughter, rich and deep.

Finally, she got hold of herself, wiping her tears. "Oh, that felt good. I needed it, too. I think this is what's known as divine intervention."

Damon's sparkling eyes seemed at once impossibly ancient and like those of a newborn baby. "Aye, more than you know, my fair maiden."

"If I'm the fair maiden, then you can be my knight in shining armor. My hired knight. How does that sound?"

He dipped his head once. "'Tis a fair offer."

They exchanged a smile that left her feeling cheerful and optimistic and warm all over. Really, really warm. Then she thought: what was she saying? Her smile fell as reality set in. "I can't afford to pay much."

He lifted his hands as if to say he didn't care.

"Actually, I can't afford to pay you at all." She pushed back from the table. "I'm sorry. I made a promise I can't keep. I'll give you a ride back to town."

"I don't require money. I'll work for . . . sustenance."

She shivered at the look in his sexy eyes, the way he drew out that last word.

"Food," he clarified. "And a place to lay my bones at night."

Bones . . . bones . . . she tried to keep her mind out of the gutter. "Okay." Why was she whispering? She thrust her hand at him. "Deal."

He took her hand, and she got the most curious feeling that he'd rather lift it to his soft lips than shake it. "You've been kind to me, Harmony Faithfull. Yet, you ask nothing in return."

"Why wouldn't I be kind to you?"

The hard line of his lips softened into an expression of surprise and pleasure. "That question alone answers mine, lass." He searched her face in a deeply intense, almost intimate way that made her go all squishy inside. Then he murmured, "Your goodness, it sits around ye like a halo. Are ye sure you're not an angel?"

Her smile came partly out of pleasure from his compliments, and partly out of the irony of being viewed as an angel. While her attraction to Damon was definitely heavenly, it was anything but angelic. "Very sure. Kindness exists outside heaven, too, you know."

"I've not much experience with kindness. With goodness."

"We'll have to change that," she said, her heart squeezing again.

"Aye, we will. . . ."

He released her, then, and she slid her hand under the table. Closing her fist, she secretly held on to the feel of him.

Five

Harmony stood on the porch as Damon strode off to the barn to arrange his new home in the hayloft with bedding, supplies, and a box of Oreos (the taste of which had rendered him nearly orgasmic).

Damon held no menace—raw, smoldering male sexuality, yes, but not menace. But she was an urban girl, born and bred, and it was always wise to make sure a person didn't have a record a mile long. She considered herself street smart, observant, and never blindly trusting, but she wanted to make darn sure Damon's looks, charisma, and charm—not to mention her hot-running blood and his miraculously timed arrival—weren't interfering with her better judgment. Having his fingerprints checked out was the way to go. Any employer would do the same thing.

Harmony returned to the kitchen and wrapped the glass Damon had used with a paper towel. Carefully, she slipped it into her backpack and slung it over her shoulder. "Come on, Bubba. Let's go shopping." She needed to buy Damon some work clothes that fit, but first she'd pay a little visit to Jeanie Tortellini, the sheriff.

She cut across the field to where a stand of aspens and tall pines marked the beginning of the Rocky Mountain National Forest. After turning right, a quick walk on a dirt trail would bring her right up behind the Mysteria police station and jail.

Bubba jerked on the leash and started growling. "What, boy, another naked hunk?" At this rate, she'd have a whole staff of them working for her. Not bad for a single girl. But part of her didn't want an army of muscles at her disposal. She'd rather have Damon, who engaged her on all levels, swinging from weary and jaded to boyish and full of wonder in the space of a heartbeat.

The puppy tugged hard on the leash and tried to run into the woods. Harmony held on with both hands. "Bubba, stay!"

Jeanie Tortellini burst out of the forest with a tall blond man trailing behind her. His wrists were bound with her police belt. The loose end Jeanie gripped in her fist.

Bubba broke into a full-fledged bark. "Hush, boy!" Harmony tried to quiet the pup.

Jeanie's smile when she saw Harmony was genuine, if not a little startled. "Good morning!" She used her free hand to brush loose strands of hair away from her face. With pink cheeks, messy hair, and strangely bright eyes, Jeanie looked as if she'd been in a scuffle. But it was the woman's appearance of having dressed too quickly that puzzled Harmony the most.

Jeanie's hand went to her uniform shirt as if she, too, just realized the buttons were in the wrong holes. It must have been quite a struggle, her apprehension of the lawbreaker.

Harmony stopped about twenty feet from the pair. "I was on my way to see you. I need a favor." She stole a glance at Jeanie's prisoner. His white-blond hair swung around his waist, some strands tied in braids. And were those pointed ears peeking through the spun-silk hair? A bit of an unfortunate birth defect, because with his archer's quiver, dark green tunic, and thigh-high leather boots, he was a dead ringer for Legolas from *Lord of the Rings*. "But, I see you're busy."

"I was," Jeanie said. "But I'm not now."

Making a quiet sound, the prisoner cast Jeanie a smoldering glance, and Jeanie's mouth quirked in the barest of smug little smiles. Harmony got the feeling that there was more going on than she probably wanted to know. Par for the course in Mysteria.

"Behave." Jeanie tugged on the belt and I'm-too-sexy-for-my-suede-tunic Legolas lowered his eyes dutifully. He had the perfect male pout, sullen and sensual. "How can I help you, Reverend Faithfull?"

Harmony unwrapped her paper-covered package. "I hired someone at the church this morning—a groundskeeper." Deciding it was better to keep the lurid details of Damon's arrival to herself, she moved the paper so Jeanie could see the drinking glass. "He's not from around here, and as much as I think I believe what he's told me about his background, it pays to be sure he's not wanted for a felony. Can you check out his fingerprints?"

Jeanie took the paper-wrapped glass. "No problem." The sheriff slid her gaze over the prisoner. Harmony could almost feel the electric surge of their eye contact. "If that's all you needed, I've got to get this bad boy under lock and key."

Legolas's mouth curved. The idea of a lockdown seemed to invigorate the sexy pseudo-elf. Or did he just like being called a "bad boy"?

"Thanks, Jeanie," Harmony said, unable to keep from staring at the man's pointy ears. "Stop in for coffee this week."

"I'll be there. And be careful with your new help. If you need me, just call."

"Will do."

Jeanie grinned and gave Harmony a little salute. Then she frowned at Legolas, using the belt to jerk him forward. To Harmony, his stumble seemed a little staged.

Harmony gave Bubba's leash a much gentler tug and continued toward town, and the One-Stop Mart, which conveniently did mean one stop in the true rural tradition of general mercantile stores. Since Wal-Mart hadn't yet invaded Mysteria, and probably never would, it was the only place she'd be able to find work clothes for Damon.

Puffs of pink pollen whooshed with each of her footfalls on the path, drifting in cotton-candy mounds, a phenomenon that no one seemed to be able—or was willing—to explain to her, and that included the town physician, who Harmony swore, even if she wasn't supposed to swear, that she'd spied waving a wand as she drove past his office the other day. A wand, as in magic wand, a fairy-godmother model, too, she assumed, because it had sported a shiny star at its tip. Harmony couldn't imagine what the handsome but terminally distracted Dr. Fogg had been doing, circling the wand over old Mrs. O'Cleary's white-haired head, but the very next day, when Harmony had seen Mrs. O'Cleary at the One-Stop, not only was the old woman's arthritic limp gone, but her snow-white, overpermed pin curls had relaxed into soft, shiny blond waves! It was just the sort of weird, supernatural happening Mysteria produced in abundance.

And you expect people to come to church when the local doctor can perform miracles? How could she compete with that? *How?*

After tying Bubba's leash to the bike rack in front of the store, Harmony pushed open the door to the market. Tin chimes clattered against the glass, and air thick with the scent of vanilla, peppermint, and old cardboard hit her nostrils with her first full breath. A cloud of pollen that had collected by the threshold spun in a powdery pink tornado. Unintentionally, Harmony inhaled a stream of the stuff and sneezed. Eyes tearing, she grew warm all over. Not as warm as when she was around Damon, but the same parts were involved. It was really distracting.

Mrs. O'Cleary beamed at her from behind the counter. She looked ten years younger than the last time Harmony had seen her—before her visit to Dr. Fogg. "It looks like love is in the air today, Reverend Faithfull!"

"It's the pollen." Harmony dabbed at her eyes. "I think I might be allergic."

The woman winked. "Who's the special man?"

Harmony's heart fell to the plank floor with a thud. Or at least it felt that way. "I don't understand what you mean."

Mrs. O'Cleary winked and wagged her finger. "Don't deny it. I know just by looking at you, young lady. You're in love."

"What you see is my love for my work, Mrs. O'Cleary. I love this town and the people in it."

"Pah." She waved her hand.

"I haven't been dating anyone. I haven't met anyone." Except for Damon. Harmony's face flooded with heat. "I haven't known anyone long enough to be in love."

"Silly girl. Time makes no difference. Sometimes you just know."

Sometimes you just know. Harmony thought of Damon and her heart contracted. Then she shook her head. She couldn't let the eccentric residents of Mysteria—or the pink pollen—get to her. It was her job as pastor to be the voice of reason—of God—in this town. "I need to pick up a few things for the church," she said, changing the subject as she stepped sideways down the aisle that contained everything from baseball caps to panty hose—and a display of Hanes underwear.

"Nails? Plaster? A nice . . . long . . . screw?"

Harmony shot the old woman a startled glance. The knowing amusement she saw in those crinkly blue eyes almost made her blush. "I hired someone at the church. He needs clothes."

The old woman grinned wickedly.

Harmony tried not to react. "*Work* clothes," she explained, choosing jeans, shirts, thick cotton socks, and boots, hesitating only when she turned her attention to the Hanes display. Boxers or briefs?

Harmony could feel Mrs. O'Cleary's eyes boring into the back of her head. "Do you need a particular size?" the woman inquired helpfully.

"Extra large. I mean, he's not fat. He's just . . . large." *Incredibly so*. She squeezed her eyes shut. *Just shut up, Harmony*. She chose several pairs of boxers in generic colors like beige gingham check and powder blue, studiously avoiding the designer black silks that practically begged to jump into her arms. *Would Damon look awesome in those, or what?*

Or did he look best in nothing?

In nothing, she decided.

Harmony, please. He's your employee.

Not trusting her facial expression, Harmony kept her chin buried in the pile of clothing in her arms and dumped the entire pile of clothes on the counter by the cash register.

Mrs. O'Cleary smiled at the Hanes packages as she rang them up. Harmony paid for the purchases with as much self-consciousness as if she were buying a package of condoms.

It was a relief to return to Bubba's innocent, unquestioning eyes. With several heavy shopping bags hanging from her hands, she headed home with the puppy. The closer she got to the farm, the faster she walked. And the only reason she could come up with was that she anticipated returning home to Damon a little more than she felt comfortable admitting.

Six

Sated with a belly full of the divine delicacy called Oreo—and he'd eaten every last one in the box—Damon sprawled on his back in bed in the hayloft to the rear of the vast empty interior of the barn. Sunlight leaked between the timbers and provided the only illumination. He breathed deep, sampling the air. The scent of Mysteria had not changed much in three hundred years, aside from the oily background odor of fossil-fueled machinery and the more acrid smell of electrical equipment. The barn smelled like dust and hay, and faintly of livestock that had not lived here for a year or more. Although his animal-sharp sense of smell was fading rapidly, he could still pick out the faint pungent odor of mouse droppings and that of the young black dog. Despite so many different scents, Harmony's scent stood out above all else, perhaps because he'd so focused on it. Her essence was on the wooden handles of the tools, on his very skin.

She had not the scent of another male about her; he'd noticed that straightaway, glad he'd held on to his demon's sense of smell long enough not to have to guess. She was free, unattached.

Smiling, he wedged his hands behind his head, laced his fingers together as he inhaled the lingering scent of the beautiful lass. Harmony had ordered him to get some rest, and he was trying—without much success. He had not done the labor required, he supposed. Tonight, it would be different, for this afternoon, he'd start work. Aye, but there were some other labors he had in mind when it came to Harmony Faithfull. Exhausting labors he would more than care to try.

"Ah, lass," he murmured, "ye are beautiful; no denying that. Inside and out." He liked the way she listened to him, so very carefully, how she'd taken him in and given him shelter with few questions asked.

Harmony's open and generous heart was something that not all humans possessed; but rarer still was her uncanny ability to look him in the eye and sense his needs, his fears, even—a gift that brought great risk for him. If the lass ever discovered that he had no soul, she'd be repelled by him, would even fear him.

"Everyone has a soul," she'd insisted.

Bah! 'Twas an observation based on her innocence of creatures like him, a demon that was never meant for a mortal life, a good life. He was a monster created out of darkness and intended to remain in the shadows, carrying out the Devil's deeds. The fact he was here at all was due to the Devil's whim, and the Devil's whim was never good, not in all the ten thousand years Damon had watched Lucifer in action.

There was only one solution: stay far enough away so that Harmony didn't discover his dark secret, and yet close enough to savor the way she made him feel: warm, happy, hopeful—just the sort of emotions to which he was unaccustomed and woefully ill-equipped to sort out. He couldn't have her, not in the way he wanted, but he could do good deeds for her, become indispensable in other, less intimate ways. Perhaps this was Lucifer's plan all along, this punishment of placing him within arm's reach of a woman like Harmony Faithfull, without being allowed to truly touch her.

Damon could think of no crueler sentence.

A scrabbling noise in the barn dragged him to full alert. He peered into the dim light, scanning for an obvious explanation for the brief sound. His demon eyesight was still strong enough to discern what crept down there in the shadows. Although he saw nothing, he knew he was no longer alone.

A dark creature had joined him.

With stealthy quiet, Damon vaulted off the sleeping berth and landed in a crouch, hands up and ready for battle. "Show yourself!"

"She likes you," rasped a voice from the shadows. "Yes, she does."

Hell's bells, 'twas a goblin! Useless monsters, always underfoot. "Too many eyes," Damon growled. "And too few brains."

The creature came into view. It had the dark green skin of a frog, gleaming and lumpy with boils. That the little goblin hadn't called him "Lord" reminded Damon just how far he'd fallen.

No, not fallen. *Risen.* Damon had to think differently now.

The little monster waved something at him. "I have me a souvenir."

Between the goblin's spindly fingers was a long strand of wavy dark hair. Harmony's hair. Damon's heart dropped. If the goblin brought part of Harmony back to Hell—any part: a fingernail, this strand of hair—it would forge a link between the underworld and this farm, and would make other night creatures more brazen. They'd come looking for souvenirs of their own, mementos far more precious.

Damon advanced on the goblin, snarling, but the goblin danced out of his reach. "No, no, you can't have it, mortal. It's a prize too sweet. A prize all mine. Mine, mine, mine. Soon she will like me, too. She will like me, she will, better than you." A slimy, warty tongue darted out between the goblin's lips and slid down the entire length of the hair, a sensation Harmony would feel in her sleep night after night unless Damon ended it here.

Rage boiled up inside Damon and made his blood burn. Snarling, he grabbed for the little beastie, but it slipped out of his grip. Fury was making him sloppy. In the past, he'd always acted efficiently and without emotion. Now anger drove him. Aye, anger and fear.

Slow down. Concentrate. Damon forcibly unclenched his teeth and extended an open hand. "Give."

"No, no, no. Oh, no. Mine, mine, mine. All mine, not yours."

"But all Hell-born are brothers, yes?" The mere thought of pledging a blood bond with a goblin almost made him puke. "'Tis simple. You help me, I help you." He advanced another step. "Give me the hair and no harm will come to you for your trespassing."

"Harm, harm will never come," the goblin sang. "Your powers are gone, yes, they are." Spinning in a careless little pirouette, it waved the strand of hair like a victory flag.

Damon watched. Waited. His gentler tone had made the thing careless. Lost in celebrating, the goblin spun closer.

Damon bolted forward and grabbed the creature by its skinny wrist before it could dart away. The goblin shrieked in surprise; its lips pulled back in fear, revealing rows of yellowed, needle-sharp teeth. "Ouch, mortal. Hurts—hurts, it does!"

Damon brought his face very close. "Unfortunately for you, I'm not yet mortal enough to care."

With the wriggling, screaming goblin in one hand, he strode across the barn. "No, no, no!"

"I think yes." Damon reached for a bucket and threw it under a spigot, turning on the water. A few drops splashed onto the creature's belly and sizzled like hot oil.

The beastie screamed in agony and fright. "No! Not that! My lord and master, not that."

"Ah, so I'm your lord now, eh?" Methodically, Damon filled the bucket. "Interesting how desperation breeds respect."

"Master, Master, please. Let me go!"

Grim, Damon shut off the water and turned to the goblin dangling from his grip. Its eyes were wide, each blinking at different rates. Thin, blistered fingers curled around his forearm. Damon could feel a rapid pulse in the press of its fingertips. Harmony's hair still curled from one knotty fist.

One dunk was all it'd take to silence the despicable creature forever.

Frantic yellow eyes searched his face. Damon knew he looked fearsome to the goblin, what with the rage he felt glowing in his gut.

Sensing its demise, the goblin went very still. "I'll do anything, Master, anything."

Damon lowered the goblin until its bare feet hung inches from the water. Fear trembled through its thin frame. "Mercy," the goblin wailed. "Oh, please. Mercy!"

Damon went very still. *Mercy* . . .

Harmony's words echoed in his memory. *"You're a true man of mercy."*

But was he? Damon swallowed, frozen to the spot, almost forgetting about the struggling goblin that was so far too panicked to sense Damon's hesitation, his weakness.

Nay, not weakness! Mercy was not a weakness. Mercy was never wrong!

'Twas it not time to prove he believed it?

Damon turned his attention to his prisoner. "Give me your prize, goblin. Give it to me and I will let you live."

The goblin's little hand unfurled. "Here, Master. Here, here. You take—please take."

Damon snatched the curly black strand and slipped it into his trousers pocket. Then he brought his nose very close to the little creature's maw. The goblin's breath was fetid and warm. Wisely, the creature chose silence, or Damon might not have trusted himself to maintain his compassion. "Never come here again—you or your cohorts. For if you do return here, 'twill not go well for you the next time." He lowered the creature, slowly, until its heels just barely brushed the water. A sizzle and a scream brought a smile of satisfaction to Damon's face. "Not well at all . . ."

He threw the goblin to the ground. "Go! Return here and ye will perish."

"Don't want to perish. No, no, I will go, go." Gasping, the goblin scrabbled, limping, across the hay-strewn floor and disappeared into a small Hell hole that opened only wide enough to allow the creature to disappear.

Sniffing the air one more time to check for subdemons, goblins, and other dark creatures, Damon had almost convinced himself there were none close by when another dark form came barreling into the barn, snorting and snuffling. A breath away from flinging the creature into the wall, Damon saw that the intruder was Harmony's dog.

Bubba leaped up on him, black eyes shining: a wriggling, roiling mass of pure eagerness—eagerness to see him, to smell him, and above all to please. Damon scratched him behind the ears. "Aye, I'm glad to see ye, too."

Next, Harmony swept through the door, her arms filled with bundles. She'd changed clothes from earlier. Her blouse was pink and form-fitting, worn over faded blue pants that hugged every inch of her long, firm legs. The flesh of her ankles peeked out between the pants and pink-and-white rubber-soled shoes.

"Down, Bubba!" Harmony's hair bounced in a mass of dark ringlets around her shoulders. "Damon does not want to be mauled."

Mauled by the dog, no, Damon thought. *But mauled by you, lass, well, that would be an experience to be savored, indeed.*

"I'm sorry, Damon. He's all over you."

"'Tis not a bother." Damon took the pup's head in his broad palms and held eye contact with the squirming animal. *Be still, boy. Be still.*

The dog immediately sat on its rump. Only its tongue fluttered.

Harmony laughed. "How do you do that? It's amazing. I'm going to start calling you the dog whisperer."

"'Tis a lot like whispering," he conceded, sorry that the talent to communicate with animals would soon leave him. With one last affectionate rub behind Bubba's floppy ears, he turned his full attention to Harmony. His heart gave a little leap at the answering spark of interest he saw in her eyes.

She was full of life. She filled him with life.

Harmony smiled and reached for him, and his breath caught as he waited for her touch, but all she did was pluck a piece of straw from his shirt. "I thought you were going to rest."

He glanced at the portion of the floor where the Hell hole had opened. It was gone. Only displaced straw indicated where the struggle had taken place. His shoulders sagged as he dashed an unsteady hand across his forehead. He hadn't been weary before, but he was now. Battle, he'd overheard many a mortal warrior state, exhausted a man.

But his weariness was more a mental matter than a physical one. After tonight he might no longer be able to detect such monsters before it was too late. *How then, will you protect Harmony?* Hopelessness threatened to swamp him. Like the tumultuous sensations coursing through him in Harmony's presence, he did not know quite how to quench such emotions. *You must fight to control them, then.* Aye, fight as he'd earlier fought to control his desire to take Harmony to the kitchen floor and make wild love to her. A shudder ran through Damon at the thought. In the silence of his mind, he tried to pray, though he knew not how. Who would listen to a prayer from a soulless demon? Certainly not God. As for the angels, he'd made enemies of most of them. Instead he simply made a plea: *Help me to keep the lass safe. Give me the strength.*

"You're exhausted," he heard Harmony say.

"I've rested long enough, lass. It's time to put me to work. You name the task, anything at all, and I will devote myself to its thorough completion."

Another contemplative spark flashed in her brown eyes, quickly quenched, but not before he felt the answering heat in his loins.

Hell's bells, living in her presence was going to be torture. *Lucifer, you have truly crafted the ultimate punishment.*

Rather hoarsely, Damon said, "Show me where I might find the tools of my labors."

Harmony's gaze dropped. Then the red patches on her cheeks flared and she cleared her throat. "Oh, tools. Right. Everything's over here." She walked away very fast, but somehow he knew she wanted him to follow. "Everything you need. Thanks to my brothers and Home Depot."

"The men in your family have chosen well for you." Damon selected a shovel, hefting it into his hand, and heard the tear of fabric. He glanced down with dread at the same time Harmony made a small sound. His shirt had split, exposing much of his chest and torso.

Harmony ran off. For an instant he wondered if he'd scared her off for good, but she hurried back to him with the bundles she'd carried into the barn. "These are for you, and none too soon." She shoved the packages into his hands, her attention shifting somewhere else, as if she were both tempted and afraid to look at the strips of fabric hanging from the ruined shirt. "New work clothes—and in your size, too. Now you don't have to worry about them coming off until they're taken off!" Her eyes squeezed shut, as if the comment about taking off clothing had embarrassed her.

"Lass, you've given me too much as it is—"

Her hands came up to stop his protest. "Don't worry about the cost. We'll work it out."

"Aye. That we will."

She met his eyes and blushed deeply, and he wasn't sure why. Again, Damon tasted the air, trying to gather more information to help understand her baffling reactions—and his. She desired him, as he desired her. She could not hide the fact. It hung in the air, it permeated his senses.

Harmony's attraction to him, combined with his for her, was sharp and powerful, fueling passionate thoughts of sliding his hands under the garments she wore to feel the heat of her bare skin, which only exacerbated the sexual hunger building with each breath he took. As if that wasn't bad enough, he reacted physically with the thought, growing rock hard with a new-to-him ache that left him barely able to breathe. It reminded him of the sensation when Lucifer set fires so intense that they sucked all the air from the chambers of Hell. Only this was nothing close to suffocation!

Damon clutched the bundle of clothes to his lower abdomen, sharply relieved at having a way to cover up as sexual desire, a cataclysm of need, boiled up inside him. Never before had he been forced to face his reactions to a mortal. To a woman. To anyone.

But ye will have to behave. You're a man now. A good man.

Good, good, good, good. If he chanted it, it might sink in. Good men did not drag women like Harmony to their mouths to kiss deeply as they fell, clothes scattering, to the ground, where he'd kiss her everywhere else—

Damon made a sound in the back of his throat. *Good, good, good . . .*

A chiming little tune rang out from Harmony's pants, startling Damon as much as it did the lass.

She tore her eyes from his, mumbling something about taking a "call" on her "cell phone" as she pulled a little silver rectangle from her pocket. "I should have guessed," she said, reading the glowing numbers. "What is it about fathers and timing?" She pushed a button and spoke into the phone. "Hi, Daddy!"

While Harmony was otherwise distracted, Damon, trying with all his might to block the distraction of her scent, grabbed a pickax off a hook on the wall.

She had a family, he thought, and then wondered at his surprise. Of course she had a family. All humans did. Unlike him, they weren't born of shadows and darkness, the Devil's spawn.

"I'm doing great. How are you and Mama? And Great-grandma?" Harmony nodded, smiling as she listened. Then her grin faltered. "What did Great-grandma say?" Harmony's gaze shifted to Damon and darted away. The red patches were back, one on each cheek. "No, I haven't had much time for a social life. No, really! I've been too busy—yes, busy with the church. Oh, yes, the people here are wonderful. Just great. I'm so happy—you're *what*?" She almost dropped the cell phone. "You're coming here? In August?" she squeaked. "No, it'll be no trouble. I can't wait to see you, Daddy. Look, I gotta run. Church business. Give my love to Mama and everyone else. Miss you."

Harmony sighed as she wedged the cell phone into her pocket. "Why did I do that?"

Damon shook his head. "Do what, lass?"

"My father's coming for a visit, in less than two months. With the entire family!" She pressed her fingertips into her temples, muttering, "And they're dying to see the thriving church community I just told him about."

"You dinna tell him that," Damon pointed out tactfully. "I was listening."

"My father made a guess based on what I told him, and I didn't deny it. That's just as bad! I lied to a pastor—and I *am* a pastor!" She glanced heavenward, appearing truly repentant as she murmured a prayer. Then she wiped her hands on her pants. "Well, there's only one thing to do, Damon, and that's to make what I told my father true. Somehow, I'm going to come up with a way to reel in the townspeople to this church on Sundays—and fast." She started walking to the door. "When all else fails, cook on it."

"Cook on it?" he asked and she laughed from where she stood near the open door encircled by sunshine streaming around her like a halo.

"When I have problems to solve, I head to the kitchen. I think the best when I'm cooking things. Always have, always will. Since this is a big problem, you'll have a big dinner to look forward to."

Damon remembered the food from the midday meal and salivated. His stomach grumbled so loudly that he was surprised she didn't hear it.

"Home-made fried chicken," she muttered as she walked away, already deep in thought. "Mashed potatoes and gravy . . . buttered corn . . . peach cobbler for dessert . . ."

He watched her go. *Well, lass, ye are not in this alone, no matter what ye think.* This was his chance to help her, to prove himself worthy of her generosity. If his fair maiden needed a knight in shining armor, then that was what she'd get. While he worked at his assigned labors, he'd come up with a way to help her, though he knew not how a former demon could help fill a church with the faithful.

Aye, but he'd figure it out. Yes, he would, and quickly.

There was no time to change into his new clothing. In his new and very mortal life, there wasn't a moment to waste. Not having eternity before him cast everything in a different light, in fact. Although he'd developed a certain respect for humans when he'd committed his crimes—no, his deeds—of mercy, only now that he was one of them did he fully appreciate the humans' courage in facing a finite life. With the puppy trotting after him, he strode out into the sunshine with the promise that he, too, would brave his mortality like the man he was—or at least like the man he hoped one day to be.

And so it was that Damon of Mysteria officially began his new life as a mortal: by digging postholes to shore up a weakened section of the front fence.

Seven

After an hour of working outside, the weather grew so hot that sweat soaked through his ruined shirt. Tossing aside the tattered garment, he continued bare-chested.

After a dozen more strikes of the pickax, he scented something new and different in the air—something far more pleasant than his sweat. Damon looked up, the ax held in midair. Three women stood across the fence, staring at him.

Their sexual interest washed over him in pheromone-laden waves. There was the aura of the dark arts about them but not evil, nay, none of that, but sorcery and magic. And their brilliant hazel eyes were afire with a light all of their own. For one panicked moment, he thought they'd figured out what he was; then he realized they were more interested in what he was now. Or at least what of him existed below his neck.

Bubba didn't growl, which told Damon that Harmony knew these women even if he did not.

Slowly, Damon lowered the pickax. "And who might you pretties be?"

The wench with long dark hair stepped closer to the fence. Her face was serious, but her sensuality smoldered. "Genevieve Tawdry. And these are my sisters—Glory and Godiva."

"Hello, stranger." Glory twirled a finger in her red hair as she licked her lips. Her bosom was ample, would make many a man happy, and she eyed him with the kind of come-hither smile that had remained unchanged down through the ages. Mortal men would take it as an invitation to share in the bounty of her body. *You are now mortal, too, Damon, are you not?*

Aye, he was. But as much as he found all three wenches attractive, it was only Harmony he desired.

The wench named Godiva observed him with perceptive eyes. She had a powerful magic about her, this silver-haired witch. Could she tell his origins? He hoped not. If Harmony were to find out through her friends that he'd come from the depths of Hell, she'd banish him from her church for good. He wouldn't lie to her, when that time came, but the longer he could put off the truth, the better. "If I'd bumped into you before," Godiva said, "I'd have remembered. You're new here."

"Aye, I am." 'Twas not really a lie. It had been three hundred years since he was last here; it was almost like being new in town all over again. He stood proudly, the ax resting on his shoulder. "I'm the new church groundskeeper."

"Really." Glory exchanged a speculative glance with her sisters. "We didn't know there'd been an *old* groundskeeper."

"There wasn't. I'm the first." Damon folded his hands on the tip of the shovel handle and three pairs of hungry eyes shifted to his bare chest. Their sexual interest thickened the air.

The trio paused to whisper among themselves, glancing at him often, sometimes even his face, but mostly from his neck down. Damon noticed the shopping bags they carried. They'd been on their way home from shopping when they'd spotted him and stopped dead in their tracks. If townsfolk regularly passed this close to the church, why then couldn't they spare a few moments more and visit on Sundays?

An idea began to form. A magnificent idea. Harmony needed a way to lure the townsfolk inside the church. Perhaps he was the answer to that problem.

His body had been put to far worse uses, certainly. And he'd spent ten thousand years planting doubts and fears. Could he not do the same with the women in the town, but planting interest to attend Harmony's church instead? He wouldn't be able to convince them in his typical fashion, for he'd lost the ability to circumvent free will when he was banished from Hell, but he could influence others, especially female others, in a much more primitive way. Aye, an *age-old* way.

Damon's mouth curved in a slow smile he was sure all three women felt to the very tips of their toes. Then, stretching his arms over his head, he worked a kink out of his back. The women looked faint as he hefted his pickax. "Alas, I cannot dally any longer. I am behind in my labors. Reverend Faithfull will beat me if I dinna get back to work."

Glory's lush mouth fell open. "Harmony beats you?"

"Only if I misbehave," he confided in a deep and sexy burr.

One of the witches made a small, soft sound.

"But I'll be doing maintenance on the church on Sunday—Sunday morning."

"What time?" Glory whispered.

"A quarter to nine." Damon winked at her, picked up the pickax, and went back to work. When he next glanced up, the sisters had walked away, but as they disappeared around the bend in the road, he saw them murmuring and giggling among themselves.

Aye, he'd planted his seeds of interest. If things went as he hoped they would, by next Sunday, Harmony would be reaping what he'd sown.

Eight

On Sunday, Harmony stood on the front lawn of the church, watching in happy amazement as woman after woman filed in for the nine A.M. service. Smiling and shaking hands, she welcomed the women she'd previously seen only at the One-Stop, the gas station, or on the streets of the town.

In uniform, Jeanie Tortellini walked up to her. Harmony couldn't help thinking of Legolas. In fact, the other day when she'd visited the sheriff, the jail cell had been empty. Although she often wondered what had happened to the sexy elf, she hadn't come up with a tactful way to ask the question.

"You've got yourself a nice crowd this morning, Harmony," Jeanie said.

"I do." Harmony tried to keep the bewilderment from her voice. It was only 8:45 and the pews were already one-third filled. With eager women. "And you're here, too, Jeanie. I thought you had to work Sunday mornings."

"I do. I'm here on official business."

Harmony lifted a brow. "What kind of business?"

"Crowd control."

Before Harmony could ask how the sheriff knew there'd be a crowd at church, Marie, the UPS driver, poked her head in their little huddle. "Where did you hide him, Reverend?"

"Hide who?"

"Your new groundskeeper."

"You mean Damon?"

Jeanie shook her head as if Harmony was beyond all help. "Yes. Damon. He's hot. If you haven't noticed."

"And if you haven't noticed," Maria put in, "you might want to stop by Dr. Fogg's office and take a gander at the eye chart, because I would say you need those peepers examined."

"Or get her heart checked to see if she has a pulse," Jeanie teased.

Harmony supposed it shouldn't surprise her that it hadn't taken long for word to get around about Damon. Almost as much as they appreciated the attributes of a good-looking man, the women of Mysteria loved juicy gossip, particularly when the latter concerned the former. Everyone, it seemed, even the pets, had a libido running in constant overdrive. Maybe it was that strange pink pollen. Nevertheless, she mumbled something about it not being professional to view her new employee in *that* way, which was such an obvious lie that the sheriff's eyes twinkled in merry amusement.

"Ooh, there he is now." Maria hurried off to where a small crowd of women had gathered around Damon, watching as he fiddled with a repair to the door frame at the front entrance of the church. Why was he doing that now, of all things, right when services were about to start? He'd been busy with the fence all week, and she'd assumed he'd take Sunday off, which was his free time by rights.

Laughter rang out from the group of women surrounding Damon. He appeared to be charming the panties off them as he ushered them inside. As if he'd sensed she was watching, he turned and caught her gaze. Immediately, his expression changed into something warmer, more personal, telling her that he viewed her differently from the other women.

Differently, because he thinks you're a nun, Harmony.

Harmony shifted her attention to Bubba, who sat adoringly at Damon's feet, the cute little traitor. But who could blame the dog? Damon occupied Harmony's thoughts day and night, too. Especially at night. She'd added an extra two miles to her daily jog, but it didn't seem to be helping.

Jeanie lowered her voice and spoke in her ear. "If I can tear your attention away from the groundskeeper hunk for a second, I have the information you requested."

Harmony's heart skipped a beat as she whirled around. "Damon's fingerprints."

"Uh-huh. And I don't have anything on him."

"Great!" But Jeanie appeared more troubled than relieved. Harmony frowned. "Isn't that good?"

"I mean I have *nothing* on him, Reverend. Nada. Zilch. We ran his prints and not a thing came up."

"What are you saying—that he doesn't exist?"

Jeanie spread her hands. "My research went beyond prints. I have friends in high places, and they helped. As far as the government goes, no. He's never applied for a passport, or registered to vote. He's never paid taxes, either, but then he's never held a job that required even the simplest background check. It goes without saying that he's never seen the inside of a prison—which was what you were worried about, right?"

Harmony thought back to the day it seemed that Damon had literally appeared out of nowhere in the garden. "What if he switched identities? What if he's a fugitive trying to escape his past?"

"We'd have picked it up. Prints are prints. I had an expert check them out, too, a CIA buddy who owed me a favor. Your hunk's fingerprints showed no evidence of being altered surgically or by any other method." The sheriff shrugged. "I don't know what else to say, but that he's clean. Real clean. Count your blessings."

"I will." Harmony took a steadying breath. "Speaking of blessings, I'd better get this service started."

She left the sheriff's side in a happy daze. "He's clean," she whispered to herself. "Real clean." Her intuition had been right—she wasn't falling for the devil's spawn, after all. Next time she had her doubts about anything, she'd listen to her instincts. *Thank you, Great-grandmother Eudora!*

Harmony breezed past Damon, hitched herself just high enough on her tiptoes as she passed by to whisper in his ear, "Dinner at six-thirty. Inside. Dress nice."

It would be the first time since the day he'd arrived that she'd invited him to dine in the kitchen. Not knowing if he had a record or not had hardened her resolved to wait before taking the chance. Now, she knew.

The glimpse of his shock slipping quickly into pleasure lingered in her mind as she took the pulpit with true excitement coursing through her. She was finally beginning what she'd come to Mysteria to do. Her smile was contagious: a chain reaction reflected by the happy faces of the townswomen. But when her gaze settled on Damon, who stood in the doorway a few careful steps outside the church, she felt a bolt of pure energy. How could he not be heaven sent?

Harmony raised her hands and belted out a hallelujah. Her heart, filled to bursting in more ways than one, was in every single syllable.

At dusk Damon showed up at her front door with a thick bouquet of wildflowers. He'd showered and combed his hair. Although he had only work clothes to wear, he'd ironed them and she decided that no matter what he wore, everything or nothing at all, he was the most gorgeous man she'd ever seen. And tonight he was all hers.

"Thank you," she sang out, taking the flowers. "They're beautiful." The heat in his eyes was especially intense as he took in the sight of her in the red-hot form-fitting sheathe dress she'd bought on impulse in town after the service was over. Sometimes even a pastor had to break the rule of resting on Sundays. "You look very nice tonight, too, by the way." She came up on her toes and planted a kiss on his cheek. A nun's kiss. She wanted more, she thought as she stepped back.

Behave, Harmony. Be professional.

Damon's whiskey-gold gaze glinted, as if he sensed her inner battle. "You have the devil in your eyes tonight, Damon of Mysteria," she said, imitating his accent.

He looked suddenly troubled. "Sorry, lass. I dinna mean to."

"It's just an expression! You can be so literal, at times."

He flashed his famous smile, one tinged with relief. "Aye, and tonight you've got a bit of the devil in ye, too, I see."

Because I'm hoping to find a little piece of heaven in your arms.

"Sit, make yourself at home," she told him while she wedged the flowers into a water-filled glass vase and placed them on the kitchen counter because already the little eating table was half-filled with plates. On the stove in a cast-iron pan, four bone-in country ham slices, each a quarter-inch thick, sizzled in butter. While she finished cooking, she chattered from nervous excitement. The artificial barrier she'd erected between herself and Damon, one held in place by her lingering worries that he was a criminal, had crashed into so much dust. "So, how about that attendance at church today, huh? It's a miracle! A real miracle."

"Nay. Take credit where credit is due, Harmony. Word about your church has spread far and wide. 'Twas only a matter of time."

"Hmm. I'd like to believe it. But where were all the men?"

Damon's smile faltered. "Were there no males present?" he asked innocently.

"Except for you and Bubba, that crowd was a hundred percent female, and don't pretend you didn't notice. It doesn't make sense. But I guess it's not gracious to look the Lord's gift horse in the mouth."

Especially not with Daddy coming. A robust church community was a source of Faithfull pride. She couldn't let her family down.

Oh, but they'd be impressed with Damon, though, she thought happily. He was such a gentleman, so much like her brothers. And when all-seeing Great-grandmother Eudora stepped through the front door, one look at Damon and she'd see him for what he truly was!

Oh, yes, things were looking up. Yes, indeed.

She tried to forget about the strange gender imbalance at church and instead focused on the pleasure of cooking and Damon's company.

With a spatula, she flipped the ham steaks. "I'm fixing us ham and red-eye gravy. A Faithfull family favorite. Ever tried it?"

"Nay, lass. But I canna wait." Damon closed his eyes and inhaled the aroma. Even from the stove, she could see the shudder that rumbled through him.

She couldn't help laughing. "In all my life, I can't say I've ever had more pleasure cooking for anyone."

His smile was brilliant, as if he savored her compliments as much as he did his food.

She bustled about the stove, crashing pots and pans onto the burner as she hummed to the music playing on the stereo. Damon watched her with an affectionate, amused gaze that made her heart beat even faster. "My mama made me and my sisters help her with Sunday supper since we were little girls. We'd turn up the radio and listen to our favorite songs. Sometimes we'd dance more than we'd cook, and Mama would scold us." Harmony gave her butt a defiant little shake. Her tight, red-sheathed butt.

The look on Damon's face sent heat shooting up and down her spine. *Harmony, behave yourself.*

Do I have to?

It was almost like being a teenager again, except that the voice of reason she battled was her own.

She turned back to the stove and heard a loud scratching noise behind her. Damon growled, "Trolls—be gone!" Then there was a splash, a prolonged sizzle, and an abbreviated squeak.

Nine

Whirling around, she caught Damon just as he sat back in his chair. He looked shaken and was trying to hide the fact.

Harmony's brows went up. "What was that? What just happened? What did you mean by a troll?"

Damon flushed. She'd never seen his face color like that before. "'Twas a . . . mouse," he explained. "We call them trolls in Scotland."

"Oh." She pondered that. Then she glanced around her clean kitchen, the spatula gripped in her hand like a weapon. "Where's the mouse? I haven't had a problem with mice before." That's when she saw the puddle. And on the table, Damon's empty glass.

"I chased it off," he explained. "They dinna like water." As if he were reloading a six-shooter, he refilled his glass from the pitcher on the table.

Harmony stared at the puddle. "That's weird."

"What is?"

"The water's smoking. No, that's steam."

"Condensation."

"Hmm. Well, it is a little humid tonight after that thunderstorm." Before she could get to the puddle with a dish towel, it had evaporated. Humidity wasn't the problem. But she wasn't sure what was. Except that there had been a mouse that Damon called a troll that had disappeared as quickly as the puddle he'd made on the floor.

Keeping her eyes open for rodents, she mixed brown sugar, a half cup of brewed coffee, and a cup of water for the gravy, stirring until the sugar dissolved.

From behind, she heard Damon's chair scrape backward. *Not another one.* A splash and a startled squeak signaled a hit. Almost too fast to register on her retinas, something larger than a mouse but smaller than a bunny darted out through Bubba's doggie door, something that had appeared to run on two legs, not four, though she was sure it was a trick of the eyes.

Delighted barking from outside told her that the puppy had given chase to whatever it was. "Damon, I don't think they're mice."

Panic flashed in his eyes, as if he didn't want her going down that road. "What else would they be, lass?"

"I mean, I think they're rats. Why are you acting so worried? Is my hulking, six-foot-five knight afraid of little rodents?"

"Nay." *I am afraid for you,* his eyes said.

What a sweetie. He took his role of protector so seriously that it had extended to pest control. She wanted to hug him, but her hands were sticky with sugar. "I don't like mice, but I'm not afraid of them, Damon. The desert rats we had in Iraq were way worse, and I saw cockroaches in Biloxi that were as big as small horses, so don't worry about me." Despite her big talk, she did react with a little shudder as she envisioned mice scampering through the house at night, popping out of the medicine cabinets in the dark, nesting between her bed-sheets. "Do you know where they're coming from?"

"I've seen one or two in the barn," he mumbled.

Where he slept. Again, she shuddered. "I'll buy some traps tomor-row. Or a cat—a hungry cat! I just want them gone before my family gets here."

"Trust me, lass. I dinna want the little beasties around, either." He said it like he meant it, too. She was confident that tomorrow, the rats would be history.

Harmony drizzled gravy over the ham steaks. Red-eye gravy was thin in consistency but potent in flavor. Her mouth watered in antici-pation. Careful not to step on any stray creatures, she carried the platter to the table, setting it down amid bowls of mashed potatoes, vegetables, and biscuits.

"Oh, I baked us a special dessert, too." She carried the cake to the table and announced proudly, "Devil's food!"

Damon choked on the water he'd just sipped.

"What's wrong? It's just chocolate on chocolate, and I know you love chocolate."

"Aye, I do," he rasped. "The name—it merely startled me, lass."

"You're so darn cute sometimes, Damon of Mysteria." Tossing aside her apron, she grabbed a book of matches and stood next to his chair to light some candles. He smelled clean, like coconut soap. His skin radiated heat and his personal scent that she found so distracting. She wouldn't mind a chaste kiss. *Get real.* She craved a real kiss, a hot, deep, toe-curling kind of kiss, the kind she daydreamed about when she was supposed to be working on her sermons.

His hand slid around her waist. "Cute? I dinna know if I'm that, lass, but ye do make me happy. Very happy."

He's never felt like this before. He's never been this happy. She shook off the strange, unbidden thought. Why were those things jumping into her head? It always seemed to happen when he touched her.

Harmony tried not to think about latent seer genes coming active, and instead turned around in the circle of Damon's arms and slid her arms over his shoulders. "You make me happy, too."

They'd never touched like this, so casually, so intimately. It had never been for the lack of wanting to, of course, but suddenly she wondered what in the world she was waiting for when it came to that real kiss she'd been wanting. And so she bent down and brushed her lips over his.

Just a taste, that was all she intended, but his lips were soft . . . warm. Perfect.

Damon made a soft sound of pleasure in his throat, opening his mouth to hers as his fingers slid into her hair at the back of her head to bring her closer. Her tongue brushed his, and soon they were kissing more boldly, her hands framing his jaw.

The next thing she knew, she was in his lap with her butt nestled between his hard thighs. Damon didn't just kiss; he savored her, relished her, drawing out the tender kiss the same way he'd delighted in every morsel of food from the day he arrived. Maybe even more so, made her feel as if she were the best thing he'd ever tasted, that his appetite was endless, insatiable, and that it wouldn't stop here, that he'd want more and more and . . .

Damon released her like a hot potato. "Good, good, good," he mumbled into her hair.

Laughing and gasping, Harmony rested her cheek against his jaw-bone. "Good. It was definitely that. Good, good, good."

"I dinna disagree. 'Tis why I'm trying to remind myself to behave."

She rubbed her thumb across his lower lip. "A good man, you are, Damon. A gentleman."

He glanced away, as if suddenly afraid of what she'd see in his eyes. "I haven't always been good, Harmony."

"The corrupt job with the corrupt boss . . ."

"Aye."

"But you're starting over. You have a new life." *You're clean,* she almost blurted out, but she couldn't tell him that, couldn't admit she'd checked up on him. It seemed a betrayal of everything he'd been so far, which was nothing less than, well, than good. "Only God's perfect, Damon. The rest of us do the best we can."

It always amazed her how his smile transformed his face. His bone structure was strong, and he could look almost cruel when his expression was serious, but whenever he grinned, he became so roguishly handsome it took her breath away. "I will always do my best for you," he said, pulling her close again. "Better than best."

Folding her in strong arms, he hugged her to his chest for the longest time, as if she somehow anchored him here on earth. The thought made her heart ache when she remembered how lost he seemed when he'd first arrived. Then, he pressed his mouth to her forehead in a kiss so achingly tender that it left her awash in goose bumps all the same.

Bubba crashed through the dog door, and they jumped apart.

"He's got something in his mouth." But Harmony only caught a glimpse of the rat-sized thing in Bubba's mouth before Damon blocked her view with his big hand. "Hey!" She tried peeling his fingers from her eyes. "I want to see."

"Nay. 'Tis not a pretty sight." Damon held her head to his chest with his left hand as he threw something with his right. She heard more water splash and a shriek. Did rats shriek? Several pairs of paws scrabbled on the floor. Then two loud swishes of the dog door and a lot of barking told her that whatever Bubba had caught managed to escape.

Harmony wriggled off Damon's lap. "I'm going after Bubba."

"Nay, lass. He'll be fine."

"What if the rat bites him?"

"The troll—er, rather, the rat—'twill have disappeared underground before the pup catches up."

"Underground? What are they—part gopher?"

From outside, Bubba yipped in frustration. Apparently, the rodent had indeed disappeared down its hole.

Harmony tugged on the hem of her blouse to recover some of the modesty she'd thrown to the wind. To forestall any further interruptions of dinner, of kisses, or of anything else, she shoved an empty chair in front of the dog door. Then she plopped down in her chair, clasped her hands under her chin, and whispered a quick and silent prayer to compose herself before saying grace. "Thank you, Lord, for the bounty we are about to eat. Thank you for bringing Damon here to help me." *And thank you for making him the most amazing kisser in the whole wide world!* "Amen."

For the first time in her presence, Damon murmured "amen," too. It sounded rusty on his lips, as if he'd not had much practice with prayer. It didn't trouble her; she'd seen inside his soul. He was cleaner and purer inside, where it counted, than some pastors she'd run across.

"Sometimes, lass, I dinna know if I have brought you help or harm."

She shook her head in confusion.

"Your thanks to God," he explained. "You gave thanks for my help, such as it is." He waved at the chair blocking the dog door. "It seems I have brought you more harm than good."

"You mean the rats? You can't blame yourself for that. We probably stirred them up when we cleaned out the hayloft."

He made a scoffing, grumbling sound in his throat.

"We'll get rid of them tomorrow. Besides, like I told you, they don't bother me that much. They bother my mama, though, so as long as you eradicate them before she gets here, I'm happy."

"I will try," he said with such pained seriousness that she put down her fork and knife to stare at him. "I'll do everything I can, lass. Everything. Until then, you must promise me never to be alone with them. Never fight them without me at your side."

"They're not monsters, Damon," she said with a laugh. "They're rats!"

He laughed weakly.

"And I know you'll slay them for me, brave knight, right?"

"Aye, fair maiden," he said with more vehemence than what seemed to fit the task. "'Tis my job to slay the beasties."

Nevertheless, through the rest of the supper, Damon acted edgy. Peering around the kitchen as he ate, he squinted at the corners, studied crevices, kept watch on the dog door she'd blocked.

When they'd finished, they didn't linger over conversation. Damon appeared too distracted. Harmony walked him to the back door. The air was warm for nighttime in these parts. Distant thunder echoed from somewhere over the Rockies. "It's going to be a hot one tomorrow," she observed, trying to act casual though she was acutely aware of his body so close to hers.

He turned to her. "Thank you for tonight."

"My pleasure."

"Aye, your pleasure will always be mine, lass."

Harmony gulped. Sigh. He had no idea. . . .

He stood there for a moment, studying her with a look that ping-ponged between desire and regret, then, chanting "Good, good, good" under his breath, he bid her good night as any respectable gentleman would a nun and walked away.

It was all she could do not to follow him back to the hayloft.

Behave, Harmony. Although she wasn't sure how much longer she'd be able to do so.

Pressing a cool glass of water against her cheek, she watched him go, wondering just what it was going to take to bring out the devil in Damon.

Ten

The next Sunday the men began trickling into church to see where the women were going. With every passing week more townsfolk came, until Harmony had to ask Damon to build her some more pews.

He did so gladly, though it took him away from his pet project, the installation of an expansive automatic sprinkler system surrounding the church. "The beasties don't like the water," he'd explained.

He must be right: ever since the water had been coming on every night, there hadn't been any more problems with rodents in the house. And as a side benefit, the lawn looked great, too. Unfortunately, they now had a glut of water-loving garden slugs to deal with. But at least those hadn't tried crashing dinner. Yet.

It was Sunday, T-minus one week and a day until her family invaded Mysteria, and Harmony was in the midst of delivering her sermon to a full house. Standing a few careful steps outside the half-open door, her loyal knight Damon stood guard, his arms folded over the end of a pitchfork as he leaned against the outside wall. Although he never stepped foot inside the church—"'tis not right," he'd insist so mournfully—he always listened carefully to her weekly message. Often she'd work in little things she hoped might help him escape his dark, mysterious past, something he remained reluctant to share. "I wasna good," he'd say in his brogue. Yet, without a criminal record anyone could unearth—and Jeanie had never stopped trying—how bad could he have been?

No sooner than Harmony conjured the thought than an unseasonably cold breeze whooshed inside the church. "Bad, bad," the wind seemed to whisper, a crackly, desiccated noise like the scratch of crinkled brown leaves on the sidewalk in autumn. With one hand fisted in the fabric of her cotton skirt to keep it from flying up, she tried to snatch back her papers from the whirlwind, but it only blew harder, whipping her hair around her face. "Evil," it hissed, drawing out the word. "Evil demon, baaaaad."

Then the wind surged in velocity, gushing between the pews, tossing off hats and whipping hair, until it hit Harmony full on and whirled around her like her own personal tornado, scattering the pages of her sermon. "Bad . . . bad . . . bad . . ."

Something pressed in on her mind, bitter, distasteful, like a taste of bile. She mentally flung it away. "The basement's unlocked," she shouted to her dispersing flock. "It may be a tornado. Get inside, take shelter!" But the wind erased her words.

"Baaaaaaaaaaaaaaaaaad," it rasped.

Stay away. Harmony shut her eyes and shoved. She didn't know what it was that she heard in the wind, only that whenever it touched her mind, she shuddered, repulsed.

"Reverend!" Jeanie Tortellini tried to assist her but the wind blew the woman backward.

"I'm okay!" But was she? She had to squint against the whistling gale in order to see. Damon was no longer at the door. Knowing him, he was outside helping others. "Find Damon. You two make sure everyone's okay. Get them in the basement if you have to." Barking the orders, the blind trust, it reminded her of when a missile had struck outside the field hospital in Iraq and she and the doctors were trapped inside. "Go, Jeanie! You know what to do. I'll be right there."

Jeanie ran off. As Harmony struggled as if swimming upstream to follow, she glimpsed Dr. Fogg, as calm as could be, observing the scene like the scientist-physician he was, jotting down notes on his Blackberry as he evacuated the building along with the rest of the townspeople.

Finally, Harmony fought her way outside to the porch. Outside, shadows arced and swooped. Birds. First a rodent invasion, now a bird invasion?

The wind subsided the moment Harmony exited the church, as if it had tried at first to keep her from doing so before giving up.

That's a weirder thought than the talking wind. No more of that, okay?

"I'm sane," she muttered. "Really I am. I just live in Mysteria, that's all—" She froze on the top step, her mouth falling open. The scene before her was so inexplicably impossible that her mind almost couldn't process it.

What at first glance she thought were birds weren't. "Flying monkeys?" she whispered. Good heaven, they were! From their little gold-trimmed suits to their Dixie-cup hats, they were replicas of the winged assistants from the movie *The Wizard of Oz*.

As if that weren't bad enough, Damon stood in the eye of the furry hurricane, fighting back as if the whole thing were personal.

Eleven

Damon swung his pitchfork at the flock of subdemons. "Be gone! Back to your Hell hole!" But with his powers reduced to what he could conjure as a mortal man, he could do little more than issue threats.

The subdemons had started emerging from a Hell hole in Harmony's vegetable garden while she was preaching. More and more of them. Damon had tried to get them all stuffed neatly back down the pit before church was over. He could turn on the sprinklers, aye, and wash them all away, but what a muddle it would make, melting, sizzling subdemons everywhere. And how would he explain the little articles of clothing left behind? Nay, 'twas better to scoop them up by the pitchforkful and shove them back to Hell before Harmony emerged from the church.

He'd actually gotten ahead of the game when the winds began. Filled with dread, Damon turned around, a wriggling subdemon, caught by the collar, still dangling from his pitchfork as townspeople poured out of the church.

Hell's bells. He should have known Lucifer would not let him win, would keep trying to sabotage the trust Damon had built in Harmony.

For if Damon were to win over Harmony Faithfull, Lucifer would lose. Over the past few weeks, the Devil had shown no signs of giving up on his quest to assure the defeat of his ex–demon high lord.

How many incidents such as this had there been over the past months? Too many to count. First there'd been the goblin in the barn, then the minitrolls in Harmony's kitchen. Now this, a flock of subdemons in the middle of the lawn in broad daylight on a Sunday morning, the most brazen violation yet! Well, except for the naked incubus he'd found sneaking through Harmony's bedroom window one night, but that may have been only a coincidence, the wrong window on the wrong night for the unfortunate dark creature.

Damon redoubled his efforts to get rid of the subdemons, but they swarmed. He'd seen a lot of scenes during his long years working for the Devil, but few as chaotic as this one unfolding on the front lawn of Mysteria Community Church. Townsfolk ran every which way, complicating his efforts to chase the beasties from the churchyard. Damon attended to the subdemons while simultaneously trying to joke about the infestation to impart calm to the crowd. Even for Mysteria, this was a strange happening, although many of the locals took it in stride. It would not be so in any other town.

Competing with the subdemons' raucous noise were the howls of the O'Cleary great-grandchildren, who ran wild like little demons themselves. Damon fancied that he'd like a family of his own someday, but two minutes spent with the O'Cleary offspring was almost enough to convince a man to drop all thoughts of procreation.

And then there was Dr. Fogg. His hair windblown, his tie whipping in the breeze, he pushed spectacles up the bridge of his elegant nose with one hand as he crouched down low, attempting to entice a subdemon with a broken Saltine cracker. Consorts with elves, that one does, Damon thought. The same with the sheriff. Damon could smell an elf a mile away, and even with his demon's senses almost gone, he knew well what the doctor and especially Harmony's friend Jeanie did in their spare time. Elves, too sexy for their pointy ears, they were. The town jail stank of them.

Damon knocked several more subdemons unconscious and dragged them to the Hell hole, shoving them back into the earth. "Tell your master his efforts are in vain. He'll never destroy me. He'll never turn me back the way I was before!" A derisive sound came up through the Hell hole, like a deep belch. The warm, moist breeze ruffled Damon's hair. 'Twas Lucifer himself answering him.

Damon's lips pulled back over his teeth. "Are you such a coward that you send your minions to do your dirty work? Why don't you come out and fight me yourself?" Damon raised the pitchfork. "Come on. Come up here and fight like a man. I may be mortal, but I'm ready for ye."

"Damon, who are you talking to?"

At the sound of the familiar voice, Damon's heart plunged into his stomach.

Harmony sounded poised at the razor's edge of hysteria.

"Dinna be afraid, lass!" With a sweep of the pitchfork, he took out several of the more brazen of the subdemons before her eyes, her wide, brown, disbelieving eyes. Some of the creatures lay dazed on the ground. A few crawled, pulling their broken bodies toward the Hell hole in the garden. Damon puffed up his chest and assured her, "They'll soon be gone."

"Gone . . ."

"Aye." That's when he noticed how brightly her eyes glowed, how her lips were so pale and tight, contrasting with her flushed cheeks. But what he noticed most of all was the shovel gripped in her white-knuckled hands, as if she meant to clang it against the side of his head. Nay, she was not frightened, not at all; she was as furious as the wind that had whipped her long hair and skirt only moments before.

Harmony's glare intensified. "Gone, like those so-called rats you found in my kitchen?"

Instinct told him no answer he gave would be the right one.

"Gone where, Damon? To the south, maybe? Isn't that where you told me you were from, Damon? Farther south than I've ever been? You weren't talking about Mexico, were you?" Harmony ducked as a subdemon swooped low overhead. Then she advanced on him, her nostrils flaring. "Were you!"

Damon hesitated, the pitchfork raised in midair as his heart sank.

A thousand alternate explanations came to mind, but with those excuses, would he not be slipping back into the lies that so characterized his previous life?

"Nay," he said gently. "I was not talking about Mexico. But I can explain. I . . ." *Say it*. He jerked his pitchfork at the sky. "I was one of them."

Harmony's eyes went wide. "A flying monkey?"

"Nay, lass! I was a demon."

Twelve

There was a terrible pause. Then Harmony asked, "A *demon* demon?"

"Aye, a demon demon."

"This is the truth, Damon. You swear?"

"I do."

Harmony made a strangled sound and raised her shovel high. For a moment, Damon was sure she'd whack him in the head, but she struck at a low-flying subdemon instead, and then another as they wheeled overhead, taunting him.

"Why didn't you tell me?" *Clang*. A subdemon fell to earth, another victim of Harmony's vicious swing. "Why didn't you?"

"I did! That very first day. In the kitchen. Ye thought I was lying." As she stared at him, he saw her gaze turn inward and knew she remembered. "But ye took me in all the same. Deny it you might, lass, but ye are as close to an angel as I've ever encountered."

She snorted. "What do you know about angels? You're a demon."

"*Was* a demon, lass. I was fired. Terminated without benefits."

Crash. Thwap. A little red hat sailed down to the grass. "Benefits. Oh, please. Hell has a retirement plan?"

"They did, once," he muttered. "No longer, it seems."

"Is nothing sacred anymore?" Her sarcasm was as sharp as a blade. "Well, there's always social security." *Thump*. Another subdemon dropped from the sky.

Water erupted from the grass, engulfing them in a drenching cold spray. Shrieking accompanied the deluge, but human shrieking this time. Semihuman, Damon qualified. Mrs. O'Cleary's great-grandchildren had somehow turned on the sprinklers. Any subdemon unlucky enough to be hit hissed and sizzled, screaming as they dissolved into little piles of doll-sized clothing.

"Who turned the sprinklers on?" Jeanie Tortellini ran across the churchyard, yelling, trying to regain control. The preteen Desdaine triplets, Withering, Scornful, and Derisive, whooped in delight. "How come no one's watching these kids?" she demanded of the parents who were wisely hiding behind some lawn chairs.

"Wait!" Harmony yelled to the woman. "Leave the water on! It's . . . it's killing them." She swung her glare around to Damon. "Just like what happened to the wicked witch in *The Wizard of Oz*. She melted. You knew this all along; you prepared for it by installing these sprinklers. And here I thought you were just a fan of irrigation!"

At that moment, Damon again understood that the best answer was no answer.

The lawn turned into a sea of mud. Children squealed with laughter as they grabbed the sprinkler heads and aimed water at the subdemons. Harmony's pumps made sucking noises. She snarled and threw her shoes one at a time at the creatures, striking one and knocking off its little red-and-gold hat. A jet of water clanged off the handle of Damon's pitchfork. He lost his balance. Harmony tried to steady him, but she slipped. They went down hard in the mud.

He turned to find her lips an inch away from his. His body was wrapped around hers as they lay sprawled on the ground, the same body that now reacted rather briskly to that pleasant discovery. He'd come to enjoy the sensations of his new body—advantages to being mortal that he'd never realized. But also disadvantages, one of which was poor timing, he decided quite quickly upon noting the fury contorting Harmony's face. "I should have been happy talking to the dog!"

Damon shook his head. "I dinna follow, lass . . ."

"I should have been satisfied with the simple things, the solitude, but no, I had to want more. A full house on Sundays." She gulped several breaths. "But what did I get? Demons and flying monkeys!" She threw down the shovel.

Her face was streaked with mud. He reached up to wipe her cheek with his thumb, but she recoiled as if she feared him. Feared what he was. He couldn't blame her.

"I kissed you, Damon!" she accused. "I kissed you!"

Aye, and he'd not stopped thinking about it, either.

"I cooked for you. I bought you underwear. I . . . I wanted to *make love* with you!"

You could have heard a pin drop in the sudden silence. Damon wasn't sure which one of them looked more shocked by her confession.

Then there was a loud whoosh. Water gushed out of a hijacked sprinkler and, aimed by mischievous little hands, ricocheted off a metal fence post, zinged overhead, and clipped off one of the chains holding the Mysteria Community Church banner over the church door. As if in surrender, the banner slid off the wall.

A fitting end to a terrible day.

Harmony watched the sign fall. Looking as if she were about to cry, she stopped herself and dashed the heel of her palm across her eyes. Muddy water streamed from her hair and dribbled down her ruined dress.

"Lass . . . ," he tried, lifting a hand to her. Then he hesitated, fearing her vulnerable stance was deceptive, that if he touched her, tried to hold her, she'd snap like a too taut spring and fly away from him. As it was, she pushed to her feet without another word and went to join Jeanie in restoring order.

Damon watched her go. So much had changed since he'd come to Mysteria, and yet so little. He was as much a reason for doubt and second thoughts as he ever was.

An oddly pitched scream tore into his self-pitying thoughts. He saw an O'Cleary child go down under the weight of several angry subdemons, a situation missed by others in the chaos. Subdemons were dark creatures with little power, but enough of them could kill a small human. Could kill a child.

Damon surged to his feet, the pitchfork in hand. A half-dozen strides brought him to where the child's thin legs kicked. Damon grabbed one beastie by its collar and threw it to the ground. Then he dragged the remaining creatures off the frightened child.

The little girl's face was without color, her blue eyes wide and tear-filled. "Are you hurt, little one?"

She shook her head, but her lower lip trembled. "Scared?" he asked gently, coming down on one knee.

She nodded, her mouth wobbling. Damon lifted her fist, which was still clamping a plastic water gun. He smiled. "Would ye like to get them back?"

She grinned. "Yeah!"

"Then let's do it." He hoisted her under his arm. "Fire away!" With the child pumping water out of the little toy gun, he chased fleeing subdemons to the Hell hole, followed enthusiastically by a wildly barking Bubba and a herd of miniature O'Clearys. When every last one had either melted or vanished into the depths of Hell, Damon lowered the little girl to the ground. Her skinny shoulders felt so delicate under his hands. A sudden rush of emotion threatened to swamp him, a sensation still so new. This child encapsulated all that was fragile and good on this earth; all that he'd hoped to protect, to cherish. "What is your name?"

"Annabelle," she answered in a tremulous voice.

"Bullies, that's all they are, Annabelle. Ye canna be afraid. Your goodness, 'twill always win out. Ye are stronger than them. Far stronger. Do ye understand?"

Annabelle nodded, and he touched a fingertip to her little freckled nose before rising to his feet. His breath caught in his throat when he realized Harmony had been watching him the entire time, her face so full of pain that he had to turn away from her horrified gaze.

Damon trudged to the sprinkler timer box to shut off the water, but before he reached the shutoff valve, and as everyone began to come up from the basement and from behind chairs and under tables—just as everyone thought it was safe—little Annabelle O'Cleary fired off one last salvo with the hose, aiming the water at her parents as her brothers and sisters, not appearing a wee bit sorry, fled the scene.

Damon wrested the hose from Annabelle's little hands. "Off with ye now, little hell-raiser." With grudging admiration, he sent her on her way. Then he tended to the shaken townspeople, working his charm as best he could to coax assurances that they'd return to church the next week. All the while he felt Harmony's gaze on him, and his face burned in shame.

Jeanie sauntered up to him. "I've seen a lot of unusual goings-on in this town, but not this. What were those animals?"

"Are they not from Mysteria?" Damon tried charming the sheriff with one of his smiles, but her gaze sharpened.

"It won't work, Damon. Not with me. And just for your informa-tion"—she bobbed her chin in Harmony's direction—"it won't work with her, either. I want the facts, not the glossed-over version."

"Aye, I know," he said with a sigh. "I'd tried to keep it from her so I wouldn't lose her, but now that I have, secrets do me no good. In Satan's army, there is a hierarchy. At the apex are the demon high lords, Lucifer's commanders. Then there are the foot soldiers, the scores of classes of underlords, demon worker-bees, and subdemons. They can take the form of almost any monster, from ant-size on up, and with more ways to intimidate, frighten, and kill than can be counted. New versions are created every day."

"Like . . . Demon 8.0," Jeanie joked, jotting down the information.

"That is a way to look at it," Damon said sadly, gazing over at Harmony, who refused to meet his eyes.

Jeanie noted the exchange and put down her notepad. "You're in deep shit, aren't you?"

"Deep, really deep, aye."

"We Mysteria women call it doghouse deep. And there's only one thing you can do. Go fix it."

"I dinna know if it's possible."

"Her job is to forgive, Damon. That'll be the easy part. All you have to do is to convince her to put her heart into it." She chucked him on the arm. "Good luck. I know you can do it."

Could he?

Damon found Harmony in the barn, washing mud off her hands and face at the work sink. Harmony turned around, wiping her hands on her soiled skirt. Water and tears had smudged the makeup under her wide, expressive brown eyes. She studied him for a moment, as if he were a stranger. Then she blew her nose in a paper towel. "No wonder you didn't like devil's food cake."

His chest hurt. "Yes, I have a past, of which ye know little."

He told her everything, as best a man could summarize ten thousand years of walking the earth.

"Ten thousand years." Harmony's voice came out as a squeak. "A *hundred* centuries."

"Aye, but I've lived more in these past few months than in all the time before." He told her the story of the starving settlers of Mysteria, how he'd given them the Will-to-Go-On, how he'd repeated such acts all around the globe until Lucifer found out and captured him. He told her about the torture, his being made mortal, and finally how he'd woken, dazed and naked, in her garden, terminated and pensionless. "I thought he was done with me, then, Lucifer was. But 'tis clear he's not yet finished. And for that, lass, I am truly sorry . . . for what you've suffered as a consequence. And 'tis about you, for the Devil does not want me to have something good, you see. Then I'll have won. If there's one thing I know about Lucifer—he does not like to lose."

"Is everything okay in here?" Jeanie Tortellini poked her head in the barn.

"Fine!" they both shouted a little too quickly.

The sheriff shot Damon a you-poor-bastard wink. "The water's off, Reverend; I locked up the church. Everyone's gone home—it's a ghost town out there." Jeanie clamped her mouth closed, as if realizing that was a poor choice of words, given Harmony's profession—and mood. She held up a little gold-trimmed red coat. "But on the plus side, there are enough doll clothes left behind to supply every little girl's collection in Mysteria." She sniffed at the garment and grimaced. "Once they've been through the wash, that is. Hey, I'll be down at the jail, so call me if you need me." Jeanie waved good-bye and slid the door closed.

Damon sighed. It was time to pack up his things, tidy the hayloft, and leave. But there was one last thing he had to say. "I am sorry, lass. I know those words do not come close to making up for all the disasters I've wreaked here, but know this: What I did, what I said, I did in hopes it would keep ye close—close to me. Know that. But I see now what I feared most has come to pass. I've lost you," he finished valiantly and turned away.

"Damon, please."

He stopped.

"You haven't lost me."

His head snapped around. "Say it again, lass. I dinna think I heard you."

The ends of her luscious mouth curved slightly. "You haven't lost me."

A harsh breath escaped him. He hadn't lost her; somehow, he hadn't chased her away.

What if Lucifer learns of this?

Damon squeezed his eyes shut. *Dinna think of it.* Like he'd told the child Annabelle, good always triumphs over evil, and he must summon the faith to believe in it.

"I lost sight of something today, something very important." Harmony brought her hands together, clasping them tightly as if she were nervous, nervous as he. "The best sermons are lived, not preached. I'll never forget the day my great-grandmother Eudora said that to my father, when she disagreed with something he'd done. She'd have scolded me today, told me the same thing, when she saw how quickly I wanted to condemn you. Seeing that God's forgiven you, it might be a little arrogant if I didn't. Ya think?"

"Only God's perfect, Harmony," he said, reminding her of her words to him shortly after he arrived in Mysteria. "The rest of us do the best we can."

"Yes, we do." Her eyes were luminous with tears as she walked to him and lifted a trembling hand to his cheek. He pressed his hand over hers as his emotions soared to heaven. "It doesn't matter what you were before, Damon. It doesn't. I had a calling to come here, and when I did, nothing was what I'd expected. But I knew God watched over everyone who lived here, whether they chose to see it or not. And then you came, and through you I fulfilled my calling here, through love. You're so full of love, Damon. What went down before doesn't matter. You're a beautiful man with a beautiful soul, and that's all that counts."

His mood crashed immediately. A beautiful soul? "Lass, I was a demon, born of shadows. I know you've insisted that all humans have a soul, but I was not created as you were. The Devil crafted me, not God."

She propped her hands on her hips. "Is this why you've never wanted to step inside the church?"

"I feared holy retribution—plagues, lightning strikes, and the like."

Harmony snorted. "Oh, puleeze. You'll have to find another excuse." She poked him on the chest with her index finger. "You can't fool me when it comes to souls, sir. I'm a Faithfull. Knowing souls is in our blood. I saw what you did to help little Annabelle O'Cleary. A man with no soul never would have done that, alleviated a little girl's fear, or have run around afterward, convincing everyone they needed to come back to church next week, and not to be scared—and they believed you, Damon. A man with no soul never would exude the zest for life that you do, or the energy, your ability to make people laugh and feel comfortable. A man with no soul never would have . . . never would have . . ." Her finger trailed down his stomach, and she blushed deeply.

"Never would have what, lass?" he coaxed.

"Never would have made me fall in love with him." She smiled softly. "With *you*."

Damon's heart crashed against his ribs. She loved him! 'Twas everything he'd ever wanted, for so many hundreds of years, to know love, to experience the pure and simple joy of it, the giving and receiving. To be human enough to share himself with someone else, to sacrifice. And now that it was placed before him, this miracle, he was all but paralyzed for fear of breaking the spell.

"Oh, lass," he managed stupidly. "Are ye sure?"

"Never been more sure of anything in my life."

Slinging an arm low around her waist, he drew her close. "Never been more sure," she whispered against his lips. In the next instant, he was kissing her, falling head over heels into the well of joy that was this woman, who said she loved him. *Loved him!* Who said he had a soul.

From the conviction in her voice, he believed her. He remembered the feeling that had surged into him the moment he'd defied Lucifer. But even that explosion of joy and rightness dimmed with the knowledge that Harmony Faithfull loved him. Wanted him.

Then something Harmony had said earlier came crashing back into his mind. "Lass, forgive me if I misunderstood you out there on the lawn, but didn't you mention you'd wanted to make love with me?"

"Yeah, I did." She grabbed his butt and hauled him close. "And if I don't do it soon, I might explode!"

"Hell's bells, so will I." Grinning eagerly, he swept her off her feet and carried her swiftly to the bedchamber in her house.

Thirteen

Together they fell onto the bed. Harmony laughed, exhilarated; being with Damon was like riding a roller coaster, and now it was perched precariously on the highest hill.

Damon's weight pressed her deep into the mattress. It felt delicious. *He* was delicious! Her hands slid everywhere, his muscled back, his abs, the thickly muscled arms. That amazing body, she had it all to herself—and everything else that came with it. Yes, everything else, and God forgive her for going after it so greedily.

"Kiss me," she told Damon, her fingers curling in the damp fabric of his shirt. She dragged him down to her mouth and kissed him, hard and deep. Dark, sweet heat. Slick and wet. The rasp of his whiskers as she explored with her tongue. He was the best thing she'd ever tasted, and she was hungry for more.

A deep sound rumbled in his chest in reaction to her eagerness. Shyness hadn't entered her mind, only that she'd wanted him like this for so many weeks.

A beautiful man. A beautiful soul.

But he was a demon! Satan's helper.

He's starting over. A new life. He's clean, real clean, remember?

As for his kiss? Hoo boy, it burned so hot it made Hell look cold. She'd gladly pay penance for that decidedly unholy thought—but tomorrow. Not now.

"Mmm," she murmured as they kissed. "Mmm." Smiling, she tore through the buttons on his shirt.

The scrape of Damon's teeth on the side of her throat made her shiver as he fumbled with the waistband of her skirt. His hand slid up her inner thigh, and she could feel him tremble. When he touched her between her legs, the spasm of pleasure was so intense that her body gave an involuntary little jerk. If that was what his fingers could do, then she could only imagine—

"Too many clothes on ye, lass." Her panties came off next, and the rest of their clothes went every which way.

Damon flipped her over, kissed her behind her knees and made her giggle. "'Tis my first time, ye know," he told her as he trailed kisses up her spine, pausing to lick a sensitive little place between her shoulder blades that she never knew existed.

"First time what?" she gasped, delighted with his creativity with all the places he found to touch with his tongue and his lips.

"My first time making love."

Harmony rolled over to stare at him. Sometimes lip reading helped with communication, especially when the messages were garbled. "You're not a virgin."

"Aye, I am."

"Listen, if this is something you've come up with to make up for the whole demon thing—"

"Hush." He pressed a finger to her lips. "'Tis the truth. Ye are my first." He didn't seem bothered by the fact in the least, nor hindered by any lack of confidence, she thought, as he pulled one bra strap down, then the other, lowering the lace until he found her nipples, lavishing each with attention as if they were made of the finest, most delectable chocolate. "No need to worry, lass. I know exactly what to do."

She tipped her head back to the pillow and moaned. "I can't argue that, baby." Her sexy Scottish hunk was a virgin! She nearly whooped with delight. "You don't act like it's your first time."

"I've experienced little, aye, but have seen much," he murmured as he concentrated on pleasuring her. "Pagan lovers mating inside stone circles on Midsummer Eves . . . Viking wedding nights, the harems of Arabia . . . Roman orgies."

Pagan mating rituals? Harems? Roman orgies? "Damon, honey, I don't know if we're on the same page."

"I know the difference, love, between what I saw and this. Trust me. My instincts are good." His arms bulged with muscles as he did a push-up over her, dipping his head to kiss her neck. Then he flipped her over and bit her on the butt. She squealed, and he laughed, soothing where he'd nipped her with kisses, then tossing her over again only to enter her, thickly, deeply. Her breath caught as her back arched, and she made a little gasp of surprise. Damon's expression shifted from astonishment to tenderness to hunger; his eyelids fell half-closed, and the softest groan of pleasure slipped out after he breathed her name. Although she could feel the intensity of Damon's emotions pressing on her mind, all she needed to know was right here, written on his face, everything he felt being with her, out in the open.

Her belly squeezed as he pushed slowly deeper, filling her, stretching her. She was glad he was going slow. It had been a long time for her, and she hadn't expected he'd take her this quickly. But maybe foreplay wasn't as popular in ancient times as it was now. Then again, she hadn't been waiting ten thousand years to "do it." Only since college, which had sometimes felt as long.

Yet, her body was ready for him—whoa, more than ready. The mere weight of his body pressing her into the mattress had her panting in anticipation.

"Ye are my first," he squeezed out in a harsh breath. "My first, aye, my only, and my last." Clutching her hips possessively, he pushed all the way home, sending shockwaves clear down to her toes.

He moved slowly, at first, not hesitant but most definitely reined in. She drew her knees higher on his hips, squeezing him with her thighs, to hold him there, to hold him close. Gradually, he gained confidence with her moans of delight. And when he finally found his rhythm, it was all she could do to hold on and ride the storm.

Just when she thought it couldn't get any better, he rolled onto his back, pulling her with him, somehow remaining deep inside her.

She straddled him, astonished, her hair tumbling over his chest. But he moved her backward so his hand could slip between their bodies. And watched her, as she'd watched his reactions earlier, his fingers dipping between her legs where she was so wet, teasing, circling, as he thrust faster and deeper. Her head fell back. "Damon . . ."

Tremors fluttered in her stomach, sharpening, hot, so hot. The quivering built to an ache that swelled until it was almost unbearable. She couldn't breathe, couldn't speak. Heaven help her, she never knew it could be like this. Never knew it could be this good.

Damon touched her again, and her climax took her; she cried out, grabbing the bedsheets, as if to keep herself from flying away.

In the midst of it all, Damon went rigid and gasped her name. It seemed to go on for a long time for him, his release, powerful and intense. Then, as he collapsed in a panting heap on the mattress, he reached blindly for her and pulled her close.

Sweat dampened his skin, and hers. Exhausted, she kissed him, tasting salt, inhaling his scent.

"Ah, Harmony, love." His deep voice vibrated in his chest, his breath hot against her ear. "Ah, my sweet angel."

She came up on her elbow and smiled at his stunned expression. "Happy?"

"Aye . . ."

"So, it was everything you hoped it'd be?"

He let out an amazed chuckle. "If this is what it feels like to be human, lass, then I've but one thing to say."

She grinned, trailing her fingertips over his lips. "What's that?"

"Immortality is highly overrated."

* * *

Much later, they lay abed, dozing, limbs tangled after making love yet again. Damon couldn't get enough of Harmony, but was trying to control his appetite so as not to hurt her. She didn't seem to have suffered overly much, though, he thought with a smug smile.

He gathered her in his arms as she slept. Deny it she might, but Harmony Faithfull was as close to an angel in human form as he'd ever encountered. And he would know. It'd been many thousands of years since he'd crossed paths with the angels, and even then it was to do battle with the archangels, like Michael and Gabriel, fearsome warriors, equals to him in all ways of war. But it was the stories of the lesser angels that had always captivated him through the long centuries. Sweet, they were said to be, and mysterious, beautiful enough to bring a mortal man to tears, he'd overheard some humans say. Some of the angels were so pure of heart and intentions that they could lure a demon from the inexorable pull of the depths of Hell to the plains of the mortal world. Aye, Lucifer raged for many days after losing one of his best demon high lords in such a fashion. Pompeii was the result of that particular tantrum. Damon knew, because he'd been dispatched on assignment to do Lucifer's dirty work immediately after. Memories boiled up: *Fire . . . the stench of cinders and death. A sky roiling with black, sulfurous smoke.* Damon had walked the destroyed streets of the city, feeling nothing, simply doing what he'd been brought into existence to do: planting fear, doubt, and second thoughts, and accomplishing it with no emotion at all. He may have lost his demon's heightened senses, but not the memory of how it felt to have the darkness inside him, the coldness. How it felt to be empty.

"Unlike now," he murmured, burying his face in Harmony's curls. "Unlike now . . ."

Time seemed to stand still as the sun slowly rose. It reached the level of the windowsill and spilled into the bedroom, waking Harmony. "I suppose we should get up." Her voice was thick from sleep and spent passion.

Damon pulled her close. Slid his hand down her warm belly to find her moist and hot. "Why not stay abed a while longer?"

"Mmm." Harmony turned in his arms and they kissed, and then he loved her, slowly, carefully, savoring her. Afterward they drowsed in each other's arms. Damon had never imagined this sort of contentment existed. This happiness. He did not want the day to arrive and interrupt it all. And apparently, neither did his lover.

They dozed a while longer until Bubba came to the bedside, whining to be let out. Since more than dogs could squeeze through the dog door in the kitchen, Harmony kept it locked at night.

Damon offered, "I'll take him." Naked, he flung open the door to the solitude of the backyard, scratching his chest as he yawned and waited as the dog trotted onto the lawn.

Bubba lifted his leg and did his business, but instead of returning, he darted across the lawn, barking his announcing-visitors bark.

"Who's here?" Harmony called from the bed.

Damon squinted toward the road. "Someone's driving through the front gate. 'Tis a large, silver boxy vehicle."

"Is it a Humvee?" Harmony's voice sounded a wee bit strange.

"I dinna know," he said. "But the license plate says . . . #1 Pastor."

"Oh, no! No, no, no." Harmony leaped out of bed, tripping in the tangled sheets as she shoved one arm into her robe and then the other. Damon's heart sped up at her panic. "They're here. I can't believe they're here. Why do these things always happen to me? I try to live a godly life, and I do . . . well, except for last night, and I don't regret that for a moment, but this—this is just so typical of my life." She whipped the robe around her lush body. "I am so busted."

Damon grabbed her shoulders and steadied her. "Tell me. Who is in that car?"

"My father. My family. They showed up one week early!"

Fourteen

After the initial burst of panic from the shock of her family's unexpected arrival blew past, Harmony forced herself into combat mode. It was like the time in Iraq when the shell hit right outside the hospital.

She shoved the rumpled quilt over the sheets, collected scattered pillows, and arranged them hurriedly, wondering where she could arrange Damon where no one would notice him but quickly coming to the conclusion that not a single nook or cranny in the farmhouse would hide a six-foot-five-inch-tall ex-demon.

The doors to the Humvee slammed. Her heart tumbled as she peeked around an eyelet curtain. "They're unpacking the car, they always do it before coming in, and they're slow. It'll buy us some time, but precious little. Just enough time for a shower, I think." She slapped her hands on his gorgeous bare butt and pushed him toward the bathroom. "We have about two minutes. Maybe less. So I'm coming with you."

Damon appeared delighted by that fact, until remembering the car in the driveway. Harmony pulled him under the gushing water with her. "This is going to be the fastest shower you've ever had."

They soaped each other hastily.

Harmony grabbed blindly for two towels as water from her soaked hair streamed over her face. "Here's the plan. I'll get dressed and go meet them. You go out the side door—grab anything, tools, whatever, make it look like you were working—and I'll bring them inside and distract them with breakfast."

He brought his hand to her cheek, a calming touch. "I willna do anything to embarrass you."

"I know, honey. I know. You'd never embarrass me, Damon. I'm proud to be with you. It's just that . . ." She waved at the bed. "This isn't exactly proper behavior for a pastor, and especially for Reverend Faithfull's daughter."

He pressed a hurried but heartfelt kiss to her lips. "You dinna need to explain. I know what to do."

Harmony uttered a prayer of thanks for Damon's understanding as he grabbed his clothes and hurried out the side door.

Somehow she got herself together, pulling on yoga pants and a T-shirt. She secured her thick mass of soaking wet curls atop her head, jamming in a couple of pins to hold it in place, and burst outside, where Bubba pranced and jumped around her family and their suitcases. Car doors slammed, and her family bustled around the luggage, chattering and laughing, clearly excited to be there. Harmony smiled, her heart filling at the sight of them: Daddy tall and graying, but still so handsome, looking strangely underdressed in his sweatshirt and ironed Levi's; Mama, regal as always in her role as Reverend Jacob Jethro's wife but as light on her feet as the star athlete she once was when she met her husband at their high school track meet; Harmony's oldest brother, Jake Jr., was busy unloading the trunk—one thing about the Faithfulls, they didn't travel light. And Robbie had come, too, at sixteen the youngest Faithfull, attentive and respectful as he helped Great-grandmother Eudora step down from the rear passenger seat.

Harmony gulped, her stomach dropping. What would the woman see? What would she know? Too much already, Harmony thought, remembering the phone call with her father, when Eudora seemed to know about Damon.

Walking carefully, methodically, Eudora leaned on her cane. As always, she was dressed to the nines: a sapphire blue skirt set, with clusters of pearls clipped on her ears and around her neck, and a chocolate brown wig slightly askew. Step by careful step, she walked around the front of the truck, sucking on her false teeth. Her cane sank into the squishy, damp grass, and she stopped. Frowning, she shook her head in disapproval. Wheeling a bright red suitcase, Mama joined her to stare at the clods of displaced sod, the gouges and skid marks, the broken sprinkler heads, pieces of tattered cloth, and someone's forgotten sneaker.

The ruined yard.

"Hell's bells," Harmony whispered. She hadn't realized so much damage had been left behind. Her shaking hand crept up to the little cross she wore around her neck. *Lord, give me strength—oh, and the creativity—to come up with some really good answers to their questions.* Then, with her mouth formed into the biggest, most welcoming smile she could muster, she glided out to them, her arms wide open. "Wow, isn't this just the best surprise!"

In the next instant, she was swallowed up in a huddle of love, hugs, and kisses.

"We were going to spend this week in Rocky Mountain National Park," her father explained, "but when we saw the exit leading to Mysteria—"

"We simply couldn't pass it by," Mama finished for him. "I had to see my baby."

Eudora grasped Harmony's hands in hers. Her skin was once the color of rich caramel; now it was almost transparent over a network of bluish veins. Despite mild palsy, her grip remained as powerful as her intense gray-brown eyes. "Ah, you're happy, girl, aren't you?"

"I am, Great-grandma," Harmony replied shyly. "Very happy." *She knows what you did last night.* The thought popped into Harmony's mind, clear and simple. Her first instinct was to look away, to break the eye contact, but she stayed strong. Fact: Eudora knew what was going on between her and Damon. No way could she hide it. The best Harmony could hope for was for Great-grandmother not to say anything.

"What happened here?" Mama waved a manicured hand at the lawn.

"Um, a circus," Harmony blurted. *Good one.* "Yes, we had a bit of a circus here yesterday after services." That wasn't really lying, was it?

Mama brought her hands together in delight. "Isn't it wonderful, Jake? Our girl's as creative in spreading the good word as you."

Harmony shrank back in shame as her father puffed himself up. "I'm proud of you, Harmony. So proud of what you've done here in so short of a time."

Oh, boy. If you only knew.

"You got someone to put in sprinklers," Jake commented. "Looks like a first-class job. You didn't do it yourself, did you?"

"I did," said a familiar deep voice.

Harmony's heart bounced as Damon strode toward the group, a length of PVC pipe and a new sprinkler head in one hand, his other hand extended in welcome. "I'm Damon, the church groundskeeper." Dressed in clean clothes, his hair brushed neatly away from his freshly shaven face, Damon looked so bright and alert that no one would ever guess he'd been doing anything other than . . . well, than what he'd been doing all night.

Harmony blushed; she couldn't help it. "I'd been looking for someone to hire, a handyman and groundskeeper, when Damon came along looking for work. He's been wonderful, such a help, a blessing, truly."

At her gushing, Damon seemed almost bashful. The part that touched her the most was that it wasn't an act. "Reverend Faithfull needed someone for the heavier work so she could concentrate on the church. I've been busy making repairs and working in the fields"—he pulled a plump ear of corn from his overalls pocket, to the obvious delight of her family—"and once Harmony approves the plans I've drawn up for the barn, Mysteria Community Church will have a new social hall and gym."

"We will?" Shocked, Harmony watched Damon withdraw a folded piece of paper from his pocket. On it was a detailed drawing that he'd clearly spent a lot of time on and that she'd known nothing about. "Well," she said, "as you can see, Damon is indispensable."

Eudora cackled and patted his hand. "I see a lot of things about Damon."

Harmony's smile was wooden at best. Why, oh, why did she have to have a seer as a great-grandma? Why couldn't she have a normal family, who wouldn't be able to tell that she'd acquired a decidedly out-of-the-ordinary boyfriend?

"You're a good boy," the old woman said. Then she winked. "Good, good, good."

Damon coughed. It was the first time Harmony had seen him blush.

Eudora ran an admiring gaze over Damon's muscular frame, nodding, her eyes crinkling, then she gave Harmony an admiring, conspiratorial he's-hot wink before hobbling away to lead the clan to the house.

Harmony sidled up to Damon as her family walked on ahead. Pointing to her eyes, she whispered, "She's a seer. She can read thoughts sometimes. Just don't say it out loud."

"But she knows, lass. She knows what I am."

"She knows what you *were*." Harmony took a deep, calming breath. "And all we have to do is keep the rest of the family from finding out."

It was like old times with the family hanging around the kitchen counters and table just like they did in the big house in Oakland. After everyone had had a tour of the property, the church, and the house, Harmony prepared a late brunch, laughing and catching up.

Bacon sizzled in a cast-iron pan; grits bubbled thickly in a pot, while Mama stirred gravy for the fluffy, towering biscuits in the oven. Eudora sat at the table, sucking on her false teeth, while the men argued about basketball. "We didn't have basketball in Scotland," Damon was telling them.

"Hoops after breakfast," Robbie decided.

Her father wouldn't hear of letting Damon sneak away to work, and held him captive in the kitchen as if he were already a member of the family. Damon soaked up the noise and laughter. Harmony's heart squeezed tight when she realized that this was something he'd never had—a family.

This was all going much better than she'd expected. When was the other shoe going to drop?

It's not going to drop. After yesterday's disaster, what could happen today that would be worse than that? Smiling, Harmony set the table, expanded with two extra leaves, and placed a strawberry dipped in powdered sugar as a garnish next to each person's antique china coffee cup.

She straightened, admiring the festive look the fruit and china brought to the table, and was about to tend to the bacon when in the corner of her eye she saw something move.

She blinked. Surely it was lack of sleep playing tricks with her vision. *Please, Lord, let it be that.*

She waited for more movement. Nothing. She was seeing things.

As soon as the food was ready, everyone sat around the table. Damon, bless his sweet heart, pulled out her chair, taking cues from her father and brother Jake, who did the same for Mama and Eudora.

Even though only one-third of the Faithfulls were in attendance, they were a noisy group, and the conversation filled the small kitchen. Dishes were passed around. When everyone's plates were filled, they joined hands to say grace.

In the hush that came over the room, Harmony's coffee cup scraped sideways. Her hand shot out, stopping it. "Fly," she explained urgently, her heart in her mouth. "They're really in abundance this time of year."

The moving cups had been no trick of her eyes. She prayed for inspiration, for an excuse, an explanation, anything at all to hop into her head and out her mouth, but the prospect of monsters from Hell appearing while her family was here had all but paralyzed her.

"Hold Great-grandma's hand, baby," her mother urged. "Your father wants to say grace."

Ever so reluctantly, Harmony withdrew her hand from the cup and slid her fingers back into Eudora's cool, dry palm. As Reverend Faithfull's resonant voice boomed, everyone's eyes were closed, except for Harmony's. Eyes wide open, she stared at the cup. But from across the table, she heard a soft scrape. Heart pounding, she watched three of the cups slide across the table, pushed by the strawberries. Switching positions, the cups moved around in some sort of paranormal shell game. Harmony made a squeak, and both Eudora and Damon squeezed her hands.

"He plays with you because you don't know how to fight him," the old woman whispered. Instinctively, Harmony knew her great-grandmother meant the Devil himself. "If you fight his evil with goodness, he'll lose interest and cease his games. Not forever, mind you, but for now."

Damon murmured back, "My powers, they are gone."

Eudora clucked in disapproval. "They're different now, your powers, not gone, and stronger than ever for the enemy you will face for a lifetime."

Mama opened an eye. "We will discuss the flies once your father is done speaking."

They were silent for a moment, then their furtive whispering continued.

"Harmony has never accepted she has powers," Eudora continued, "but she's come into them now. It's what drew you to her, Damon, and her to you. And what still attracts Satan to you both. He feels the power, the power of good, and it threatens him."

With that scary thought lingering in the air, Harmony's father finished grace. "Amen," they all said, and with a clattering of plates, silverware, and voices, the brunch began.

Harmony's appetite had vanished. Damon sat tense and ready for battle.

"Who moved the strawberries and mugs during grace?" Jake Jr. asked, laughing. "You, Robbie?"

His little brother looked indignant. "It wasn't me."

"When we were kids, we used to play pranks when everyone's eyes were closed during grace," Harmony explained to Damon. To the others, she said, "I . . . um, thought it'd be fun to take a trip down memory lane."

Everyone moaned at her. "Harmony . . ."

Her laugh was brittle. "Sorry, it was too much fun to resist," she said, thankful for the chance at an excuse for the displaced cups.

Then her strawberry bounced into the air. She snatched it. Before she could take a bite out of it and pretend nothing was wrong, she saw a tiny green creature hanging from the stem.

A little green man.

"Ah!" She dropped the berry into her grits with a noisy plop. Her mother glanced at her sharply. "A caterpillar," she explained breathlessly. "The countryside is full of them." Where did the green man go? Was it drowning?

Then Damon's cup jerked forward. His hand slammed over it.

"Aye, nothing we do seems to stop them." Then he leaned over and whispered in her ear. He sounded sick at heart. "Snotlings."

"What are those?" Her voice sounded strained and shaky, and a little bit crazed. "Wait, it doesn't matter. How do we get rid of them?" She reached for the pitcher of water, and he caught her hand.

"Water has no effect," he whispered. Harmony could see her family trying to catch a snatch of their hushed conversation. "They are the smallest of the green-skinned races. The orcs and goblins use them as slaves for simple tasks because they're not intelligent creatures."

A snotling peeked out from under her father's plate. Harmony watched in dread as her father cut into his strawberry with his knife and fork. "They seem smart enough to me."

"I mean, they are not a threat on their own to other creatures. They form gangs to attack."

Jake Jr.'s strawberry rolled to the edge of the table. He caught it in his palm before it leaped off the edge. "Your table needs leveling, kiddo," he informed Harmony. "The food is rolling off."

She made a weak laugh. "There's still so much to do around here." Something green darted across her plate. She squished it under a biscuit. Her mother frowned at her, as if she were a child playing with her food. But that impression was better than the alternative.

The fork on Great-grandma's plate rattled. Utterly calm, Eudora covered it with her napkin. What if Daddy's plate was attacked next? Or Mama's? What if they saw they weren't caterpillars or flies? Perspiration trickled between Harmony's breasts. Her heartbeat was erratic. She was never going to make it through this meal without passing out. Short of screaming fire, how was she going to evacuate her family from the kitchen?

"Bullies," Damon muttered softly. "That's all they are. Ye canna be afraid. Goodness will always win out. We are stronger than them. Far stronger."

"Then why do they keep returning?" Harmony whispered.

"Because they can," Eudora said. "Damon is correct. You have the power to eliminate them."

"We've tried. Nothing works."

"Call a pest control company," Jake Jr. suggested, biting into a piece of bacon.

"Monday," Harmony mumbled. "I'll give them a call. If I'm not dead by then."

The old woman frowned. "Satan torments you because your panic makes it fun. Take away the reason for his amusement, and he'll forget about this place and move on. Not forever, mind you, but for now."

Harmony tried to read the woman's mysterious expression. "How do you know so much about Satan?"

Her eyes seemed suddenly ancient. "Oh, we've crossed paths before."

"Grandma . . . please." Daddy shook his head. "Let's keep our mealtime conversations on happier things. Heaven, for instance, as opposed to Hell."

Eudora placed her hands in her lap, primly, but Harmony didn't buy it for a moment. "It's always good to be grateful for what we have so much in abundance in this family," she reminded him. "Our goodness."

Murmurs of agreement went around the table.

Eudora continued with her little homily, addressing her father, even though Harmony knew the lesson was intended for her and Damon. "Because of your position and power, Jake, Satan toyed with our family more than once. He places temptation in our path, tries to ruin us, but I'm always ready for him. Always ready."

She took Harmony's hand and Damon's and brought them together under the table. Damon's fingers were hot and dry. Her body gave a little leap, remembering the feel of that hand sliding over her bare skin, doing the most amazing things. . . .

A cup clattered against a plate. Harmony squeaked and tried to pull away, but Eudora hissed at her. "No."

"But—"

"No!" Eudora placed her arms over Harmony's shoulders, Damon's, too, and drew them close. "Believe in your power to defeat him, and you will. Fill your minds with goodness, and together push it outward. He'll not be able to stand against you."

"That sounds too simple."

"It is. That's what too few people remember. Good and evil. Right versus wrong. Yes versus no. There's nothing complicated about it. Good repels wickedness. If it were otherwise, the world would have gone to hell in more ways than one eons ago."

"Aye," Harmony heard Damon murmur, as if he understood.

"Hold it right there, you three." Robbie pushed back from the table. "Great picture!" He snapped a shot on his digital, and in the distraction of showing everyone the image, Eudora spoke under her breath to Harmony and Damon.

"Whenever it seems the Devil is near, join hands and think of goodness—of God."

"Like a séance?" Robbie asked.

Eudora frowned at him. "Eat your eggs. Go on," she urged Harmony and Damon. "The two of you. Try it. You are weak alone and most powerful together against the force of evil. Gather the light of goodness around you, the power, and then use it to fight Satan— to thrust him away. Let the light expand out from you, then push. Together, you will not lose."

"Grandmother," Daddy warned.

"Hush, boy! Can't you see I'm teaching a lesson here? What is it with this family sometimes?" Eudora made a cluck of annoyance. "Together you can fight him off. And in fighting him off, you can fight *them* off."

"The snotlings," Harmony whispered.

"Now, let's practice. Close your eyes and hold hands."

Damon's hand closed over Harmony's as he shut his eyes. Their arms rested on Eudora's lap, on the bright blue wool of her skirt.

"You, too, girl. Close your eyes."

"Yes, Great-grandma." Oh, how she didn't want to listen! Not with little green men on the loose. If her mother were to see them, or Daddy, then the explanations would have to follow, and they'd learn about Damon—

"Now," Eudora growled.

Harmony squeezed her eyes shut.

She could hear something scratching on her plate. Maybe the snotling was trying to dig out from under the biscuit. If she could just squish it back down . . .

But Damon held fast to her hand. Eudora pressed her hands over their clasped ones. "Think of good . . . as hard as you ever have."

Harmony pursed her lips and concentrated, thinking of heaven and light, of faith and eternity . . . and the quiet hush of a snowy morning, of the softness of a baby's head, the ripple of grass in the fields . . . the tenderness of Damon's kiss, and that way he looked at her that morning in the twilight of dawn, when he'd held her so close. . . .

To her amazement a sense of assurance came over her, a strange and quiet confidence. And then, she sensed the press of Damon's mind against hers, the first time she'd felt him reaching out to her with his thoughts. Taking a deep breath, she opened up and let him in.

A burst of light exploded behind her eyes. Damon's hand convulsed in hers, and Eudora made a quiet sound of approval. "Yes, children. That's what you do. Now fight. Push."

Gather the light, Harmony thought. *Gather the light and throw it outward.* In her imagination, she visualized pooling her strength with Damon's, and together they chased away the shadows, letting the light seep into every crevice, letting it pool and overflow, until there was no darkness left.

The table started vibrating. Harmony's eyes shot open. The orange juice in everyone's glasses shook, and the silverware rattled.

"He's angry," Damon murmured.

The shaking continued and Mama made a gasp. "What is it, Jake? An earthquake?"

"A small aftershock to one we had some time back," Damon explained with utter calm.

The little kitchen chandelier swung crazily, and juice splashed on the tablecloth. But Harmony wasn't afraid anymore. She had control now. "Bring it on," she told Lucifer and gripped Damon's hand with all her might. "I'm ready to kick some devil's ass."

"Harmony!"

Harmony smiled a bit sheepishly at her mother's incredulous glare. "Sorry, Mama. It just slipped out. Great-grandma's got me all fired up about good versus evil."

Her brothers laughed.

A tearing noise dragged all their gazes upward. The tremors had knocked the chandelier loose. Plaster sprinkled down. It dropped a couple of inches, swinging on its wire. Then it plunged to the table with a mighty crash.

The tremors stopped. Bracing herself, Harmony glanced around the table with the fallen chandelier looking like a gaudy centerpiece. The strawberries were behaving like strawberries were supposed to behave. Same with the cups. And no little green men cavorted over the tablecloth.

"Yes," Harmony whispered. "Yes. Thank you, Great-grandma."

Cackling softly, Eudora patted Harmony on the thigh and resumed eating her breakfast. Jake Jr. moved the chandelier to the floor, and Mama plucked a piece of plaster out of her coffee. After a few nervous comments about the rarity of earthquakes in the Rocky Mountains, the conversation returned to its normal volume and enthusiasm.

"A toast," her father called out and raised his glass of orange juice. "To getting to know our daughter's new friend. Damon."

"Do you think you can join us for Christmas, honey?" Mama asked him. Then her apologetic gaze swerved to Harmony. "Or will that be too soon?"

Harmony smiled. "No, not too soon at all. I'm kind of hoping he'll be staying around for a while."

The look in Damon's gold-brown eyes was one she'd never forget. "Aye, lass. I'll be around for a while. As close to forever as heaven allows."

Harmony was terrified no one would ever return to church after the flying monkeys, but as the week went on the casseroles started arriving, brought by sympathetic townspeople, and even cookies, baked, incredibly, by the terror triplets Withering, Scornful, and Derisive. Jeanie stopped by, of course, and the Tawdrys, Mrs. O'Cleary, and her great-granddaughter Annabelle, all impressing the Faithfulls with their good words about Harmony and Mysteria Community Church, while Damon devoted his energy to acting the part of the perfect

suitor, an ex-demon trying to win the hand of the preacher's daughter. It drove home the uniqueness of Mysteria. Everyone was welcome here, no one was ostracized, no matter who—or what—you
were.

When the crowds returned that next Sunday, Harmony smiled
from the pulpit at her father, looking so proud as the guest of honor
in the front pew. Next to him were her brothers, Mama, and Great-
grandmother Eudora, whose hand rested affectionately, and rather
appreciatively, on Damon's rock-hard thigh.

Later that night, after the Sunday dinner dishes were cleaned and put
away, and her family was gathered around the television in the living
room, Harmony and Damon sneaked outside.

Taking her hand, Damon led her to the garden and under the apple
tree where he'd landed naked only a few months before. Fireflies floated
all around them. Frogs and crickets provided a ceaseless chorus. Damon
slung his arms low around her waist and pulled her close. They stood
there simply holding each other. With soft, warm lips, he nuzzled her
neck. "Good, good, good," he murmured.

She giggled. "They'll be gone tomorrow and we'll finally have
some private time to . . . well, you know."

"Aye, I do know. How could I forget? I've thought of it day and
night, lass. Day and night." He slid his hands over her butt and pulled
her closer. Yes, he was thinking about their lovemaking, no doubt
about it. His body made that fact obvious.

She tipped her head to gaze up at him. "At one time, you weren't
too happy about being mortal in Mysteria. Does this mean now
you are?"

Damon chuckled. "Aye. 'Tis all I ever want to be."

"When I used to look at this church, all I could see was its emptiness, but it was my emptiness that was the problem," she confessed.
"And then you came and everything changed."

His handsome face was luminescent with love. "This is only the
beginning. 'Twill get better and better with us." Swallowing nervously,
he crouched down on one knee. "Forgive me if I dinna do this prop-

erly." Then he clasped her hands in his. "Harmony, will you do me the pleasure of one day taking me as your husband?"

She whooped then slapped a hand over her mouth. "Yes," she mumbled joyfully through her fingers. "Yes."

He lifted her up and swung her around, kissing her hard. Then, with devilish intent and one hell of a bad-boy grin, he carried her swiftly away from the house to where the lights didn't reach.

And so, the fair maiden married her dark knight the following spring, and all was right between them . . . or as right as life could be in the strange little hamlet of Mysteria.

That was, until they began to wonder if demon genes could be passed on to their children, the first of which arrived within the year. But that is a story for another day. . . .

ALONE WOLF

MaryJanice Davidson

ACKNOWLEDGMENTS

Thanks to "the girls": Susan, Gena, and P. C. for their support; they made this such a fun project, I was bummed when it was time to turn it in.

Thanks also to our editors at Berkley for their enthusiasm for Mysteria and its, ah, interesting inhabitants. Without their thumbs-up, this book wouldn't be here.

Thanks also to all those who wrote me asking about the goings-on in Mysteria; the girls and I got kind of curious about that, too. So here you go.

AUTHOR'S NOTE

The events of this novella take place three months after the events in *Bewitched, Bothered, and Bevampyred*, available at www.triskelion.com, and a year after the events in *Derik's Bane* (Berkley Sensation).

Also, triplets aren't necessarily evil. And most horses don't behave like the night mare. But there are, of course, exceptions.

Prologue

The house sat in the center of two gently rising hills, looking like a jewel on a beautiful woman's bosom. It was, in fact, the color of crushed rubies; the shutters were black. It was a two-bedroom in the Cape Cod style, two stories, one and a half bath, with an assumable mortgage at a fixed rate; the heater and central air were both up to code.

Inside, the walls were the bland color of good cream; the floors were oak. There was a dishwasher, but no garbage disposal. The house was built in 1870, and so was sorely lacking in closet space. Still, at sixteen hundred square feet, it was of a respectable size; the perfect starter home.

Of course, it was haunted. In 1914, one of the roofers (hired to fix the holes brought by the Big-Ass Hailstorm of the Spring of '14) fell off and, after dying, had the bad manners to linger. But she was helpful, really; a squeaky door would magically fix itself, the heater, though thirty years old, ran without a hiccup. If her views on the doings of the Mysteria City Council were noisily and frequently expressed, it was a small price to pay for never having to call a handyman.

The backyard went straight back, like an arrow, and the garden sat at the top of the yard like an arrowhead. It had grown over, of course, but could be brought back again; it was the right size for a salsa garden, or perhaps some cutting flowers.

The front yard ran straight up to the road and was small, almost an afterthought. There was no sidewalk; just a paved driveway that led to the small detached garage.

In the front yard was a sign: white, with stark black lettering. It looked like a For Sale sign, but the largest letters read FOR CRYING, and the rest of the sign read:

. . . out loud, think about what you're doing! This is a weird weird weird town. There's a reason this house has been on the market going on ten years. Think carefully before you so much as set foot on the lawn.

(It was a large sign.)

Then, in smaller letters, accompanied by a red smiley face: DON'T FORGET TO TAKE A BROCHURE!

The house sat like a jewel, and waited.

One

His first memory was of the moon, a shining, broad black face with the whitest teeth and the darkest eyes beaming down at him. When he checked his medical records years later and did the math, he figured out it would have been his third trip to the hospital; his second broken arm.

Mama Zee, the most sought-after foster mother in the county, had taken him home after signing all the paperwork (her righteous name, according to the most-helpful chart, was Ms. Zahara J. Jones) and put him in the battered wooden crib in her tiny third bedroom. (Willie and Konnie were in the other bedroom, and Jenna slept on the foldout couch in the living room.)

He did not remember the foster father breaking his arm, or the other foster father breaking his *other* arm, and he did not remember doctors or the hours of pain, but to the end of his days he would remember her smiling face. That, and waiting. It seemed he was always waiting: for a ride, for a class to start, for a job, for a hug, for a friend.

He was just a dumb baby then, and didn't know what the moon really was, but for a long time that was how he thought of her: Mama Zee, the moon.

In the end, he always came back to her. He loved the moon, but could not stay: for one thing, the noise drove him fucking nuts. Mama Zee *always* had kids around. There were always toys underfoot; the cupboard was always stuffed with little applesauce containers. Even as a small boy, at four, at six, at nine, he would have to get out, wander about on his own for a while.

After a while, the cops never ever caught him; he was too quick, and too quiet. But he always came back, and after the first two times, when Mama Zee saw that no matter how many times she smacked him with the dish towel or yelled, no matter what she did or how she worried, he would leave, he was compelled to go. But he always came back. And so she didn't worry. Or, if she did, she never spoke to him about it.

She even gave him a book once (well, she gave him lots of books, many times, but this one he remembered especially) about a kid named Jack who could travel between dimensions; his family called him Traveling Jack. "That's like you," she told him, "you just can't stay in one spot, boyo. And that's fine."

Well, no, he thought. *I can't stay here, is what it is.* But he didn't say it out loud. He'd bite off his own fingers before he'd say something so mean to her.

In fact, the entire neighborhood treated Mama Zee as a bomb that might blow up in their faces, because they knew *he* was quick, and quiet. And strong.

Mama Zee had all the help she needed getting groceries delivered (and because she usually had between three and seven foster kids at any one time, the milk bill alone was staggering), all the extensions needed to pay local vendors, and nobody ever broke in.

Occasionally, on his travels, Someone Bad would take it in their head that he might have something they wanted. It always went badly for Someone Bad and the older he got, the easier it got.

At first he put up with it, because he knew the bloody nose, the black eye, the whatever, would be all better in a day or two, sometimes less, depending on the moon. It was the price you paid for choosing not to sleep under a roof; that, and cold feet.

And then, one day it was like he had a lightning flash, only inside his brain. And the flash was made up of words: *Not today, pal.* He was nine when he realized he could make a grown man cry. It was shockingly easy.

He wasn't a bully (Mama Zee would have smacked him half to death with that dish towel), but he'd crunched up quite a few of them.

He wasn't very good in school—something about sitting still in a classroom reminded him of Mama Zee's noisy, toy-strewn living room. But he was good at other things.

When he got big—and thanks to Mama Zee's cooking, he got *really* big—he found out people would pay to get and keep a bully out of their lives. Pay a lot, sometimes. And sometimes it wasn't a bully; it was an ex-husband or a mean boss or a bad cop (but really, under their outside skin, they were all bullies). And the older he got, the more they paid him. Almost like if he didn't do the job, they were afraid he'd do them, so they practically threw money at him.

Of course he wouldn't; he was still a little nervous about Mama Zee's dish towel, though he had twelve inches of height and sixty pounds of muscle on her, and she was old; she was fifty-four. But the people didn't know that, and so they gave him money.

He didn't know what to do with it; he tried giving it to Mama Zee, but she only took enough to pay off her little house in Revere. He knew better than to talk her into retiring; the moon did not get tired of changing the tides, and Mama Zee loved kids. And she wouldn't move to a nicer neighborhood. She wouldn't take a car, either; not that a person needed one in that area.

He paid for Jenna's college; she was grown now, and still sleeping on the couch. She took it with thanks, and moved out, and Mama Zee didn't say anything, but he heard her crying later. Only it was the good kind of crying, so he wasn't sure what to do about that. In the end he did nothing.

Finally, Mama Zee said to him, "You're grown, boyo. Don't you want a place of your own?"

He just shrugged; his skin was itchy and he kept looking at the door. The new kid, Bryan, had colic. It was noisier than usual in the small house on Winthrop Avenue.

"Stop that twitching and pay attention to me; you can go soon enough. Don't you ever think about getting a girl and settling down?"

"No," he told her, and it was the truth, naturally. He couldn't imagine lying to her. Like he couldn't imagine taking a woman for his own, and cursing her as he was cursed. He would never.

That made her look sad, for some reason, and she slammed a cup of applesauce in front of him. She felt better when he ate.

He hated applesauce.

He got a spoon and started eating.

"You should take some of that money and buy a house of your own," she finally said. She watched him eat every bite of the pulped fruit. "Your own house, where it can be as quiet as you want it. And then, maybe . . . the rest will come."

"Okay," he said.

"Because—I've been thinking about this a lot, boyo, and you can't be the only one. The only one in the whole entire world. Right? You can't."

He shrugged.

"Just because you never ran across another werewolf," she added sharply, as if he had contradicted her, "doesn't mean there aren't any others out there. If only your birth parents—"

She stopped talking, and he was glad. He had never known them, but he didn't like them. They had been killed in a car accident, and left him.

"You need to go," she added, nicer. "Go and find someone like you, maybe a whole bunch of people like you. Not that there's anyone exactly like you, boy." She looked at him closely. "No, you're one of a kind."

He grunted.

Mama Zee got up, opened the fridge, unwrapped a raw hamburger, put it on a clean plate, and handed it to him. "Thank you for eating the sauce. I don't think you—"

"Get enough fruit and vegetables in my diet," he finished for her. He used the same spoon to wolf down the raw meat.

"Don't be smart, boyo. You gonna do what I said?"

"Sure," he replied.

TWO

Cole Jones stared at the small red house, then looked back down at the map of Colorado folded in his hand, then back up at the house.

Mysteria.

Specifically, 232 Roselawn Lane, Mysteria, mail code 678. No city, county, or state.

He had literally followed his nose here; for that matter, he wasn't entirely sure where *here* was. Certainly, the small town hadn't been on any map. Small, charming, and quiet, he had found it mesmerizing and interesting. And the smells! The fields smelled like newly mown hay (a good trick in autumn), the main street smelled like fresh pie, shit, even the town dump hadn't been bad. Just interesting.

And it was so quiet. The little red house sat alone on the lane, and there wasn't a crying baby for miles—downtown Mysteria was almost five miles away. A true country house. He had assumed, being city born (well, city raised) that he wouldn't like the country, but the quiet seemed to him like the most marvelous thing.

There was, in fact, only one house for sale, and he was looking at it. He had read the puzzling yard sign three times, and almost smiled. It didn't frighten him; it made him want to sprint to the bank and throw all his money at the first teller he could sniff out.

And speaking of sniffing, he could smell the small car seconds before he heard it. And in another minute, there was the groan of poorly maintained brakes, a door slamming, and he turned to see a short, chubby brunette with a nipped-in waist, wonderful deep breasts, and sweetly plump thighs

(ummmm)

hurrying toward him.

"I'm sorry," she called to him in the flat accent of a Midwesterner, probably upper North Dakota or Minnesota, "have you been waiting long?"

"Yes."

"Oh." She appeared to mull that one over for a moment, then said, blinking, "I'll be glad to take you inside for a tour."

Her eyes were the exact color of oak leaves, greenish brown, and large. Her brows were a shade darker than her hair, almost black. She was very pale, like a marshmallow. A juicy, gorgeous, mouthwatering marshmallow. He was almost knocked over by the—by the *intensity* of her. It was like she was more there than other people. He had never smelled anything like it.

"That's fine," he said, trying not to be overtly sniffing. Maybe she'd think he had a cold. Or was hooked on coke. That would be great!

"What's fine?"

Juicy and intense, but not the sharpest claw in the pad. "A tour. But you don't have to. I'll take it."

"You *what*?"

She was staring at him, but that was fine; he was used to it. It used to make him mad when he was younger, to have someone gape right into his eyes, challenging, gawking—it always made him feel like hitting, or biting. But he didn't mind anymore; he figured he'd outgrown his youthful temper. He was old, twenty-seven.

"I have a cashier's check," he added helpfully.

"Er, what? I mean, great. The down payment—"

"For the asking price." He pulled out the piece of paper and tried to hand it to her, but her arms were frozen at her sides and she was opening and closing her

(red-lipped, rosy, like berries, like ripe berries)

mouth like a bass.

She looked down at herself, and he looked, too. A green suit, a white blouse. No stockings. Black pumps. Then she looked around, as if wondering if what was happening was actually happening. Finally, she said, "Er, yes. Ah, look, Mr. Jones, I have to tell you, this—Mysteria, I mean—this isn't—I mean, it's a great town, the greatest town in the world, but—but it's—I mean, it's—" She took another look at him, audibly gulped, then smiled. A real smile, one that made her eyes crinkle at the corners and a dimple pop up in her left cheek. He couldn't help it; he smiled back.

"On second thought," she said, "I think you'll fit right in here."

"No," he said, "but I like the house anyway."

"I'm Charlene Houtenan."

"I know," he said, and shook her hand, and ignored the impulse to nibble on her knuckles and tell her she smelled like wet clover.

Three

". . . And if you'll sign here . . . and here . . . and here . . ."

He signed patiently: *Cole Jones. Cole Jones. CJ. CJ.*

". . . and we've got the cashier's check, and these are your copies— I must say, this is the fastest closing I've ever done, and I've been a Realtor since—for a long time."

He ate more pie, and tucked the wad of paperwork into the folder she offered him, then dropped it on the seat beside him. They were doing the closing at Pot's on the main drag in Mysteria. He was glad. The pie was amazing.

"And I guess that's it." Charlene was resting her small chin on her hands and staring at him as he wolfed down his third piece. "Congratulations, Mr. Jones."

"Cole," he told her again.

"Right. And I'm Char."

"Right."

"Do you know what her secret is?" she almost whispered.

"No."

"She puts seaweed in the crust."

"Umm."

"And she also sells them to go," Charlene added, "in case you wanted, you know, not to worry about fixing supper tonight."

Pot "My full name is too hard to pronounce" herself came up to their table. She was awesomely tall, the tallest woman he had ever seen, and too thin. He could see her skull beneath her face; see the bones stretching through on her limbs. Her hair was the greenish color blondes got when they spent the summer in the pool. Her eyes were the oddest green he had ever seen on a person, the color of the Boston harbor on a good day. Her eyebrows were so light and fine, they nearly disappeared into her face.

"Fourths?" she asked, drumming abnormally long fingers on their table. Her voice was low and slurring. Her nose was a blade.

"No. But I'd like two more chicken pies to go."

She placed two blue pie boxes, tied neatly with white string, on their table, then put the check on top of the box.

"Thanks, Pot. I've got it," Charlene said quickly, snatching the check before Cole could put down his fork. Pot nodded and made a graceful exit.

"You don't have to," he said, chewing. If Mama Zee could see him talking with his mouth full, there'd be hell to pay. "I have money."

"Ha! You're a homeowner; you're poor now."

"Okay."

The café door opened and three girls trooped in and, though he knew it was rude, he stared a little. He had never seen identical triplets before; they were like preteen Barbies: all blonde hair, perfect teeth, and tans. They were identically dressed in khaki clam diggers, red shirts, and white flip-flops, as if it was August instead of September. As one, they looked at him with their blue, blue eyes, then marched up to the counter where there was a pickup order waiting.

Over the muted hum of voices, he heard one of them ask, "Who is *that*?"

"Someone too old for you," Pot replied.

"Oh, yuck," the second one said. "Pot, that's gross."

"New guy?" the third one asked.

"Obviously," Pot said, popping open the cash register and dropping the triplets' money into the drawer.

"Touch-ee! What's wrong, Pot, red tide getting you down?"

"As a matter of fact, yes. Good-bye, girls."

"Nice," the first one said.

"So rude!" the second one said.

"One day we'll learn to cook as good as you," the third one threatened, "and then you'll be out of business."

Pot laughed at them, the sound like a spring trickling through the woods.

"You'll rue the day," the first one said mildly, trotting out behind her sisters.

"Those were the Desdaine triplets," Charlene said as the door whooshed closed behind them. She was grinning a little. "You should be nice to them; when they take over the world, they might spare your life."

"Umm," he said, scraping the plate. Seaweed in the crust? Whatever was in the crust, it was buttery, flaky, tangy and salty and mouthwatering. The chicken was tender and juicy, the vegetables perfectly cooked.

He could hardly wait to get to his new house and reheat another one. Assuming he had a microwave. Or a kitchen. Maybe he should have had the home inspected after all. . . .

"Excuse me," Charlene said as she got up to pay the bill. Another woman was manning the cash register, and Pot glided up to his table. She smiled at him and he saw her teeth were small, like pearls, and pointed, like thorns.

"Hello," he said politely.

"Mr. Cole."

"Will you come over to my house tonight?" he asked.

"Indeed. Eleven o'clock?"

"Yes. It's—"

"I know which one it is," she said, then glided past Charlene, who was looking at him with not a little hurt in her gaze. It puzzled him, and as usual, when he didn't know what to do, he did nothing.

Four

He did have a kitchen. Spotless, with the longest counters he'd ever seen, and the smallest microwave. A chicken pie just fit.

He prowled around the house, extremely satisfied, and made a mental note to get the computer and land lines hooked up in the morning. He had already called Mama Zee to tell her he had moved, er, somewhere, and was now a homeowner full of pie. She had been surprised, but delighted, puzzled over his address, but determined to send him a case of applesauce as a housewarming present. He would rather have a case of manure, but of course didn't tell her that.

When the ghost spoke, he was so startled he nearly fell down the stairs. He'd had no warning; it wasn't like she had a scent.

"Just so you know, your name on the deed doesn't mean this is your house."

"That's exactly what it means," he replied, recovering.

"Okay, well, what I meant was, it doesn't mean you belong."

"I've never belonged anywhere."

The ghost yawned. "How sad, boo-hoo."

He was looking out windows, in closets, smelling corners, and peeking into bathrooms. "Where are you?"

"Mind your own business, homeowner."

"Char told me a roofer was killed working on the house."

"So?"

"So, what do you want?"

There was a long, puzzled silence; Cole had the sense no one had asked her that before. "I guess I want what anybody wants: to putter around in my own house, to be left alone."

"Okay."

"Chatty, aren't we?"

"Um. What's your name?"

"Also none of your business."

"But we're roommates. You probably know my name."

"It's Rae, all right? And don't go thinking we can get all chummy and such. You're still green, homeowner, talk to me when you've been in this town for a decade or so."

"Okay."

"And no women coming and going at all hours of the night, either!"

"Pot is coming at eleven."

"Goddammit!" the ghost cursed, then sulked and wouldn't talk to him anymore, which was a relief.

Pot was early and, interestingly, did not knock. Just walked right in. She smiled like a shark when she saw the two empty pie plates on his counter.

"Hello," he said.

"Hello."

He cast about; what was polite? What did normal people *say*? "Thanks for coming."

"I couldn't resist. I'm sorry to be so early, but I was very anxious to see what was on your agenda."

Right. Time to get to it. He appreciated her directness; it was a trait he rarely ran across. "I'm different," he said, "like you."

"Not like me."

"Okay."

"I'm a river nymph," she explained patiently, "you're a werewolf."

"I don't know what that is," he admitted, as startled as when the ghost had first spoken.

"Which one?" She opened his fridge, sighed happily when she saw it was full of food and drink, and helped herself to a bottle of water.

"A river nymph."

She drained the bottle in two gulps, something he had not thought physically possible. "Couldn't you tell by looking at me? By my scent?"

"You smell like the deep end of the pool," he told her.

She grabbed another bottle, popped the top, chugged it down. "Yes, indeed. There are two rivers that run parallel to Mysteria—"

"There are?" He was startled; he'd only seen one on his way in.

She grinned again, showing her pointy teeth—good, he imagined, for eating raw fish. "You have to really be looking to find the other one. Or, I have to be inclined to let you see it. Never mind, it's not the point. Potameides Naiad, that's me, and have you noticed how dry it is in here?"

"Potameides is much nicer than Pot," he told her.

"I don't care," she told him, working on bottle number three, "and I doubt you do, either."

"Why do you make pies and run around in a hot kitchen all day?"

"Mysteria is my home; in that small way, I contribute to the community."

"But why are you here?"

"I had planned to ask you the same thing. This is my home now, that's why." She looked at her floor, and her long, greenish blonde hair fell forward, obscuring her face. "I saw you and thought—maybe—we were kindred spirits."

"Are you looking for others like you, too?" Perhaps they would team up. They'd have to stick to the coast, of course, and he would be sorry to see his red house go, not to mention Charlene, but the entire reason he was even here was to—

"No. I know where my people are; they can come to me whenever they wish. I was banished."

"Banished from the river, Pot?"

"From a particular river, so I came here." She lifted her head and stared at him defiantly; he felt like he might slip and drown in her glare. "And it's Queen Potameides, werewolf."

"Sorry." A displaced queen! Who was a river nymph, no less. Evil triplets. Gorgeous Realtors with heart-shaped butts. And it was only his first day. "Maybe your people will relent, soon."

She laughed without humor. "I doubt it, Mr. Jones. I've been here for over a hundred years. Not long for my people, but long to be away from friends."

"I'm sorry."

"It isn't your problem. Why were you sent away? That's really what I must know. Particularly if your people are having the same, ah—difficulties—as mine."

"Oh. I wasn't sent away." He didn't think. "I was raised by ordinary humans." If Mama Zee had heard him refer to her as ordinary . . . he shuddered, then went on. "I never knew my birth family."

"And you're a werewolf? But that's terrible!" Queen Potameides seemed genuinely distressed, which was pleasant, as she'd just met him. "Did the humans ever lock you up, or—"

"No. My foster mother understood. She's the one who made me go away. In a nice way," he added, since the river queen looked alarmed again. "To find others like me."

"Oh. Well, there's a werewolf in town—"

"There is? Where?" He looked around as if the creature was hiding in his kitchen.

"His name's Justin, but calm down, he's actually out of town right now. But he could answer your questions when he returns, I'm sure."

"Thank you, Queen Potameides."

She smiled shyly. "I am pleased you don't share my particular woe. When you find your people, will you leave?"

Er. Uh. Good question. Back in Revere, he had assumed Mysteria would be a stepping-stone. Now he wasn't so sure. He liked the house. He liked Charlene. He loved the pies. He liked the river goddess. In one day, he'd felt more at home, more real, than in his entire childhood in Massachusetts.

Maybe he could commute to the werewolves. Maybe they wouldn't insist on his living with them. Maybe—

"Hey, Pot, looks like you're done. Don't let the door hit you in your damp ass on the way out."

"Shush, Rae," the queen said sternly, and the ghost hushed. "You don't have to put up with that one if you don't want," she added to Cole. "There's an exorcist in town who could get rid of her like *that*." She snapped her fingers, which squished; the ends were wrinkled and damp, as if she'd been swimming all day instead of baking.

"Ha!" the ghost crowed. "He wishes. He's been trying to exorcise me for years."

"It's true," the queen added in a low voice. "His heart really isn't in it. He knew Rae in life, you see."

"Also," Rae summed up, "he couldn't exorcise a ghost if you threw them in a blender together."

"You're mistaking compassion for weakness," the queen said. "Again."

"Has anyone ever told you, you smell like wet dog?"

"You *dare* speak to me that way again, dead thing, and I'll . . ."

"Drip through me? Make water stains on the floor? Hock a big ole salty loogey into one of your pies, which I can't eat anyway, so why would I give a crap?"

"Ladies, ladies. Don't fight. It's all right," Cole said, wondering what he would do if they did fight. Try to stop them? Leave? Distract the queen by filling the bathtub? "It's all right," he said again.

"How?" the queen demanded. "How is it all right?"

"She—the, you know—" He gestured vaguely to the air.

"The *ghost*, you idiot," the air snapped back.

"She doesn't make any trouble," he finished unconvincingly.

The queen sighed. "That's what they all say."

"Squirt it out your ear, Potty."

"Thank you," she replied with the dignity of a centuries-old royal line, "for your hospitality, *Mr. Jones*. No need to see me out."

Fortified with Aquafina, the queen left, every step a squish. Cole took a minute to mop up the tracks, feeling oddly cheerful. There was a werewolf in town (well, would be soon), he had a roommate who never gave him any trouble (so far . . . and not too much) and didn't eat baby food (probably) or get colic (again, probably), the queen could cook, and the realtor had a terrific body. It was like a smorgasbord of thought: where to go, what to do, what to think about first?

Exhausted, he went to bed.

Five

The next morning, after breakfast at the café, he asked where Charlene was.

"The range," one of the triplets told him. They were sitting across from him in his booth, watching with amazement while he ate. He was a little amazed himself at their interest.

And his own, in Charlene. He'd stopped by her small Realtor's office (on the outside, it looked like a small, weather-beaten Cape Cod, though they weren't on Cape Cod . . . right?) on the way to breakfast, but it was locked, with a Closed sign hanging in the window. Well, after her commission from yesterday, she could probably afford to take a day off. And he was used to eating alone.

Not that he was eating alone this morning. "The range?" he repeated, mopping up the juice from his blueberry pie with the crust from his apple pie.

"The shooting range. East end of town. Where do you put it all?"

"I run it off."

"Oh," the second triplet said. They were again disconcertingly dressed alike, this time in felony schoolgirl outfits of red plaid skirts, white blouses, white knee socks, and black loafers. If they didn't smell so strongly of immature female, he might have been in trouble. As it was, he pitied their parents: it would be hard to keep the boys away. "You know, there are other places to eat in town."

"Yes. Where is the range?"

"We'll show you."

"That's all right, Withering. Just give me directions."

"I'm Withering," the third one pouted, kicking one of her long legs. "That's Derisive."

"No, it's not."

"How do you know? We got up and switched around when you were ordering your lunch delivery."

He shrugged. He had no intention of explaining to the preteens that they had distinct smells, and slightly alarming ones: cinnamon, cloves, and nutmeg. Sharp smells, and not comforting in females. He preferred his women to smell like flowers, grass, or—

"Charlene."

"What?" Scornful asked.

"Where is she?"

"We really will show you—no tricks," Withering promised.

"But you have to tell us something," Derisive added.

"Your deep dark—"

"I'm a werewolf," he said, already bored with their preteen weirdness. He hadn't liked seventh-graders when he *was* one.

"That's it? Just like that? 'I'm a werewolf.'"

"It's not a secret," he explained.

"It's not?" the triplets chimed. "We have all kinds of secrets," Derisive added. "You'd lose your hair just thinking about them."

"It's not a secret," he reminded them. "It's why I'm here. To find more of my own kind."

"Well, that's admirable and all, but you probably shouldn't just blurt it out to anybody you see."

"Not even here?"

"Welllllllll . . ." The sisters looked at each other. "Maybe here is okay. Goddess knows it's a weird place. But still, if we didn't have to drag it out of you, or trick you . . ."

"We couldn't trick him," Scornful said.

"Yes, you could," he corrected. "I'm not very smart."

"About that," Withering said, looking at him thoughtfully, "I wouldn't be so sure. You're staying for a while, Mr. Cole? You bought Rae's house?"

"It's my house."

"Right," Scornful said.

"Better run that one by Rae," Withering added.

"Or just run," Scornful suggested.

"Welcome to Mysteria," her sisters finished in eerie unison.

Six

He found Charlene at a small outdoor shooting range on the east end of town. The triplets had, at the last second, disdained to accompany him, instead giving him a map that disappeared as soon as he saw the range with his own eyes. Disappeared like a trick: *poof*. He spent five minutes trying to find it in his car before giving up. He wasn't in Kansas anymore, Toto.

Not that he had needed it; the smell of gunpowder and spent casings was very strong on this end of town; he would eventually have stumbled across it himself. Still, it was good to know the triplets could be helpful when they wished.

He had seen silver slices of the mysterious second river on the road out of town, but every time he got close, it turned out to be a mirage. He could smell water, but it could have been from the river on the other side of town.

Meanwhile, Charlene was gamely plugging away at a series of turkey-shaped silhouettes about fifteen feet away from where she was standing. The silhouettes were made of iron, and he could hear the bullets plinking and whining off of them, and smell the stench of gunpowder. It was so bad he almost didn't go up to her, but the fact that she overwhelmed even those bad smells decided him. Also, the sight of her butt in denim.

He found a spare set of earphones at the shooter's table, slipped them on, then said, between her shots, "Shouldn't you be a little farther away?"

She didn't turn around, just kept banging away in the general direction of the targets. The gun in her hand was so big she could barely hold it upright. It made him feel slightly ill to look at it. Hunting with lead and pieces of metal seemed kind of . . . he wasn't sure. Cheating?

If you couldn't bring someone down with your hands and feet and teeth, it—

"Don't you have a hot date with Pot?"

"No."

She slipped the earphones off her ears, popped the cylinder on the revolver, set it on the small, waist-high stand, and turned to face him. "And you better watch out for the triplets. They could get a guy like you in big trouble."

"Thank you for the advice."

"Is it true?"

He blinked. "Is what true?"

"That you're a werewolf?"

"Sure."

"Is Pot helping you—you know—find others of your kind?"

"No."

"Oh." Interestingly, her scent went from sharp suspicion to sweet surprise—honey over oatmeal. It made for a pleasant change from the gunpowder. "Well, maybe I can help you. I've, uh, had some experience in this stuff."

"Selling houses to werewolves?"

"No, no. I'm a . . ." She paused dramatically, then rushed out with, "I'm a vampire slayer!"

"But I'm not a vampire," he said mildly.

"That's okay, I'm not really a slayer. I'm more like a vampire beater-upper. I don't like killing them. Hey, the undead are people, too."

She was lying. But he was so used to it—people lying like they breathed—that it wasn't especially alarming. He assumed that she was stressed and tense about her job(s), and couldn't tell him the full truth about her night business. But a vampire beater-upper might be handy, if she could—

"I've run into lots of werewolves," she assured him. "I bet I could help you find some of your kind."

"One of my kind lives in this town," he reminded her.

"Right, right. But I meant, your herd. Find your herd."

"Oh." He almost smiled at her, and didn't at the last minute. His smile made people afraid. "That would be good."

"Yes, indeed, I've seen more creatures of the night than you can shake a stick at," she continued, slipping her tinted shooting glasses off her face. And now she was telling the whole truth . . . probably a truth anyone living in Mysteria could tell. "We'll get you hooked up."

"I'd like to get hooked up," he said, and this time he did smile. Oddly, she wasn't afraid; instead, she blushed prettily, and he wondered just how important finding the others really was.

Seven

"The first thing we ought to do," Charlene was telling him after they had parked in front of a small house north of Main Street, "is leave Justin a note."

"A note?"

"I told you, I'm pretty sure he'd be helpful to you, but he's out of town right now."

"For a vampire slayer—"

"Vampire beater-upper."

"—you're not very aggressive."

"I'm a little bit of a pacifist," she admitted, scribbling something on a piece of stationery and getting out to slip it into the mailbox.

"Now what?" he asked.

"Uh . . . we wait until Justin reads his note?"

"Isn't there anything else we could do? Isn't there an underground contact you can call, or e-mail?"

"Oh, sure, *loads* of them. Tons. But right now, they're all sleeping. See?" She pointed to the sun, fat on the horizon and tinting the clouds orange. He couldn't believe it was almost evening. They'd been driving around and chatting all day as she gave him a tour of his new town. "Everybody's resting up for their nightly battle against the scourges of the underworld."

"Oh."

"So, why don't you come over to my house for supper? I stuck a roast in the Crock-Pot this morning; there'll be plenty."

"Oh." He thought that one over. If he went to her house, there would be food, and her company, and that would be pleasurable. But he would want to—

"I guess you don't want to," she said, and blood had rushed to her face again, that charming blush.

"I do want to," he assured her. "I'm just not sure I'd want to leave."

"Well," she said, blushing harder and starting the car, "who said you'd have to leave?"

Pot roast was awkward, but delicious. He couldn't get what she'd said out of his mind. She was so *there* it was driving him crazy; he wanted to be done with potatoes and carrots and meat and just get her on the floor and fuck her until they were both slick with sweat and out of breath.

But you didn't just do that. He was pretty sure. There were women in his old neighborhood, of course, but nobody like Charlene. What was the protocol? Goddammit!

He was never more aware of being a werewolf than when he wanted to get laid. Sex made the difference between species yawn like a chasm, a bottomless one. Because he knew when the woman wanted to do it, but she rarely came out and said it.

So he had to sit there (at the movies, at dinner, at a car show, whatever) and pretend he couldn't smell her lust. And she pretended she wasn't giving off enough hormones to make him feel like he was losing his mind. The whole thing made his balls hurt.

Charlene wanted him. He wanted her. She'd joked about him spending the night. She'd made him supper. She was helping him find his—what was the term? Herd. His herd. And she'd been helpful in a hundred other ways, too, professionally and personally.

So—what? Jump on her? Ask for seconds? Get a refill on his milk glass? Ask her out for the next night and go home and try to sleep with a raging hard-on? (He didn't know about other werewolves, but masturbation had always seemed to him silly and wasteful.) What?

"Do you want a refill?"

"No," he snapped.

"Cripes, sorry. Well, why don't we just get to it, then? But let me clear the dishes first."

He sat like a lump while she cleaned off the small kitchen table, rinsed dishes, put the milk back in the fridge.

Had he heard her right? Get to it? Get to what? Maybe she had a slide show all prepared, or puppets in the closet, or something. It sure as shit couldn't be what he was thinking. Nothing in his life had come easy; he didn't expect things to change now.

He caught another whiff as she went by

(ummmmm)

and then realization hit and he backed up so fast his chair fell over. "You're ovulating!" he cried, and it was as much an accusation as "You're the killer!"

She blinked owlish eyes at him; her pupils were enormous, and ringed in dark green. *Nocturnal*, a voice in the bottom of his brain told him, a voice that didn't speak up very often.

"What?" she was asking. "I mean, I am, but how can you tell?"

"Because you smell like peaches in syrup. I was so distracted by all the other smells, I didn't—no, no!" He backed away from her. "I have to go home now."

She pouted. Her full lower lip actually poked out and he thought about sucking it into his— "But I wanted you to spend the night."

"No way. Not if there's a chance you'll get pregnant."

She blinked again, slowly. "But I'm on the Pill."

"You're lying." It would only occur to him later to wonder why she had lied about such a thing.

"Well." That seemed to give her pause. "You could wear a condom."

"No."

"Oh, so you're one of *those* guys."

"I don't know what you're talking about, but they don't work," he explained, as patiently as he could while climbing over the coffee table to stay away from her. "I guess latex doesn't stop werewolf sperm."

"Oh." Weirdly (what the hell was going on?) she seemed pleased at the idea. "I guess you won't believe me if I tell you I've got a diaphragm in the bathroom."

"I'm leaving now."

"But we haven't had dessert!" she wailed, gesturing to the dishes of fresh pie.

And I plan on keeping it that way.

Eight

Annoyingly, she could drive as fast as he could run, or almost, because he had barely slammed and locked his front door when she was hammering on it.

"Cole! Come on, don't be a baby. Let me in and we'll talk about this!"

"No!" he yelled back, resting against his front door. If he let her in, they were going to mate. If you put your hand in the fire you got burned, if you jumped into mud you got dirty, and if an ovulating female got too close to a werewolf, he got laid. They both did.

"Why are you acting like this?"

"I don't want a baby!"

"Then stop acting like one!"

Argh. Faulty human hearing. "I didn't say I wasn't acting like one, I said I didn't *want* one."

"But why don't you?"

"Because I don't even know you!" he lied. Of all the reasons not to mate with a healthy, gorgeous, sweetly rounded, helpful, intelligent female, not "knowing" her was the least of it. "Now get back into your car and go away!"

"You know, the full moon's over seven days away," she said. "I looked it up. It's not like you're going to burst into hair right this second."

"It's four days away," he corrected her. "Get lost."

"Are we really going to have a conversation like this through your door?"

"Not if you get lost."

She was silent. Thank God! He slumped to the floor, still throbbing, still wanting her. But he could never do that to *any* woman—curse her with a half man/half beast, a child who didn't know, and a father who couldn't help—never mind someone like Charlene. He wouldn't go near her while she was ovulating. In fact, he was starting to think it was a good idea to stay away from her altogether.

The thought made his heart hurt, actually cramp like when you swam too long and your legs burned. He ignored it; his personal feelings about someone he barely knew—

(yes, that's right, you don't even know her)

(is that the human in you, or the werewolf? maybe werewolves make up their minds a little quicker)

He slapped his hands over his eyes and shook his head. How would he know? Anyway, it was a perfect example of why he shouldn't knock Charlene up. What if his son or daughter wanted to know these things in twenty years?

What the hell could he tell him or her? "Sorry, I was supposed to find out but I got your mom pregnant and settled in Mysteria instead, and never got around to finding my people. Well, good luck and all."

Never.

He could hear Charlene rustling around the side of his house, doubtless looking for a way to get in. Silly bunny; she had no chance. He wished she would give up and break a window. Argh! He meant give up and go home, yeah, go home, that's what he wanted.

He heard a double click, and instantly realized what had happened. As Char stepped through the back door, he howled, *"Rae!"*

"What?" the ghost asked petulantly. "Nobody's gotten any in this place for decades. I think you should go for it."

"I had no interest in it before—"

"So—what? That's an electric drill in your pants?"

"—and I'm sure not doing it if you're going to watch!"

"Oh, calm down, princess. After all these years, I've decided sex is fundamentally boring, at least from a voyeur's point of view. I'll be in the basement. Did you know the tap's been leaking since last night?"

"Go fuck yourself, Rae!"

No answer. Just as well. Somewhere, Mama Zee could probably sense he had been swearing, not to mention rude to a lady. A dead lady, but still.

Charlene was stamping down the hall toward him, her breasts jiggling with every stamp. He tried to look at her face for about a second, immediately gave up the battle, and turned to scrabble at the locked door. His fingers were suddenly too big, the lock the size of a pin head.

If the neighborhood could see him now, the neighborhood enforcer scrambling to escape from a woman who barely came up to his chin . . .

Her arms were around him and she was raining kisses on the back of his neck. He groaned and fought the door as if it was a living thing, but it stubbornly resisted him.

"Come on," she said, and there was a note of sad urgency in her voice. "I need you. In more ways than you can ever imagine."

"We can't," he groaned. He stopped clawing at the door, and stood still in her arms, leaning his sweaty forehead on the (annoyingly closed) door.

"We have to. I have to."

"I can't do it to you."

"I think," she whispered, reaching around and cupping his jeans where the zipper came together, "you can."

"You have no idea what you're getting into."

"That's okay," she said, turning him around. He kissed her, sucked on her full lower lip, even nipped her lightly. She just wriggled closer. "Neither do you."

Nine

"God, God . . ."

"That's funny, that's just what I was saying," she teased. They were resting on the living room floor, clothes strewn everywhere, and she had slid a chubby thigh over his legs and was stroking his ribs. "Repeatedly. Loudly."

It had been, to put it mildly, a hectic half hour. Kissing and sucking and stroking and sliding . . . and then they had really gotten down to business. She had been everything he imagined: athletic and indefatigable, with the lips of a devil and the hands of an angel. He wanted to go again. He *would* go again. Except . . .

"What if you're pregnant?" he asked anxiously.

"Boy, you are *really* harshing my buzz. No afterglow at all, huh? No?" She saw he was leaning over her propped up on an elbow in a pose of tense waiting, and answered him, obviously quite puzzled. "Cole, what is the big deal? I told you I was on the Pill."

"Yes, but that was a lie."

She pressed her lips together. "And the pitiful remnants of the afterglow . . . gone. Yes, okay, it was a lie. I admit, I wanted to get you into bed. Forgot about that damn nose of yours for two seconds. But I still don't understand what the big deal is. I wouldn't tie you down—what year do you think this is? What town, for that matter?"

"But the baby—"

"Ah, the baby." She said it with such admiration and longing, he was a little afraid of her.

"What if it's—like me?"

She smiled. "What if it is?"

He got up, starting putting his clothes on. "You're not getting this at all."

"Obviously. So explain it to me."

"I could never make you understand. Now get out." He paused. "Please."

"Okay, okay." She slipped into her blouse, found her underpants wadded up in a corner, stepped into them. "Your postcoital grumpiness has been duly noted."

"So has your total indifference toward the consequences of intimate relations."

"What are you, a woman now? And nobody held a gun to your head, I might add. *And* I might not be pregnant, you know. Maybe you're not the big ole stud you think you are. How about *that?*"

"I am, though," he said gloomily, holding the door open for her. She hopped out, half-dressed and trying to slip into her sneakers.

"Don't call me!" she yelled as he shut the door.

"Don't worry," he muttered.

It was only after she left that he remembered she was supposed to take him around to other supernatural creatures, try to track down his herd.

His lifelong dream, his goal, and it had all flown out of his head right about the time he ripped off her bra. Fucking great. Reason #238 to stay the hell away.

✒

Ten

The child—not a child anymore, a woman in her thirties—had dark hair, long strong legs, and Charlene's owlish eyes. "Anything?" she was asking him, keeping well away from him, as was her habit. "You can't tell me anything?"

"I'm sorry." His voice surprised him; it was old, cracked. "I came here and met your mother and that was the end of it."

"But what about our people?"

He shrugged, then coughed an old man's cough. Though they were sitting on the porch of his beloved red house, the paint had long faded; now it was his beloved pink house. Many of the windows were broken, but he was too indifferent to fix them—he didn't feel much in the way of cold, anyway.

Charlene, of course, was years dead. It was just him and the whelp, a woman who avoided him—lived in Reno, of all places—unless she needed something.

"What about my grandparents?"

"Dead." The black mare was standing patiently on the porch next to his rocking chair and he reached out a wrinkled hand and stroked her velvety nose. "They're all dead."

"But these—these *things* happen to me all the time, things I can't control."

"I know."

"And I'm stronger than everybody. And faster. Everyone else seems like a clumsy—I don't know—it's like they're monkeys or something. I don't really feel like I belong with them."

"I know."

"I can't marry one of *them*."

He yawned. "Then don't."

The mare nickered into his palm and he saw the For Sale sign was up again in his yard, facing the house instead of the road, and this time it read DEATH LIVES HERE.

"Dad, you have to help me."

"I can't."

"Dad."

"Sorry." The sign changed while he watched: HA. HA. HA.

"But who am I?" the woman asked as she faded from sight, like a ghost.

"I don't know," he told her fading figure. "I never knew myself, either."

The mare nickered again, almost like laughing. The sign now read: TOO BAD, SO SAD, LIE DOWN AND BE BAD.

"Gosh," Rae's voice said from behind him. "Don't you think you should wake up now? This is a doozy of a nightmare. I mean, blech."

He blinked and coughed his dry old man cough again. His hands were wrinkled claws. He looked at the horse, standing so patiently by his chair.

"Shoo!" Rae said. "Get lost! Go scare somebody else, you creepy nag!"

Startled, the horse clopped down the steps and galloped off.

And he woke up in the middle of a sweaty bed. His hands were normal. He was still young. It had all been a—

"Fucking night mares, they're always causing trouble," Rae said from nowhere, and was that a note of sympathy in her voice? "It was just a bad dream, Cole."

Or a vision of things to come. He leaped out of bed, intent on finding Charlene. He'd been avoiding her for three days, but he had to warn her. Make her understand. And if she didn't understand, he—he didn't know.

But . . . like she said, maybe she wasn't pregnant. Maybe the situation would be salvaged. He would have to leave Mysteria, but the alternative was worse. He had no animosity toward the night mare; she had shown him a future he wanted no part of, a future he needed reminding of, and given him time to fix things.

"I've got to see her," he told Rae, striding toward the door.

"Good plan, Cole. May I suggest clothes? Or at least boxers?"

"Oh. Right. Thanks again."

"I must say, you're the most interesting roomie I've ever had. Everyone else usually moves out by now."

"Can we talk about this later, please?"

"Oh, fine, ignore the ghost, see if I care. It's not like I have feelings or anything!" That last was almost shouted as he slammed the door on his way out. He made a mental note to make it up to her—how, exactly, does one make it up to a ghost?

A problem for later. Right now: Charlene.

Eleven

He bounded up the steps to her house and, before his fist could land on the door, it opened and he fell through the doorway.

"For a werewolf," she observed, looking down at him, "you're remarkably clumsy."

"Buh," he replied, because she was wearing a Vikings jersey and nothing else. He had never had much interest in organized sports, but he had a sudden urge to watch every Vikings game ever televised.

"You do not," she observed, "look well. Everything all right?"

He climbed to his feet. "Sorry about barging in on you like that." A lie, but he had to start somewhere.

"You didn't really barge," she pointed out, walking toward the kitchen, big hips rolling sweetly beneath the purple and white. "I heard you jogging down the lane—don't you ever drive? We live five miles apart, you know. Then, zip! Like the Marathon Man. Is it safe? Anyway, I had the door open by the time you came up the walk."

"Uh-huh." It all went over his head, and who cared? He had other things to worry about. He followed her, trying not to obviously sniff. "Why are you up so late? Oh, of course. Vampire beater-upper business."

"Ah. Yes. About that. I'm not."

"Not pregnant?"

She froze in the midst of pouring a glass of milk for herself. "Now how would I know that already? It's been, what? Half an hour since we did it?"

"Seventy-six hours."

She gave him an odd look and he crept closer. He needed a really good whiff of her hair or her neck, skin on skin would be even better. In fact, best of all would be—

"Riiiiight," she replied. "Anyway, I'm not a vampire beater-upper. I made the whole thing up."

"The whole thing?"

"Yes."

"You don't have dealings with the, uh, depraved underworld of the dead?"

She shook her head. He literally didn't know what to think: his mind was as blank as a broken TV. The enormity of the lie actually distracted him from the other problem. "But—why?"

"Why do you think? I wanted an excuse to be close to you. You picked out the one house for sale and bought it so damn fast, I had to think of something else. Something you wanted. The truth is, I wouldn't know a vampire if he came up and slapped me in the face."

"You're pretty close to that now," he said, getting pissed.

"Oh, Cole, stop it. You'd suck up your own barf before you'd hit a woman. And I'm sorry to sound like such a bitch."

Her switches in temperament were dazzling. "What?" he managed.

"Well, it was a crummy thing to do. I've been just sick about it and I wanted to—you know. Get all the cards on the table, as the saying goes."

"But—"

"Justin really is a werewolf, though," she added anxiously, watching his face.

Justin—some strange male werewolf—was the last thing on his mind right now. "I don't—" he began.

"I'm sure he can help you. I can't, though. I've got other stuff to worry about. Stuff you can't even dream of, so don't bug me about it," she added, going from truthful to contrite to defiant in about ten seconds.

He stared at her. "I knew you were lying about part of it, but I didn't think you were lying about all of it."

"How does it work, exactly?" she asked. "It's not like your nose is a lie detector—I mean, it is, and obviously a pretty good one compared to most people's equipment, but how could you know exactly what was a lie and what wasn't?"

The irony of the woman who claimed to be able to help him find his herd asking about something as fundamental as scenting was not lost on him.

"I just assumed you were anxious about your work—I was distracted by, uh, other things." He looked down at his hands. He should, by rights, be strangling her right now. But he had gone along with the lie, hadn't he? To get laid. To see those fabulous breasts. To be with her. The most important quest of his life and he hadn't asked any questions. The neighborhood was right: all muscle, no brains.

Charlene put a chubby hand over his, looked up at him earnestly, and said, oblivious of her milk mustache, "I really did have my reasons. I don't blame you for being mmpphhh-phargle."

She mmpphh-phargled because he tugged her into his embrace and buried his nose in her hair. Then he held her at arm's length and almost shouted, "You're pregnant!"

"I am?" She looked thrilled. "Noooooo. Really? You can really tell so quickly?"

"Dammit! Dammit! Dammit!"

"Yes!" She broke out of his embrace, clasped her arms around herself, and spun around in a tight circle. "I don't suppose you can tell whether it's a boy or a girl?"

"Charlene, this is a very serious business. You have to stop—stop dancing around your kitchen and listen to me."

"It's more serious than you know," she reminded him, "but I'm listening."

He stopped. What was there to say now? Stay or go; it was still the same choice it had always been. Only now infinitely more complicated. He didn't handle complicated well. He tended, in fact, to handle it by leaving.

"What do you mean, more serious than you know? What's your agenda?" he asked, stalling for time. Stay or go? Have sex with her or throttle her? No, wait. That wasn't the question.

"I have to have a baby," she explained. "Do you want a glass of milk?"

"No. Why?"

"I'm a mial."

He blinked. The name meant nothing to him. "What?"

"A mial."

"A meal?"

"Mee-*all*."

"Yes, but what is it?"

"What's a human?" she retorted, scrubbing her fingers through her loose hair and almost glaring up at him. "What's a werewolf, what's a warlock, what's a night mare? What's a witch, what's a dryad, what's a vampire? What's a fairy, a goblin, a troll? It's just another creature sharing the planet, that's all."

"Yes, but what *is* it?"

"Oh, right. Uh. That's a tough one to explain. We're just—we're just another species here. There's about . . . um . . . ." Her eyes slitted as she thought. "Maybe half a million of us on the planet?"

He thought of Pot, the triplets, the night mare. "What kind of magic can you do?"

She smiled. "No kind. We're pretty boring. The only thing interesting about us is our life span—the average mial lives to be about twelve."

"Twelve?" he almost shrieked. "How old are you now?"

"I'm old," she said wistfully. "Old to be having a baby. Four next month. Don't worry," she added, "it's not creepy or anything that we did it. We reach maturity at ten months."

"Wh—but—wh—"

"But Cole, listen!" She grabbed his forearms. "Listen to this! If I have a baby with a human or a human hybrid—like a werewolf or a witch or whatever—he or she will have an *enormous* life span! Fifty or sixty years, at least! Think of *that*! That's practically forever." For a moment she was looking through him, not at him. "My line could go on for centuries. We can't get a foothold on this planet because everybody else lives eight times as long, but my baby has a chance— we have a chance—"

Definitely the weirdest day ever. And this from a man who routinely turned into a wolf and ate cows. "You want to take over the planet?"

She looked shocked, as if he had slapped her. "Heck, no. We just want to have a chance. We can't get a chance, you know, because— but my baby will have a chance. My line, my name."

"Your baby won't know anything about anything," he said, almost shouting. "He'll be stronger and faster than everybody, live longer than his mother's people, be alone, die alone. You want *that*? *That's* your big plan?" He realized he was towering over her, roaring, and didn't care. "Because that's what you've got!"

"He'll have the world! He'll be able to do whatever he wants!" she shrilled back. "He'll have more than ten years to live, and that opens up anything you can think of."

"You're cursed. I've cursed you. And the baby."

"We're blessed," she snapped back, "and you're a moron. You've given the baby great gifts and you don't even realize. The life span alone is the birthright of practically everyone else here; my child deserves it, too. And she'll be strong—able to defend herself and stay safe. And *live*."

"You are," he said carefully, "a crazy person."

"Yeah, well, it takes one to know one."

"And I'm not having anything to do with this."

"Who asked you to?"

"If I walk out this door . . . ," he threatened.

She threw the empty milk glass at him; he ducked easily. "Bye!"

He walked out that door.

≈

Twelve

"And then you left?"

"Well. Yes. I said . . . you know . . . If I walked out that door I was never coming back, and then—"

"She threw the glass at you and good-bye."

"Yeah."

"And you've been in town—what? Less than a week?"

He almost groaned; the full moon was a few hours away. He had actually forgotten about the moon, that's how crazy Charlene was making him. Forgotten! Christ, what next? Forgetting to eat?

"Are you sure you won't have a piece?" Pot asked, tapping the box with a bony finger.

"No."

"It's goat," she wheedled.

"I'm not hungry."

"That," Rae announced, "is seriously screwed up."

"Hush, ghost. You're not helping."

"Come on, Potty. There isn't one part of that story that isn't weird. Charlene's a mial? Whatever that is. And pregnant? All part of her plan? And she's dying?"

At Cole's fresh look of alarm, Pot quickly said, "She's dying as we all are, Rae. Everyone has a time limit. You're just too silly to acknowledge yours."

"She can talk," Rae said as if Pot wasn't sitting right there at Cole's kitchen counter. "Her people live for a zillion years. Poor Charlene! Just think, she could be dead before Bush is out of office."

"I'm going to puke," Cole said, and went to the bathroom, and did. When he came back after brushing his teeth, Pot was still there. So, presumably, was Rae.

"What are you going to do?" the queen asked.

He opened his mouth, but no words came out.

"Boy oh boy," Rae observed. "Not the sharpest knife in the drawer."

"Enough, Rae. Well, Cole? Are you going to stay here with Charlene, raise the baby? See to its upbringing after Charlene—ah, after? Or leave them and find your people?"

"Door number two," Rae added, "makes you a gigantic loser."

"That's not true," the queen interrupted. "You have no obligation to her; she admitted she tricked you."

"Which doesn't sound like it took much effort on her part."

"Rae!"

"All I'm saying is, Einstein he's not."

"As I was saying," the queen continued, sending looks of irritation to all corners of the kitchen, "you're not mates, she has what she needs of you, she has in fact released you from any obligation."

"Yep, she's totally fine living a life alone, being a single mom, dying young, and leaving your kid an orphan. Don't give it another thought."

Cole leaned over far enough to rest his forehead on the counter. It felt smooth and cool. "Why did you come over?" he asked the Formica.

"Well . . ." The queen paused. "I don't want you to read anything into this, but—"

His front door was thrown open. "My queen, your kingdom awaits!" several people shouted in unison, which was a good trick.

"—I'm leaving town," she finished.

Thirteen

"Holy Christ on a cracker with Cheez Whiz," Rae gasped, while Cole stared at the naiads—he assumed they were naiads—milling around in his living room.

"Forgive us, Queen Potameides," one of them said, and the group—there were seventeen, severely straining his living room space—went into a deep bow. "We have been from you so long, we could not remain in the front yard a moment longer knowing you were not far away, and so we—"

The queen waved the explanation away, and the guard or whoever it was instantly shut up. "Yes, yes, that's fine."

"What's going on?" Rae demanded.

"Probably the ones loyal to her overthrew the ones not loyal to her," Cole said. At the queen's unguarded look of surprise, he added, "Violence I understand."

"Yes. Ah. Yes. My cousin is dead—"

"Long live the queen!" another one interrupted. They all, Cole noticed, looked a great deal like the queen, the same long stringy hair and watery eyes, the same damp smell and long, spidery limbs.

"Right," the queen finished. "So, I go."

"This very damned minute?" Rae asked, sounding upset.

"Rae."

"I mean, you gotta leave right now, pack a bag and your swim fins and off tonight? Without a good-bye or anything?"

"Rae."

"Because that rots!"

"Rae. The river is my home, and more, my people need me."

"Well, shit!"

"You must have known I wouldn't stay forever."

"Why not? All the other freaks in this town don't seem to be in any damned rush to leave." The ghost audibly gulped. "Uh, no offense, Cole."

"That's okay," he replied. To Pot: "So you're taking the chance to go back and be with your people?"

"As I said. Don't read anything into that. Our situations are different. I'm an exiled queen and you—"

"Are a chump if you let Charlene get away," Rae said, "but we're getting off the subject. Why do you have to leave now? Because I know that look, Pot, you cow, you can't fool me, once you're in the wind we'll none of us see you again, and stop me if you heard this already but that *rots*."

"I'm of the royal family of the Naiad," Pot said sternly, "and I do not have the freedom ordinary people have. The Mississippi is a large territory and I lost it once through carelessness and—"

"The Mississippi *River*?" Cole asked. "That's your kingdom?"

"Was," Pot replied. "And now, is again. But I wanted to come by and say good-bye. In fact, you and Rae are the last ones on my list. I can't have my kingdom and Mysteria both—don't read anything into this—so I've traded the café to the triplets and their mother for, ah, future favors, and have wrapped up my other affairs. So now—"

"Wait a minute," Rae interrupted. "We were *last* on your list?"

"Well . . ." Pot paused. "I went, ah, geographically. This house is the last one."

"Fine, go then!" Rae shouted. "I never liked you anyway!"

"I will go," the queen replied, smiling, "and that is a lie. And Rae,

I adore you, and that will never change, not if I rule for a thousand years."

"Go soak your head in the deep end!"

"I go, then."

One of her hench-naiads opened the front door, but before Pot could grandly sweep out, in the manner of a river queen, a tall dark-haired man blocked the doorway.

"What now?" Rae griped, but Cole could hear the undercurrent of tears in her voice.

"Aside for the queen," one of the naiads demanded.

"Shush," the queen said. "He's not one of my subjects, Mr., ah . . . ?"

"Michael Wyndham."

"Potameides."

They shook hands. "Pack leader," the tall man explained.

"Queen of the Mississippi River naiads," Pot offered. "Good night."

"See you."

She left. She took all the river people with her. The werewolf came in.

Fourteen

"Hi," the werewolf said. He was dark-haired and broad, with gold eyes, big hands, and a feral scruffiness that Cole felt and instantly responded to. He had the weird urge to kill a cow and present it to the stranger. *Two* cows.

"Hello."

"I'm Michael Wyndham. In case you didn't hear me at the door."

"Cole Jones." He didn't offer his hand to shake; he had the very strong sense that the man wouldn't want his hand. Instead, Wyndham was sizing him up and Cole saw his nostrils flaring as he took every-thing in. Oddly, this was in no way alarming. It was almost—comforting?

"I can't believe she just picked up and left with those other weir-dos. I didn't even like her," Rae said tearfully, "but you talk to some-one for fifty years, you get used to them, you know?"

Wyndham flinched. "Who the hell is *that*?"

"That's my ghost."

"Hey, pal." The tears instantly vanished. "I'm not *your* anything."

"Sorry," Cole said. He kept trying to look Wyndham in the face and his gaze kept skittering away. He had been raised to know that it was polite to look people in the eye when you spoke to them, but Wyndham didn't seem to mind. "My roommate."

"A ghost? And a river naiad. I've met an eleionomid before—"

"Marsh nymph," Rae explained, before Cole could ask.

"—right, they're all over the Cape where I live. Lots of river marshes out there. And lots of witches, but that's about it. Oh, and you." Wyndham smiled in a perfectly friendly way, keeping his teeth covered, and Cole, responding to the man's natural charisma, actually smiled back.

"What—" Cole began, and stopped. Still the weirdest day ever, and getting weirder. And too many damned questions. Pack leader? What was he doing here now, tonight? How had he found Cole? What did he want?

Rae saved him the trouble. "Are you—what?—the boss of all the werewolves, then?"

"I am."

"So—what? You're here to—what?"

Wyndham was recovering quickly, and didn't seem to mind being interrogated by a dead woman. "I'm here to assist a member of my Pack, if he needs it." To Cole: "You don't look like you're in any real peril to me."

"He knocked up the local Realtor," Rae offered.

"Oh. Congratulations?"

"We're, uh, still working that out," Cole said. "How did you find me?"

"Another Pack member lives here. He got in touch with me— apparently there's a vampire killer in this town? Someone who knows quite a bit about werewolves?"

"You don't sound like you believe that all the way."

"Well"—Wyndham shrugged—"I don't take chances, period. As you were new, we thought you might need a hand. And with the moon on her way"—Wyndham gestured to the window, which showed nothing but unalleviated darkness; there were no street lights this far out of town—"I thought you might be vulnerable. Normally I wouldn't travel this close to a Change, but in this case . . ."

While Cole processed this, Rae said, "Whoa, whoa, whoa. That stud wannabe Justin *told* on Charlene?"

Wyndham blinked slowly, like an owl. "My Pack keeps me informed of any potential threat, yes. Which reminds me, Cole, why didn't *you* tell me about this vampire killer?" His lips actually curled at the word "vampire," and Cole instantly knew: the boss werewolf didn't believe in vampires. But had come anyway. Perhaps he assumed Charlene was a crazy person. God knew there were enough of them in the world. Still, it was nice of him to check up, even if Wyndham had doubted anything would come of it.

And he was waiting for an answer. "My parents were killed when I was a baby," he explained. "I was raised by regular people. I mean, my foster mother." Not exactly "regular people." He prayed word of his slip wouldn't get back to Mama Zee.

Wyndham was nodding. "Yep, yep, that's what I figured. I can smell them all over you. That's not a bad thing," he added quickly. "You can probably smell them all over me—I married one."

"Ha!" Rae cried. "There you go. He married a regular person."

Wyndham laughed. "I didn't say that."

"She's no threat to you," Cole said quickly. "The vampire killer. She was just trying to—" What? What in the world could he say? Annoyingly (or mercifully), Rae remained silent.

"Are you sure? You're part of my family, even if you never knew, and I want to help you any way I can." Wyndham clapped a large hand on Cole's shoulder. It felt like a brick. "You're not alone anymore, Cole."

Then why, he wanted to ask, did hearing that—at long last—make him feel exactly nothing?

Fifteen

"That was, no joke, the most amazing thing. Pot leaves, the werewolf guy shows up, and how nice was he? I mean, wow! He had kind of an Errol Flynn thing going on, did you notice? Yummy. And where'd he go already? You guys didn't even get a chance to catch up or anything!"

"He left for his Change." Change. Pack. He could hear the capital letters in his head, sensed their deep meaning. "We don't like to be in towns or cities when the Change happens." We. Werewolves. My people. Us. Our.

"How long do you have?"

"About an hour." Fifty-three minutes.

"So you have time!"

"Time?"

"You're not fooling me, pal. I heard you sticking up for Charlene. And I heard you tell him you weren't in any big rush to get out to the Cape."

"Too many tourists," he said automatically.

"Ha! The thing you came here for, the reason you blew Charlene off, it's handed to you on a platter, and what? You're all Mr. Cool, 'Oh, well, I'd love to visit, maybe for Christmas.' Give me a goddamned break."

He said nothing.

"I mean, look at the situation," Rae continued. Christ, she loved the sound of her own voice. "You've basically got a choice: go off with your people—like Pot did—or stay with what you like and marry a local—like your boss says *he* did. And he's soooo helpful: you don't have to move in with all the werewolves on the Cape. What'd he say again?"

"There are too many in the world to live in one place," he said automatically.

"I just knew you were paying attention. Aaaaaaand?"

"Any werewolf past the age of consent can live anywhere, with Wyndham's permission."

"Which he *gave* you about five minutes ago. Aaaaaaaand?"

"I don't have to choose; I can move between worlds, as his mate does."

"Ding ding ding!"

"What?"

"Cole. For Christ's sake. What are you still doing here? You're talking like I didn't hear you puke at the thought of Charlene dying alone."

Fifty-one minutes.

"And you're talking like you have a choice. When really, you never ever did."

"That's true," he said.

"So, again. Stop me if you've heard this. What the hell are you waiting for? Does that Wyndham guy have to chisel an invite on your forehead?"

"No," he said, and practically jumped toward the doorway. But before he could get it open, it opened by itself (but not really) and like magic (but not really; she probably just drove up and he was too distracted to hear the car) Charlene was standing there. Her thereness, her concentrated punch, washed over him like a wave and he wondered why he was surprised. Of course: she had a short life span; her people jammed everything they could into a dozen years. Of course they were more there than ordinary people. And how could he ever have resisted her?

"I knew this would happen," Rae said, sounding shocked. "I think I'll see if I can install free cable."

He opened his mouth, but as usual, the smarter person beat him to the punch.

Sixteen

"Before you leave," Charlene began, "I've come to tell you that I've changed my mind, and no matter where you run to, I'll hunt you down like a rat."

"I met the head of the werewolves," he replied. "And it's pack, not herd."

"*And*, it's fine if you don't want to get married, but you're going to be with me until the bitter, gory end."

"Also," he added, "the baby is welcome with my people anytime; a drop of werewolf blood is as good as a hundred percent as far as they're concerned."

That gave her pause, he saw at once. Her brow wrinkled and then smoothed out, and she said, "You've been busy in the last few hours. Days, come to think of it."

"I was coming to get you," he told her.

She smiled, and it was like clouds blowing away from the bright, beautiful moon. "That's funny. I was coming to get you, too."

A split second later, they were in each other's arms. "You're not allowed to die in six years," he said into her hair, her dark, dark hair.

"Well, I've had some thoughts about that. This *is* Mysteria, you know. The oddest place on earth. Maybe we can find a spell or something. You're just as much on the edge as I am—what if you're out chasing rabbits and get hit by a truck? It could happen anytime. It's the risk we all run."

"Repeat," he said, kissing her throat, her cheeks, her forehead, her mouth, "after me: I'm not going to die in six years."

"Well . . ." She was busy kissing him back. "I won't if you won't. Er, how much time do we have before you grow a revolting amount of back hair?"

"Forty-seven minutes."

She laughed. "Plenty of time."

THE WITCHES OF MYSTERIA
AND THE DEAD
WHO LOVE THEM

Gena Showalter

To those of us who probably should live in Mysteria:
P. C. Cast, Susan Grant, and MaryJanice Davidson.
And to Christine Zika for a wonderful experience.

One

"Men suck," Genevieve Tawdry muttered, "and not in a good way."

She was tired, so very tired, of Hunter Knight's hot and cold treatment of her. He was making her crazy, laughing with her flirtatiously one moment (translation: stringing her along without giving her any actual benefits, the bastard), then dropping her altogether the next moment, then laughing flirtatiously with her again.

By the Great Goddess, she wasn't going to tolerate it anymore.

Unfortunately, lovesick witch that she was, Genevieve didn't have the strength to shove him from her life—which meant she would have to up her game. But how? Truly, she'd tried everything. Spells and incantations. "Accidental" meetings where she happened to be braless. "Accidentally" ramming her car into the back end of his Ford Explorer. Or the latest, an incident that happened only last night, "accidentally" tripping and falling into his lap at a mutual friend's wedding.

Nothing worked.

Last night had been a "cold" night. Hunter had taken one look at her in her brand-new white silk dress (no, she hadn't been the bride and yes, the bride had been pissed that she'd dared to wear the "sacred" color) and he hadn't been able to get away from her fast enough. She sighed.

What would it take to make herself irresistible to him? To hold his attention for as long as she desired it? To at last put an end to the heart-pounding tension that always sparked between them when they were together? Whatever was needed, she'd do it. Anything. Everything.

"God, I'm a stalker." Frowning, she tapped her fingers against the desk surface.

Moonlight spilled through the window in front of her, mingling with the soft glow of lamplight, illuminating the unread book in front of her. Incense burned beside her, the scent of jasmine curling sweetly and fragrancing the air.

She sat in the office of the three-bedroom home, aka den of iniquity, she shared with her two sisters, hunched over the desk, dark strands of hair falling over her shoulders. Behind her, the TV emitted a *crunch*, *crunch* sound, as if someone on screen was enjoying a tasty snack. A family of squirrels raced around her feet—her oldest sister's newest save-the-world-one-animal-at-a-time "project."

I don't want to be Hunter's stalker. I want to be his lover.

Over the years, he had become the bane of her existence, the mountain she'd tried to climb (naked) but couldn't quite manage to conquer. But damn it. He liked her; she knew he did. Last night, before he'd run away from her, she would have sworn to the Great Goddess he'd had an erection and had been desperate to get *to* her, not away. Desperate to touch her. Desperate to taste her.

Heat had blazed in his emerald eyes, scorching, white-hot. Enough to blister. He'd reached for her, his fingers caressing her with phantom strokes, before he dropped his arm to his side. He'd licked his lips and taken a step toward her before catching himself and striding away.

Why, why, *why* did he continually do crap like that?

If not for moments like those, she might have given up long ago and forced herself to forget him. Yet, he'd beaten John Foster to a bloody pulp for trying to kiss her. He always walked her home if he saw her in town. And it was *her* he'd called when his father had died, seeking comfort. *Her* he came to when he had a problem at work and needed help finding a solution.

That meant something. Didn't it?

"Maybe you should offer to ride him like a carnival pony," Glory said from behind her. "That always works for me."

Genevieve twisted to face her younger sister. "What are you doing in here?" she gasped out in surprise.

Glory brushed away the cheese dust on her lips. "Uh, spying. Hello. I say sleep with some other man and forget Hunter."

Always the same advice. Genevieve eased slowly to her feet. "How would you like it if I cast a spell, bringing every one of those chips to life and letting them exact their revenge against you?"

Glory's hazel eyes flashed. "You wouldn't dare!"

"Oh, really? Keep talking, then, and by tomorrow morning the entire town will be talking about the Great Doritos Death."

"Is that before or after they talk about Stalkerella and her unwilling victim?"

For several seconds, she and Glory glared at each other. Hunter was a sore spot for Genevieve; food was a sore spot for Glory.

Finally Glory expelled a deep breath, and her features slowly softened. "Evie, when are you going to realize Hunter will never want you the way you want him? He dates everything that moves and even some things that don't. But not you. Never you. He just, well, I didn't want to be the one to tell you this, but he pities you."

"He does not."

"Yes, he does."

"No, he *desires* me."

"That's delusion talking, and something *every* stalker says."

"I'm not stalking him," she said with a stubborn tilt of her chin, even though she herself had thought the very same thing. "I'm seducing him."

Her sister rolled her eyes and popped another chip in her mouth. "That's like saying murdering your neighbor is merely giving them a big send-off."

"Girls, please." Godiva, the oldest sister, strode into the room, her silver-white hair streaming behind her. She wore ripped jeans and a faded blue T-shirt, both of which were streaked with blood, dirt, and dark fur. "I've got an injured wolf in the kitchen and your arguing is upsetting him."

"You brought an injured wolf into the house?" All traces of color abandoned Glory's cheeks. "I can live with the squirrels and the wood mice, but a wolf? No way. They're dangerous killers, Diva. They like to claw witches like us into bite-sized nibblets and feast on the pieces."

"We have nothing to fear from him." Godiva anchored her hands on her hips. "He's too weak to cause us any harm."

"Where is he?" Genevieve asked, trying to push Hunter—and Glory's remarks—to the back of her mind. Her sister didn't understand. How could she? She'd never been in love, never been consumed by the emotion. Never wanted more from a man than temporary satisfaction.

"He's in the kitchen, and I could use your help."

"Of course." Following behind her older sister, Genevieve dragged a protesting Glory down the hall and into the kitchen.

Glory immediately flattened herself against the wall, surrounding herself with faux plant leaves, maintaining a safe distance from the large—very large—animal lying on the black and white tiled floor. As if she could hide with hair as vivid red as hers. Godiva bent over him, dabbing a steaming cloth over the jagged, bleeding claw wounds on his belly. He whimpered up at her, his eyes big and brown and glazed with pain.

Genevieve crouched beside her oldest sister. "What do you need me to do?"

They spent the next several hours murmuring peace spells, applying salve, and stitching the poor wolf's wounds. He drifted in and out of sleep, but through it all he responded to Godiva's every touch, recognizing her voice, her scent, and calming whenever she approached.

"He likes you," Genevieve said.

"I think he recognizes me and feels safe. I've seen him before, in the forest. I was gathering herbs, and he was watching me."

Genevieve wished Hunter responded to her half as much as this wolf responded to her sister. Since the day Hunter had saved her from gracing the dessert menu of a rabid gnome, she'd loved him.

She'd been seventeen years old at the time and he twenty-two, but she'd known she belonged with him. They'd even kissed that day, a delicious, mind-shattering kiss she'd never forgotten. Yes, she'd relived it in her dreams over and over again.

They were meant to be together, damn it. The way he sometimes treated her like a curse of hemorrhoids, no anti-itch cream in sight, had to stop! Did he think she meant to use him as a sexual toy then kick him out of her life? If so, he should love that. Did he think she meant to ruin their friendship? Well, she didn't. She wanted to love him (hard core).

She would never, ever do anything to hurt him. Well . . . she bit her bottom lip. Fine. That wasn't exactly true. Once she'd cast a seduction spell over him, hoping he would become sexually enthralled with the first woman he saw (which would have been her). Instead, she'd made nearly every woman in Mysteria, a town known for its weirdness, fall into instant lust with *him*. Even her sisters had been trapped under the spell. For days the entire female population had followed him everywhere, ripping at his clothes, begging him to make love to them.

"Even if the wolf saw you before," Glory said, the sound of her voice breaking into Genevieve's thoughts, "that's not reason enough for him to respond so favorably to you. He acts like he adores you." She frowned. "Hey, did you give him one of my love potions?"

"Of course not," Godiva said. "I think he senses that I mean him no harm."

At Glory's words, a wonderfully frightening idea danced inside Genevieve's mind, an idea she'd always discarded before—and no, she wasn't going to injure Hunter to gain his attention (although she wouldn't rule that out, the sexy bastard). What if *she* drank a love potion? What if she made herself so irresistible he wouldn't think of turning her away? She'd never dared drink one before; there were simply too many uncertain variables.

For one night in his arms, though, she was now willing to risk it. Risk the deflation of her inhibitions, the danger of enticing the love of a legion of other men. The danger of loving him forever and him only loving her for a single night. Hell, she already loved him and she didn't see an end in sight for the emotion. For Hunter, she'd risk anything. Everything. Except . . .

Genevieve uttered a sigh. Did she really want to win him because of a potion and not because he simply wanted *her*? Yes, she decided in the next instant. The stubborn man needed a push in the right direction, and she was tired of waiting for that to happen naturally. Her patience was frayed beyond repair.

Besides, if she had to watch him flirt and laugh with another woman one more time, just one more time, she'd fly into a rampage worthy of the Desdaine triplets, the town's most notorious troublemakers.

Now that she had a plan, urgency rushed through her. She glanced at the clock above the refrigerator. Ten P.M. Knight Caps, Hunter's bar, would be open for at least four more hours.

"Will you be okay on your own?" she asked Godiva.

"Hey, she's not alone. *I'm* here," Glory said with a pout.

"Oh, sorry. Will you be okay with Glory standing in the shadows and doing nothing?"

"I'll be fine." Godiva nodded. "Candy Cox should be here any minute. She's going to sit with me." Candy—oops, *Candice*—was the high school English teacher and Godiva's best friend. "My big boy is finally resting peacefully. Why? Are you going out?"

"Yes." She offered no other explanation. Neither of her sisters approved of her obsession with Hunter.

"Where are you going?" Glory asked suspiciously. She inched to the kitchen table, keeping the long length of the hand-carved mahogany between herself and the wolf.

"*I'm. Going. Out.*"

"That's not what I meant and you know it." She paused, then her pretty face scrunched in disgust. "You're going to see *him*, aren't you?"

Genevieve's back went ramrod straight. "So what if I am? You got something to say about it?"

"Nope. Not a word. Except, if you want to make a fool of yourself over him again, go for it. Just know that the town isn't laughing *with* you, they're laughing *at* you."

Her fists clenched at her sides. "You're just begging for a piece of me, Glor."

Awakening, the wolf raised his head, his lips pulling tight over his fangs.

"Don't listen to them," Godiva cooed at him. She smothered her fingers over his thick fur, giving her sisters a pointed glare. "They're both going to rot in the fires of hell, just like Pastor Harmony says."

"Harmony didn't say we were going to hell," Glory said. "She embraces every one of every religion, and she says only evil people go to hell."

"Exactly."

As they argued, anticipation and nervousness zinged through Genevieve's veins. Not for the proposed trip into hell, but for the coming night. Now that she'd decided to do it, to love-potion the pants right off of Hunter, she didn't want to waste another minute. "Glory, I'd like to talk with you privately," she said sweetly. She motioned to the living room with a tilt of her chin. "I don't want to fight."

"I don't believe you."

"Okay, stay here then. I'm sure the wolf won't regain full strength soon and be disoriented and afraid. He won't fly into a rampage and—"

Glory jolted backward with a gasp. "Alright. Fine." One tiny step, two, she scooted around the table, around the wolf. "I'll meet you in the living room."

Dissatisfied with such a gradual pace, Genevieve reached out, grabbed her younger sister's hand, and tugged her into the next room. In the center, she whirled. She was almost bubbling over. Tonight might be the night all her dreams came true. . . . Glory's love potions were legendary. Each sister specialized in a different area of magic. While she herself wielded the darkest power, that over vengeance, Godiva's strength was in healing, both spiritual and physical, and Glory's was in love.

"I want to drink one of your love potions. And don't say no."

Glory pursed her lips and crossed her arms over her chest. "How about: hell, no."

"Please."

"Nein. Nay. Non."

She pushed out a frustrated breath. "Why not?"

"Evie," her sister said, her expression softening, "he's not good enough for you. When are you going to realize that? I'm more inclined to turn him into an impotent troll than help you win his affections."

"It's one night, Glor. What can that hurt?"

"It wouldn't be one night for you. You'd want more."

True. So true. Deep down, she hoped Hunter would be so enthralled by her that he'd become addicted to her touch. "If he doesn't want me after the potion, I'll take a blood oath never to speak to him again." A small lie, really, since she only planned to leave out one word. Never.

"Sorry."

"Please. I'll bake those eye of newt muffins you love so much."

"Oh, you bitch. I love those." Several minutes passed in thick, brooding silence, before she shook her head. "Nope, sorry. I simply can't allow you to endure more hurt because of him."

"I'll wreak vengeance upon your greatest enemy. I'll go total witch on their ass."

Glory opened her mouth, then closed it with a snap. Opened. Closed. Her hazel eyes gleamed hopefully, glowing with otherworldly power like they did just before a spell. "Horrible, painful vengeance?"

"Yes."

"Even if it's, say, against Falon Ryis?"

"Hunter's best friend? *He's* your greatest enemy?" Genevieve blinked in surprise. "I didn't know you and Falon had even spoken to each other. Ever."

Glory's jaw clenched stubbornly. "I'm not going to explain. You make his life miserable, I'll give you the potion. Take it or leave it."

She didn't have to think about her answer. "I'll take it."

Glory slowly smiled. "Then the potion is yours."

"Thank you, thank you!" With a joyous whoop, she threw her arms around her sister. Sometimes family was a wonderful thing.

"What's going on in there?" Godiva called.

Glory said, "Genevieve accidentally conjured a male stripper, and we're placing dollar bills in his G-string. Just ignore us."

"Ha, ha. Very funny," came the muffled reply. Then, "I'll be there in a sec."

"Come on." Glory extracted herself from the bear hug and flounced down the candlelit hall, through thickly painted shadows, toward their bedrooms. "It's in my room. I really hope you know what you're doing," she murmured.

Did she? Genevieve mused. Not really. Did she care? Hell, no. Thoughts of lying naked in Hunter's arms eclipsed all else. He'd trace his fingers over her breasts, roll her nipples between his fingers. He'd kiss a path down her stomach, lingering, licking . . . "Uh, can we put a rush order on that potion?"

Glory unlocked her door with a quietly muttered "Open" and a wave of her delicate hand. Instantly the thin slab of wood creaked open. They stepped inside the room.

Genevieve's jaw nearly hit the ground. She rarely ventured in there and was momentarily shocked by the total chaos. Clothes and empty food cartons were scattered all over the floor, a sea of reds, blues, greens, and sweet and sour chicken orange.

"I need a minute," Glory said, already tossing shoes and other items aside as she scrounged through the mess.

"No, you need a maid." She pinched the 38D bra hanging from the lampshade between her fingers before dropping it on top of the matching panties at her feet.

"I've been depressed and haven't cleaned. Big deal." Pause. "Ah-ha! I found you, you little sneak." Smiling, Glory jumped up. A red bottle dangled from her fingers. "Love potion number thirteen."

Genevieve frowned. "I want love potion number nine."

"Trust me. Nine sucks. You want to ride a man like a bronco at peak rodeo season, you go with thirteen."

"I'll take it." Genevieve grabbed the crimson container and gently rolled it between her fingers. Dark liquid swirled inside, mesmerizing her. This was it, the answer to her prayers. Her heart drummed in her chest, faster, faster, then skipped a beat. This innocent-looking bottle was about to gift her with the best night of her life. Eager to begin, she reached for the cork, but her sister's next words stilled her hand.

"Drink half just before you walk into the bar, not a moment sooner. Only half. Understand?" Urgency rang from her voice like a clarion of bells.

"Yes. Why?"

"Uh, hello. You'll have every man in Mysteria following you and fighting for your attention if you drink it now. And the full bottle will cause . . . too much passion in you. Now go. Get out of here before I change my mind."

Genevieve needed no further prompting. "I love you." She kissed her sister's cheek and raced to her room. Quickly she changed into the sluttiest outfit she possessed. A black dress with a V neck so low it nearly touched her navel. The hem dangled mere inches below the curve of her ass. A little uncomfortable with the amount of skin showing, she slipped on a pair of tall hooker boots that hit just above her knees.

She left her hair down, the brunette tresses hanging along the curve of her back in sexy disarray. She spritzed jasmine perfume between her breasts and swiped fuck-me-hard red gloss over her lips. There. Done.

After grabbing a quarter, she grabbed her broom and skipped outside. Flying would be faster than driving. A cool night breeze kissed every inch of visible flesh—and boy, was there a lot of it. Amid the romantic haze of moonlight, insects sang a welcoming chorus, interspersed prettily with the buzz of fairy wings. Once she'd settled on top of the skinny broom handle, careful to cover her butt so she didn't moon the entire town, she commanded the contraption to fly.

"High, high my stead will soar. Touch the ground we shall no more." As the words left her mouth, the broom inched higher and higher into the air, then sped forward, moving faster than any car. Long tendrils of dark hair whipped her face, slapping her cheeks. Plumes of pink pollen whizzed past her, leaving behind an erotic scent.

When the lights of the town square came into view, framed by towering, majestic snowcapped mountains, she lowered and slowed. She stopped at the One-Stop Mart and bought a package of condoms from the pink-haired kid at the register. Outside, she popped back onto her broom and stuffed several foil wrappers in her dress.

Ever upward she soared again, past the tall pines. Whitewashed wooden buildings, dirt roads, and friendly people came into view, each weirder than the next. Psychics, vampires, trolls, fairies—Mysteria turned no one away.

As she flew over the town's wishing well, a lovely arching marble structure that glittered in the moonlight, she swooped low and dropped her quarter inside. "Let tonight be exciting," she said, wanting the wish to come true with every fiber of her being. Wisps of magic ribboned in the air, curling into the sky, making her shiver. She grinned.

Soon Knight Caps entered her line of vision, the tall stone structure bursting with people, laughter, and gyrating music. She slowed. Her heart raced when she finally stopped at the side of the building. Her palms began to sweat as she hovered, hidden by the shadows. What if Hunter was somehow able to resist the potion? She swallowed the sudden lump in her throat. What if she failed to attract him? What if—

Her teeth ground together. No. No thoughts of failure. Not tonight. Tonight wishes came true.

Stiffening her shoulders, she hopped to the ground. Her broom fell with a thump. Already she could sense Hunter's presence inside. His warm essence swirled around her, layered with a subtle fragrance of sex appeal and man. With shaky fingers, she studied the bottle one last time, only then seeing the warning label on the side.

"May cause dizziness," she read. "This drug may impair the ability to drive or operate machinery. Use care until you become familiar with its effects. Seek medical attention if liquid comes into contact with eyes."

Nothing she couldn't handle, she thought, popping the bottle's cork. "Bottom's up, Evie." She drained the contents. If half would make Hunter love her for a night, just think of what the full bottle could do. There was no such thing as too much passion. The bitter liquid tasted foul on her tongue, and she felt its quick descent into her stomach. Burning, burning. So hot. She coughed and doubled over. Her blood boiled, setting fire to everything inside her. She squeezed her eyes shut and tried to scream, but no sound emerged.

Thankfully the burning soon faded as if it had never been.

Blinking, Genevieve straightened and took stock of her physical being. She didn't *feel* any sexier. Didn't feel irresistible. Still, she inched to the front entrance. *I can do this. I'm a sexual cauldron of lust.* She pushed open the doors. *I'm a sexual cauldron of lust.* The sound of inane chatter and frantic music filled her ears. Smoke wafted around her, blending with the shadows and creating a dreamlike haze.

A small part of her expected everything male to attack her as her gaze searched the room for Hunter. No one paid her any heed. Where was—her heartbeat skidded to a stop. There he was. Behind the bar. For a moment, she forgot to breathe. He was serving drinks to a twittering, giggling fairy threesome. A rush of jealousy hit her. Each fairy possessed a startling, delicate beauty, with glittery skin and gossamer

wings that entranced human men, bringing out their protective instincts. Not to mention lust. These fairies were completely pink, with
fuchsia hair, rose skin, and seashell garments.

Hunter looked magnificent. His disheveled black hair tangled over
his forehead and hit just below his ears. Silky. Tempting. His sharp
cheekbones hinted at some foreign lineage. Probably royalty. A ruth-
less conqueror. His nose possessed an endearing bump and a scar
nicked the right corner of his lips, most likely souvenirs from a barroom brawl.

He was probably six-foot-five, a veritable giant to her five-four.
Obviously he worked out. A lot. His delicious biceps stretched the
fabric of his black T-shirt. Overall (and quite surprisingly) he was not
a handsome man. He was too savage looking. *Predator*, his mesmerizing green eyes proclaimed. An irresistible proclamation. She wasn't
sure why he'd come to Mysteria, or what made him so different from
other males that she had to have him. Only him.

He laughed at something one of the stupid flirting fairies said, and
her jaw clenched. He must have sensed her presence in that moment
because even as he laughed, his gaze traveled across the distance and
locked on her. His smile grew even wider, and he waved in a welcome—
until he saw her outfit. His eyes, suddenly blazing with fire, narrowed.
His smile faded into a fierce frown; his hand fell to his side.

He turned away from her.

Oh, no no no. There would be no ignoring her tonight. No giving
her the cold shoulder. *I'm a sexual cauldron of lust*, she thought, stepping into the bar.

TWO

I'm dead, Hunter Knight thought. *So fucking dead*.

His blood heated as his gaze drank in the vision that was Genevieve Tawdry. Actually, he didn't have to look at her to know her appearance. He'd memorized it long ago. Long, dark brown hair that glinted red in sunlight framed a serious little face. Pert nose, huge hazel eyes that sometimes glowed and were always fringed by the prettiest lashes he'd ever seen.

As usual, she mesmerized him.

Right now, in the dim strobelight of the bar, she appeared lovelier than ever. Her barely-there dress—holy hell, she might as well have been naked. Every muscle in his body (even his favorite) hardened to the point of pain. A pair of black boots stretched up her calves, just past her knees, leaving several inches of delicious thigh visible. Cleavage spilled from the deep V of her top. *Come over here and lick me*, that cleavage said.

What he would have given to take that cleavage up on its offer.

Every time he saw this woman, he experienced an inexorable urge to strip her and ride her. Hard. Ride her till she screamed his name. Ride her till she spasmed around his cock. Now was no different. Her slender body, with its hide-and-seek curves, would fit perfectly against him. Over him. Under him.

His teeth ground together. He wanted her desperately. He'd always wanted her.

And there was no way in hell he could have her.

Loving Genevieve would destroy him. Literally. Being psychic sucked ass. One touch of Genevieve's lips at their first meeting and he'd known, *known*, she would somehow kill him if he let himself get involved with her romantically.

That didn't stop the cravings, however, didn't stop her image from constantly haunting his dreams. Hell, in that scrap of black material she now wore, she might very well cause his heart to stop or his dick to explode.

"Hunter, will you get me a sex on the beach?" a high-pitched female voice said in front of him. Fairy laughter erupted, ringing like dainty bells.

He forced his gaze away from Genevieve, forced his lips to edge into a semblance of a smile, and met the impish gaze of one of the fairies. "Sure thing, sugar. Sex on the beach, just for you. I'll even add Knight's special ingredient."

More giggling. The girlish sound grated on his every nerve.

He thought he might have slept with one of these horny pixies (maybe all of them?) at some point last year, but at that moment he couldn't remember when. Or who. Or if they'd had a good time. He didn't care anymore. Couldn't get hard unless he thought of Genevieve.

What was it about her that so obsessed him? She was pretty, but other women were prettier. Maybe it was her amazing smell. No one smelled as sweet and intoxicating as Genevieve. Or maybe it was her eyes, so vulnerable. So determined.

He mixed the requested drink and slid it across the counter. From the corner of his eye he watched Genevieve saunter to the bar, her hips swaying seductively. She eased onto a stool, mere inches from his reach. Every nerve ending inside him leaped to instant life, clamoring for her. A touch, a press. Something. Anything.

"I'll have a flaming fairy," she said. Her voice dipped huskily, soft and alluring. Menacing.

The fairies gasped at the implied threat.

His lips twitched. Genevieve arched her brows—they were two shades darker than her hair, nearly black—silently daring the fairies to comment. They remained silent. He watched the byplay in amusement, admiring Genevieve's spirit and strength. Fairies were delicate creatures, at times human in size, at others merely flickering pinpricks of light. They adored sex and alcohol, gaiety and games, but they rarely fought. Most resided in the surrounding forest and Colorado mountains, visiting Mysteria when they grew bored.

"Are you refusing to serve me?" Genevieve asked him.

"Of course not," he said, realizing he hadn't moved an inch since she'd requested her drink. He grabbed a glass. He didn't allow himself to look at her and the tempting cleavage she displayed. Lately it was becoming harder and harder (literally!) to send her away.

Maybe he should not have cultivated a friendship with her, but he'd been unable to completely push her out of his life. He just, well, he wanted to spend time with her. She amused and exhilarated him.

At least she hadn't killed him. Yet.

Every time he saw her, he asked himself a single question: is she worth dying for? Always the answer was the same. No. No, she wasn't. Not then, not now. He might crave her, he might enjoy her, but he would *not* die for her. He lifted a bottle of rum.

"Sooo . . . how are you, Hunter?" she asked him.

Stay strong, he mentally chanted. *Fight her appeal.* But damn it all to hell, the urge to wrap her in his arms and give them both what they wanted was stronger tonight than ever before. "I'm good. Busy, though. I really need to see to my other customers. You'll have to excuse me."

He turned his back on her.

Silence.

Horrible, guilty silence where everything faded from his mind except the look of pain that passed over Genevieve's face. He wished he could take back the words and say something else. Something innocent like, You look nice. Something honest like, It's great to see you. As it was, hurt radiated from her and that hurt sliced through him sharper than any knife.

"Genevieve," he said, then pressed his lips together. If he told her he was sorry, he'd only be encouraging her.

"I still need my drink."

"Of course." Well, hell. He didn't know how to handle her anymore. Always his resolve teetered on the brink of total destruction—now even more so. He needed to send her away, but he wanted her to stay so badly. *She's not worth dying for, remember?*

He inhaled deeply, meaning to relax himself, but her scent filled him. More decadent than ever before. Pure temptation. Forbidden desire.

Total seduction. Hot and wild. His eyelids closed of their own accord, and his hands ceased all movement, her drink once again forgotten.

"Hunter?"

His cock jumped, hardening further. Again, his name coming from her lush made-for-sin lips was torture. Too easily could he imagine her screaming his name while he pounded in and out of her.

Snap out of it, asshole, and fix her drink.

Hunter pried his eyes open and mixed vodka, peach schnapps, and cranberry, orange, and pineapple juices into the rum. Without ever glancing in her direction, he struck a match and lit the top on fire. Yellow-gold flames licked the rim of the glass before dying a hasty death. He slid the drink to Genevieve and turned away.

"What do I owe you?" she said in that breathy voice.

"You're my *friend*." They both needed the reminder. "It's on the house." If her fingertips brushed his while she handed him money, he'd come right then, right there. And he'd be willing to bet it would be the best orgasm of his life, no penetration required.

"Falon," Hunter called. Falon, his employee and best friend, was busy cleaning tables, but the tall, muscled male sauntered to the bar.

"Yeah?" Falon smiled a mysterious smile.

The three fairies trembled in reverence, bowing their heads in acknowledgment.

Falon had uptilted violet eyes, perfect white teeth, tanned skin that sometimes shimmered like it had been sprinkled with glitter, and shoulder-length blond hair with a slight wave. While human women lusted for him, fairy females were awed by him. They treated him as if he were a king, a god. Hunter had no idea why. Every time he asked, Falon shrugged and changed the subject.

Falon wasn't human, Hunter knew that, but he didn't know exactly what type of creature Falon was. There was an unspoken rule in Mysteria: if you can't tell, don't ask.

"Do you mind taking over?" Hunter asked him. "I've, uh, decided to call it a night."

"I don't mind at all. I like the view from the bar." Falon's gaze strayed meaningfully to Genevieve. "I've been meaning to call Genevieve, anyway. So this works out perfectly."

Falon and Genevieve? Hunter froze in place, lances of possessive-ness and jealousy blending together and spearing him. *Nothing you can do about it, man. Leave. Now.* Muscles clenched tightly, he strode toward the storeroom. His home was above the bar, and the only door to the staircase was there. He'd go upstairs and seduce a few bottles of Jack Daniels. Maybe then he could wipe Genevieve's image from his mind. Not to mention the hated image of Genevieve and Falon.

"Thanks a lot, Tawdry," he heard one of the fairies murmur. "You scared Hunter away, just like you always do."

Genevieve growled. "If your greatest wish is to be bitch-slapped, color me Genie in a Bottle because I'm about to grant it."

Hearing the embarrassment in her tone and the shame she tried so hard to hide behind bravado, he stilled. Another wave of guilt washed through him. He'd rejected this woman at every turn. He'd embar-rassed her in front of the entire town more times than he could count. And she'd never been anything but sweet to him.

He knew she was shy around men. The way her cheeks pinkened, the way she sometimes stumbled over her words and gazed at anything but him, proved that. Yet she'd worked up the courage to approach him time and time again. How could he hurt her yet again?

"I, for one, am glad Hunter left," Falon said, his tone seductive. "I've wanted to get Genevieve alone for a long time."

Get her alone? That poaching bastard. *Stop. Don't think like that.* Hunter rolled his shoulders and drew in a deliberate breath. Still, the thought of Falon and Genevieve together flashed through his mind again, the two of them naked and writhing. Rage seethed below the surface of his skin.

Maybe his psychic abilities were wrong. Maybe Genevieve wouldn't be the death of him. Maybe— He ran his tongue over his teeth. His instincts were never wrong, and he knew better than to fool himself into believing a lie. He had to keep pushing her away.

Except, pushing her away might send her straight into another man's arms. Something he'd always feared.

Yes, he'd always dreaded the day she would *stop* coming to him. That would mean she was ready to move on and accept another man. His hands fisted at his sides. He hadn't meant to, but he'd cultivated a tentative friendship with her to keep such a thing from happening. Was it wrong of him? Yes. Did he care? Hell, no. The idea of her with another man always blackened his mood and set him on killing edge.

If she went to someone else tonight, to Falon, he'd—he'd—no way in hell he was letting that happen, he decided.

Determination rushing through him, he spun on his heel. Genevieve still sat at the bar, her shoulders hunched, her face lowered toward her empty glass as Falon spoke to her. Her hair tumbled over her shoulders, shielding her delectable cleavage.

"Genevieve," he called before he could stop himself.

The music skidded to a halt, the band members too interested in what was happening to play. In fact, everyone present went silent and locked eyes on him. Everyone except Genevieve, that is. She continued to stare into her glass, her gaze faraway, lost.

"Genevieve, you beautiful thing, I need your attention."

Finally her chin snapped up and she faced him, shock filling her luscious hazel eyes. "Did you say beautiful? Are you talking to me?"

"Is your name Genevieve?"

"Well, yes."

Oh, how she enticed him. She was all innocence, yet she possessed a wild, sex-kitten allure. It was a lethal, contradictory combination that always intrigued him. "Why don't you have a seat at one of the tables, and I'll join you in a minute."

"Thanks a lot, Hunter," Falon said, but there was a glimmer of amusement in his tone. Scamming bastard.

Genevieve's nose crinkled and her brow furrowed, the planes of her face darkening with suspicion. "Why?"

"Because."

"That's not an answer. What do you want to talk about?"

He flicked a pointed glance to their avid audience. "It's private."

"I don't understand." Then her lips—her lush, kiss me, lick me all over, fuck me all night lips—pressed together. Comprehension dawned in her eyes. She smiled slowly, seductively, yet somehow she appeared even more sad.

Now *he* was the one confused. What had made her happy and sad all at once? What did she comprehend?

"I would love to 'talk' with you," she said.

He gulped. She made it sound like they'd be going at it like wild animals on the tabletop. Maybe they would. If only she didn't tempt him on every level. Why did the Fates have to be so cruel? He desired this woman desperately, but he couldn't have her as anything more than a friend.

She eased to her feet, and he choked back a laugh when she flipped the rose-colored pixies off. His laugh died a sudden death when he saw that her dress barely fell below the curve of her bottom. His fingers itched to touch.

None of the tables were empty. Everyone watched her curiously as she crossed her arms over her chest. "You have five seconds to give me a table or I'll conjure your spouses into the bar. They'll find out what you've been doing and—"

Before the last word emerged, everyone at the tables jolted to their feet—everyone except Barnabas Vlad, the art gallery owner. He didn't have a spouse. Chairs skidded, drinks sloshed over rims. "Here, take mine," rose in disharmony. Satisfied, Genevieve skipped to the table hidden in the corner, partially covered in a shadowy haven. "I'll take yours, John Foster. Thank you."

The town pervert was too busy staring at her cleavage to respond.

"Move out of her damn way!" Hunter shouted.

John nearly jumped out of his skin as he leaped away from Genevieve.

"And play some music. *Now*." Hunter scowled at the band leader. "That's what I pay you for, isn't it?"

A few seconds later, soft, romantic music drifted from the speakers. His scowl deepened. Resisting Genevieve was hard enough; throw in a romantic atmosphere . . . God help him.

The three fairies were frowning, he noticed, and Falon was leaning his hip against the bar. "You're putting on quite a show tonight," his friend said.

"I'm glad you find it entertaining." He paused, looked away. "I'm taking a break."

"That's nice."

"You're still in charge."

"That's nice, too."

"Yeah, well, you're an asshole and if you don't wipe that smirk off your face, you're fired."

Falon's deep laughter followed him as he stormed to Genevieve's table and plopped down across from her. Once again, her delicious scent enveloped him. He shouldn't have instigated this, but now that he had he was helpless to stop.

"What did you want to talk about?" She propped her elbows on the table and leaned forward, granting him another spectacular view. Sweet heaven above, she wasn't wearing a bra.

Had he suggested they talk? Perhaps a better suggestion would be that he shoot himself here and now and just get his death over with. "We've known each other a long time," he began, fighting past the friction of sexual need working through him.

"Yes."

"And we've never discussed—" What the hell was a safe, nonsexual topic?

"Yes?" she prompted, grinning.

Her teeth were two rows of pearly white perfection. And she had a dimple. Why had he never noticed it before? *Probably because you've rarely given her a reason to smile at you, moron.* He yearned to nibble on the delectable little morsel.

"We've never discussed—" He paused yet again. The weather? No, he'd only picture her naked in the rain. Favorite places to shop? No, he'd picture her shopping naked. Favorite books? No, he'd picture her reading naked.

Ah, hell.

Is she worth your life? Now, this moment, he couldn't say no so easily.

"There's got to be *something* you want to talk about." She licked her lips, her pink tongue as lethal as any weapon of mass destruction.

They could talk about taxes at this point and he'd be aroused. "I—how have you been doing lately?" he asked. He leaned as far back in the stool as he could, hoping distance would clear his foggy senses.

"Good."

"How are your sisters?"

"They're good." She tapped a finger to her chin, her oval nail glinting in the light. "Hunter, is there something else you want to say to me?"

He tangled a hand through his hair. Hell, yes, there was something he wanted to say to her: get naked.

How did she twist him into knots like this? He saw her, and he wanted her. He caught a whiff of her sweet fragrance, and he wanted her. He closed his eyes, and he wanted her.

Is she worth dying for?

He stared at her, watching the way shadows and light played across her lovely, serious little face. Watching the way hope flickered in her eyes, lighting the hazel to an otherworldly green.

Before the night was over, he was going to have this woman's thighs around his waist. Or head. He wasn't picky. He was going to know what it felt like to touch her curves, to know her taste. He was going to know how her expression changed when she climaxed. The future be damned.

Not giving himself time to consider the ramifications, he shoved to his feet and held out his hand, palm up. "Genevieve, would you please dance with me?"

"Really?" Disbelief and awe rained over her face before she frowned. "You don't plan to leave me in the middle of the song, do you?"

His chest constricted. He'd done that to her on numerous occasions. In his defense, he'd become so aroused holding her in the curve of his body he'd had two choices: leave her on the dance floor or fuck her on the dance floor. "We'll dance the entire song. I promise."

Slowly she grinned. "Yes. Yes. I would love to dance with you."

The moment she placed her fingers atop his, his senses screamed with approaching danger. He ignored the warning. Here, in this moment, nothing mattered except cherishing Genevieve the way he'd yearned to cherish her all these many years.

Was she worth dying for?

Hell, yes.

Three

Oh, Great Goddess, it had worked! The love potion had actually worked.

Her hand in his, Hunter led her onto the dance floor. Where their skin touched, she tingled. He'd asked to do this; he'd even said please. She hadn't begged—not that she would have. (Okay, she might have.)

They stopped in the center of the floor, paused for a moment, facing and watching each other. Their breath intermingled—his was shallow, hers was coming in fast, erratic pants. Multihued light pulsed from the strobe above, caressing his face, and music flowed seductively.

Something she'd never seen before flittered over his expression. Something infinitely tender. Her stomach flip-flopped. What thoughts were rolling through his mind? He reached out and sifted a strand of her hair between his fingers, then brushed it from her temple. His touch electrified her.

The need to breathe was forgotten. Only Hunter existed, only Hunter mattered. His fingers slid down her shoulders, along her arms, and circled her waist. Her lips parted on a sudden gasp of pleasure. His strong arms locked around her, gathering her close. Heat zinged and crested, then his hands were, anchored on her lower back.

"Hunter," she said, unsure why she'd whispered his name. It was there, in her mind, in her blood, branded on her cells.

"Genevieve," he returned softly. "So lovely."

Throughout the years, she'd prayed he would accept what was between them. She would have prayed even harder if she'd known the sheer magnificence reality would be. Her chest pressed to his, nipples hard and aching; his strength seeped through her scanty dress. And he didn't jerk away from her, didn't run. The scent of him, heat and man, enveloped her.

Together they swayed to the erotic rhythm of the music. Several times, his erection brushed against her. Delicious. Welcome. Their gazes never strayed. Constantly sizzled.

Emboldened, she rasped her hands up the buttery soft material of his T-shirt. He sucked in a sharp breath. "I've wanted to be your lover for so long," she admitted.

"I've wanted that, too. So badly."

Her fingers played with the hair at his neck. "Some days I would have sworn you desired me. Some days I would have sworn you hated me."

"I always desired you. You're total pleasure, sweetheart." He paused. Frowned. "You're eternity."

Eternity . . . With that one word, joy and sadness battled for supremacy inside her. Joy because he was talking about forever with her; sadness because it had taken a love potion to get him to this point. However, she shoved the sadness away. Tonight was a night for magic and love. She would allow nothing else to intrude.

Tomorrow the sadness could return and erode the precious memories she had formed. As for now, she would take what she could get, however she could get it.

She'd wanted him too long.

"I'll give you eternity," she said. "I'll give you anything you ask for."

He broke eye contact and pulled her the rest of the way into his body. Her head rested on the hollow of his shoulder. "I've watched you grow from pretty teenager to exquisite woman."

A shiver stole over her skin. Was he speaking true, or did the love potion beckon him to lie and say anything that might please her? "Why did you constantly push me away, then?"

He ignored her question. "Every time you walked into a room, you consumed my attention. If you had known just how much I desired you, you would have pursued me all the more. And if you'd pursued me any more, I wouldn't have been able to resist you."

Sparks of exotic sensation pulsed through her. Unable to help herself and craving the taste of him, she grazed her lips over his neck. Her hands clutched at his back. Mmm, his skin tasted good, like expensive wine and twilight magic.

"There was no reason to resist me," she said. "I wanted to be with you."

"You amaze me." He nuzzled her nose. "You could have any man you want, but you never gave up on me."

That sad little gleam returned to her eyes, and Hunter knew he'd do anything to get rid of it. "What if I swore to never run from you again? Would you smile for me?"

In lieu of an answer, she brushed her lips over his neck once more. This time, however, she let her tongue explore, twirling, circling. He cupped her butt, lifting her slightly, and his erection rubbed the crevice between her legs. A moan tore from her. They were fully clothed, yet they were managing to make love on the dance floor, despite the people circling them.

Genevieve bit his ear. "Help me understand why you ran. Did you think I would use you? Did you think we would no longer be able to remain friends?"

He laughed, the sound devoid of humor. "No. I knew you wanted more than sex from me. I knew our friendship could survive."

"Then . . . why?"

"Genevieve," he said. The grief in her voice sliced through him, more lethal than a blade. He couldn't tell her the truth because it would frighten her away. If she knew she was going to be the death of him, she would leave him.

Now that he had her in his embrace, he wanted to keep her there. *Would* keep her there. He couldn't believe he'd pushed her away for so long. Stupid. A mistake he'd never make again. Never had a woman felt more perfect in his arms.

After all the years he'd hurt her, she deserved romance from him. Sweetness, tenderness, more than he'd ever given another.

"You have the most amazingly expressive eyes." He allowed his fingers to crawl down the curve of her bottom and play with the hem of her dress. "Have I ever told you that?"

She sucked in a gasp of air; then, as she released the breath, she relaxed against him fully. "No. You never told me."

"More fool me. Your eyes are so intoxicating, sometimes green, sometimes velvety brown, and I always feel like I'm lost in them." He brushed the side of her face with his, tickling her softness with his slight beard stubble, relishing the contact. He kissed the tip of her nose. Not dipping lower and tasting her lips proved nearly impossible. "Did you know you have three faint little freckles on your nose? When you're angry or sad, those freckles darken. I've wondered over and over again if you have freckles on the rest of your body."

"I could . . ." She gulped. Her eyes widened and filled with eagerness. "I could show you."

"Yes. I would love that." *I'm not an honorable man.* He stilled with the thought. Here she was, offering him a paradise he didn't deserve. His mouth curled into a frown, and he stared down at her. She deserved a man who could love her forever, a man who hadn't hurt her for years.

So what? he thought in the next instant. She wanted him; he wanted her. He wasn't a martyr. For what short time they had together—he knew his death was certain now, but he was past the point of caring— he would give her everything. His heart, his attention, his affection. He'd love her so thoroughly she'd savor the memories for the rest of her life.

"I truly am sorry for how I've treated you in the past, sweetheart."

"I forgive you," she said, her features sincere.

His brows arched in surprise. "That easily?"

"We're friends, aren't we?"

"Genevieve." He groaned her name as he meshed his lips into hers. She immediately parted for him, welcoming him inside. Her decadent flavor filled his mouth, so much richer than he'd ever imagined. She moaned, a needy sound, a greedy sound.

Urgency roared to intense life. Shards of her magic flowed into his cells, awakening pieces of him he hadn't known existed, crowning him with power and vitality. Warming him. He felt the pinprick rasps of her nipples against his chest and had to clench his fists in the material of her skirt to keep from kneading her breasts. Had they been anywhere else but a crowded barroom, he would have taken her. Would have pushed them both over the sweet edge of seduction.

"I want you," she breathed. "I want to make love with you."

"Hell, yes." He'd place her gently in his bed and smooth his hands over her. Work his way up and down her body with his tongue. Her legs would part, revealing the wetness of her arousal. "Stay the night with me." *Stay forever.*

"Yes. With all my heart, yes."

His cock jerked in reaction. Passion blazed in her eyes—passion for him. Only him. She smoothed her tongue over her lips, taking his taste with it. Her eyes closed in surrender, and she was the very picture of desire. Of lust and love and his most private dreams.

"Tell me what you're going to do with me, once you have me in bed," she said in a needy, aroused whisper. As if she had to know right then or she'd combust.

"What would you like me to do?" If he did half the things floating through his mind, they wouldn't walk for a week.

"Everything."

He rubbed against her, the action causing pleasure/pain flickers through his body. "Kiss you?"

"Mmm-hmm." She bit her bottom lip.

"Touch you?" He wanted so badly to drag her up to his room, to kiss and touch her *now*, but he was going to dance the entire song with her if it killed him. And it just might.

A tremor slipped down her spine. "Where would you touch me?"

"Everywhere."

Another tremor. "Yes, do that. Touch me everywhere."

"I'll taste you everywhere, too."

"Please, yes."

He licked the shell of her ear. "I'm going to make you come so many times, you'll—"

The double doors suddenly bounded open and a horde of . . . creatures burst inside the bar, surrounded by a palpable air of menace. Instinctively sensing their danger, Hunter shoved Genevieve behind his back. The music screeched to a halt. At the bar, the three fairies instantly shrunk to their tiniest size, puffs of glitter-smoke wafting from them.

Short, winged monsters with long fangs, more fur than a bear during hibernation, and razor-sharp claws formed a line in front of the doors, blocking escape. Their eyes were red and glowing; their angled, grotesque features were misshapen. Hideous.

They were subdemons, he realized.

Though different breeds were formed every day and he'd never encountered this type, Hunter recognized their scent: sulfur. As a monster hunter—pretending to be nothing more than a bar owner—he'd stalked and killed their kind most of his life. Demons, vampires, predators of the night—the scum of the earth, in his opinion. They were creatures who survived on human carnage. They were pure evil, and he despised them all.

Killing them had always been one of his favorite pastimes.

"Did someone wish for excitement?" one of them asked.

Genevieve gasped. "Oh, my Goddess. No, no. I take it back. No excitement."

"I suggest you leave," Hunter told them, the actual words nearly undetectable, laced with rage. Genevieve slipped her hand into his, and he felt a tremor rush through her. "Don't worry, sweetheart, I'll take care of this," he assured her quietly.

"No." The demon who had spoken, the tallest of the bunch— which wasn't saying much, since he only reached Hunter's navel— stepped forward and grinned slowly, anticipatingly. "I think we'll stay."

The grainy, high-pitched voice sent shudders through him. "Your kind isn't wanted here."

The creature's stance became cocky, arms crossed over his chest, legs slightly parted, his expression taunting. His dark, broken wings fluttered like an erratic heartbeat. "Your woman doesn't agree. She wished for excitement, so excitement we'll give her."

"I've changed my mind." Fighting past her fear, Genevieve stepped beside Hunter. She maintained her hold on him. Inside, her magic churned and swirled, dark and dangerous, ready for release. Sometimes the darkness of her powers frightened her more than her opponent; now she felt only fear for Hunter's safety. "He asked you to leave nicely. If you don't, I'll wreak such horrible vengeance upon you that you'll go home crying to the devil like little girls."

"We're not going anywhere until we've granted your wish. Master's orders." Laughing, the demons broke apart, knocking over tables, throwing chairs, climbing up and down the walls, and tearing off chunks of stone. Men and women, fairies and gnomes, gasped and raced (or flew) out of the way. That the gnomes, stumpy, trunklike monsters with more brawn than brain, were scared, added to her worries.

"Go upstairs and lock yourself in my room," Hunter demanded.

"I won't leave you to deal with them alone. I can make them go away." Amid shrieks of horror, the frantic pitter-patter of frightened people, and the evil vibrations of demon laughter, Genevieve raised her hands high in the air. "Burn to ash these demons shall, never a night again to prowl."

As she spoke, the demons flinched, anticipating the bombardment of her magic.

"Pain and suffering you will endure," she finished, "of this I am very sure."

Nothing happened.

Shocked, frowning, she tried again. Again, nothing.

The demons smiled slowly. "Looks like the witchy-poo has lost her powers."

More shock pounded through her; she uttered the spell for the third time. Still, no results. Why? "I—I don't understand." Why wouldn't her magic work? A side effect of the love potion? No, surely not, but Glory had told her to only drink half. The demons should be writhing balls of fire. Instead, they were chuckling and amused.

"Playtime is over," a grating voice proclaimed. The demon snarled and flashed his dripping fangs. "Get her!"

"Genevieve!" Hunter shouted as a creature lunged for her. Hunter grabbed it by the forearms and tossed it to the ground. He kicked and hit the demon with expert precision. His arms arched through the air so quickly the movements were barely visible. He ducked and spun, leaped and struck with poetic menace.

Falon joined the fray, stabbing at the monkey wannabes with broken liquor bottles and wood shards.

With the men occupied, another demon dove for her, slamming her into a table and knocking every ounce of air from her lungs. Dizzy, she sank to the ground. The only people she'd ever fought were her sisters, yet they hadn't wanted to actually kill her. Still, she knew the basics of self-defense and how to fight dirty.

Her opponent jumped astride her, pinning her where she lay. It licked its lips and tried to wrap its claws around her neck. She put her newly filed nails to use and poked it in the eyes. It howled, its attention on its pain, and she smashed her palm into its nose. In the next instant, Hunter kicked the demon away from her and grappled the hell spawn to the ground.

"Demons of the night," she chanted, standing, arms high in the air, "you will die now, I don't care how."

The fight continued without interruption.

Damn it! She glared down at her hands. Why wasn't her magic working? She felt the power of it inside her, as potent as ever, yet it refused to be released.

From the corner of her eye, she saw a demon's razor-sharp claws lengthen and slash at Hunter's chest. He didn't move in time, and blood began to ooze from the gaping wound. She gasped. Screamed. Fury and fear bubbled inside her.

"Run, baby," he panted, struggling to keep the creature from his throat.

"No, I won't leave you." Nearing panic, she grabbed a long, splintered wood shard and raced toward the battling pair just as Hunter punched the bastard in the face and rolled away. "Catch!" She tossed him the shard.

He caught it, and when the demon advanced, Hunter stabbed it dead center in the chest.

The creature burst into flames.

As the orange-gold flickers licked the walls and dissolved into ash, the tallest of the demons stopped tormenting a screaming gnome long enough to focus narrowed eyes on Hunter, who was pushing to his feet.

"You'll pay for that, human." Two other demons approached the leader's side, each of them glaring with hostility. "Oh, you'll pay."

Genevieve grabbed a beer bottle, broke the end on the bar, and held the jagged amber glass in front of her. "You'll have to fight me, as well," she said bravely. At least, she hoped she sounded brave.

"With pleasure, little witch," was the delighted reply.

"Damn it, Genevieve," Hunter said. "When this is over I'm going to teach you to obey my orders." He closed in on the demon, and a bleeding Falon closed into step at his side. Both men wore expressions of certain death—demon death.

Her heart drummed in her chest. *What should I do, what should I do, what should I do?* When she'd wished for excitement, she hadn't meant *this*.

Distracted as she was, she didn't notice as one of the demons sprinted to her. It reached her and knocked the glass from her hand before tossing her to the ground. Suddenly breathless, she lay still for a long while. Or perhaps she lay for mere seconds. Her attacker jumped on top of her and she fought like a wildcat, kicking and scratching. As it attempted to subdue her, its rancid breath fanned her face.

"Be still!" it hissed. Its forked tongue slithered from between thin lips.

She bit its arm, the taste of salt and ash filling her mouth.

"Bitch!"

"That's *witch* to you." She worked her arms free and clashed her hands together, then backhanded the creature across the face.

"Dead witch." Its sharp, lethal fangs emerged, dripping with . . . what? Not saliva. This smelled bad. Worse than bad. Evil. Like death. It gripped her wrists and held them down, its head inching toward her. She knew it was moving quickly, about to sink its fangs into her neck, but her mind processed it in slow motion.

She pulled her knees to her chest and slammed her feet into the demon's chest. Surprisingly, it flew backward and propelled across the bar. Gasping for air, trembling in fear, she jolted to a sitting position.

"You okay?" Hunter panted, at her side. He dropped to his knees. Sweat and blood dripped from his temples. His gaze roved over her body frantically, over her ripped dress, searching for injury.

"I'm fine. But you—"

"Look out!" Falon shouted.

Hunter whipped around; Genevieve gazed, horrified, past his shoulder. The demon she'd kicked was flying at her, hate in its eyes, a long shard of glass in its outstretched hand, mere seconds away from reaching her. Instinctively, she dove to the side. Anticipating such a move, the demon moved with her. Hunter, damn him, sprang in front of her, taking the blow himself.

"Hunter!" she screamed.

Eyes wide, he looked down at his chest.

"Got him." Laughing, the demon and the rest of his cohorts raced away. Some jumped through windows, the sound of tinkling glass echoing from the walls. Others rushed out the same way they'd entered. Hinges squeaked as the front doors burst into shattered pieces.

Genevieve's mind registered only one thing. "You're hurt. Hunter, you're hurt." Still on her knees, she scrambled in front of him. Blood dripped from his chest, the glass embedded so deeply she could only see the tip.

"I'll be fine." Weakness and pain tinged his voice. "Did they hurt you? Are you cut anywhere?"

"I'm okay, damn you. I'm okay." He looked so pale, causing her panic to intensify. Not even when she'd first spied the demons inside the bar had she felt this much fear. "You should have let him stab me." Her chin trembled. "You should have let him stab me."

"I'm glad you're well." His eyelids drifted shut for a long moment. "I'd have to become a ghost and do the revenge thing if they'd harmed you."

"I need to pull out the glass and bandage your wounds, okay? I need to—"

"It's too late. Demon saliva . . . is poison, and one of them managed to bite me. Genevieve," Hunter said, his voice so raspy she had trouble hearing him. "I want you . . . to know, you were totally . . . worth it."

Her arms anchored around him, her head burrowing against his chest. His heartbeat thumped weakly, sporadically. "Hunter, listen to me. You're going to be okay. Let's get you to my sister. She's a healer." She gazed at the bar, wild and desperate. "Someone call Godiva. Call her right now."

"I'll do it," Falon said.

"My head is spinning." Hunter's forehead bobbed forward. "Help me lie down, sweetheart."

His full weight fell into her. She absorbed it as best she could, locking one hand at the base of his neck and the other at his lower back. Leaning forward, she slowly and as gently as possible lowered him. Seconds dragged by. By the time he lay completely prone, her arms burned and shook with exertion.

"I wish I could have had more time with you," he said. He didn't open his eyes. "That's my only regret."

"Stop. Don't talk like that. You're going to be fine." Her chin trembled all the harder; her blood ran cold. She tore the shirt from his chest and studied the rest of his wounds. What she saw made her mouth dry up. Long, jagged scratches ran like bloody rivers over his ribs. Several teeth marks adorned his neck, the skin already black. Already dead.

She covered her mouth with her hand to cut off her horrified cry. "I love you, and I need you. Tell me you're going to be okay."

His lips lifted in a weak smile. "I wish . . . I wish . . ." As his voice tapered to quiet, his head drifted to the side.

Genevieve screamed. "No." She gripped his shoulders and shook him. "You're going to be okay. You're going to be okay." Violently, she continued to shake him. "Open your eyes, damn it. Open them right now or I'll curse you to live in a monastery."

He didn't respond.

Falon approached slowly and crouched down. He reached out and placed two fingers over Hunter's neck. Tears filled his eyes. "I'm sorry, Genevieve, but he was dead the second the demon bit him. They produce a poison that no human can survive."

"No. No. When my sisters get here, we'll cast a spell and he'll be fine. You'll see. He'll be fine." A huge lump formed in her throat, making it difficult to breathe. "He's going to be fine," she whispered raggedly, more for herself than Falon.

Yet even after she and her sisters cast their spells, Hunter remained motionless. Lifeless. Dead.

Yes, Hunter Knight was dead. And there wasn't a damn thing she could do about it.

Four

"Uh, Mr. Collins. I think you should know something."

Roger Collins, owner and operator of Mysteria Mortuary—as well as a closet shape-shifter (spotted owl)—looked up from his desk and faced his apprentice, a freckle-faced boy with a pasty, almost gray complexion. "What's happened, hoo hoo, now?"

"Hunter Knight's body has disappeared."

Exasperated, Roger scratched his shoulder with his nose. Things like this were always happening, and he was tired of it. "Let's keep this between us, hoo hoo. No reason to alert the town." They'd only cancel the burial, and he'd be out a hefty chunk of change. No thanks. "Knight's funeral, hoo hoo, will happen as scheduled."

"Huuunnnterrrrr. Hunter Knight, you silly boy. Wake up, *s'il vous plait.*"

The voice called to him from a long, dark tunnel. Hunter tried to blink open his eyes, but it hurt too badly so he left them shut. Did lead weights hold the lids down? His mouth was dry, and his limbs were weak. Most of all, his neck throbbed.

What had happened to him?

He remembered fighting the demons, remembered Genevieve leaning over him. Remembered a black shadow swooping him up and carrying him away. And then, nothing. He remembered nothing after that.

"*Mon dieu!* Aren't you just the prettiest little thing." A soft hand smoothed over his brow. "I could snack on you all day and come back for leftovers."

That hand . . . His ears twitched. He could hear the rush of blood underneath the surface of skin. He could even hear the faint *thump*, *thump* of a heart. His mouth suddenly flooded with moisture. Hungry, he realized. He was so hungry he could have gnawed off his own arm.

"Well, don't just lie there. I know you're awake. Pay some attention to *moi*, you naughty boy. I saved your life, after all." A pause. "Well . . . I kind of saved your life. Maybe a more truthful saying would be I saved your death."

The voice was deep enough that he knew it belonged to a man, but it was surprisingly feminine. And that horrible French accent . . . Despite the pain, Hunter forced his eyelids apart. Dank blackness greeted him. But slowly, very slowly his eyes adjusted, and he was able to make out a rocky cavern and a silhouette. The silhouette became a body . . . the body became a man . . . and then he saw everything as clearly as if the sun were shining.

"Hello, my little love puppet," the man said. "We're going to have *the* best eternity together, *oui.*"

"Barnabas?" Hunter asked, rubbing his eyes.

"None other," he said with a proud lift of his chin.

Barnabas Vlad, owner of Mysteria's only art gallery ("art," of course, meaning pornographic photos); Hunter had come across the man only a few times. Last time he'd seen him, the man had been inside the bar. Something about him had always set Hunter's nerves on edge—something besides the fact that Barnabas often hit on him like a sailor on leave.

Right now Barnabas was dressed in a black, Oriental-styled gown, and he twirled a black parasol in his hand. Usually he wore huge blue sunglasses, but he wasn't wearing those now.

His eyes glowed bright red.

Hunter jumped to his feet, behind the stone dais he had lain upon. He winced in pain, but held his ground. "You're a vampire." He spat the word, for it was a foul curse to him.

"*Oui, oui.*" Barnabas's glossed lips stretched into a happy, unconcerned smile. "What do you think of my outfit? It's new. Very *china doll* meets *modern society*, don't you think?"

"I think your dress needs a hole in it," Hunter snarled. "Right in the vicinity of your undead heart." His gaze circled the cavern, searching for anything he could use as a stake. There were no rocks, no twigs. Damn it. What he would have given for his COTN—creatures of the night—arsenal at home.

"Why are you looking at me like that?" Barnabas's smile became a pout, and he splayed his arms wide. "You're a vampire, too, *mon ami*."

"No, I'm not."

"*Oui*, you are."

"No, I'm not."

"*Oui*, you are."

"No. I'm. Not. I'm a vampire *hunter*, you disgusting, vile, rotten piece of dog shit."

Barnabas took no offense and laughed, actually laughed. "Not anymore. Feel your neck. I drained your blood and gave you mine."

There was truth in the vampire's expression, truth and utter enjoyment. Everything inside Hunter froze. No. No! He couldn't be a vampire. He'd rather die.

Hesitant, hand shaky, Hunter reached up. He could taste blood in his mouth, it was true, but the rest . . . His fingertips brushed over the small, very real puncture wounds on the side of his neck. He knew exactly what that meant. *No*, he thought again. He hunted vampires; he hated them. Before Genevieve, it had been his only purpose in life. "Now . . . you putrid sack of undead flesh." Glaring, he pointed a finger at Barnabas, wishing it were a stake. "Why would you make me a vampire? Why didn't you let me die?"

With a guilty flush, Barnabas hopped onto the dais. "I was in the bar the night those demons attacked you. When you fell, you were covered in blood and, *mon dieu*, you looked so tasty. I didn't cop a feel or anything, if that's what has you so worried."

"That's not what I'm worried about," he shouted. *I'm a monster now. I'm the very thing I despise.* He knew a lot about vampires. They were—had been—his business, after all, and he'd seen many people make the change from human to beast. Oh, they tried to fight the urge to drink.

They never won.

Always the thirst for blood, for life, seduced and consumed them.

They killed the people they once loved—and everyone else around them. *I can never allow myself to see Genevieve again.* The wretched thought nearly dropped him to his knees. Nearly felled him.

Barnabas has lived in Mysteria for a long time, and he hasn't slaughtered the population. Hunter paused, blinked. How seductive the thought was and he grasped onto it with desperation. Maybe he was wrong about vampires. Maybe vampires didn't kill—

He squeezed his eyes closed. Such rationalizations were dangerous and could get Genevieve slain. No, he couldn't see her, couldn't risk it.

"Are you worried that you will no longer have a sexual appetite? You will, I assure you." The vampire's eyes stroked over him, stripped him, glowing a brighter red with every second that passed. "Despite the myths, you will function as you always did—except for the sunlight thing and the blood thing. Small prices to pay, really."

"Considering what?" he snarled. "There are no advantages that I can see."

"There are most certainly advantages." Barnabas tapped a black-gloved finger onto his chin. "You'll get stronger every day. Faster. You'll be a force no man—uh, woman—can resist. Like *moi*. After a while, you'll even enjoy taking blood. I pinky promise."

"I'll be a killer." This wasn't happening, couldn't possibly be happening. He tangled a hand through his hair.

"You won't be a killer."

"Yes, I will."

"*Mais non*, you won't."

"Yes. I. Will. Your continued arguing is really starting to piss me off."

"Do you want to fight me?" Barnabas asked hopefully. "I'm always up for naked wrestling."

Hunter bared his teeth in a scowl. As he did so, his incisors elongated. He actually felt them do it, sliding down, sharpening. He smelled the metallic twang of blood in the air—blood from a recent feeding Barnabas had enjoyed. How thirsty Hunter suddenly was. He shook with the force of it. "I can't drink blood. I just can't."

"You smell me, don't you? You want to sink your teeth into me? Go ahead. I already gave you blood, but you were asleep and didn't get to taste the sweetness of it." Barnabas motioned him over with a wave of his hand. "Taste it. You might like it. But you had better hurry. Soon my heart will shrivel up again, the blood gone, and there'll be nothing left for you to taste."

Hunter's stomach twisted in revulsion—and eagerness. He found himself stepping toward Barnabas, closing the distance between them, unable to stop himself. He found himself leaning down, teeth bared, mouth watering.

Genevieve's beautiful image flashed inside his mind. *She's in trouble.* The knowledge flooded him, his psychic ability attuned to her. Even in death. He straightened with a jolt. Blood was forgotten. Only Genevieve mattered. "Show me the way out of this cave before I kill you, vampire." He'd save her, then leave her.

Barnabas frowned. "You're not ready to leave."

"Yes, I am."

"*Mais non*, you're not."

"Yes, I am. And you're not French, so stop with the accent."

"I haven't taught you the way of our kind yet."

Rage poured through him as if he'd drunk it. "*Your* kind, vampire. I will never be like you."

"*Oui*, you will."

"No. I. Won't. Stop arguing. My woman is in trouble, and I *will* save her."

"Fine. Go. I've already fed you, so you don't have to worry about drinking for a while yet." Barnabas's eyes flashed red with jealousy. "But when the hunger hits you, you'll come back to me. I know you will."

"She hasn't stopped crying for three days."

"She refuses to eat. She barely has the energy to sit up and drink the water I force down her."

"What should we do?"

"I don't know. Great Goddess, I don't know."

Genevieve heard her sisters' hushed voices and stared up at the hole she'd blown in the ceiling yesterday. Why couldn't she have done that the night of the brawl? The morning after Hunter's death, her magic had returned to full operating capacity, but she hadn't needed it. And now she didn't care.

"Should we call a doctor?"

She rolled to her side, placing her back to her sisters. Why wouldn't they leave her alone? She just wanted peace—from their voices, from life. From the flashing, bloody images of Hunter's death.

"Genevieve, sweetie, we know you're awake. Talk to us," Godiva begged, her tone tinged with concern. The wolf she had saved plopped at her ankles and nudged her hand, wanting to be petted. "Tell us how we can help you."

"Bring Hunter back to life." Her throat ached from her crying. Raw, so raw. Like her spirit. "That's all I want."

"We can't do that," Glory said softly. "Raise his body from the ground, yes, but the risen dead become predators. Killers. You know that. The longer the dead walk the earth, the hungrier for life they become. He would eat you up and spit out your bones."

Yes, she knew that, but hearing it tore a sharp lance of pain through her. One moment she'd had everything she'd ever dreamed, the next she had only despair. *Hunter*, her heart cried.

"The surviving demons are destroying Mysteria," Godiva said. "We need your help to stop them."

"I can't." Strength had long since deserted her. More than that, any concern she'd had for the town and its citizens had died with Hunter. "I just can't."

Glory claimed her right side, and Godiva sat at her left. Surrounding her. "His funeral is today. Do you want to go?"

"No." She didn't want to see him inside a casket. A part of her wanted to pretend he was still alive, simply hiding somewhere. "Why did he have to die? Why? The love potion had worked. He wanted me as much as I wanted him."

"Uh, um." Glory looked away, at anything and everything but her sisters. "Humm."

Godiva's eyes narrowed. "What did you do, Glor?"

Pause.

"Glory!"

"Well, Evie asked for a love potion. I didn't think Hunter deserved her, and knew if he loved her for one night, then dumped her the next day, she'd be devastated."

"What did you do?" Godiva repeated.

Another pause.

"Don't make me ask again," Godiva said, raising her arms as if to cast a spell.

"I, uh, sort of gave her a power depressant instead."

"Sort of?"

"Okay, I did. But I didn't mean any harm. I thought it would be okay. I didn't think she'd need her powers."

The sorrowful fuzz around Genevieve's brain thinned. *Power depressant,* echoed through her mind. How many spells had she attempted with no results? One spell, that's all it would have taken to save Hunter. One spell, and the night would have ended differently.

She squeezed her eyelids closed, wave after wave of fury hammering through her, each more intense than the last. "He's dead because I couldn't help him. He's dead because I couldn't use my magic."

Her younger sister's cheeks bloomed bright with shame, then drained of color with regret. "I didn't think you'd need them. I didn't even think you'd notice." She clutched Genevieve's hand. "I'm so, so sorry. You have to believe I'm sorry. But think. Hunter wanted you. Not because of a potion, but because of *you.*"

Genevieve's fury fizzled, leaving only despair; her muscles released their viselike grip on her bones and she sank deep into the mattress. Hunter had wanted her. Truly wanted her, without the aid of a love potion. All the things he'd said to her had come from *him.*

That made the pain of his death all the harder to bear.

I killed him. I killed him! If she hadn't decided to make Hunter love her, no matter the methods used, if she hadn't made a wish for excitement, he would still be alive. *My fault. All my fault.* Hot tears slid down her cheeks.

"Please. Leave me alone for a little while. Just leave me alone."

Hunter's funeral had begun an hour ago.

The digital clock blurred as Genevieve's eyes filled with tears. Any moment now, they would lower his casket into the ground and the cycle of his life—and death—would be complete.

Sobbing, she turned away from the glowing red numbers and mashed her face into her pillow. She'd never been so miserable. Her sisters had gone to the funeral. Genevieve simply wasn't ready to say good-bye.

She cried until her ducts could no longer produce tears. She cried until her throat burned and her lungs ached. Then she remained utterly still, absorbing the silence, lost in her sorrow. Minutes later, or perhaps an eternity, a buzzing sound reverberated in her left ear, and a fly landed on her cheek. Weakly she swatted the insect away.

"Bitch," she heard.

"Murderess."

"I wish *you* would have died instead."

Genevieve rolled to her back and blinked open her tired, swollen eyes. Three tiny fairies swarmed around her face, flashing pink. All three were female and scowling. She recognized them from the bar.

"You killed him," one of them hissed.

"You killed him," the others reiterated. "You could have used your magic against the demons, but you didn't. You killed him."

You killed him. Yes, she had. "I loved him." She'd thought her ducts dry, but stinging tears beaded in her eyes.

"How could you love him? You don't care about him. The demons have sworn their vengeance upon him for killing their brethren and are even now desecrating his grave, yet here you lie, doing nothing. Again. Someone even took his body from its casket."

"What?" She jolted upright. A wave of dizziness assaulted her, and she rubbed her temple with her fingers. "Desecrating his grave, how? And who dared take his body?"

"Does it matter?" *Buzz. Buzz.* "Your sisters are fighting the demons off, but they cannot do it without you, the witch of vengeance."

Without another word, Genevieve leaped out of bed. Her knees wobbled, but a rush of adrenaline gave her strength. Arms shaking, she tugged on the first pants and T-shirt she could find, then raced through the hallway. The wolf—what had Godiva named him?—

trotted to her, following close to her heels. He was almost completely healed, and his brown eyes gleamed bright with curiosity.

"There's trouble at the cemetery," she felt compelled to explain. Trouble she would fight against. Heart racing, she grabbed her broom and sprinted outside. No one—no one!—was going to destroy Hunter's grave. Whoever had taken him *would* return him.

Moonlight crested high in the night sky, scooping low. The citizens of Mysteria did everything at night, even funerals. A cool breeze ruffled her hair and kissed her fiery hot, tear-stained face. Moving faster than she ever had in her life, she hopped on her broom and flew toward Mysteria's graveyard. When she passed the wishing well, she flipped it off. When she passed Knight Caps, closed for the first time in years, she pressed her lips together to silence a pained moan.

Soon the graveyard came into view.

Monuments rose from the ground, white slashes against black dirt. Only a few patches of grass dared grow and the only flowers were silk and plastic. Death reigned supreme here. Broken brick surrounded the area with a high, eerie wall. The closer she came, the more chilled the air became, heavier, laden with the scents of dirt and mystery.

Her eyes narrowed when she saw the open, empty casket. Her eyes narrowed further when she saw the group of demons taunting her sisters and spitting on Hunter's grave.

Hunter's mourners must have already escaped, for there was no trace of them. Her sisters were holding hands and pointing their fingers toward the short, monkeylike horde of demons whose wings flapped and fluttered with excitement as they tried to claw their way through an invisible shield.

Both Godiva and Glory appeared weakened and pale, their shoulders slumped. Genevieve dropped to the ground, tossing her broom aside as she ran to them. She grabbed both of their hands, completing the link. Power instantly sparked from their fingertips. In pain, the demons shrieked.

"Thank the Goddess," Glory breathed. Her hands shook, but color was slowly returning to her cheeks. "I wasn't sure how much longer we could hold them off."

"There weren't this many left at the bar." Right now Genevieve counted eight. "Hunter and Falon killed a lot of them."

"They keep multiplying," Glory said. "I have a feeling we can kill these, too, but more will come. You're the vengeance witch, Evie. Do something."

Genevieve focused all of her rage, all of her sorrow into her hands. They burned white-hot. Blistering. Her eyes slitted on her targets. "Burn," she said. "Burn."

One of the demons erupted into flames, its tortured howl echoing through the twilight. Another quickly followed. Then another and another turned to ashes, until only one remained. "Go back to hell and tell the others if they ever return I'll make their deaths a thousand times worse."

The creature vanished in a panicked puff of black smoke.

So easy. So quick. Exactly what should have happened at the bar.

Finished, depleted, she allowed her hands to fall to her sides. Weakness assaulted her as it always did when she used her powers to such a degree. She should have felt a measure of satisfaction. She should have felt vindicated. She didn't. Inside, sorrow still consumed her.

"Everyone must have raced home," Godiva panted. She hunched over, anchoring her hands on her knees. "We need to do something to prevent more demons from attacking."

"Like what?" Glory settled on the ground, her hand over her heart. "Genevieve warned them. What more can we do?"

Genevieve stared up at the stars. "A part of me wants them to return." Her tone lacked emotion, but the cold rage was there, buried under the surface. "I want to kill more of them."

Arms folded around her, comforting arms, familiar arms. "That puts other citizens at risk," Godiva said softly. "If Hunter were still alive, you'd want him protected. Let's give everyone else the same consideration."

She closed her eyes at the pain those words brought—if Hunter were alive—but nodded. Always the voice of reason, Godiva was right. If Hunter were alive, she would do whatever was necessary to protect him. "Do you know who took his body?" She gulped, the words foul on her tongue.

"No." Glory.

"No." Godiva.

Genevieve fell to her knees in front of the empty casket. Tears once more burned her eyes. There was a fresh mound of soil beside her, the spot Hunter was supposed to rest in for all of eternity, a gift to Mother Earth.

He's lost to me. No, no. She could not accept that. *Would* not accept that. "I want to raise the spirits of the dead to protect Mysteria," she found herself saying. No matter where Hunter's body was, his spirit would be able to find her—*if* she raised it. In that moment, she would have sold her soul if it meant seeing him one last time. "They can guard the town against the demons."

Pause. Silence. Not even insects dared speak.

"I don't know," Glory hedged. "Spirits are so unpredictable."

"Genevieve . . . ," Godiva began.

"Please. Do this. For me."

Her sisters glanced at each other, then at her, each other, then her. Concern darkened both of their expressions. Finally Godiva nodded. "Alright. We'll raise the spirits, but only until the next full moon."

Elation bubbled inside her, not obliterating her sadness but eclipsing it. *Hunter,* her heart cried again. *We'll be together again soon. If only for a little while.*

Five

"Let's begin the spirit-raising spell." Godiva removed the band from her hair, letting the long pale strands cascade down her back. She breathed deeply of the night air. "We need to be naked for this one, so no part of our magic is trapped in the clothing fibers."

"Oh, great," was Glory's reply. She remained still, *not* stripping. "This is the twenty-first century. Do we still need to strip?"

"Yes. Now hurry and take off your clothes. I need to get home and feed Romeo." Romeo, the perfect name for her injured wolf. He'd charmed her with only a look.

Already Godiva missed him. He'd become her constant companion, a comfort in these last dark days. She wished there were something she could do for Genevieve, anything to remove the haunted glaze from her sister's eyes.

Remaining silent, Genevieve removed her clothing. Godiva unbuttoned her dress and shimmied it down her voluptuous hips. The buttercup yellow material pooled at her feet. A chill night breeze wisped around them, and with a sigh, Glory, too, stripped.

"There," she said. "Now we can begin. Form a circle and clasp hands."

The tortured howl of a wolf cut through the darkness. Godiva stilled. Had Romeo somehow gotten out of the house and now stalked the woods, searching for her? Another howl erupted through the night.

"Oh, Goddess." Losing all trace of color, Glory shoved her hair out of her face. "The wolves are out. Maybe we should go home."

"We'll be fine," Godiva said, though she was worried. For a different reason. She didn't fear the wolves; she feared for Romeo. What if he got in another fight and was injured again? He might not survive this time. Her need to hurry increased.

She was just about to grab her sisters' hands when, a few feet away, her gaze snagged a silver phone and a masculine arm. Her mouth fell open. A cold sweat broke over her skin. "Girls," she whispered frantically. "Someone is taking pictures of us."

"Did you say someone is taking pictures of us?" Glory's silver eyes narrowed. "Nobody takes secret pictures of me unless I've had time to diet."

"Don't worry. I'll handle this." Cold and emotionless, Genevieve raised her hands into the air, a dark spell slipping easily from her lips.

A startled scream echoed through the night.

"What did you do?" Glory bent down and swiped up her broom. "See for yourself."

The girls closed ranks on the tombstone, circling the intruder and blocking him from escape. They found the flip phone hovering in the air in front of a trembling, horrified man, the phone clamping and snapping its way down his body. Only after it had bitten his favorite appendage (twice) and he screamed like a little girl (twice) did it fall to the ground.

"John Foster," Glory gasped. "You big pervert. Does Hilde know you're out here? And staring at our breasts, no less?"

"Please don't tell her—your breasts are so big." Eyes widening, he said, "I mean, I don't want her to know—I want to touch your breasts." He shook his head, but his gaze remained glued on Glory's chest. He licked his lips. "What I mean to say is—double-D fun bags are my favorite."

Glory smacked him over the head with her broom. "Letch!"

"Bastard!" Godiva grabbed her own broom and popped him dead center in the face.

"This was the wrong day to piss me off, John." Genevieve didn't have her broom in hand, so she raised her arms high in the air and uttered another incantation. "You like breasts so much, you can have a pair of your own."

His shirt ripped down the middle as a huge pair of breasts grew on his chest. He stared down at them, his mouth gaping open. "What the hell! Get them off, get them—hey, these are nice." Closing his eyes, he reached up and kneaded his new breasts, a rapturous smile spreading across his face. "Mmm," he muttered.

"Undo the spell!" Glory scowled. "Undo the spell right now. We'll punish him another way."

"No, this is punishment," he cried, covering the man-boobs protectively. "I swear. Don't take them away. I've got to learn my lesson."

Genevieve did as Glory suggested, and John's chest shrunk back to its normal size. He bawled like a baby the entire time. He even tried to dart out of their circle, but Godiva locked his feet in place with a wave of her hand.

"Not so fast," she said.

His eyes widened with horror. "What are you going to do to me? I didn't mean any harm. I only wanted a peek at your boobies."

Without saying a word, the three sisters tugged at the rest of his clothing, peeling it from his middle-aged body until he wore nothing but a few teardrops. Since he'd gotten a look at their goods, it was only fair they got a look at his.

"Ew, gross," Glory said. "Maybe we should dress him again. I'm throwing up in my mouth."

"That will just waste more time," Godiva replied. "We're going to cast our spells around you."

Glory's gaze darted between his legs. "Yes, *little* John, we're going to cast our spells around you and you're going to stand there like a good boy and pray the Goddess takes mercy on your soul."

That dried his tears. "You mean you're not going to hurt me, and I get to watch you dance? Naked?" He tried real hard not to grin. "Thank you, Great Goddess. Have mercy. Oh, have mercy. Lots and lots of mercy and breasts and mercy. Amen."

"I swear," Genevieve said, "you're the scum of the earth."

"Ignore him," Godiva said after another wolf howl echoed through the night. "We need to get to work."

"Fine."

"Yes. Let's hurry." Genevieve found her broom half buried in a mound of dirt, snatched it up, and rejoined the circle.

The three sisters closed their eyes, blocking out John's image and his voice, and in perfect sync began their protection spells. Round and round they danced, their hips undulating, their hair swaying, their brooms raised high in the air. Each one chanted under her breath.

While she danced, Godiva stumbled over the spell's words, unable to push Romeo from her mind. That last howl had sounded pained. Was he hurt again? Should she go looking for him? He was one of the biggest, strongest, fiercest wolves she'd ever seen, but he possessed a gentle and loving nature and other beasts of the forest might trample him.

Suddenly Glory stopped, her breasts jiggling with the abrupt halt.

"What are you doing? Keep moving," John whined. "I'm still praying."

She frowned. "Does it feel like the ground is shaking?"

Godiva stilled, followed quickly by Genevieve. In the next instant and seemingly without provocation, Glory stumbled backward and landed on her butt.

"What's going on?" Godiva gasped as dirt began cracking at her feet. Grass began splitting. Flowers tumbled off of tombstones . . . and then the tombstones themselves tumbled to the ground. "What's going on?" she asked again, her tone more frenzied.

Glory popped to her feet, and Genevieve paled. "I think—ohmygoddess—I think the bodies are rising!"

"That can't be." Glory sucked in a breath, whirling around to scan the surrounding area. "We only called forth their spirits."

"Well, the dirty bastards didn't listen!"

"I don't understand. Did we say the wrong words?" Godiva asked.

A bony hand shot through the cracked dirt and latched onto John's ankle. Startled, he screamed and would have dropped into a fetal ball and sucked his thumb if his feet hadn't been frozen in place. All over the cemetery, bodies rose. Most were completely decayed, but all still wore their worm-eaten burial clothes. As they emerged, they limped, lumbered, and trudged toward the sisters. Deadly moans echoed across the distance.

"What should we do?" Glory gasped out, holding out her broom like a sword. "What the hell should we do?"

Agnes McCloud—a woman everyone knew had once been John's mistress—climbed all the way out of the ground. Seeing her, John started shaking like an epileptic. "Help me," he cried. "Please, help me. Free my feet."

Godiva swatted at the skeleton with her broom. "Shoo." Big chunks of dirt fell out of the dead woman's hair. "Get back in the ground. I command you."

Agnes was only recently dead from a car accident, and her face lifted into a grin when she spied John. "John! Oh, my darling Johnnie. I missed you so much."

"We've got to send them back." Glory's mouth formed a large O as she counted the number of bodies headed toward them. "They're multiplying like rabbits!"

"Demons of the Dark," Godiva shouted, "return to your graves!"

They kept coming.

"Spirits of the Netherworld, be gone!"

Still, they kept coming.

Meanwhile, Agnes had pounced on John and was feasting on him like he was a buffet of sensual delights and she had been on a year-long fast. Except, the man looked like he would rather eat his own vomit than the dead woman's tongue. That didn't stop Agnes.

If she'd had time, Godiva would have snapped a picture of the two with the flip phone. As it was, the rest of the dead bodies finally reached them and closed her and her sisters in a circle, moaning and groaning and reaching out to caress them. Having been without human contact for so long, they were probably desperate for it. Or maybe they were simply hungry and she and her sisters looked like a triple-stacked Egg McMuffin.

Glory shrieked. Godiva swatted at the bony hands with her broom. And Genevieve stood in frozen shock. "Is that . . . Hunter?"

A male form broke through the line of trees, just beyond the cemetery. His skin was intact, his features normal. Except for his eyes. They glowed a bright, vivid red. Obviously, he wasn't a corpse. But . . . what was he?

"Hunter!" Genevieve called excitedly. "Ohmygoddess, Hunter, over here!"

He turned toward the sound of her voice, and his lips lifted in relief. "Genevieve!"

They sprinted to each other, avoiding dead bodies and Genevieve threw herself into his arms. Godiva couldn't hear what they were saying. She watched as Hunter flung Genevieve over his shoulder and carted her straight into the forest.

"Godiiiiiva," Glory gasped. "Don't just stand there. Help me!"

She shook her head and continued to fight off their molesters with her broom, all the while uttering spell after ineffectual spell. Well, not so ineffectual. Each spell conjured something—just not the help they wanted. A fairy. A gnome. A gorgeous demon high lord. Why were their spells messing up? She still didn't understand. Each creature materialized at the edge of the forest and stood, watching the proceedings, grinning. One of them even produced a bowl of popcorn and a large soda.

"Two dollars says the one with worms in his eyes snags the witch on the left," the demon said.

"You're on," the gnome agreed.

Suddenly a fierce growl overshadowed every other noise, and a pack of wolves raced into the graveyard, snapping and snarling.

"Romeo," Godiva cried, her relief nearly a palpable force when she recognized her pet.

His teeth bared in a menacing scowl, Romeo leaped up and latched onto the bony arm reaching for her and snapped it off before sprinting away.

"Give that back," the corpse shouted, chasing after him.

The rest of the wolf pack chased the skeletons in every direction. All except Agnes, who was still sucking John's face. Godiva and Glory dropped to the ground in relief.

"I never thought I'd be grateful to the wolves," Glory said. "Should we be worried for Genevieve?"

"No. I think she'll be fine." More than fine, actually. "Here, take my hand. We have to send these corpses back to their graves."

Glory intertwined their fingers. Without the fear of being eaten, they were able to concentrate on their spell. As they chanted, magic began to swirl around them, drifting through the cemetery and luring each dead body back to its grave.

Suddenly, Falon—who had not come to Hunter's funeral, for some reason—burst from the forest and came running toward them. Rage consumed his features. Godiva blinked over at him in surprise—she'd never seen him move so quickly or so lethally—and from the corner of her eye she saw Glory jolt up, panic storming over her expression.

"I'm naked," Glory said, her voice frantic. "Where are my clothes? Falon can't see me naked!" Her movements jerky, she searched the dirt, found the yellow dress Godiva had worn, and tugged it over her head.

Falon skidded to an abrupt stop in front of Glory. "Are you alright?"

His gaze focused on Glory, and Godiva was amused to realize she herself could have been a bloody, writhing mass and he wouldn't have noticed. Still, she scrambled for the clothing littering the ground, a pair of stone-washed jeans and a pink sweater.

"We're fine," Glory said stiffly. She pushed to her feet and smoothed her hair out of her face, looking anywhere but at Falon. "How did you know we were in trouble?"

A tinge of color darkened his cheeks. "I sensed it."

Well, well, well. Godiva had never seen the two exchange a single word, yet here they were, acting as if they knew each other. How interesting. Sexual attraction sparked between them, white-hot, intense. Nearly palpable.

"Well, you're too late," Glory told Falon. "We took care of everything ourselves."

Just then Romeo appeared in front of Godiva, claiming her attention. "There's my good boy," she said, reaching out for him. He dropped an arm bone at her feet as if it were the greatest prize in the world and nuzzled her with his nose. She luxuriated in his soft black fur as his tongue flicked out and licked her collarbone. "I'm glad you're okay."

"Eww." Glory balled her fists on her hips. "I know I've said your boyfriends were dogs in the past, but hello. This one *is* a dog. Don't let him lick you like that. Have him neutered, at the very least."

"He's my special sweetie." She rubbed her cheek against his. "My hero."

Glory turned on her heel. "I'm outta here," she called over her shoulder.

"I'll walk you home," Falon said.

She didn't bother glancing in his direction. "No, you won't."

"I wasn't asking. I was telling." The determined man strode to Glory's side, keeping pace beside her.

"I don't need your help, jerk-off."

"I'm giving it anyway."

Their voices faded. Romeo growled at Glory's retreating back, then looked up into the sky and howled. As he howled, his body elongated and his fur fell away. Godiva gasped and jerked away from him. Skin and muscled ridges were forming. Ribs, fingers, and toes. Bronzed skin.

"Romeo?" she asked, frightened. Her mouth went dry, and her heart pounded against her ribs. He was . . . beautiful. "Romeo?" The name emerged on a breathless catch of air this time.

Dark gold *human* eyes were suddenly staring down at her, and she drank in the most beautiful face she'd ever seen. Perfectly chiseled cheekbones, perfectly sloped nose. Full, lush pink lips made for kissing. Her gaze traveled downward, taking in the rest of him. His chest was wide and muscled, like velvet poured over steel. And his—"Oh, Great Goddess." Hello, satisfaction.

"I've been dying to do this all week, but was afraid you'd stop coddling and petting me." He grinned wickedly. "You are not mad?"

His voice was rough and husky, and so sexy she shivered. Gulping, she blinked up at him. "Not mad. Promise."

"I would like a chance to coddle *you*. Let me take you home."

To bed, echoed in her mind, unsaid. "Yes. Take me home."

Six

"You're here," Genevieve said as Hunter slid her down his body. "You're really here." She circled him, disbelief, joy, and sexual hunger eating at her. Pink pollen twirled around them.

Hunter remained utterly still. He was as harshly gorgeous as ever, only somehow more savage looking. Her heart thrummed with excitement, even as confusion rocked her. "How are you here? You aren't a corpse and you aren't a spirit, but you've been gone for three days."

Trees swayed around them, and the scent of moon-magic and jasmine wafted headily through the air. Rays of muted light illuminated the clearing.

"I . . . didn't die," he said. He stared at her neck, his eyes red. "I should leave."

"No! Stay." She bit her bottom lip. Never had she been more overjoyed, more confused. "Why are your eyes red? Wait, the red is fading. I don't understand. What happened to you?"

He didn't answer.

She forgot the question, anyway, as she reached out, hands brushing his jacket to the ground. *She* was already naked; she wanted *him* naked, too. Nothing else mattered really. Next she unbuttoned his shirt. It, too, pooled at their feet. Her fingers met his chest, paler than before but strong.

"I missed you so much," she told him. "When I thought you were dead, I wanted to die, too."

"Genevieve," he said, the sound of her name a moan of pleasure-pain. He squeezed his eyelids together. "I should go. You're safe now."

"Don't leave. Stay with me. Please."

"Something happened—"

"However you survived, I don't care. I just want you." She flattened her palms over his chest, his nipples deliciously abrasive. "Mmm. So good."

His hands tangled in her hair, and their gazes locked. "I want to kiss you."

"Do it. Kiss me."

He leaned toward her and nuzzled his nose over her neck. "You smell so good. Better than I remembered." The more he spoke, the more slurred his words became.

"Kiss me, Hunter. Please."

He paused only a moment before straightening and crushing his lips against hers. His tongue slid into her mouth, already heating, already slick and flavored with passion. He tasted like urgency. They'd been apart so long—days that seemed to have stretched beyond eternity.

Her hands tore at the button on his pants, and in seconds, he was naked. All the while, he rained little kisses over her entire face. Desire rushed through her blood. "No more waiting," she said breathlessly.

"No more waiting," he agreed. Something dark blanketed his expression, his eyes suddenly going red again. "I'm not going to hurt you," he said, his voice rough, filled with determination.

"I know."

"Good." He tumbled her to the ground. His lips clamped around her hard, aching nipple, and his hand trailed down her stomach, raising gooseflesh. He stopped at the apex of her thighs, dabbling at the fine tuft of dark hair.

"Yes, good," she moaned.

She kneaded her hands down his strong torso, reveling in the hard muscles hidden under male skin. Power radiated from him. *My lover,* she thought dazedly. *My man. Mine, all mine.* The passion, the desire, the pleasure he gave her surpassed her wildest imaginings. And he hadn't even entered her yet.

He began sucking her nipple, his teeth surprisingly sharp, wringing another gasp from her. He licked away the delicious sting. "I'm not going to hurt you, I'm not going to hurt you, I'm not going to hurt you," he chanted.

"You can't. As long as you're with me, you can't."

"How did I push you away all these years?" His voice was strained, laden with carnal intent, heavy with arousal.

She arched into his fingers, silently begging him to move them inside her. No, wait. She stilled. Before she forgot everything but his touch, she wanted to fulfill the fantasy that had been floating through her mind for years. "I want to take you in my mouth."

Like a sea siren of long ago, she rose over him, her hair falling like a dark curtain. She walked her fingers down the muscled ridge of his chest. Scars slashed left and right over his ribs, jagged badges of past pain. This was not the body of a bar owner. This was the body of a warrior.

He sucked in a breath when she licked each of his nipples. He moaned when she cupped his testicles.

"You aren't just a bar owner," she said, voicing her thoughts and blowing a hot puff of air on his abdomen. His muscles quivered. "You're much more."

"Yes, but I don't want to talk about it. Move a little lower, sweetheart, and help me forget." He growled, and hearing that desire-rough growl made her shiver.

"Besides running the bar, what is it you do?" she persisted. She wanted to know him. She didn't want to simply be his lover, she wanted to be his confidante. His . . . everything.

A muscle ticked in his jaw. "Hunt vampires, demons, and other creatures of the night. That's how I got my name."

She circled his navel with her tongue. His hips shot toward the sky.

"Have you destroyed very many?" she asked.

"Many." An aroused breath shuddered past his lips, and his eyes closed. "Then I met you and decided to settle here and now I think it'd be a really good idea if you moved a little lower. I don't want to talk about the past anymore."

Shock brought her to an instant halt. "You settled here because of me?"

"Yes."

Surprised, happy, she sucked the entire length of his penis into her mouth. He was so big, her mouth stretched wide.

He began to babble. "I was afraid another gnome would try and hurt you, couldn't let that happen, had to stay near you, damn you feel so good, I need to get inside you. Oh, that feels good. Your mouth. Heaven."

"I love you," she said, never ceasing her up and down strokes.

His hips shot up, and he growled low in his throat. Hoarse. Animalistic. She worked him, savoring every sensation, every taste.

"Holy hell, I can't stop," he managed to gasp.

She sucked him dry.

When he lay limp, collapsed against the dried leaves and twigs, she crawled over him. Feminine power filled her, and she grinned slowly, wickedly. "I've wanted to do that for a long time."

"Not nearly as much as I wanted you to do it." Twin circles of pink painted his cheeks. "I didn't mean to go off so quickly. That just felt so good, and it's been so long, and it made me forget—" He cut himself off and pressed his lips in a thin line.

"How long has it been?" The question sprung from her before she could stop it. She didn't want to hear about his other women. Wanted him only to think of her. Her body, her mind. Her heart.

"About a year," he admitted sheepishly.

He pushed her to her back with quite a bit of force, and she smashed into the ground with a gasp.

Instantly he frowned. "I'm sorry, baby. I didn't mean to push so hard."

"Don't be sorry. I'm not hurt." Smiling seductively, she stretched her arms toward him. "I like it when you're rough."

His expression softened, and his gaze raked over her. Desire blazed all the hotter in the blue depths of his eyes. No longer red, she realized happily. Why did they turn red? Was he a demon now? If so, she didn't care. He bent between her legs, his warm breath fanning the very heart of her. Her mind blanked. Already she trembled for the first stroke of his tongue, for the ache she'd always dreamed about, for the completion she'd always wanted. Needed.

He tasted her. His tongue circled her clitoris, an erotic dance that spun her through madness, through heaven. "Hunter," she cried, arching against him.

"That's it, baby." His voice was strained. "Go all the way over the edge."

Her legs wrapped around his neck, locking him in place. The pressure . . . the building . . . an unstoppable crescendo. When he brought his fingers into play, sinking them deep inside her, she realized the pleasure had only just begun.

"I won't hurt you, I won't hurt you, I won't hurt you." His voice vibrated through her. "You taste so good."

She continued to arch, writhing, screaming her pleasure to the twinkling stars. Her magic acted as a live wire, shooting fireworks in her blood. Then, everything crested. High, so high. Her inner walls spasmed; heat exploded inside her. So much sensation, more than she could bear, yet not enough and somehow everything.

She must have squeezed her eyelids tightly shut because Hunter was suddenly hovering over her. His eyes were red again, and sweat trickled down his temples. Lines of tension bracketed that sweet mouth of his, as if he'd endured all he could and needed satisfaction.

"I'm going to enter you now, but I won't hurt you. I'm going to fill you with me, but I won't hurt you."

"Yes. Please, yes!"

"I won't hurt you." Slowly he slid inside her, his cock stretching her, filling her as he'd promised. He moaned. She gasped. Tension tightened his features. "You're so tight. I didn't expect you to be this tight."

"More. I need more. Do it, take me the rest of the way."

He required no further encouragement. He pushed the rest of the way home. Her legs tightened around him. Squeezed his waist. Her virginity tore. Destroyed perfectly. Wonderfully.

"Virgin," he said, shocked. His eyes closed. Pleasure blanketed his expression. "Never felt this . . . good. This right. I can smell the blood. So good." He licked his lips as if he'd never experienced anything so delicious and wanted to savor the sensation. "So good."

"Only you would . . . do. Harder," she rasped.

"No, savor," he intoned. "I won't hurt you. Won't . . . hurt . . . you."

Her hands gripped his butt at the same moment she rocked her hips upward, "Savor," she allowed, barely able to get the word out. She wanted him inside her forever.

His teeth bit into his bottom lip. "No, harder."

"Yes, yes. Harder."

He slammed inside, pulled back, and pounded home.

"Yes!" she shouted, loving the feel of his in-and-out penetration.

"Not. Hurt. Not. Hurt." He moved so quickly his balls slapped her. She threaded her fingers in his hair and jerked his face to her. Her tongue thrust into his mouth. Taking. Giving. Pushing her even closer to the edge.

"You can't hurt me, I swear."

He reached between their bodies, rubbed his thumb over her clitoris, and that was it. The end. She erupted. Spasmed. Arched. Screamed. Her ecstasy vibrated into his body, propelling him to the end, as well.

"Genevieve," he howled. His features tightened further and he pounded into her a final time.

Minutes passed, perhaps hours, before their breathing settled. His eyes were so red they lit up the entire forest, and he was staring at her neck. He licked his lips. She didn't move. Couldn't, for that matter. Satisfaction thrummed and swirled inside her, the madness gone, delicious lethargy in its place. "I love you," she said.

Hunter suddenly jerked from her as if she were poison. "I have to leave, Genevieve. I'm sorry." His expression was tortured. "I'm beginning to lose control. Barnabas was right. When the hunger hit . . ." He spun away from her.

"What—what are you talking about?"

"Good-bye. I'll never forget you." He jolted into a lightning-fast run, never once looking back.

Seven

If not for her witchy powers, Genevieve never would have caught him. He moved unbelievably fast. As it was, she uttered a transport spell under her breath. One moment she was lying on the forest floor, the next she was standing in front of Hunter.

He snarled in his throat and ground to a halt. "Get away from me!"

"Tell me what's going on," she commanded. Moonlight shimmered between them, painting the forest in a magical golden hue. "Are you part demon?"

Hunter shoved a hand through his hair and turned away from her—exactly like he'd done in the past. "I lied to you earlier, Genevieve. I *did* die. After the fight with the demons, Barnabas Vlad took my body to an underground cave. He—he turned me into a vampire." His voice was laced with pain and sounded . . . tortured.

Ah. Now she understood the red eyes. She owed Barnabas a smorgasbord of human delights dinner, no doubt about it. "This is a good thing, Hunter. We can be together now."

Gaze rounding, he whirled on her. "I'm a monster. I want to drink your blood."

"Well, I'm a witch and you accepted me for who I am."

"Stop. Just stop. It's not the same. I could kill you, but your powers can't harm me."

"Yes, they can." Determined, she raised her arms in the air and summoned forth a small beam of light. Not enough to burn him, just enough to prove her point. Golden rays began to ribbon from her fingertips.

He raised his hands to shield his eyes. "Fine. Your powers can destroy me. You, at least, can control them."

She dropped her arms to her sides and the light dimmed completely.

"Even now I'm close to jumping on you and sinking my teeth into your neck, Genevieve. I'm thirsty, and I can smell the sweetness of your blood. I'm vile and disgusting and *terrible*."

"Hunter," she said, exasperated. She threw her arms in the air. Men—correction, vampires—could be so foolish. "If you want to drink from me, I don't mind." She flicked back her hair, revealing the sensuous line of her neck. "I promise."

"Argh." He spun away quickly, his body stiff, his hands clenched. "Don't do that again."

"Or what?"

"You don't know vampires like I do. Once they get a drop of blood in their mouth, they can't stop. I could take too much. I could kill you."

"You won't hurt me," she said in utter confidence. "You said so yourself, a thousand times. Bite me. Do it. Blood, blood, blood. I'll keep saying it until you get over here and bite me. Blood, blood, bl—"

Hunter pivoted on his heel and closed the distance between them. He captured her face with his hands, his eyes fierce, but he didn't bite her. He bared his teeth, sharp and white, but still he didn't bite her. "Shut. Up. I would rather live eternity without you than to know I drained you."

She saw the depth of his concern for her, and desperation churned inside her. If she didn't show him the error of his thoughts, he was going to leave her. Forever. "If you walk away from me, you're going to hurt me."

A pause.

A heavy, sickening pause.

"Genevieve." His fingers traced her mouth, then dipped to her neck. He fingered the pulse hammering there. "I won't allow myself to become a killer."

She wrapped her arms around his waist, locking him in place. "I barely survived our first parting. How am I going to live without you?" The idea alone filled her eyes with tears. After all the years she and Hunter had been apart, they deserved a happy-ever-after.

"You'll live. That's all that matters." He spanned his hands around her waist, holding her with such fervency she had trouble drawing in a breath, but she didn't care. What was breath without Hunter's scent? What was life without her reason for living?

"Bite me," she commanded him. As she spoke, she arched her head to the side. She *had* to prove to him that he wouldn't kill her. "Blood, blood, blood, bloo—"

With a pained growl, he swooped down as if he'd reached the edge of his tolerance and sank his sharp teeth into her vein. There was a stinging prick, and she gasped. A minute passed, then another, but he didn't stop. The sensations began to feel good, so good. He drank and drank and drank, and her mind began to grow foggy. Her limbs became weak. Black wisps twined around her thoughts.

"Hunter," she gasped. "I'm . . ."

He jerked from her as if she'd screamed. She slumped to the ground. Panting, he stood over her body. Blood dripped from his mouth and guilt filled his eyes. "I'm sorry. Sweet heaven, I'm sorry."

"I'm fine, I'm fine." She was panting. "I swear. You stopped in time."

"No. Too close. In the morning, I'm going to walk into the sun," he said, his voice so ragged with determination it emerged as nothing more than a feral snarl. "There's no other way. I'll keep coming for you otherwise, I know I will."

In the next instant, he was gone.

"Hunter. Hunter!" Weak, she lumbered to her feet. She screeched a transport spell, but it didn't work. Her magic had weakened with her body.

Genevieve scanned the forest. Where was he? Where had he gone? *I'm going to walk into the sun*, he'd said. "I'm okay. I survived. You didn't hurt me, only weakened me a bit." Not allowing herself to panic—yet—she stumbled through the trees. "Hunter, please!"

Branches swayed on a gentle cascade of wind. Birds scattered, soaring into the night sky, their wings striped with every color of the rainbow. If morning came before she found him . . .

"Hunter! Hunter!" She twirled as she shouted, still searching. Minutes passed. Horrendous, agonizing minutes.

He never reappeared.

Hunter made it to the caves in seconds. He'd moved so quickly that the world around him became a blur, that the five miles seemed like less than one.

Barnabas was still there, still sitting on the dais. The cave walls were rocky and bare. Bleak. Like his emotions. Hunter didn't know why he'd come here. Here, of all places. With *this* man. He simply hadn't known where else to go. He'd bitten Genevieve and had almost drained her. If she hadn't uttered his name . . . Shame coursed through him.

"Couldn't stay away, I see," Barnabas said smugly.

Dejected, Hunter wiped the sweet, magical blood from his mouth. "I'm walking into the sun, vampire. I'm too wretched to live."

"I told you the hunger would hit you, and you wouldn't be able to control it." Barnabas used his too sharp teeth to tug off one of his black gloves. "You should have listened to me, *oui?*" He *tsked.* "Now. Would you like to play a game of strip poker? I brought cards."

"No cards." Hunter could still smell Genevieve on him, could still taste her mystical-flavored blood in his mouth. His hands clenched at his sides, and he found himself stepping toward the entrance, ready to go to her again. "Damn it." He froze. "Morning can't get here fast enough."

Barnabas sighed, and the sound dripped with dejection. "I'm going to lose you one way or the other, aren't I? Through death or through your woman, and I think I would rather it be your woman."

Hunter's eyes narrowed. "What are you talking about?"

"Sit down, and I will tell you a secret. . . ."

* * *

At last giving way to her panic, Genevieve raced into the thankfully empty cemetery and gathered her clothes. Her neck ached; she didn't care. Her fingers shaky, she tugged on the pants, the shirt. All of the gravesites were in complete disarray, dirt crumbled, headstones overturned. Where was Hunter? She had to find him before it was too late. Her fear intensified, joining ranks with her panic. Her gaze scanned the area until she found her broom. She hopped on it and commanded it to fly.

It didn't work. Fine.

Holding on to it, she ran, just ran. By the time she reached the center of town, her lungs burned and her heart raced uncontrollably. People were in their yards and on the streets, cleaning up damage the demons had caused. No one paid her any heed.

She spotted John Foster hiding behind a tree in his front yard, watching the lusciously ripe Candy Cox rake her garden. "Have any of you seen Hunter Knight?" Genevieve called.

John squealed in horror and sprinted away.

"No, sorry," Candy replied with a frown. "Hunter's dead, sugar. I doubt I'll be seeing him for a while."

Panting, Genevieve ran to Knight Caps. She searched every room, every hidden corridor, but the place was empty. Nothing had been cleaned; everything was the same as on the night Hunter died. Overturned tables, liquor spilled on the floor. Pools of dried blood.

She sprinted back outside and down the long, winding streets. Finally she reached the white picket fence surrounding her home. She pounded up the porch steps and shoved past the screen door, tossing her broom aside. "Godiva! Glory!" She was so short of breath she had trouble getting the words out.

A few seconds later, Glory stumbled out of her room. She rubbed the sleep from her eyes. The buttercup yellow flannel pj's she wore hung over her curves like a sack. "What's going on?" She yawned. "Are you okay?"

"Have you seen Hunter?"

"No. I thought he was with you. What's with his red eyes, anyway? Is he a demon?"

She didn't bother with an answer. "Where's Godiva?"

"In her room. With Romeo."

"Who?"

"Romeo. Her wolf." Glory stretched her arms over her head and gave another yawn. "I think they're having sex. Again."

"Stop playing around and tell me where Godiva is. Please. I don't have much time."

"I told you. In bed. Nice hickey, by the way." Glory paused, her gaze skidding to the kitchen. "Oh, look. Doughnuts." She breezed past Genevieve and headed into the kitchen, where a box of Krispy Kremes waited on the table.

"Godiva!" Genevieve shouted. "Get out here right now."

The handle to Godiva's bedroom rattled, then the door pushed open. Out toppled Godiva, tightening her robe around her middle. She wore an expression of concern, yet underneath the concern was utter satisfaction. "Is everything okay?"

"Have you seen Hunter?"

"No, I thought he was with you."

A warrior of a man stepped from the room and approached Godiva from behind. He wrapped his strong arms around her waist. Dark hair tumbled to his shoulders, framing a face of such golden-eyed beauty Genevieve found it difficult to believe he was real. Her mouth fell open as realization struck her. *This* was the injured wolf?

"What's going on, Evie? Is everything okay?" Godiva repeated. "Your neck is bleeding."

"Hunter is a vampire, and he plans to die with the morning sun. I have to find him. Can you transport me to him?" She covered her face with her hand, fighting tears. "I can't let him kill himself."

"You know we can't transport other people. I can transport myself, though, and—"

"You are not transporting yourself in front of a vampire, Godiva," Romeo said, his voice deep, gravelly. "We will search together. I can track humans—even dead ones—in ways you cannot."

Grateful, Genevieve nodded. She would have ridden on the broom with Godiva, but Godiva couldn't find hers. "I must have left it in the graveyard," her sister said. Genevieve still didn't have the strength to fire hers up, and Glory couldn't hold both of them. They walked.

They kept pace beside Romeo, who took wolf form. They ended up searching all night, stopping only to drink. No one had seen Hunter, and only a few people seemed surprised that they were asking about a dead guy.

Finally, only thirty minutes till sunrise, Romeo caught a trace of him. "This way."

"Hurry. Hurry." She wanted to scream in relief, in frustration, in agony. But when Romeo led them back to her house, she did scream. "Damn it! Why did you bring us here? He's—" She gasped as her gaze snagged on the man standing on her porch.

"Genevieve," he said starkly.

"Hunter? Hunter!" With a cry, she raced to him.

Eight

Hunter opened his arms and welcomed Genevieve as she threw herself at him. He twirled her around, reveling in her luscious female scent, the soft curves of her body.

"Where have you been?" she demanded. "You stupid, stupid man. I've been so worried about you. You didn't hurt me out there, okay? You didn't hurt me. You stopped in time."

"I *could* have hurt you, and that was enough reason to die." He pulled back and cupped her face in his hands. Would he ever get enough of this woman?

Tears streamed down her face. "Why are you here, then? Why?"

"I talked to Barnabas. His creator hated and feared blood like me, so he took something called a blood-appetite suppressant. I didn't think it'd work, but I took it and my cravings went away. I won't hurt you now. I know it sounds too good to be true," he rushed on, "but it's true. Trust me not to hurt you. Please. I want to be with you."

"Why do you want to be with me?" she interjected. In that moment, her relief and joy overflowed, but she needed to hear the words.

His expression became tender. "I kept picturing your face and I began to realize that even in death, you would haunt me. I began to realize that leaving you would be more vile than drinking from you. I began to realize that I couldn't leave you again. You're my reason for being. You're my everything."

She blinked through her tears, barely daring to breathe.

"Will you have me, Genevieve Tawdry? Vampire that I am?"

"With all of my heart." Laughing, she kissed him over and over again. Loving kisses, happy kisses. Relieved kisses.

Hunter hugged her fiercely. That laugh of hers . . . glorious, uninhibited, he would never get enough of it. "I want you. I want you naked."

"Uh, Genevieve," came a female voice.

Genevieve's cheeks reddened, and she pressed her lips together. She'd forgotten about their audience, he realized with satisfaction, just as he had.

"Hunter, you know my sisters."

He nodded in their direction, but his eyes were only for Genevieve. "Godiva. Glory. Nice to see you again." His fingers played with the silky soft hair at the base of Genevieve's neck. He couldn't stop touching her. He still didn't like the fact that he was a vampire. He still didn't like that he had to drink blood, even though the cravings could be controlled. But he would put up with anything to be with his Genevieve.

"You, too," they said simultaneously.

"The man with Godiva is Romeo," she said breathlessly. Her eyes closed and a look of rapture blanketed her expression. "You can meet him later."

Romeo nodded in acknowledgment. He placed a protective arm around Godiva, as if Hunter might leap off the porch and attack at any moment. Hunter tried not to take offense. He had better get used to people fearing him.

"Hunter and I are going to my room," Genevieve said. "To, uh, talk."

"Dirty," Glory added.

He allowed Genevieve to take his hand and lead him inside, down a hallway and into her room. It was a neat, tidy space with everything color-coded and organized. The bed was made for sin, however. Black silks, crimson pillows. Cerulean velvets. "You want to talk?" he asked with a chuckle.

Her lips lifted in a sensual grin that caused his stomach to clench. She hurriedly secured all of the drapes over the windows so that when the sun rose, it wouldn't hurt him. "We can talk while you're inside me." She raced to him and tugged at his clothes. "I need you so desperately."

He slipped her shirt over her head, then pushed her pants to her ankles. She stepped out of them, completely naked. The sight of her naked beauty almost made him come, right then, right there. Supple curves, ripe nipples, milky skin. The long length of her dark hair provided a mesmerizing contrast.

"I can't wait," he said raggedly.

"No waiting," she agreed.

He took her quickly, with all the urgency he felt inside. Filled as he was with blood and the suppressant, he didn't have the slightest urge to bite her—except in pleasure. They rolled atop the bed, panting, growling, straining. Her breasts filled his hands. Her legs anchored around him as he pounded in and out.

"Hunter," she screamed as a sharp peak tore through her. He felt every spasm and it fueled his own.

He spilled inside her with a loud roar.

Someone banged at the wall. "Enough already," he heard one of her sisters say. Glory, most likely. Godiva was probably otherwise occupied. He chuckled into Genevieve's neck. Nope. He still didn't want to bite her. Relief consumed him.

Playfully she bit his collarbone. "I love you so much."

Her words filled his mind as surely as he'd filled her body. Even his heart stopped beating—or maybe it had never started up again after his death. Women had said those words to him before, but he'd never felt them in his bones. Even Genevieve had said them before. He'd never returned them.

"I love you, too, sweetheart."

She sucked in a slight intake of breath. "Do you really?"

"I've loved you from the first moment I saw you."

"Then why did you push me away for so long?" she asked with a frown. "You never really answered that question."

He placed a sweet kiss on her temple. "Sweetheart, the answer doesn't matter anymore. Let's just—"

"Please. Tell me."

Unable to deny her anything, he explained. As he spoke, she paled. Tremors reverberated through her by the time he finished. "You should have told me the truth years ago," she said. "I would have left you alone."

"I know, and that's exactly why I didn't tell you. I didn't want you to leave me alone. I loved you too damn much."

"What a pair we make, hmm? The dead man and the witch."

He chuckled. Life—or death, rather—was ripe with promise. He was happier than he'd ever been and he owed it all to the sweet, sweet witch in his arms. "I'm looking forward to spending eternity with you."

Slowly she smiled. "Eternity with Hunter Knight. Now that's something I can look forward to."

CANDY COX AND
THE BIG BAD (WERE)WOLF

P. C. Cast

For S.L.,
with a smile and a wink.
Thanks for the . . . inspiration.

ACKNOWLEDGMENTS

I'd like to thank Berkley, and especially my talented editor, Christine Zika, for publishing this author-created anthology. It's wonderful when your publisher believes in you.

Thank you to my agent and friend, Meredith Bernstein, who said, "Absolutely!" when I called her with this idea.

And a big THANKS GIRLFRIENDS to Gena Showalter (my partner in crime in the inception of this anthology), Susan Grant, and MaryJanice Davidson. It was such fun to work on this with the three of you. Let's do it again soon!

One

"Godiva! Wait—wait—wait. Did you just say that you and your sisters called forth the dead two nights ago?" Candice said, rubbing her forehead where it was beginning to ache.

"Yeah, but you missed the important part. Romeo was . . . *spectacular*," Godiva said breathlessly into the phone. "Who knew that poor, wounded wolf would turn into something—I mean, some*one*—so delectable."

"So he actually did more than hump your leg this time?"

"Candy Cox—I swear you haven't been listening."

"You know I hate it when you call me that."

"Fine. *Candice*, you haven't been listening," Godiva said. "He's not just a wolf. He's a *were*wolf, which means he has an excellent tongue and he humps a lot more than my leg."

Candice kept muttering as if Godiva hadn't spoken. "It's not like I don't get enough of that name crap at school. Why I ever decided to attempt to teach high school morons I'll never know." She cringed inwardly, remembering the countless times some hormone-impaired sixteen-year-old boy had made a wiseass remark (usually replete with sophomoric clichés) about her name. God, she was truly sick and tired of Mysteria High School—Home of the Fighting Fairies.

"You could have kept one of your ex-husbands' names," Godiva said helpfully.

"Oh, please," Candice scoffed. "I'd rather sound like a porn star than keep any reminders of ex-husband numbers one through five. No. My solution is to change careers. As soon as I finish my online master's in creative writing I can dump the fucking Fighting Fairies and snag that job in Denver as assistant editor for Full Moon Press."

"Honey, have I told you lately that you have a very nasty mouth for a schoolteacher?"

"Yes. And I do believe I've told you that I *have* said nasty mouth *because* I'm a schoolteacher. Uh, please. Shall we take a moment to recall the one and only day you subbed for me?"

Godiva shuddered. "Ack! Do not remind me. I take back any form of criticism for your coarse language. Those teenagers are worse than a whole assortment of wraiths, demons, and undead. I mean, really, some of them even smell worse!" Just remembering had her making an automatic retching sound. "But Candice, seriously, I don't want you to move!"

"Denver's not that far away—we shop till we drop there several times a year. You know I need a change. The teenage monsters are wearing on me."

"I know," Godiva sighed. Then she brightened. "Hey! I could work on a spell that might help shut those boys up whenever they try to speak your name. Maybe something to do with testicles and tiny brains . . ."

"That's really sweet of you, but you know that magic doesn't work on or around me, so it probably wouldn't work on my name, either." Candice sighed. It was true. As a descendant of one of the few non-magical founders of the town (his name was, appropriately, John Smith), Candice had No Magic at All. Yes, sadly, she lived in a town full of witches, warlocks, vampires, fairies, werewolves, et cetera, et cetera, and her magic was nonmagic. It figured. Her magic worked like her marriages. Not at all. "Men are such a pain in the ass."

Without losing a beat at her friend's sudden change in subjects, Godiva giggled. "I agree completely, which is why I know exactly what you need—a werewolf lover."

"Godiva Tawdry! I'm too damn old to roll around the woods with a dog."

"A werewolf is not a dog. And forty is not old. Plus, you look ten years younger. Why do you think high school boys still get crushes on you, *Ms. Candy Cox?*"

"Put boobs on a snake and high school boys would chase after it. And don't call me Candy."

Godiva laughed. "True, but that doesn't make you any less attractive. You've got a killer body, Ms. Cox."

"I'm fat."

"You're curvy."

"I'm old."

"You're ripe."

"Godiva! Do you not remember what happened last time I let myself commit matrimony?"

"Clearly," Godiva said. "It took ex-husband number five less than six months to almost bore you to death. And he seemed like such a nice guy."

"Yes, I admit he did seem nice. They all did at first." Candice sighed. "Who knew that he would literally almost kill me? And after my brush with death, I decided that I. Am. Done."

"Okay, look. You accidentally took an unhealthy mixture of Zoloft, Xanax, and pinot grigio. It could happen to anyone, especially when she's being bored to death by a man scratching himself while he incessantly flips from the History Channel to CNN—"

"—And pops Viagra like they're M&Ms and thinks that the telltale oh-so-attractive capillary flush constitutes foreplay," Candice interrupted. "Yeesh. I'm going to just say no from here on out. Truly. I've sworn off men."

"No, I remember exactly what you said. 'Godiva'—here you raised your fist to the sky like Scarlett O'Hara—'I will never marry again.' So you've sworn off marriage, not men. And anyway, a werewolf is not technically a man. Or at least if he is, it's only for part of the time. The rest of the time he is the most adorably cuddly sweet furry—"

"Fine." Candice cut off Godiva's gushing. "I'll think about it."

"Really?"

"Yes." *No*, she thought. She hurried on before Godiva could press the point. "I've really gotta go. I'm deep in the middle of Homework Hell. I have to turn in my poetry collection to the online creative writing professor next week, and I still haven't figured out a theme for the damn thing. I'm totally screwed if I can't get rid of this writer's block."

"Well . . ." Godiva giggled mischievously. "I don't know how it'd work on writer's block, but Romeo sure unclogged me last night."

"You're not helping."

"I'm just saying—a little werewolf action might fix you right up."

"You're still not helping."

"Sorry. I'll let you get back to your writing. Remember, you said you'd think about a werewolf lover."

"Yeah, I'll think about it right after I think about my poetry theme. Uh, shouldn't you and your sisters be frolicking about the graveyard checking on the dead or whatnot?"

"Oh, don't worry about it. Our little screwup actually ended up being a good thing, what with those horrid demons on the prowl; the town could use the extra protection. And anyway, it's only temporary and the dead have already quieted down. Uh, but since you mentioned it . . . are you planning on going jogging today?"

"Yes."

"Do you think you could take a spin through the graveyard and keep your eyes open for my broom? I must have forgotten it in all the excitement that night, between Genevieve scampering off into the woods with Hunter—whose eyes, by the way, were glowing bright red—and my Romeo morphing from wolf to man rather unexpectedly. Anyway, if you see it would you please grab it before somebody flies off with it? You know a good broom is hard to find."

"Yeah, sure. If I see it, I'll get it for you. But wait, isn't Hunter Knight supposed to be dead?" Candice said.

"Well, kinda. Actually, he's a little undead."

"Isn't that like being a little pregnant?"

"Don't be a smart-ass. It's embarrassing enough for me to admit that my sister's getting some vampire action. God, I wish the girl had better taste in men, alive or dead."

Candice sighed. "Hey—don't be such a prude. If I'd chosen one of the undead I might not be unmarried."

"Candice, honey, I love you, but you are a hopeless piece of work. Now be a doll and go find my broom. Bye."

Godiva hung up the phone and sat tapping her chin with one long, slender finger. Candy was getting old before her time. Goddess knew, she really did need a lover. A young lover. A young werewolf lover. A hot, naughty affair would be the perfect thing to keep her from moving to Denver. Her fingers itched to swirl up a little love spell, but magic wouldn't work on her friend. Godiva's eyes widened and her full, pink lips tilted up. Magic wouldn't work on Candy, but it definitely would work on a werewolf. . . .

Two

Candice would never get this damn assignment done.

"You'd think after teaching for almost twenty years I wouldn't have any problem doing homework." She grumbled at herself and ran a frustrated hand through her thick blonde hair. "Poetry themes . . . poetry themes . . . poetry themes . . ." Death, time, love, heartbreak, the soul, happiness, sex . . . "Sex," she muttered, chewing the end of her well-sharpened #2 pencil. "That's one I can't write about. Like I've had sex in—"

She clamped her lips shut, refusing to speak aloud the ridiculous amount of time it had been since the last time she'd been laid. As if the last time even counted. Ex-husband number five had been, in politically correct terms, penis impaired. Spoken plainly, he'd had a pathetically small dick, and an incredibly large wallet. Unfortunately, one did not make up for the other. Candice grimaced. Quite frankly, women who said size didn't count had clearly never been with a man with a small dick. And, as if their, well, lack of substance wasn't bad enough, SDM (small-dicked men) had the same problems short men had. They were mad at the world. Like it *helped* to make up for said unfortunate shortage by being a jerk? Sometimes men just didn't make sense.

"Theme!" she said, forcing her thoughts back to the blank notebook page. She wanted to create poetry that would dazzle her professor, replete with complex symbolism, witty phrasing, and possibly even a few clever slant rhymes. What she had come up with was exactly—she glanced at the naked page—nothing.

She was, indeed, screwed (figuratively speaking).

"Okay, so write something . . . anything . . . write what you know. . . ."

What the hell did she know? She knew she was sick of teaching the Fighting Fairies and she knew she would never get married again. Well, she certainly didn't want to write about high school, which left . . .

"What the hell. At least it'll get me writing."

She drew a deep breath and let her pencil begin moving across the blank page.

> Keep your Errol Flynns, Paul Newmans, Mel Gibsons
> all puppets—empty masquerades.

She blinked and reread the first two lines. Not Shakespeare, but it did have a certain ring to it. Candice grinned and continued.

> Tom, Dick, and Harry, too
> the boy next door
> I want no more.

Wasn't that the truth! Her pencil, with a mind of its own, kept moving.

> You ask, what now?
> Well,

And the self-propelled pencil stubbornly stopped. What now? What now? What now? She jumped as the clock in her study chimed seven times. Seven o'clock already? How long had she been on the phone with Godiva? Now she'd have to hurry to get in her five-mile jog, complete with graveyard detour, before the sun set. Crap! She absolutely didn't want to be outside alone after dusk. Weird things had been going on around town lately—and it took some doing for anything to be classified as "weird" by a Mysteria native. Candice put down her pencil and began pulling on her running shoes.

The beat of her shoes against the blacktop road was a seductive lure. The sound beckoned to him. He'd heard it while he was still deep in the woods. It had called him away from the young thing he was still licking. She snarled after him, disgruntled and unsatisfied at his premature departure. He called a hasty apology and promised to meet her and her twin sister later. Right now he had to follow the beat of her running feet, even though it was unlike him to leave such a delicious tidbit. He prided himself on his ability to satisfy. Like a modern Don Juan, his lovers could count on him for romancing as well as consistent orgasming, but the steady slapping sound seemed to somehow have gotten into his body. It pulled him away from his lover with an incredibly powerful singularity in thought.

You (beat) need (beat) her (beat). You (beat) can't (beat) stay (beat) away (beat).

The rhythmic lure thrummed with his pulse . . . his heartbeat . . . it pounded through his loins, making them feel hot and heavy. He scented the warm evening breeze. Woman . . . hot, sweaty, and ripe. And not far ahead of him. He wanted her with a single-minded intensity that he hadn't felt for anything or anyone in years. Growling deep in his throat, he hurried to catch her.

Jeesh, gross. Candice kept glancing nervously from side to side as she sprinted through the graveyard, totally annoyed that she'd promised Godiva she'd look for her broom. Not slowing down, she gritted her teeth and peered into the creepy shadows that flitted past the edge of her vision. Nope. No broom. Also no walking corpses, trolls, goblins, or fairies (whom she disliked with an intensity she knew was unreasonable—they hadn't asked to be made the school mascot and she shouldn't hold it against them, but she did). Nothing untoward at all. Just lots of spooky graves and silence. Thank God. Sometimes it was damn disconcerting to be normal in a town filled with abnormals. She shivered and increased her pace, wanting to leave the graveyard and (hopefully) anything that wasn't 100 percent human behind her.

Lengthening her stride, Candice thought that the burn in her muscles actually felt good. Godiva had been right about one thing—she did have a killer body. Sure, she'd like to lose a few pounds. Who wouldn't? But thanks to her lifelong love of jogging, her legs were long and strong. She also still had excellent boobs. No, they weren't as perky as they had been a few years ago, but they were full and womanly, without boulder-hard, anatomically impossible enhancements. And—best of all—she had seriously big blonde hair that was light enough to hide the encroaching gray without requiring too many touch-ups.

With a burst of speed, she shot out of the graveyard and pounded down the empty blacktop road that would eventually circle around and lead back to her house, which had been built, log-cabin style, at the edge of town. Maybe she could keep up this pace the rest of the way home. Hell, she might even run an extra mile or so!

Which was a lovely thought until the cramp hit her right calf.

"Shit!" She pulled up. Hobbling like Quasimodo she looked around for anything that might resemble sanctuary. Breathing a sigh of relief, she realized that the little rise in the road was the bridge that covered Wolf Creek. She could sit on the bank and rub her calf back into working order. So much for sprinting home.

She had just pulled off her shoe and thick athletic sock when she heard the growl. Low and deep it drifted to her on the breeze, tickling up her spine. It sounded too big to be a dog. It was probably a werewolf. Sometimes the damn things were thick as rabbits in the mountains around Mysteria. Candice rubbed harder at the cramp. She wasn't actually afraid. Werewolves were rarely more than annoying. They tended to come and go in packs—unerringly drawn to the town's preternatural nature, but except for a couple of gainfully employed families (surprisingly, werewolves tended to be excellent restaurateurs—must have something to do with the whole pack mentality and their love of meat or whatever) they usually didn't stick around long, and didn't interact with Mysteria residents, especially while they were in their wolf forms. They certainly didn't pose a danger, unless one was made nervous by big dogs. Candice didn't mind big dogs (as evidenced by her choice in ex-husbands one and two).

"Did you hurt yourself?"

His voice was deep, with a rough, husky sound that was very much man, not wolf. She swiveled around in time to see him step from the edge of the pine trees. And her mouth flopped unattractively open. He was easily six-foot-four and probably 230 pounds. At least. Broad shoulders seemed to stretch on forever, and a wide, scrumptious chest tapered down to a well-defined waist. And those legs . . . even through the relaxed jeans she could see that they were lean and muscular. His face was in shadow, so all of her attention focused on his body and the way he stalked toward her with a strong, feral grace that made her breath catch and her mouth go dry.

Then, as if he'd walked into an invisible tree, he stopped. He hesitated, and seemed almost confused. She could see him run his hand through his hair. He wore it long and loose and it framed his shadowy face as if he was an ancient warrior god that had only partially materialized in the modern world.

"Ms. Cox?"

"Yes!" she said on a burst of breath, totally surprised that the warrior god knew her name.

"It's me, Justin."

He started toward her again, and she blinked up at him as his face emerged from the shadows. And what a face it was! Strong, well-defined cheekbones and a rugged, masculine chin. His sand-colored hair was thick, with a sexy, mussed curl. His eyes . . . his eyes were an unusual shade of amber and were almost as inviting as his beautiful mouth.

"Justin Woods. You know . . ." He hesitated, then flashed an endearingly warm smile that was just the right mixture of mischievous and nervous. ". . . I had you for sophomore English."

She mentally recoiled. What the hell had he just said? An ex-student! So the warrior god was really a fucking Fighting Fairy. Didn't it just figure? Candice frowned, trying to pull her thoughts from the bedroom into the classroom.

"Oh, that's right. Wow. Time sure flies," she said with forced levity, feeling suddenly old and as out of date as an eight-track tape. She looked up at him, shielding her eyes from the setting sun with her hand. Yep. She vaguely recognized the echo of the gawky teenager within the man. "What was that, five years ago?"

"More like ten." He crouched next to her and nodded at her bare leg. "Did you hurt yourself?" he repeated.

"Oh, no. It's nothing. Just a cramp." He was so close to her that she could feel the heat of his body and smell him—young and virile and masculine. Holy shit, he was one wickedly sexy young man!

"I can fix that," he said. "I like to jog and I'm prone to leg cramps, especially when it's hot out like this. I know just what to do to make it go away."

Without waiting for her to respond he took her foot and propped it in his lap. Then he began to massage her cramping calf. His hands were strong and his touch was warm and experienced.

"Lie back. Relax." His voice had dropped to the deep, throaty tone he'd used when he'd first come into the clearing. "Let me take care of you."

She stared at him. She should tell him to take her foot out of his crotch and take his hands off her leg. But his touch was doing the most amazing things to her body. His fingers were sending little ripples of shock from her calf up the inside of her thigh and directly to her crotch, filling her with an unexpected rush of heat and wetness.

"Don't fight it. There's no reason to. It's just me," he said. His breath had deepened and his eyes kept traveling from her mouth to her breasts. She glanced down at herself and saw that her aroused nipples were clearly visible through her damp T-shirt and sheer white sports bra.

What would it hurt? It had been years since a beautiful young man had rubbed anything on her body. Years . . .

The thought of realistically just how many years it had been since a man this young had touched her had Candice sitting straight up and pulling her tingling leg from his warm hands. She flexed her foot and refused to meet his eyes as she pulled on her sock.

"Thanks!" she said with considerably more perkiness than she felt. "That's fine. Good as new."

"Well, at least now I know how you stay in such great shape."

"Yeah, that's me. Miss Great Shape." She cringed. Miss Great Shape? What the hell was she saying?

"I had a huge crush on you in high school," he murmured.

Her eyes widened with surprise and finally lifted to meet his. He had leaned back on his elbow and he was watching her with an intent expression that was anything but boylike.

"I thought you were the sexiest woman I'd ever seen," he said.

Candice was trapped by his frank, masculine appraisal, and the fact that he clearly liked what he saw. Her mouth felt dry and she couldn't seem to find her voice.

"You're still the sexiest woman I've ever seen."

She felt excitement slither low and hot through her belly. Lord, he was delicious! Her gaze slid from his beautiful eyes to his lips. He smiled, confident and handsome and just a little bit teasingly.

Candice blinked. *Reality, girl! Snap the fuck out of it!*

"You shouldn't say things like that," she said in her best teacher voice, forcing her gaze from his lips and pulling on her shoe.

"Why not?"

"Because you're my ex-student!" she blurted.

He flashed the smile again and scooted forward. Brushing her hands gently aside, he began slowly tying her shoe.

"I'm of age. Well of age. I'm twenty-six."

"Twenty-six!" her voice sounded shrill. "I thought you were twenty-seven." As if one year actually made a difference. He was an infant! Practically a teenager.

"I'll be twenty-seven if you want me to be," he added huskily.

"Uh, no. A year really doesn't make that much difference." Thank God, he was done tying her shoe. Candice started to stand, only to feel his strong hands under her elbows as he helped her to her feet.

"I agree with you. A few years don't make much difference."

He kept his hands on her arms, holding her close to him. He smelled so damned good. She could feel his thumbs rubbing slow, soft circles above her elbows. That simple caress spread electric sensation from her arms all the way down to her crotch. He was wearing a plain gray T-shirt, worn thin and soft by many washings. The outline of his chest was clearly visible beneath it. He was strong and firm and deliciously big. She wanted to lean into him and lick him through the damn shirt. And then bite him. Yeah, she'd like to nibble her way down his body.

What the fuck am I thinking? She stumbled back out of the seductive cocoon of his arms.

"Our age difference is more than a few years, Justin." She tried for her teacher voice again. Unfortunately she sounded more like a breathless Marilyn Monroe.

He shrugged broad shoulders and grinned at her. "You're really cute about that."

"About what?" Her mind didn't seem to be processing correctly, and she inanely added, "And I'm not cute."

"About our age difference. And you are cute about this one thing. Other than that you're sexy and beautiful." He brushed a strand of thick blonde hair that had escaped from her ponytail out of her face. "May I walk you home?"

Candice batted at his hand. "No, you may not."

"Why not? And don't say it's because I'm too young. My age should work for me when it comes to walking." He grinned and added, "Or jogging. I don't imagine many older men can keep up with you."

"Actually, they can't," she said. Despite herself she was thoroughly enjoying their flirty banter.

"Just as I thought! So there's no reason why I can't walk you home."

"Yes, there is. I've sworn off men," she said firmly.

He threw his head back and laughed, a sound that was as seductively masculine as it was youthfully exuberant.

"That's perfect, because I'm not a man."

"Exactly the problem," she countered, finding that she was unable to keep herself from smiling in response. "You're a boy, and I don't go out walking with boys."

His amber eyes darkened. With a quick movement that was feral in its grace he closed the space that had grown between them. He took her hand in his and, without his eyes leaving hers, he turned it over, palm up, and kissed her at the pulse point on her wrist. His lips were so close to her skin when he spoke that they brushed her arm, making her shiver with the warmth of his breath. "I'm no boy." Then, eyes shining, he nipped her gently. "But I am a werewolf. So you can go out walking with me—or anything else you might like to do—and still be sworn off men."

Three

What harm could letting him walk her home cause? It wasn't like he was a stranger, and he was right. He wasn't a teenager anymore. Really. He was twenty-six. And a half.

Plus, she was having fun. Justin was making her laugh with stories about botched meat deliveries at his family's restaurant, Red Riding Hood's Steak and Ale House, which bragged it was "the best darn steak place this side of Denver." She hadn't remembered him as being this charming or witty in high school. Little wonder—the only thing more self-absorbed and boorish than teenage boys were teenage girls.

Laughing, she made squeamish noises as he finished the story about the fist-sized hunk of fur that had been found in a package of ground buffalo meat, and how his dad hadn't figured out that it was really buffalo fur and not wolf fur until after he'd sheared the pelts off of each of his brothers.

"Thankfully, I was out of town on one of my many buying trips for the restaurant." He rubbed a hand through his thick hair. "I know it grows back, but still . . ."

"So, that's what you do? You work at your family's restaurant?"

"Yeah."

"Do you like it?"

"I guess."

She studied his handsome face, wondering at the sudden change in his attitude. And then an old memory surfaced. "Wait! Aren't you an artist? Don't I remember you winning the PTA Reflections Contest at the state level your sophomore year?"

He moved his shoulder and looked uncomfortable. "That was a long time ago. I don't do much art anymore."

"Why not? I remember that you were very talented."

"Just lost interest. It started to feel like just another chore—like washing dishes at the restaurant. Whatever." Then he seemed to mentally shake himself and his expression brightened. "Enough about that. I want to hear about you. So you're still teaching?"

"Not for much longer, I hope," she said.

He laughed. "How are you going to escape from the Fighting Fairies?"

"Ironically, through education. I'm working on my MFA. As soon as I finish it, I'm off to Denver to snag a job as an editor."

"Well, it'll be the Fairies' loss."

"Right now it doesn't feel like the Fairies need to worry. I'm in the middle of a poetry class that's trying to kill me; sometimes I don't think I'll ever get through it."

"Really?" He rubbed his chin, amber eyes shining. "Let's see if I remember. . . ." He cleared his throat and gave a quick, nervous laugh.

She raised her brows questioningly. What was he up to? Then he began a recitation. At first he spoke the lines hesitantly, but as he continued his confidence grew.

If it be sin to love, and hold one heart,
Far 'mongst the stars above, supreme, apart,
If it be sin to deeply cherish one,
And hold her rich and rare as beams the sun
Across the morning skies,
Then have I sinned, but sinning gained
A glimpse of Paradise.

His voice was rich and deep and his eyes lingered on hers, causing the poet's words to seem his own. And he effectively rendered her speechless for what seemed like the zillionth time in just the short while they'd been together.

"Did I get it right?"

"Yes!" The word burst out of her stunned mouth. *Get a grip on yourself and say something intelligent before he starts thinking he's talking to a prematurely aged teenager.* "Yes, you did," she said in a more grown-up voice. "That's 'If It Be Sin' by DeMass, isn't it? Are you a poetry fan?"

Laughing, he took her hand and planted a quick, playful kiss on it.

"What I am is a man with a pretty good memory who had one hell of a hard sophomore English teacher who terrified him and pounded poetry into his head so thoroughly that more than a decade later it's still stuck there."

"Oh, God. I did that to you?"

"Yes, Ms. Cox, you certainly did."

Unexpectedly, Candice blushed. "What grade did I give you?"

"A 'C,' and I was grateful for it. And I do believe you might have also given me an ulcer as well as several painful hard-ons that semester, too." He laughed. Then, before she could sputter a reply about the C, the ulcer or (embarrassingly) the hard-ons, he glanced around them. "Isn't this your place?"

Surprised, Candice realized that they were standing in her driveway. "Yes, it is." She smiled at him and had to press her palms against her legs to stop her hands from fidgeting. "Thanks for walking me home."

"Entirely my pleasure." He studied her for a moment, and his charming smile faltered as his expression grew more serious. "I'd—I'd like to see you again," he said quickly, then held up his hand to cut her off when she automatically opened her mouth to tell him no. "Wait. Before you shoot me down I'd like you to answer one question for me. Did you enjoy talking to me?"

"Yes." The answer came easily.

"Because I'm an ex-student or because you think I'm a man who is interesting and maybe slightly charming?"

"That's two questions," she said.

"Nope—it's the same question, just with two parts. Kinda like some of those hellish essay questions you used to torture us with."

She smiled begrudgingly at him, and decided to tell him the truth. "Because I find you interesting."

"And maybe a little charming?"

"Maybe . . ."

"Then why not agree to see me again?"

"Justin, I'm forty."

He waited, looking at her as if there had to be more to it than that.

She sighed. "Justin," she tried again, "I'm forty years old and you're—"

"Yes, I know. I got a C in English, but I did better in math. You're fourteen years older than I am. You're also smart and funny and easy to talk to and very, very sexy. Seriously, Candice. Try finding all those qualities in girls half your age. It's next to impossible." When she looked like she wanted to argue with him, he took her hand and said, "Okay, if our age difference bothers you that much, how about let's not call it a real date? Let's call it . . . an exercise appointment."

"An exercise appointment?"

"You jog every day, don't you?"

"Almost."

"Will you be jogging tomorrow?"

"Probably."

"Then how about we make an appointment to jog together tomorrow?"

"Okay," she heard herself say. "I'll jog by Wolf Creek at about sevenish."

"You're awesome! See you tomorrow." He shot her a blazing smile, kicked into a youthful, athletic jog, and disappeared into the fading light of dusk around the curve in the road.

Awesome? She cringed. *Like, wow. I am, like, totally awesome.*

Laughing softly at her own silliness, she skipped lightly up the stairs into her house. Refusing to berate herself for being a horny middle-aged letch, Candice poured herself a cold glass of water. She had the whole day tomorrow to consider if she really was going to show up for their "appointment" or not. She wouldn't think about it now. And anyway, her eye caught sight of the notebook and pencil sitting on her desk where she'd left them. She had homework to do.

Candice grinned.

She also had lines of poetry unexpectedly popping into her mind. Godiva had been partially right. Being in the presence of a werewolf had certainly unblocked her—even if an evening of conversation hadn't been exactly what her witchy friend had been recommending. Eagerly, she sat down and put pencil to the unfinished page, taking up easily where she'd left off.

You ask, what now?
Well, love comes with the night,
in the most inexplicable places
leaving the most unexplainable traces.

Candice giggled, and kept writing.

You see . . . a wolfman is the man for me!

Hmm . . . maybe she would meet Justin tomorrow.

Four

He thought about her a lot more than he'd intended to. He was supposed to show up at a keg party in the forest—rumor had it that several of the not-so-innocent high school seniors from the cheerleading squad were curious about just how well werewolves could use their tongues . . . not an invitation he had declined in the past. But tonight it felt, well, *wrong* to be rolling around the forest with girls Candice had probably taught in English class—and not a decade or so ago.

Actually, if he was being really honest with himself, his life had begun to wear on him. Or, more accurately, to bore him. He hated the restaurant. His older brothers were already firmly ensconced in management positions—hence the fact that he had been relegated to making purchasing runs for them. Not that anyone expected more of him. He'd always been "that Justin—so incorrigible and handsome!" He'd never been taken seriously. But, then again, it hadn't really mattered to him. He'd always been into having fun . . . feeling good.

When had that started to change?

He wasn't really sure. But he knew he hadn't been giving Candice a slick line tonight when he'd told her that she was smart and funny and sexy. Very, very sexy. And that he hadn't found that combination of qualities in twenty-something girls. She challenged him. She made him think. And she turned him on. He'd had no idea what a lethal mixture those things were before he spent an evening in Ms. Cox's stimulating company. He wanted to see her again. Badly. More than that, he wanted her to want him. If a woman like that could want him . . . what couldn't a man accomplish if he won the love of a woman like that?

So tonight, instead of joining the orgy in the woods he was much more interested in searching the back of his closet for an old textbook from a freshman lit class he'd taken before dropping out of the Denver Art Institute. Funny . . . he hadn't thought about his failed attempt at an art major in years. But those eyes of hers. They'd made him remember. They were mossy green—a color that cried to be painted.

Those eyes . . .

Justin grabbed the literature book and then flipped open his laptop. A few simple clicks took him to the website of Mysteria High School—Home of the Fighting Fairies. He smiled triumphantly. Sure enough, there was a complete list of faculty phone numbers.

Candice jumped when her cell phone made the little three-tone sound it did when she had a text message. She wiped her eyes, stuck her reading glasses on top of her head, and reluctantly took her nose out of Tanith Lee's *Silver Metal Lover*.

"Why do you insist on reading and rereading this book? You know what happens, and you know it makes you cry. You," she told herself sternly before blowing her nose, "are a ridiculous romantic. And you're old enough to know better." She sighed. Ridiculous or not, she truly loved the story of a robot finding his soul through loving a woman. Not that it could really happen. Even putting aside the fact that it wasn't possible to make humanlike robots, it was an impossible dream that a man could really become . . . well . . . *more* simply through the love of an exceptional woman. After all, she was exceptional (wasn't she?) and she had the unquestionable proof of ex-husbands one through five being total turds—despite her loving attempts.

Of course, a little voice whispered through her conscience, maybe she hadn't really loved any of them . . . maybe true love *did* have the power to create souls and make miracles.

"Please," she scoffed aloud at herself, "grow the fuck up."

Then, remembering what had interrupted her, Candice reached for her phone. Flipping it open she keyed up the one new text message.

Looking forward to our "appointment" tomorrow @ 7:00. J
P.S. you have beautiful eyes

She felt a rush of sweet excitement—a heady, intoxicating feeling she hadn't experienced in years. No matter how *ridiculous*, she had a date with a twenty-six-and-a-half-year-old man.

It took forever for it to be evening. Candice had chosen, vetoed, and rechosen what she was going to wear. Then she'd cursed herself over and over. Why the hell hadn't she agreed to a normal date? One where she could drive up in her chic Mini and meet him at a nice restaurant somewhere out of town. (Way out of town.) She'd have chosen her sexy little black dress that displayed all of her assets and hid most of her imperfections. Her makeup would have been meticulously applied. And her hair would have been Truly Big and Ready for Flirtatious Flinging About. She could have dazzled him with her experience and good taste in choosing excellent wine, and then ordered from any menu with the confidence and flair that can only be earned through maturity and experience. She, in short, would have had the upper hand.

Instead she was trying to figure out which of her rather old sports bras was the least tattered, and which cotton panties weren't totally grandma-ish. As if there was such a thing as an un-grandma-ish cotton workout panty. Why, oh why hadn't she bought new sports bras at the last Victoria's Secret sale? Oh yeah, she remembered . . . *they don't have real, usable sports bras at Victoria's Secret!*

Oh, God. Would he see her bra and panties? Just the thought made her feel like she wanted to puke her guts up.

No! Of course he wouldn't see her panties! She was meeting him for a quick jog, not a quick fuck.

Regardless, somehow she found herself in the bathroom. Naked. Staring through her fingers into the full-length mirror at her body as if she was watching a horror flick.

Looking at myself totally naked and under fluorescent lights just can't be healthy. But she continued to stare and criticize.

Sure, she wasn't awful looking. Candice forced the shielding fingers from her eyes. Okay. She wasn't really that bad. She'd been thinner and tighter, but her skin was soft and smooth, and she was definitely curvy. Maybe even lush. She shook her head, as if to clear the bizarre notions from it. "Lush" and "curvy" were not "young" and "tight-assed." There was just no way she was going to get naked in front of and have sex with a twenty-six-and-a-half-year-old. No. Fucking. Way.

Maybe he wouldn't be there. He probably wouldn't be there. Why would he want to be there? He could have just been being polite yesterday. He probably was just being nice. She had misinterpreted. He hadn't really flirted and come on to her. It was silly, really. He was so damn young. Sure, she was attractive, but please. She was almost fifteen years older. No way was he *interested* in her. Not like *that*.

"Hey there, beautiful."

She'd told herself that she was ready to see him—or ready for him to stand her up. Either was fine. Really. Whatever. Who cared? But then he was there, calling her beautiful and smiling his sexy, boy/man smile, and she felt the same dizzying rush of excitement she'd felt when he'd sent her the message the night before. And, dear sweet Lord, he was even more handsome than she'd remembered. Had she been blocking? Was it temporary amnesia? How could she not have been obsessing all day over his height and the incredible width of those shoulders, and that amazing jawline. . . .

"Hi," she said breathlessly, glad that she'd agreed to meet him at the creek so that she had an excuse other than just the sight of him to be breathing hard.

"How do you feel about trying something new today?"

His flirty smile made her stomach tighten. Oh, God, if only he knew.

Never mind. It was probably best that he didn't know.

Be normal! Talk to him!

"What do you have in mind?"

His eyes sparkled as he jerked his head, pointing his chin away from the road and into the forest. Then, with a confident, deep voice he recited, "'I shall be telling this with a sigh somewhere ages and ages hence: Two roads diverged in a wood, and I—I took the one less traveled by.'"

He was actually quoting poetry to her. Again. Her cheeks felt warmed by more than the short jog through the graveyard. "A little Robert Frost?"

"A very little, I'm afraid. And don't be too impressed. I freely admit to memorizing it this afternoon."

"You know, I don't remember you being this interested in poetry in high school."

"Would it help if I made my voice crack and stared, slack-jawed, at your boobs?"

"Only if your intention is to scare me out of the forest."

His smile was intimate. "That is not my intention."

She almost asked what his intentions were . . . but she didn't want to know. What if he gave her a blank look and said, "I thought we'd be friends"? She'd fucking die. But whether it'd be from relief or disappointment, she wasn't sure. She only realized that she'd been standing there silently staring at him when his smile faded and his tone became more serious.

"Candice, if you don't want to go off into the woods with me, all you have to do is say the word. I'll understand. I just thought that you might like exploring a hiking path I know about. That way we could get our exercise and still be able to talk. I don't know about you, but I've never mastered the talent of jogging and talking at the same time."

She met his eyes. His gaze was open and honest—vulnerable, even. Could he be as nervous as she felt? And then came the startling revelation—he had to be *more* nervous. She was almost fifteen years his senior and his ex-teacher. She was more experienced and more confident. She could reject him with a neatly turned phrase and a patronizing, disdainful look. She definitely had the high ground, even if she wasn't perfectly coiffed and perched on a posh chair at an elegant restaurant. Disregarding the rather ridiculous question of whether or not this was a real date, Justin had put himself in a position where he could be thoroughly humiliated and ultimately rejected by her, yet here he was, with a sweet smile on his handsome face, looking for all the world like a man who was doing his best to woo a woman.

"Do you remember the rest of the quote?" she asked, smiling softly at him.

"The Frost quote? No—I just memorized that far." His cheeks flushed a little with the admission.

"Frost concluded it, 'I took the one less traveled by, and that has made all the difference.' How about we take your path—the one less traveled by?"

Refreshingly, he didn't attempt to hide his relief with a suave turn of phrase or a knowing look. Instead he just smiled and said, "I promise that it will make all the difference."

Justin took her hand and led her into the forest.

Five

"All this time I've been jogging by the creek, and I had no idea a hiking path like this was so close."

"That's one good thing about being a werewolf. I have definitely gotten to know these woods."

He'd spoken nonchalantly, but she could feel his look and the expectant silence that screamed, "I'm waiting for you to freak out because I'm a wolf!" So she didn't respond right away. Instead she picked her way carefully over a large log that had fallen across the trail.

"You're right. Knowing the secret paths in the woods is one good thing about being a werewolf. What's another?" she asked, matching his nonchalant tone.

He hesitated only a moment. "The physical power."

"You mean when you're in your wolf form?"

Justin slowed down and studied her face. "Do you really want to know, or are you just making polite conversation?"

"I'm intrigued," she said honestly.

"There's physical power in both forms, and in both I can tap into the magic in these hills pretty easily. In this form I'm stronger than a human man. And not just physically. My senses are more acute. My memory is better." He grinned a little sheepishly. "I guess that means I should have made better than a C in your class."

"Nah," she said. "You weren't a man then. You probably hadn't attained all of your"—she paused and made a vague, fluttery gesture at him with her hand—"uh, Spidey senses yet."

His infectious laugh rolled around them. "Spidey senses? On a werewolf? Are you thinking I might be a hairy Peter Parker?"

"Oh, God, no!" she said with mock horror. "If I was going to fantasize about walking through the woods with a superhero it wouldn't be one that was really just a dorky kid. Let's try Bruce Wayne, shall we?"

"How about a happy medium? How about walking through the woods with a grown-up superhero who is modestly employed—I don't exactly have Batman's resources." The trail took a sharp upward turn and Justin stopped, pulling her gently back to his side when she started to climb ahead of him. "Want to test my superhuman powers?"

She narrowed her eyes at him. "Does this involve either: one, me being unattractively carried away by any type of a creature who has more than two arms, or two, your having the ability to see through any article of my clothing?"

He rubbed his chin, considering. "No and no."

"Then fine. I agree to the test."

"Okay. You have to hold totally still."

He walked a tight circle around her and Candice instantly noticed the difference in the way he moved. His body language was once again that of the man who had entered the clearing the day before— the warrior god who had not known who she was. He positioned himself behind her, standing so close that she could feel him draw in a deep breath. Then he bent, and whispered huskily into her ear.

"You don't wear real perfume."

She started to turn to answer him, but his words, which were spoken hot against her neck, stopped her.

"You must hold totally still."

She froze, whispering back. "What do you mean by not real perfume?"

"You don't buy that packaged and bottled stuff other women like so much and spray too much of on their bodies. Not you. Instead, you put drops of pure lavender oil behind your ears, on your wrists"—he drew another breath, then exhaled the warmth of his words against her neck—"and between your breasts. Am I right?"

"Yes, you're right."

Slowly, his hand rose to lightly, lightly caress her hair before he gently fisted it and pressed his face into it, taking a deep, hot breath.

She focused on not trembling, and thought how glad she was that she'd conveniently "forgotten" to pull it up in a ponytail.

"You never blow-dry your hair. You let the air dry it. And you prefer the night air to the warmer, daylight breeze."

This time she was truly amazed. How the hell could he know that?

"Am I right?" he asked again.

"Yes," she whispered. "How did you know?"

"Your hair smells like moonlight and shadows, and I know those scents intimately." His hands were still in her hair. "Why do you prefer the night air?"

"It's something that started when I was a little girl. In the summer I'd wash my hair at night and then sit on the porch with a flashlight and read. My dad used to laugh and say that the moonlight made my hair wavy like the tide. I guess it's a habit that stuck."

"I'm glad. I like moon wavy hair," he said.

"Do you?"

Justin gently nuzzled the ear he was whispering into. "Yes."

His breath sent chills down her body that lodged in her thighs, making her legs feel wobbly and semidrunk. She was relieved when he took his mouth from her ear and moved back around in front of her. Smiling, he was once more just a handsome young man.

"Impressed by my superpowers?"

"Very."

"Good. You'll love my next display of EWP."

"EWP?"

"Extrawerewolfory perception," he said, with only a slight glint in his eyes. "So. Are you hungry?"

"If I say yes are you going to grow fur and chase down some poor helpless rabbit?"

"Maybe another time. Right now if you said you were hungry I'd simply clap my hands twice and then help you climb up the rise in the path so I could show you that I made your wish come true."

"Okay, I'll bite. I'm hungry."

He waggled his eyebrows and leered at her. "Be careful, Ms. Cox— mine is the species that bites."

Before she could respond with the pithy reply she was formulating, he grabbed her hand and pulled her up the incline. Candice glanced around, surprised that the dense woods had suddenly given way to a lovely meadow of soft grass that was dotted with blue wildflowers. Fireflies flitted in the dim evening light, looking like miniature fairies. (Candice squinted her eyes and made certain that they weren't actually fairies. God, she hated fairies.) And then her surprise doubled. Not far from the path someone had spread a large plaid blanket, on which sat a huge wicker picnic basket and a bucket filled with ice and a bottle of white wine.

"You see what happens when you date a superhero?" he said.

"This isn't a date. It's an appointment," she said automatically.

"Well, I think that depends."

"On what?"

"On the good-night kiss."

Smiling, he led her over to the picnic dinner he had so meticulously chosen, packed, and then brought out into the forest just for her.

Six

The dinner was scrumptious. Candice was amazed by the obvious care he'd taken with everything. From the excellent dry white wine from Venice and the real crystal goblets he served it in, to the decadently tender prime rib sandwiches and fresh fruit—everything was better than perfect. And that included the conversation. She couldn't believe how easy he was to talk to. He was actually smart! A closet history buff, he told her stories about the settlers who had founded the various cities in Colorado—something she knew little about because she'd always focused on European instead of American lit.

And he noticed everything. Not just the details of the meal, but he noticed when the inflection of her voice changed, when she was distracted by the beauty of the blue wildflowers (which he promptly picked for her), and when she talked about her new passion—finishing her master's and moving to Denver. He discussed the aspects of her new future animatedly. Unlike Godiva, he didn't try to talk her into staying or dissuade her from following her dream. Justin honestly seemed to understand her need to move on.

But what surprised Candice most was how easy it was for her to forget he was so young. She wasn't sure when it happened—somewhere between their discussion of the stupidity of the underfunded state education initiatives, and their mutual (and, on her part, rather blasphemous) agreement that the *Lord of the Rings* movies were actually better than the books—but Candice Cox totally stopped thinking of him as ohmygodhe'ssofuckingyoung Justin, and started seeing him as the man she was out on a date with.

"So, how's the poetry assignment coming?" he asked.

"Better, I think. At least I got a little written last night." She sipped her wine. Maybe it was the third glass of wine, or the intimate silence that surrounded them, but it felt easy for her to speak half-formed dreams aloud. "You know what's weird? I'm doing this whole master's thing so I can get a job reading other people's writing, but I think I'm finding out that I actually like doing the writing part myself."

"You want to write a book?"

"I don't know. Maybe. Right now all I know is that I'd like to write something that—" she broke off, suddenly embarrassed.

"That what?" he prompted.

She met his amber gaze. He was so sincere. Rarely had she known a man who listened as well as he did. There was something about the way he looked at her, and spoke to her—as if he thought she was interesting and smart and he honestly cared about what she had to say.

It was more intoxicating than the Venetian wine.

"I'd like to write something that would have the ability to make people feel. It could be a book, or short stories, or maybe even poetry. What it is isn't important. What is important is that what I write evokes feelings in those who read it."

His gaze was hot and intense on hers as Justin leaned toward her, resting his hand on her knee. "I know exactly what you mean. That's how I always felt about my art. I didn't care if I was painting or sculpting or just sketching with plain charcoal. I wanted people to feel what I felt."

"Why did you stop, Justin?" she asked softly.

"I don't really know. . . ." His eyes dropped from hers. "One day I was a college freshman at the Art Institute—the next I'd washed out. I'm pretty sure it had something to do with me changing my major from art to beer and women." His lips twisted in self-mockery. "A double major actually. I made stupid choices—a string of stupid choices—and then I was back in Mysteria working at the restaurant."

She wanted to tell him that it wasn't too late for him to go to college, that he could get a portfolio together and get back into the Art Institute, but she hesitated. Did he really need her to turn into a teacher and lecture him? She didn't think so, and she also didn't want to. She liked being his date and not his mentor. Candice put her hand on top of his.

"Sometimes it's easy to get lost. You let your art get lost when you dropped out of college. I let good sense get lost when I committed serial matrimony. I suppose all either of us can do is to learn from our mistakes."

"I'm glad you're divorced." He smiled and added, "Again."

"Well, I'm with you on that one."

"Do you mind if I ask why none of your marriages worked?"

"I don't mind you asking, but I'm not sure I have an answer for you, even though I should because the ending of each of them felt the same—so you'd think I'd learn how to define the problem, if not fix it." She sighed. "I stopped loving them. Each one. Actually, it's more accurate to say that I stopped liking each of them first, *then* I couldn't love them anymore. They were five different kinds of men, and, as much as I kid around about it, none of them were bad men. I wouldn't have married a bad man. Still, it didn't work out with any of them, which, naturally, points to the one common denominator—me." She glanced up at him. He was watching her intently, and not in that patronizing "I'll just let the woman talk so I can get into her panties" kind of way. His amber eyes were interested—his expression plainly said he was involved in what she was saying. Candice drew a deep breath. "I'll tell you something I've never told anyone. I think I fail at relationships because I don't have any magic."

His brow wrinkled. "But most places aren't like Mysteria. Outside of here lots of people don't have magic and they manage to have happy marriages."

"Nope. I don't think so. I don't think you have to live in totally bizarre Mysteria to have magic. See, I think the ability to have a successful, happy marriage is a special kind of magic, and that special magic exists all over the world. The problem with me is that I'm doomed because I have nonmagic, just like I have nonmarriages and nonrelationships."

"Maybe"—he reached up and cupped the side of her cheek with his hand—"you just need to quit trying so hard."

Then, amazingly, Justin leaned forward and kissed her. It was a gentle kiss, not accompanied by any intrusive thrustings of tongue and teeth. She'd worried about that when she'd allowed herself to think about kissing him. Would a twenty-something be a bully kisser? Would he blindly stick his mouth on hers and proceed to grind any and all available body parts against her? It'd been too damn long since she'd kissed a man this young—she couldn't remember how they did it. But she needn't have worried. The boy/man/wolf kissed like a dream . . . a deliciously erotic dream. His mouth was a warm caress against hers—not a demand, but a seductive question.

"You taste like lavender and wine," he murmured, his lips lingering near hers.

"You taste like sex," she whispered back before her better sense could stop the words. "Erotic and decadent, and very, very male."

He chuckled and his lips moved to her neck. "That's because I'm still using my superpowers on you." His tongue flicked out to tease the gentle slope of smooth flesh where her neck met her shoulder. "But maybe you don't believe me. Maybe you need more proof first."

"If I say I do, does that mean you won't stop?" she said breathlessly.

"I won't stop unless you tell me to."

"Then we may be here all night," she moaned.

He pressed her down into the blanket and slid his hand under her T-shirt. "I'm good with all night."

She let her hands travel up his arms to his chest. God, his body was hard! And more than just between his legs (although it was already decidedly obvious that he didn't suffer from the same unfortunate and very flaccid problem her last ex-husband had). Utterly fascinated, she tugged at his shirt until he took his hands from her long enough to pull it over his head.

Dear sweet Lord—she'd died and, despite her numerous sins and bad language, gone straight to heaven. He looked better unclothed—and that was one hell of a compliment because he had looked scrumptious with his shirt on. He was truly a beautiful man.

Then his hands were tugging up her shirt. She started to help him . . . and remembered: 1) that she was wearing her least stretched out and frayed sports bra—"least" in no way meaning that it was attractive, and 2) she was forty. Suddenly he was, once again, ohmygod-he'ssofuckingyoung Justin.

"Uh, wait. I'm—I'm not completely okay with this," she said quickly, smoothing down her shirt while she avoided meeting his eyes.

Instantly, he stopped. But he didn't pull away from her. Nor did he throw a fit because he had a hard-on and needed to have sex now. He just shifted his weight so that she was resting comfortably in his arms. Then he lifted her chin with his finger, gently making her meet his gaze.

"Did I do something wrong?" he asked.

"No. It's not you."

He cocked an eyebrow at her and smiled crookedly. "Is there someone else here I don't know about?"

"Of course not."

"Then is it that you don't want me?"

"Of course not!"

"Candice, I'm going to be honest with you. For the past several years I haven't been connected to much—not another person or a job or even a place. I've been playing at life and just letting time pass. But with you I feel a connection, and that's something I'm not used to. I want to see where it takes us. If that means going slow physically, I will. But I have to tell you that the truth is I want you more than I've ever wanted any woman in my life."

His amber eyes had darkened to the color of aged Scotch. She could feel the sexual tension in his body. She loved the intensity with which he looked at her, and the way his hands lingered on hers. And she knew if she didn't make love to this beautiful young man that she would regret it forever.

Deliberately, she sat up and, keeping her eyes fixed on his, she pulled off her shirt. Then she reached behind her and undid her sports bra, shrugging it off her shoulders. The late evening air was cool against the heat of her skin, and her nipples puckered. Justin's gaze dropped from her eyes to her naked breasts. He reached forward and took her heavy breasts in his hands, lifting and caressing them.

"God, you're beautiful," he said huskily. "Look at you! You're not some plastic girl who hasn't lived enough to know there are sexier things than fake boobs and lace bras that match their thongs that match the color they paint their toes." He bent and kissed the swell of her breast, then let his tongue tease her already aroused nipple while she moaned and arched into him. "You're an earth goddess, rich and ripe and desirable."

He pressed her back into the blanket again, his lips and tongue teasing her breasts. His mouth moved slowly down her stomach, kissing the waist of her shorts. Before she could begin to get nervous about the fact that her stomach wasn't as flat as it had been ten years before, she heard him murmur, "Your skin is like silk, and you taste like lavender-scented honey."

She probably would have let him pull off her shorts then, but he slid down, until he knelt at her feet. Smiling at her, he took off her running shoes and socks. When he kissed the arch of her foot she had a moment to think about how desperately glad she was that she'd had a pedicure just two days ago, then he moved from her foot to her calf, kneading it much as he had done the day before. Only now he interspersed his caresses with soft kisses as he made his way slowly up her leg.

"Justin . . ." His name was a moan, and all thoughts of statutory rape and moral turpitude permanently flew from her mind.

"Sssh," he breathed against the sensitive spot behind her knee. "Let me worship you like the goddess you are, and allow me to teach you what I've learned since I left your class."

"A little role reversal?" she asked breathlessly, making no move to stop him as his lips grazed her inner thigh.

"Absolutely, Ms. Cox. It's time you quit worrying about marriages and relationships and nonmagic and just relax and enjoy a man who appreciates what an exceptional woman you are and can make you feel as good as you deserve to feel." He nuzzled the leg of her shorts up so that when he spoke his mouth moved, hot and insistent, against the very top of her inner thigh. "What I've learned is how to use my tongue and mouth to bring a woman to orgasm before I fill her body with mine and stroke her into another climax and then another."

"Do you do this often?" The thought of the possibility that she might be just another in a long line of female conquests began to dissipate her horny haze.

"No," he moaned, his mouth on her skin. "Don't think that. It's you I want to taste—you I want to pleasure. I've fantasized about you for years. You have no idea how much I want you and how special you are to me. Let me make my fantasies real. Let me taste you."

When he pulled at the waist of her shorts, she willingly lifted to make his job easier. As she settled back against the blanket, her eyes were drawn over his shoulder to the darkening sky and she felt a little jolt as she realized how close it was to sunset . . . which would be followed by moonrise . . . and a nearly full moon rise at that.

Observant as ever, Justin read the new tension in her body. He saw her eyes fixed on the sky and the clear concern in her face.

"I promise that you have nothing to fear from me."

Reluctantly, her gaze left the sky and met his eyes. "But when the full moon rises, you're a wolf, aren't you?"

"Actually, there's always a little of the wolf in me, full moon or not," he said, nipping her stomach gently and then lowering his head to taste her with a long lick of his tongue.

Her breath caught in surprise and she had to bite her lip to stifle a breathy moan.

He kissed her thigh and then smiled up at her. "Remember, your magic is nonmagic. Which means I am unable to shift my shape around you. I am in man form right now, and as long as I'm close to you I'll stay in that form." He nuzzled her thigh and kissed her again. "Let me make love to you, my sweet Candy," his voice caressed her name. "Let me be your lover."

"*I know exactly what you need . . . a werewolf lover.*" Godiva's voice whispered through her mind. Maybe her friend was right. And why not? Justin appreciated her. He listened to her and made her feel beautiful and desirable. What was wrong with her taking a young, virile lover who wanted to worship her like a goddess? . . .

With a triumphant smile, she made her decision.

"If you can't change form as long as I'm close to you, I guess the right answer is for me to keep you *very* close to me." She pulled the young werewolf to her and let his victorious growl vibrate against her naked skin.

Justin had been right. He had learned a hell of a lot since he'd left her classroom. And his tongue . . . not only did he use it between her legs with such enthusiasm that her vibrator would forever after seem a weak substitute, but his ability to listen (amazingly enough) hadn't stopped when his dick hardened. He listened and responded when she showed him the secret place low on her stomach that was so ultrasensitive. He paid attention to that spot at the base of her neck. And his kisses . . . his kisses were an erotic adventure.

When he'd brought her to climax three times he finally moaned that he couldn't wait anymore, and she'd reveled in the hard length of him as she guided him within her slick, ready folds. He'd tried to hold back—tried not to be too rough. She'd bit him on the shoulder and told him fiercely that she wasn't a breakable young girl—that she wanted him—all of him. His growl had been sensual music. She gripped his hard hips with her legs and met his thrusts with equal strength, urging him on until he cried her name and spent himself within her.

Seven

Godiva had known what she was talking about. Having a werewolf lover was *spectacular.* Especially such a young werewolf lover. God, she'd almost forgotten the incredibly sexy strength of a young man's body. And recovery time! Jeesh. That *boy* had been better than a recharged vibrator. Way better. She was so glad it was the weekend and there was no school the next day. They'd made love for hours, and he was still nibbling at her neck when he'd walked her home. She jumped the steps into her house two at a time. He made her feel twenty again. No! She took that back. She didn't feel twenty again—no way did she want to feel that stupid and unconfident again. Justin made her feel fabulous and forty, which was exactly what she was.

Candice had taken a long bath, delighted with the unaccustomed soreness of her body. And then, replete, she'd slept till noon. Noon! And only woke up then because her cell phone had toned at her, telling her she had a text message. She flipped it open, feeling a rush of pleasure even before she saw the text.

Are you busy tonight? I have a surprise for you.

What was he up to now? She grinned and replied:

More spidey sense?

His reply was a single word.

Better

She laughed out loud. This was fun! And, no. She wasn't going to go on and on with herself about how long it'd been since she'd had this kind of fun . . . and that she might be having *too* much fun *too* soon. No. She was just going to enjoy herself.

I think I can fit you into my schedule.

She waited impatiently for the tone that signaled his reply, and when it came it sounded like beautiful music—even though she was completely aware of how ridiculously romantic that seemed.

Be on your deck at dusk. And be ready . . .

Be on her deck at dusk? And be ready for what? But she forced herself not to text him back and ask for details. She wanted to break her old habits. She overanalyzed things ("things" being defined as "men"). She knew she did it, and she knew she had gotten worse as she'd gotten older.

"Not this time," she muttered as she fixed herself a cup of her favorite green tea and stuck a couple pieces of toast in the toaster. "This time is going to be different. This time I'm not looking for a husband; I'm looking for fun."

Candice took her tea, toast, a pencil, and the pad of paper she'd started writing her poem on the day before out onto the wonderful wood deck that wrapped the length of the back of her house and looked out into the woods that surrounded Mysteria. She curled up cross-legged on the comfortable wicker rocker that sat beside the little wicker table.

It was such a beautiful day! The woods, always magical (literally and figuratively) looked like a romantic dream come to life. All that it lacked was the knight and the white horse and . . .

Good lord! What was happening to her? She was making her own self sick.

"Snap out of it and get to writing so you can get to the good stuff tonight." Then, humming "Tonight, Tonight" from *West Side Story* she looked at the partially written poem.

Keep your Errol Flynns, Paul Newmans, Mel Gibsons
all puppets—empty masquerades.

Tom, Dick, and Harry, too
the boy next door
I want no more.
You ask, what now?
Well, love comes with the night,
in the most inexplicable places
leaving the most unexplainable traces.
You see . . . a wolfman is the man for me!

She smiled and began to write from there.

True, hair in the sink is copious,

Two hours later she should have been frustrated and annoyed. She was, after all, staring at the same line she'd written earlier and nothing else was coming. Well, not exactly nothing. She'd written line after line after line, but nothing seemed to work. Nothing could begin to capture the new, crystal bright feeling of happiness and expectation that was building inside of her, and that was the feeling she wanted her poem to evoke.

"Ah, hell! Never mind. I'll write it tomorrow." She had a date to get ready for, a really hot date at that, which called for eyebrow pluck-ing, leg shaving, a full pedicure and manicure, and lots of hair primp-ing. Not to mention that she was going to dig through some of the boxes she'd moved into the basement to find what she'd done with her really sexy lingerie.

"Tonight I will not be wearing a sports bra and grandma panties," she promised the air around her. Had she not been so busy trying (unsuccessfully) not to giggle like a girl, she would have noticed the gaggle of pink-winged fairies who, overhearing her, had taken off in a burst of silver glitter and musical laughter out over the trees, head-ing in the direction of their favorite witch's house.

Justin wanted to do something special for her. He'd been up most of the night thinking about what he could do—and about her. Her skin and her body . . . he'd never felt anything as lush and inviting. So this was what it was like to be with a woman versus a girl! Twenty-somethings paled in comparison to Candice. And he could talk to her! He'd actually talked with her about dreams he'd thought were long dead. He couldn't remember the last time he'd even thought about painting, yet here he was, heading to her place with the huge book he'd checked out from the library, one with glossy, full-color pictures of famous pieces of art, tucked under his arm. With his other arm he carried a bag filled with several cuts of prime fillet steaks from his family's restaurant, each broiled and spiced to perfection, and one of the brightly checked tablecloths they used in the dining room. He smiled as he got closer to her house and left the road to circle around to her backyard. When he could peer through the thick trees and just barely make out her deck, he put the book and the bag down, spread the tablecloth out over the leafy ground, and opened the boxes, letting the aroma of expensive steak waft in the light evening breeze.

He didn't have long to wait. He heard their giggles and the whirring of their wings before he saw them. Then, poof! He was standing in the center of a cloud of fairies who, as soon as they spotted the steaks, squealed with pleasure and began a dive-bomb-like descent.

"Wait!" He growled menacingly and stood protectively over the delectable meal. The fairies paused, midswoop. "If you want the steaks you have to do something for me."

Four of the glittering miniature nymphs glided toward him. They were only about as big as an outstretched hand, but their beauty was not diminished by size. They smiled coquettishly at him.

"We know you, wolfman," the four trilled together, magically harmonizing. "We've often watched you pleasure females in the forest." They ran their hands suggestively down their naked bodies. "We would be happy to do *something* for you."

He quickly put his hands up, as if fending off an attack. "No, no, no. You don't understand. The favor I need is not quite so personal."

"What a shame." They pouted prettily.

"Do you want the steaks or not?" He already knew their answer. Fairies craved red meat, but they never got enough. They could really be a pain in the ass; they were almost as bad as termites or fleas. His dad had to spray the restaurant for them monthly.

"We want the meat!" the entire group answered together.

"Good. Then this is all I need you to do." He picked up the thick art book and then hesitated before he opened it to one of the three pages he'd marked earlier. "Do you know the teacher who lives in the cabin right there?" He pointed through the trees at Candice's house.

As a group the fairies nodded.

"You know what she looks like?"

They nodded again, causing their long, shining hair to sparkle and glisten and float around them like slightly tarnished, then glittered, haloes.

"Excellent. Here's what I need you to do . . ." Justin opened the book. The fairies flocked around him, making curious little cooing noises as he gave them their orders.

Candice was going to be totally surprised!

Candice was sitting in her wicker chair sipping an excellent glass of chilled chardonnay when he stepped out of the forest and onto the grass of her backyard. There was just enough light left in the dusky sky to see that his smile was reflected by the sparkle in his amber eyes.

"Hello, Ms. Cox," he said mischievously.

"Hello, Justin," she said in her best teacher voice. "Did you stop by for a little detention?"

"I don't know." His grin widened. "I think I've been a pretty good boy lately."

"Yes, you certainly have," she said, feeling suddenly very warm.

"Not that I wouldn't like being locked in a room alone with you."

"So my surprise has to do with locks?"

"No, Miss Impatient. Nothing like that." He climbed the deck stairs and leaned down to kiss her lightly. "You look beautiful tonight. Love the short skirt."

Candice didn't think she'd ever been so grateful for having good legs.

"Thank you. Wine?" she offered.

"I'd love some, thanks."

She poured him a glass of sun-colored wine. Just before he sat in the empty wicker chair across from her he looked out toward the forest, raised his hand, and yelled, "Action!"

Instantly, the sky over the trees began to glitter like Fourth of July sparklers, and the breeze carried the sound of silly feminine laughter to them.

Candice scowled. "Fairies. What are they up to?"

"Keep watching," Justin said, sipping his wine.

"I do not like fairies," she grumbled. Still frowning, she looked back at the sparkling sky and gasped. A picture was forming from the glistening fairy dust.

"Oh, my God! It's the *Mona Lisa*!"

"Keep watching," Justin repeated.

Mona Lisa's face changed. Candice mouth fell open. "It's me!"

Justin laughed and lifted her hand from where it rested on the little table. He kissed her palm. "Yep, it is."

Candice was still staring at the glowing portrait when the picture shifted and changed. Now she was looking at a hauntingly beautiful woman with long red hair who was sitting in a small boat.

"Waterhouse's *Lady of Shalott*!" Then it, too, changed and she was watching herself frozen in time as the lady who was cursed to sing her last song as she floated down to Camelot.

Entranced, she watched the picture dissipate and begin to form again as another famous woman. This time it wasn't a painting the fairies were reproducing. It was the eternally graceful statue of the winged Nike. And then, as if the Greek gods had ordered a miracle, Candice's face and neck, even her long blonde hair, appeared to complete the glorious statue. Candice laughed and clapped her hands.

Justin hardly glanced at the fairy artwork. He couldn't stop looking at Candice. Uninhibited joy had transformed her face from pretty to stunning. Everything inside him screamed, *Her! She's the one I'm meant to be with!*

Candice gasped again as the new painting took form. "This is one of my all-time favorites! *Meeting on Turret Stairs* by Burton." She made a happy little cry. "Justin! It's us!"

Then he did pull his eyes from her to look at the sky. Sure enough, the incredibly romantic scene of the knight passing his lady on the narrow stairway had been altered so that it was the two of them. The knight was kissing his lady's arm as she leaned dramatically against the stone wall of the castle; both of them were clearly overwhelmed by a desire so real it seemed to leap off the painting and become tangible. He hadn't told the fairies to re-create this scene—just as he hadn't told them to put his face in any of the paintings—but he was glad they'd added to his instructions. He'd have to remember to bring them a couple more steak dinners. Soon.

The fairy dust painting faded slowly, leaving only the darkening sky. Finally Candice turned to him.

"How did you do that?"

Her eyes were alive and her face was slightly flushed. He wanted to push the little table that was between them out of the way and take her in his arms and kiss her until his touch was what made her eyes sparkle and her face flush.

"Magic," he said.

"But magic doesn't work on me."

"It worked on you tonight." He took her hand and kissed her palm again. "Maybe you just needed the right partner to find your magic."

"Or maybe your magic is so strong that even I can't stop it."

"I like that. I like that anything about me could be strong enough to attract you."

"Everything about you attracts me," she said, her voice low and sexy.

"Show me. Show me how much," he said.

Without speaking she stood up and led him into her house, through the cozy kitchen, the comfortably decorated den, and into her bedroom.

"I want to undress you," she said. "Is that okay with you?"

He bent and kissed her softly on the lips. "Anything you want is okay with me, as long as you still want me."

"I can't imagine not wanting you," she said, guiding him over so that he stood beside her bed while she sat on the edge of it. He was wearing a black pullover, and she skimmed it up his body and over his head, letting her fingers trail lightly down from his shoulders over his naked chest and abdomen, loving the way his body shivered at her touch. Then she unbuttoned his jeans, taking her time to slowly unzip them while her lips teased his chest and her fingers caressed the hard lump that was pushing against his pants. When she finally got his pants undone she stood, and then, hooking her fingers in his waistband, slid the jeans down, pressing her body against his as she did so.

On her knees in front of him, she took him in her hands. He was hard and hot and his body jerked and quivered under her hands. When she closed her mouth around him he moaned her name, and had to lean against the bed to stay standing.

"Your mouth," he rasped, "is a dream. A very sexy dream."

"Wet dream?" she asked when she paused.

"Oh, God, yes," he moaned.

She laughed, but before she could take him in her mouth again, he pulled her to her feet and in one quick movement, lifted her onto the bed. Lying beside her he unbuttoned her shirt.

"Now that's sexy," he said, running his finger lightly over the delicate white lace bra. "Too many women think red or black or some other godawful bright color is what men want. I don't know about other men," he murmured, "but I think white is the sexiest. You can see right through it." He circled her nipple with his finger, causing it to harden. "But there's something innocent about it. Like what it's covering has been waiting just for you." He bent over her, taking her nipple into his mouth right through the sheer lace of the bra.

Candice's breath left her in a rush. "My panties match," were the only words her lust-clouded mind could form.

Justin moved from her bra to unbutton the short cotton skirt she was wearing. He pulled it down and then knelt between her legs, gazing down at her body. She watched him closely and suddenly saw herself reflected in the desire that was so clear on his face, and knew she'd never again think of herself as old or fat or frumpy.

"Feel what you do to me," he whispered.

He took her hand and pressed it to his chest so that she could feel the racing of his heart. She let her fingers rest there for a moment, and then held the hand that had so recently covered hers against her breast.

"Feel what you do to me," she echoed.

"It's good that we're in this together," he said. "I don't think I could stand feeling all of this alone."

"You're not alone," Candice said.

"Give me a chance," Justin said. "Say you'll take me seriously, even though you think I'm too damn young."

"Justin, I don't expect—" she started.

"Expect!" he blurted. "Can't you just expect magic? Even if it's never happened to you before, can't you let me prove to you that there's more than one kind of magic in this world, and that we can make it happen together?" He leaned down and cupped her face between his hands. "I want you, Candice Cox. Not just tonight. I want you in my life. Let me make you love me."

His words scared and thrilled her. She should tell him no. Or she should lie to him and say yeah, whatever, so that they could have more good sex, and then send him on his way. But she didn't want to. It might be stupid. It probably wouldn't work. But Candice wanted more than anything else to take a chance on loving Justin. Unexpected tears came to her eyes when she answered him.

"I've waited a long time to feel like this, Justin. I can't let you go now," she said.

He smiled and wiped the dampness from her cheeks. "Well, you had to wait for me to grow up."

"Hush and kiss me." She pulled him down to her.

Soon neither of them could talk anymore. All they could do was feel.

Eight

Candice slept till noon again the next day—this time curled up against Justin's body. And she awoke to his gentle caresses and they made love slowly, whispering erotic secrets as morning gave way to afternoon. They'd said good-bye like lovers had for centuries, with lots of long looks and lingering touches.

And tomorrow . . . they were meeting tomorrow. He'd wanted to see her again that night, but as he'd been kissing her good-bye for about the zillionth time, his cell phone had interrupted them. He'd taken the call, albeit reluctantly, and after he'd hung up he'd apologized, saying that it was a call from his family's restaurant. They needed him to go to Denver tonight because . . . hell. She didn't remember exactly what he'd said. She'd been too busy floating on a cloud of sexual satisfaction.

But that wasn't all it was, Candice reminded herself that evening as she poured a glass of white wine and took it to her writing desk. She was floating on more than a sex cloud. She really liked him. Her lips tilted up in a secret smile as she remembered the text message she'd received from him not long ago. It had simply said:

Did my heart love till now? Forswear it, sight! For I ne'er saw true beauty till this night.

First DeMass, then Frost, and now Shakespeare! He was smart and interesting and so sexy she wanted to begin at his mouth and lick her way down his body . . . and then back up again. And he wanted her to be in his life—to love him. No matter how improbable or impossible, she found herself wanting the same thing. She sighed happily and sipped her wine. Creative juices flowing (along with all the rest of them), she picked up her pencil and reread the poem she'd started.

Keep your Errol Flynns, Paul Newmans, Mel Gibsons
all puppets—empty masquerades.
Tom, Dick, and Harry, too
the boy next door
I want no more.
You ask, what now?
Well, love comes with the night,
in the most inexplicable places
leaving the most unexplainable traces.
You see . . . a wolfman is the man for me!
True, hair in the sink is copious,

She grinned at where she'd stopped and, inspired, started writing.

and the house at night tends to be a mess.
But

The ringing phone jarred her. The caller ID said Tawdry, Godiva.

"Well, hi there, girlfriend. Long time no hear from." Godiva's voice was smug. "So, has anything new come . . . uh, *up* recently?"

Candice's breath came out in a rush. "Shit! You know! How the hell do you know?" Then she gasped, a horrible feeling lodging in her stomach. "Oh, no! Did you do it, Godiva?"

"Do what?"

"Don't play innocent witch with me. How did you manage it? Magic doesn't work on me."

"It might not work on you, but it definitely works on werewolves."

"You made him want me!" she shrieked, feeling even sicker.

"Certainly not." Godiva sounded offended. "All I did was to cast a lupine drawing spell right after the last time we talked. If it caught a wolf who didn't find you attractive, he would have never approached you. Think of it like baiting a hook. If the worm—which was you—

wasn't juicy and tender and appealing to the fish—or in this case, werewolf—he would never taste the bait."

"Oh." Candice grinned, feeling so relieved she was weak-kneed.

"Details, please."

"Let's just say this worm has been well eaten."

They both dissolved into giggles.

"And," Candice said breathlessly, "I'm meeting him again tomorrow. Godiva, baby, he's quoting poetry to me! *Poetry!* And he made the stupid fairies make art for me. Can you believe it? He said he wants to worship me like a goddess, and, honey, let me tell you. I definitely can't get enough of that kind of attention! But it's more than just how completely sexy he is. He's smart and funny *and* totally into me. And, Godiva, I *really* like him."

"Sounds fabulous! Who is he?"

"You mean you don't know?"

"No. I told you—I just baited the hook. I had no idea which wolf would bite."

"Oh, Godiva, it's so deliciously naughty. He's *young*, and"—she dropped her voice to a whisper—"he's an ex-student of mine."

"Oh, my Goddess! How wickedly yummy. Give. Who is he?" Godiva gushed.

"Justin Woods," she gushed.

"Who?"

"Justin Woods. You know, his family are the werewolves who own Red Riding Hood's."

"Oh, Goddess."

"What? What's wrong? I know he's young, but it's not like he's still a teenager—which would be totally and completely disgusting— he's twenty-six. And a half. Practically twenty-seven."

"Oh, Goddess."

"Godiva Tawdry, stop saying that and tell me what's wrong!" Candice was beginning to feel sick again.

"I should have known," Godiva groaned. "But how could I have known? I didn't think it would be *him*."

"Godiva. Tell me."

The witch drew a deep breath and then blurted out, "He's a slut."

"What?!"

"He's the most promiscuous werewolf in town—or out of town, for that matter. The pack tramp. Truly a dog in all the worst connotations of the word."

"Oh, no . . ."

"Oh, yes. I promise you. My Romeo has told me all about him. He's the pack joke. Thinks he's some kind of furry Don Juan. He's always licking coeds and cheerleaders and whatnot."

"Cheerleaders!"

"I'm so sorry, Candice."

"And all that stuff he said to me . . ."

"You mean about making a woman orgasm with his mouth?"

Candice gasped in horror.

"Let me guess—he licked your foot and sucked your toes?" Godiva said.

"Yes," Candice squeaked.

"That's his move. He does that with all the girls—wolves—whatever."

"I may puke." She put her hand to her forehead and closed her eyes. How could she have been so damn gullible? "How about the poetry he quoted and the fairy art? Does he use that on all of his victims, too?"

"I don't remember hearing about that, but hey, come on! Just forget about it." Godiva forced perkiness into her voice. "You had a good time, right? A little fling—an unclogging of your pipes."

"He played me for a fool." Candice's voice was quiet and intense. She let her anger build. As long as she was thoroughly pissed she could keep the hurt from blossoming like a black flower inside of her.

"No, he's just—"

Candice cut her off. "No, Godiva! It wasn't all fun and games—he made it appear to be more than that. I should have known . . . I should have been smarter, but he's not going to get away with it. I said I was too old for this kind of shit, and I am. But not because I'm dried up and unattractive. I'm too old to be lied to and manipulated. So tell me the truth. He's obviously not going on a supply run for his family tonight. I want you to find out from Romeo what he's really doing."

"Uh, if I do and I tell you, what are you going to do?"

"Well, my witchy friend, I can sum that up in one word. Retribution."

He should never have agreed to meet the twins at the full moon party. It didn't matter that his intentions had been right. He hadn't told Candice the truth, which had been bothering him ever since the family restaurant supply run lie had blurted from his mouth. He shouldn't have answered the damn phone, but he'd been feeling so good there with Candice—so right—that when the phone rang he . . .

He what? He'd answered it because he'd wanted to yell from the mountainside that he'd FOUND SOMEONE INCREDIBLE! In retrospect that seemed stupid and immature. And instead of telling the world about Candice, he'd quickly agreed to meet Brittney and Whitney at the party that night. There was little he wouldn't have agreed to just to get them off the phone before Candice heard their silly female voices on the line and dumped him right then and there.

And actually going to the party hadn't seemed stupid—not until he'd stepped into the forest and felt the moon's call on his blood. He'd answered that call automatically, embracing the sweet savage pleasure and heat of sinew and bone changing and re-forming with the power of the beast. He'd meant to show up long enough to tell the twins—and any of the other numerous females he'd pleasured—that he was officially taking himself off the market. He meant to make a clean split with his old life, so that he could begin his new one. Earlier that day he'd even gone online and looked up the Denver Art Institute. Then he'd actually begun a sketch. Just a woman's eyes. They were green and framed with thick blond lashes and soft laugh lines. . . .

Thinking of Candice, Justin let the moon caress his fur as he raised his muzzle to the sky. Surrounded by young wolves who were breaking off into intimate groups, he howled his passion for Candice into the night.

*   *   *

The full moon was so white against the absolute black of the starless sky that it almost looked silver. Sitting at the edge of the clearing, Candice breathed deeply of the warm night air and waited. It wasn't long before she heard them approaching through the trees. They weren't being stealthy—there was no reason for it. They were being young and uninhibited and very, very horny.

Godiva had been right (again). It was easy to tell which of the wolves was Justin. That thick sand-colored pelt was as distinctive as his eyes (and his tongue).

She stood up and stepped into the clearing. Keeping the hand that clutched the collar hidden behind her back, she cocked her hip and shook out her hair. With a sexy purr in her voice, she called to him.

"Justin, come here, boy!" The big wolf sitting between two blonde bitches who were drooling over him (literally) while he howled at the sky cocked his ears at her. Candice ran her hand suggestively over her body. "I have something special for you that I just couldn't wait till tomorrow to give you."

With an enthusiastic woof, he bounded toward her, his all-too-familiar tongue lolling. With one quick movement, she dropped to her knees beside him and slipped the heavy-duty choke collar around his throat.

"Arruff?" he said, staring up at her in confusion.

"Tonight you're coming with me," she whispered. When the bitches yapped at her, she grinned over her shoulder at them. "Don't worry. I'll give him back to you—but not till I've had my way with him."

He whined and squirmed as she dragged him to the Jeep she'd borrowed from Godiva. No damn way his hairy ass was going to fit in her lovely little Mini—even if she did allow dogs to ride with her, which she definitely didn't.

"Don't bother with the whining and big doggie eyes. They're not going to work," she told him. "And remember, my magic is nonmagic. You can't change as long as I'm close to you. But isn't that convenient? I hear that your favorite position is very close to a woman. Any woman. So get comfortable, fur-face."

*   *   *

"Thank goodness I caught you before you closed, Doctor." Candice smiled as she dragged the whining wolf into the veterinary clinic.

"Is there something wrong with your . . ." The vet hesitated, narrowing his eyes at the wolf.

"Dog," Candice supplied innocently. "Yes, there is something wrong with my dog. I need you to perform emergency surgery."

"Really? He looks healthy to me." The vet reached down and ruffled the "dog's" sandy fur.

Justin whined pitifully.

"You're a big boy, aren't you?" the vet said.

"He certainly thinks he is—which explains the emergency. I need you to cut off his . . ." Candice paused, glanced at Justin, then dropped her voice and whispered into the vet's ear.

"Well, I don't know. It's pretty late. I was just closing," he said.

"Surely you can fit him in. Pretty please, Doc?" She fluttered her lashes at him.

The vet smiled and shrugged. "I suppose I could for my favorite teacher. Go, Fairies!"

"Go, Fairies!" Candice chimed in automatically.

"If you wait here, I'll take him in the back and be done in no time."

"No! I mean, I'll come with you. If I don't stay close to him he'll change . . . into something that might surprise you."

"But you won't want to watch!"

"Of course not," she assured him. "I'll stay in the room, but I have a poem I need to finish, so I'll be concentrating on that while you take care of his little *problems*."

"Suit yourself, teacher," the vet said. "Bring him back."

Justin began to growl.

"Doc, I think we need a muzzle."

Candice settled on a metal folding chair not too far from the operating room table, careful to keep her back to the busy veterinarian and his unwillingly drugged patient. She ignored the tight, sick feeling in her stomach and, while Justin was being prepped, she picked up her pencil and smiled grimly as she finished her poem.

Keep your Errol Flynns, Paul Newmans, Mel Gibsons
all puppets—empty masquerades.
Tom, Dick, and Harry, too
the boy next door
I want no more.
You ask, what now?
Well, love comes with the night,
in the most inexplicable places
leaving the most unexplainable traces.
You see . . . a wolfman is the man for me!
True, hair in the sink is copious,
and the house at night tends to be a mess.
But if that wolfman breaks my heart,
if he thinks that we should part,
I'll wait until the moon is waxing full
that magic time when his change is soon,
(my love is quite helpless then, as a puppy . . .
baby . . . body in a mortuary)
I'd collar that fur-faced gigolo
and make a timely visit to the Vet.

Ah, well, I'm sure there'll never be a need.
I haven't seen a neutered werewolf . . .

Candice glanced up at where the vet obscured her view of the sleeping, spread-eagled Justin.

. . . Yet.

As the vet picked up an evil-looking scalpel, Candice closed her notebook.

"Doc?"

The vet paused, blade hovering above the spread-eagled "dog," and glanced over his shoulder at her.

"I'm sorry. I know this is going to seem odd, but I've changed my mind."

He frowned at her.

She gave a purposefully silly, girly-girl laugh. "Oopsie, sorry. I guess I just can't go through with it, no matter how . . . uh, naughty he's been. I'll still pay you for the neutering, though. Don't worry." She fished her checkbook out of her purse and hastily wrote the vet a check. Then she nodded at the sleeping Justin. "How long will he be out?"

"A couple hours."

"Perfect. Can you help me lift him into my car?"

Nine

Justin woke up in the ditch not far from the clearing where the party was still in full swing, as evidenced by the randy growls and breathless giggles that drifted on the night air. At first he was totally disoriented. His mouth felt like a bird had shit in it and he had a killer headache. What the hell? He'd gone to the party as a farewell to his old life, and then . . .

With a terrified yelp, his memory rushed back. Commanding his human form to come to him, he sat up, gasping and reaching between his legs. All there! He was all there.

What had happened? Why had Candice freaked out?

But even before Justin found the neatly folded note she'd left staked to the ground beside him with . . . he shuddered . . . something that looked disturbingly like a scalpel, he knew what had happened. Someone had told her about him. He was fully aware of his bad reputation.

He'd never really given a shit. Until now. He opened the piece of notebook paper. The full moon had brightened the sky enough for him to easily read her bold writing.

> **Girls might think it's cute or exciting to be with a man who collects lovers like a dog collects fleas. Well, that's just one of the many differences between girls and women. Gigolo men piss grown women off. I'm a grown woman. The game you played with me pisses me off. I suggest you stick to girls. Next time you may lose more than a few orgy hours. Keep in mind, "Heaven has no rage like love to hatred turned, nor hell a fury like a woman scorned." Ah, to hell with that poetic crap. Basically, I wanted to say, GO FUCK YOURSELF, JUSTIN!**

When he returned to wolf form he didn't notice the sensual stir of his morphing flesh, and he didn't rush back to the clearing to pair up with an eager young wolf to reassure himself that everything was still in working order. Instead he padded slowly home—the garage apartment his parents pretended to rent to him as part of his salary and benefits at the restaurant, which felt as empty and meaningless as his life had become.

"You should be almost done with that awful poetry class, right?" Godiva asked her friend.

Candice was sitting on her balcony, arm resting against her little table, pad and pencil beside her. She stared out at the forest while she propped the phone against her shoulder and kept doodling on her notebook paper. "Yep. Almost."

"And that means the whole MFA is almost done, right?"

"Yep. Almost."

"And snow is almost done falling out of that giant flying rabbit's ass, right?"

"Yep. Al—" Candice frowned, realizing what Godiva had really said. "Don't be such a smart-ass."

"You know, I hear he's back in town."

"I don't want to talk about it."

"So don't talk—just listen. He's back in town, but werewolf gossip has it that he's only here temporarily. Seems he's just come to collect some of his stuff to take back to his new apartment in Denver."

"And why should I care?"

Godiva kept talking as if Candice hadn't spoken. "Word also has it that he's still not slutting around. No parties. No orgies. No cheerleaders. Not even the slightest hint of a girlfriend, wolf or not."

"Godiva! I do not give a shit. I haven't talked to him in weeks."

"Well, maybe you should!"

"I cannot believe you're saying that. You're the one who told me what a slut he was. And I saw it with my own eyes. He lied to me and was fucking every bitch in sight that night."

"Girlfriend, I told you what Romeo told me—that several werewolves told him that Justin wasn't doing anyone that night. And, as far as my excellent gossip network—which includes forest fairies, and you know those little shits live for gossip and red meat—can tell, Justin Woods has not been with anyone since the three dates he had with you."

"Two dates. And one of them wasn't even official."

"Whatever. I think you should call him."

"What! I am *not* going to call that boy."

"Oh, give it up. You know very well he's no boy."

"Again I say whatever. And he knows my phone number. If he wanted to talk to me, he'd call me."

"Candice Cox, may I please remind you that the last time you interacted with him you almost had his balls cut off, you dumped him in a ditch, and you left a scary revenge note, complete with a literary quote and a go-fuck-yourself."

"He lied to me."

"True, and circumstantial evidence pointed to his definitely being an asswipe. But since then he has behaved respectably, by either man or wolf standards."

Candice sighed. "I can't call him. I feel like an idiot."

"Do you want me to cast a little—"

"Hell, no! Godiva Tawdry, promise me right now that you will not put any kind of love spell, or anything like a love spell, on Justin."

"Okay! I promise. But I still think you should call him." She brightened. "Hey, I could have Romeo talk to—"

"No! God, I feel like I'm trapped in a dream where I'm back in high school trying to figure out my locker combination and realizing I'm butt-ass naked. Just leave it alone, Godiva. If Justin wanted to see me again, he'd figure out a way to do it." And she knew it was true. Candice had only been with him for a short time, but she believed in his tenacity. He'd set his sights on seducing her, and he'd certainly accomplished his goal. If he had any desire to talk to her or see her, he'd get it done. But even though his behavior had changed drastically since the night she'd almost had him neutered, he had stayed completely away from her. Not that she cared.

"Candice?"

"Oh, sorry, what did you say?"

"I asked what your last poetry assignment was about."

"We have to write two poems about heartbreak. One free verse. One sonnet. And neither can be clichéd."

"Oh, a real uplifting assignment."

"Yeah, it's just one laugh after another over here."

"Are they done?"

"Almost. I just have to finish tweaking the couplet to conclude the sonnet. Then I'm going to set them aside for a day or so, and do a quick rewrite before I have to turn them in next week."

"After you do that, why don't you and I get all dressed up and go into Denver for some excellent Italian food? I'll even drive."

"I'm not flying on that damn broom of yours."

"I said *drive*."

"I'll think about it," Candice said.

Godiva paused. She was almost afraid to ask the next question, but she knew she had to. Her talent was, after all, healing. Resolutely, she said, "Candy, what happened with Justin really did break your heart, didn't it?" It took her friend several seconds to answer her.

"Yeah," she finally whispered into the phone. "Isn't that stupid?"

"No, it's not stupid. It's what can happen when we love someone, and you have rarely let yourself love anyone."

"Ironic, isn't it? And I'm the one who's been married a zillion times."

"You didn't really love any of the ex-husnumbers. But there was something about Justin that got to you."

"I wish . . . ," Candy began.

"What, honey?"

"I wish your magic worked on me."

"So do I, honey. So do I."

After she hung up, Godiva sat staring at the phone a long time. There had to be some way she could help her friend. After all, it was her fault this whole thing had happened. First, she'd cast the drawing spell that had brought them together. Then she'd spilled the beans about Justin's promiscuous ways. Who knew the wolf was going to have some big, hairy epiphany and learn to zip his pants? And now the gossip tree said that he was really getting his shit together. Seems he was spear-heading the acquisition of a new restaurant for his family, and the eavesdropping fairies, who seemed to have a real soft spot for the wolf, had even heard whispers that he'd reenrolled in college. Was it just her? Wasn't it obvious to everyone that Justin was trying to make himself worthy of Candice?

And Candice was moping around like she'd been stuck in a class-room with the horrid Desdaine triplets (Godiva shuddered—Goddess! What a wretched thought! Those girls were the brat pack.). Some-thing had to be done.

Maybe if Justin knew how miserable Candice was . . . maybe then he'd call her and they'd live happily ever after!

But she'd promised Candice she wouldn't cast any love spells on him. Godiva tapped her long fingernail against her chin. Then she smiled. Candice was writing poems about heartbreak. What if Justin were to read them? He wouldn't know that they were an assignment!

He'd just think she was pining over him—which she was. That was it; the fairies would be only too happy to help. . . .

Humming to herself, Godiva began gathering four-leaf clovers . . . the little dried white things from the tops of dandelions . . . a pinch of frog snot . . . and various other delightful things she would need for the spell. . . .

Candice rubbed her neck and stretched. Well, the couplet that ended the sonnet was done. Good thing, too, it was getting dark and she should move inside from her porch. But she didn't get up. She liked sitting out there. And it wasn't because she remembered another evening on the porch, one that had been filled with hope and magic and love. . . .

No. It was just that the woods were quiet, and their somberness reflected her recent mood. It was nice to sit out on her balcony and write, even if what she wrote was damn depressing. She lifted the paper that had the final draft of both poems written on it and shook her head sadly. They were good. She knew it. But if they did evoke feelings, the feelings would be sadness, loss, longing. . . .

She put the paper down, remembering how not long ago she had dreamed of writing things that evoked brighter emotions.

What was wrong with her? So she'd had a little fling that had ended abruptly and, quite frankly, not very well. It was ridiculous that it was still making her feel this sad. She closed her eyes and rested her head against the back of the chair. What was it about Justin that stayed with her? Was it just because he'd been so damn handsome? That couldn't be it. Ex-husband numbers one and four had been very handsome men. Well, was it the sex? No. Ex-husband numbers one and three had been fantastic in the sack. She'd gotten over all of them, more easily than she usually cared to admit. So why was Justin still haunting her dreams?

Against her closed eyes the warm evening breeze had picked up. It felt good, almost like a caress against her skin. It made her think of the summer, when dandelions dried and their little white heads blew all over fields of four-leaf clovers. She sighed and relaxed, feeling suddenly sleepy. . . .

. . . Until she heard the wild flapping and opened her eyes in time to see her homework papers being lifted by the crazy wind. She leaped up, grabbing at papers, sure she saw translucent pastel wings fluttering in among the notebook pages as her poetry scattered out into the forest.

"Fucking fairies!" she screamed, running after the trail of paper.

An hour later she had still not found the final drafts of both poems. Grumbling about hanging sticky flypaper and a giant bug zapper to get rid of the fairy problem, she gave up, resigning herself to rewriting the finals again. At least she'd just finished both poems that day. It shouldn't be too hard for her to remember exactly what she'd written. . . .

He'd gone for a walk. Justin hadn't even understood why, but all of a sudden it had been very important that he take a walk in the woods, and before he knew it, he was heading south. Toward her house. He'd just realized how close he was to her little log cabin when the wind changed directions and, in a flutter of iridescent wings, two papers blew straight into his hands. He felt a jolt at the familiar writing.

Poetry . . . her poetry!

Then he started reading, and his heart clenched. Candice's words were like a mirror of what was going on inside him. Could it be? Could she really care as much as he did? He read on, and images began to form in his mind, and with them a plan. Maybe, just maybe, he could find a way to reach her.

Ten

To some people it might seem counterproductive to jog to town simply to eat a triple fudge banana split. To Candice it made perfect sense. She sat outside the One-Stop Mart and tried to tune out the sounds of the arguing Desdaine triplets as they fought over God knew what. Those monsters were always into something. And that poor sweet preacher, what was her name? Pastor Harmony? She'd somehow gotten trapped in there with those little demons. Candice could hear the woman trying to end the argument before any of the three little terrors could permanently disable some hapless passerby, which was just damn brave of the preacher. No wonder everyone said she was honestly nice—that she accepted everyone no matter how magical or nonmagical (or how disdainfully horrid).

Something crashed inside the store and Candice cringed. How old were those brats now? Eleven? Twelve? She'd damn sure better be out of teaching before, like a plague of locusts, they descended upon Mysteria High. Just another reason to land that fabulous job as an editor in Denver. Candice ate her ice cream slowly, dreaming of the romantic possibilities of her future profession. She'd have three-martini lunches with authors. She'd wear amazing clothes and have a loft near downtown. She'd discover the next Nora Roberts!

"Candice! There you are. Holy bat shit! You will not believe what the vampire is displaying in his gallery!" Godiva rushed up to her friend, her large round bosoms heaving with excitement.

"More porno dressed up as art?" Candice said, interest definitely aroused. She was always up for some full-frontal male nudity. Actually, it might be just the thing to help her get over the Justin Blues. Unfortunately, Godiva shook her head.

"No. It's not porn."

"Damn. Then what's the big deal? You know I don't like those bloody pictures the vamps think are cool. I don't know why vampires are so into art, anyway. You'd think they'd choose a more, I don't know, nocturnal profession."

"Candice! Just come with me. I cannot begin to explain what you're going to see."

"Can I finish my banana split first?"

"Bring it. This can't wait."

Grumbling, Candice let Godiva shoo her down Main Street to Mysteria's only art gallery, Dark Shadows. A crowd was gathered around the front display window, and as she got closer, she realized that all of them were staring in the window, and they all were crying.

Crying? The exhibition was so bad it was making the populace cry? Sheesh.

Godiva grabbed her arm and shoved her forward so she could get a better look. At first she was so completely distracted by the beauty of the pieces and the amazing talent of the artist that she didn't understand exactly what it was she was seeing. There were two watercolor paintings on display. Her immediate impression of them was that they were dream images, and they vaguely brought to mind Michael Parks's sexy fantasy work. One was of a woman who was in a cage that looked like it had been carved from ice. All around the outside of the walls of ice were big tufts of a delicately leafed plant in full purple bloom. *Lavender*, she thought. *They're bunches of blooming lavender.* Candice looked more closely at the woman in the center of the cage. She was sitting on the floor, with one hand pressed against the nearest translucent wall, almost as if she were trying to push her way out. She was wearing only a white hooded cloak. Parts of her shapely bare legs were showing, but her face was in shadows—all except her eyes, which were large and mesmerizing with their mossy green sadness. There was something else about her eyes. . . .

Candice shifted her attention to the other painting. It, too, was amazingly rich in detail and color. It showed a woman sleeping on a bed that was in the middle of what looked to be a dark room in a castle. Mist, or maybe fog, hung around the bed, further obscuring the woman. A single tall, narrow window slit let in two pearl-winged doves, as well as a ray of moonlight, which fell across the bed, illuminating the side of the woman's face so that a single tear at the corner of her eye was visible. This woman's face was also in shadow. Her blonde hair spilled around her on the dark bed, drawing Candice's eye. What was it about her hair?

Then she realized that displayed beside each painting was a framed poem. She pushed her way farther through the sobbing crowd until she was so close to the window that she pressed her fingers against the cold glass. Candice began reading the elaborate calligraphy of the first poem.

Come, icy wall of silence
encase my weary heart
protect me with your hold, hard strength
till no pain may trespass here.
Make still my battered feelings
within your protective fortress
safe
request I this sanctuary from life's storm.
But, what of this ensorcelled heart?
Will it struggle so encased?
Or will walls forged to keep harm out
cause love's flame to flicker low
till silence meant as soothing balm
does its work too well, and
no more breath can escape
to melt the fortress of frozen tears.

Candice couldn't breathe. She felt as if someone had punched her in the stomach. Frantically, her eyes went to the second poem. It was a sonnet, and it was written in the same meticulous calligraphy.

The dreamer dreamed a thousand wasted years
Captive of wondrous images she slept
Swathed close in sighs and moans and blissful tears
Reliving promises made, but not kept.

The moon's deft watch through narrow casement fell
Its silvered light caressed her silken face
Like a dove's soft wings colored gray and shell
Shadowy thoughts frozen in time and place.

He watched her breath like silver mist depart
And he longed to join her murderous sleep
But truth rare listens to the wounded heart
Hence even hero souls must sometimes weep.

Now love's pinions can never more take flight,
Entombed forever in grief's endless night.

"They're mine," Candice whispered. Her stricken voice didn't carry above the sobs of the people around her. She tore her eyes from the window and looked frantically back at Godiva, who was standing at the edge of the crowd crying softly. She raised her voice so that her friend could hear her. "They're my poems, Godiva. I wrote them."

"Who said that?!"

Heads swiveled to the tall gaunt figure standing in the doorway of the gallery. Barnabas Vlad (a name everyone in Mysteria knew he had absolutely, beyond any doubt, *not* been born with) was swathed head to toe in black, holding a small lacy black parasol, and wearing huge blue blocker reflective sunglasses.

"Who said that she is the poetess?"

"That would be me," Candice said reluctantly.

All the heads then swiveled in her direction and Candice heard weepy murmurs of *Oh, they're so wonderful,* and *They break my heart, but I love them,* and *I have to have one of my own and the art that goes with it!*

Barnabas pointed one finger (fully covered in a black opera-length glove) at Candice. "You must come with me at once!" The vampire turned and scuttled through the gallery door.

Candice couldn't move. Everyone was staring at her.

"Let's go!" Godiva pushed her toward the gallery door, ignoring the gawking crowd. Then, still sobbing softly, she added, "And no way are you going in there without me."

Candice had been in the gallery before. It was decidedly on the dark side—walls and floor black instead of the usual clean white of most galleries. It was never well lit, and it was always too damn cold. But she liked the art exhibits, especially the gay pride exhibits Barnabas like to have. She could appreciate full-frontal male nudity, even if it couldn't appreciate her.

"Back here, ladies."

Barnabas called breathily from the rear office. Godiva and Candice exchanged glances. Both shrugged and followed the vampire's voice.

"You're sure it's your poetry?" Godiva whispered, wiping her eyes and blowing her nose.

"Of course I'm sure," she hissed at her friend. "How could you even ask me that! They're the poems about heartbreak I wrote a week or so ago for that poetry class."

"Well, it's just that . . ." But they'd come to Barnabas's office so Godiva clamped her mouth shut.

"Ladies, I'm charmed. Come in and sit, *s'il vous plaît*." Barnabas fluttered his long fingers at the two delicate pink silk Louis XIV chairs that sat regally before his ornately carved mahogany desk. When they were seated the vampire launched into a breathy speech in his trademark poorly rendered French accent. "Do *pardon* my abruptness out there, but it's been wretchedly stressful since I put up that new display. That is no excuse for *moi* rudeness, though. It is just such a shock— such a surprise. *Mon dieu!* Who would have imagined that such a magnificent discovery would have been made at my humble gallery? Oh! How rude of me. Introductions are in order. I am Barnabas Vlad, the proprietor of this humble *galerie d'art*." He peered at Godiva for a moment, squinting his eyes so that his iridescent pink eye shadow creased unattractively. Then his expression cleared. "Ah, *oui oui oui*! I do know you. Are you not Godiva Tawdry, one of the Tawdry witches?"

Godiva looked pleased at her notoriety. "*Oui!*" she said. Now that she'd stopped crying she was able to appreciate the humor of the undead guy's foppishly fake Frenchness.

He turned to Candice with a smile that showed way too many long, sharp teeth. "And you are our poetess! You look familiar to me, *madam*, but I'm sorry to say that I have misplaced your name."

"I'm Candice Cox," she said.

The vampire's pleasant expression instantly changed to confusion. "*Mais non!* It is not possible!"

"Okay, this is really starting to piss me off. I wrote the poems a week or so ago for an online class I'm taking for my master's. I can prove it. I turned them in last Friday. Now I want to know how you got them, who this artist is who has illustrated them, and why you all"—here she paused to glare at Godiva—"think it's so impossible that I wrote them. I may be a high school teacher, but I do have a brain!"

"*Madam!* I meant no disrespect." The vampire definitely looked flustered. "It is just . . ." He dabbed at his upper lip with a lacy black hankie before going on. "Are you not the English teacher whose magic is nonmagic?"

"Yes," Candice ground from between gritted teeth.

"Then that is why it is impossible that you have written the poems."

"What the hell—" Candice sputtered and started to get up, but Godiva's firm hand on her arm stopped her.

"Candice," Godiva said. "The poems have magic."

"*Exactement!*" Barnabas said, clearly relieved that Godiva had stepped in.

"Magic? But how? I don't understand," Candice said.

"You saw the people. Your poems made them cry. They made *me* cry. When I looked at the paintings and then read your words, I thought my heart would break with sadness. It was awful—and wonderful." Godiva teared up again just thinking about it.

"That is how everyone has been reacting," Barnabas said. "Since I put them on display this morning. Weeping and blubbering, blubbering and weeping."

"But where did you get them?" Candice felt as if she'd just gotten off a Tilt-a-Whirl and couldn't quite get her bearings.

"They were in a plain brown package I found by the rear door to the gallery this morning. I opened it, and my heart began to break. *Naturellement* I instantly put them on display."

"So who left the package?"

He shrugged. "It did not say. There was only this note in the package."

Candice snatched the paper from his expensively gloved fingers. Typed on a plain white piece of regular computer paper it said:

If the poet would like to work with me again I would be willing. Tell her that I will meet her here at the gallery tonight at sunset.

"But there's no signature or anything," Candice said.

"Artists." Barnabas sighed and rolled his eyes.

"Okay, none of this makes any sense. The artist seems to know who I am, but I have no idea who this person is, how he or she got my poems. I mean, I just wrote them for the online class. I typed them into the computer, attached them to my e-mail, and sent them to the creative writing professor. Then I put the originals into a file labeled with the proper class. I suppose someone at the university could have gotten to them. The only other copies were blown away one day in a freak windstorm."

Godiva shifted guiltily in her chair.

Candice shot her a narrowed look. "What do you know about this, Godiva Tawdry?"

"Nothing!" she said quickly.

"So you did not print them in such lovely calligraphy?" Barnabas asked.

"No! Not even my handwritten copies looked anything like those." Candice got up and marched to the front window. She yanked both framed poems from the easels on which they were displayed. As an afterthought she made little shooing motions at the gawking, crying people. Then she hurried back to Barnabas's office.

"Let me see them," Godiva said. Candice gave them to her and the witch studied the poems. "This is hand-lettered with a calligraphy quill—nothing computer-generated about it." She kept staring at the poetry, and suddenly her eyes widened. "It's not working!"

"What?" Candice asked.

"The magic. I'm not feeling anything." She looked apologetically at her friend as she handed the poems back. "They're perfectly lovely poems, but I'm not crying."

"So the magic's gone?" She should have known it. No way would she really have magic. She glanced at Barnabas. The vampire looked stricken.

"Wait. I have an idea," Godiva said. Flouncing herself over to the window, she grabbed one of the paintings, noting that all the criers had dried up and drifted away. She returned with the picture. "I need the poem that goes with this one."

Candice looked at the green-eyed woman in the cave of ice, and was in the process of handing the free verse poem to her friend when she gasped and stared at the painting.

"The eyes! I knew there was something about them. She has my eyes."

Barnabas looked from the painting to the teacher. "*Mon dieu!* You are right, *madam.*"

"The other one has your hair," Godiva said.

"Holy shit," Candice said.

"Give me the poem."

Candice let Godiva take it out of her numb fingers. The witch held the poem up beside the picture. Almost immediately the vampire started to sniffle. Through his tears he said rapturously, "It has returned! The magic has returned!"

"It never went away," Godiva said. "It just doesn't work without the paintings."

"That is weird as hell," Candice said.

"*Madam,*" Barnabas gushed breathily into the silence, "I would like to commission you and the artist for twelve more poetry paintings. And I would be willing to pay you this amount of money." He scribbled a number down on a piece of pink notepaper and slid it over the desk to Candice.

She picked up the paper. She blinked. And blinked again. She could not believe the amount of zeros on the paper. "You want to pay me this for twelve poems?"

"*Mais non!*" He looked offended. "I would pay you this for each of the twelve poems, as long as your artist agrees to illustrate them. "*Naturellement*, I would pay the artist the same commission. I have already called my brother in Denver. As soon as you and the artist *fini*, we will have a grand opening exhibit in the city that will be *très extraordinaire!*"

Candice wasn't sure she could breathe. "But I don't even know who the artist is."

"We're idiots!" Godiva said. "Isn't there a signature on the paintings?"

"No, *madam sorcière*. I studied each painting for the artist's signature. What I found was odd, not a normal signature at all."

"Well, what did you find?" Candice asked, staring at the painting.

"In the bottom right corner of each is a miniature reproduction of a full moon. That is the only signature the artist left."

Candice sighed. "Looks like I'll be here at sunset to meet this mysterious artist."

"But I think you should go home and change first," Godiva said. "Those jogging shorts are frayed and you spilled banana split all over your shirt."

Candice was too busy wondering at the amazing events to notice Godiva's self-satisfied little smile.

Eleven

Candice was more excited than nervous. She dressed carefully, purposefully picking artsy clothes instead of the boring teacher crap that hung in the front of her closet. *A poetess!* she told herself, *I'm going to dress like a poetess.*

She chose a silk skirt that she'd bought in a funky shop in Manitou Springs the last time she'd visited the Colorado Springs area. Its scalloped hem flirted a couple of inches above her knees and it made her feel pretty and feminine. She matched a sleeveless black top with it and then hung her new necklace around her neck. It was a waterfall of amber beads and she realized that she'd bought it only because it reminded her of Justin's eyes—but she couldn't seem to help herself. *This job will help me get over him. And if it keeps up it'll be my ticket out of here. Denver, here I come!* She pointedly ignored the fact that rumor said Justin was living in Denver. It didn't matter. Denver was a big city, and she'd never run into him. She didn't hang in the coed crowd. Instead of thinking about Justin, Candice slid on a pair of strappy black sandals, gave her hair one more fluff, and rushed out to her Mini.

The sun was just setting when she pulled up in front of the gallery. She was relieved that Barnabas had taken the paintings and poetry out of the display window. She really didn't want to wade through another crowd of crying people to get to the door.

Stepping into the gallery she was met by Barnabas, who was wringing his hands.

"The artist insists on meeting alone with you, *madam*," he said. "I will go, but I will be back in *exactement* one hour to hear your decision. *Au revoir* until later, then."

"But where's the artist?"

"In the rear gallery. That is where I have hung your work." With one more worried glance around his gallery, the vampire minced out the door.

Candice straightened her shoulders and walked to the rear gallery. He was standing with his back to her, studying the two paintings that hung beside the framed poems. *He's really tall,* was her first thought. He was wearing a dark, conservative suit that fit his broad shoulders well and tapered nicely down to his waist. His thick sand-colored hair was short and neatly cut. He didn't seem to notice that she was there.

"Hi. My name is Candice Cox and I'm the poet," she said, wishing she'd given more thought to how she would introduce herself.

"I know who you are," he said without turning around.

Candice blinked. Was she so excited that her ears were playing tricks on her? That voice. She knew that voice. Didn't she?

"Why did you write these poems?" he asked.

"As an assignment for a class I'm taking." She felt the air slowly being squeezed out of her.

"Was that the only reason?" He still didn't turn around.

"No," she said softly. "When I wrote them I tried to explain how I was feeling."

"And how was that?"

"My heart had been broken. I made a stupid mistake and jumped to a conclusion that wasn't the right one."

Finally, the artist turned slowly around. His amber eyes met hers. "You weren't all that mistaken."

She couldn't believe it was really him. With his hair cut and his suit he looked . . . he looked like a man who could take on the world and win.

"I've missed you, Candy."

"Justin, I—I . . ." She tried to put together a coherent sentence while her emotions swirled.

"I'm sorry!" they said together.

"I should have given you a chance to explain," she blurted out.

"No! I shouldn't have gone to that stupid party to begin with," he said. "I want you to know that I wasn't going there to be with another woman."

"I know that," she said.

He took a couple of steps toward her. "Did I really break your heart?"

"Yes," she whispered.

"Is there any way you could let me fix it?" he asked.

"Yes," she whispered again. Then she closed the space between them and stepped into his arms. He bent to kiss her, but her words stopped him. "You're the artist!"

He smiled. "I am."

"So you found your inspiration in my poetry?"

"No. I found my inspiration in the woman whose heart finally became soft enough to be broken, and when I did I understood that separately we are just a gigolo wolf and a burned-out teacher, but together . . ." His lips gently brushed against hers.

"Together we make magic," she finished for him.

Epilogue

The art gallery, Dark Shadows II, was located in trendy downtown Denver, nestled between a Starbucks and a posh designer jewelry shop. It was a popular place, known for its unique exhibits and for discovering talented new artists. But even for a popular gallery, tonight's opening was busy. No, not busy—mobbed. The gallery owner, Quentin Vlad (whom everyone in Denver believed to be eccentric and odd, which was partially true . . . the other part was that he was a vampire—something that no one needed to know) was all atwitter. Dollar signs were blazing in his eyes, and he didn't even mind that he'd had to hire extra security to control the crowd. Sold! Every available piece in the exhibit had been sold within the first hour of the opening.

He could hardly believe his brother's amazing find! Who would have imagined it? A nonmagical poet and an untrained artist werewolf—put them together and they create art that evokes feelings in the people who view it *even outside the boundaries of Mysteria*!

Now that was magic.

"Fifty thousand! I'll up my offer to fifty thousand dollars!"

Quentin looked into the flushed face of the sweaty man who was staring, mesmerized, at the spectacular painting and poem that hung side by side in the central room of the gallery. "Sir, I'm sorry. I told you the first twelve times you inquired as to its price. That particular piece is part of the artist and poet's personal collection. It is not for sale."

"Everything's for sale," the man quipped. "Everything has a price."

"Not that piece."

The deep voice came from behind them. Quentin and the desperate man looked back to see a tall, handsome young man dressed in dark jeans, a T-shirt, and a black leather jacket. He had his arm around a woman who wore funky, artsy clothes. Her thick blonde hair was loose, framing the arresting green in her eyes perfectly. She leaned into his side intimately.

"No." She smiled. "Not that piece."

He bent to kiss her and, arm in arm, they strolled into one of the other crowded rooms of the gallery.

The sweaty-faced man's gaze stayed with them a moment, but soon his eyes were drawn back to the painting and the poem—as was everyone's attention. The painting was wondrous, a blending eroticism and beauty so breathtaking that it, alone, would have been an attention-getter in any gallery. But mix it with the poem that was displayed in intricate calligraphy and framed beside it, and wondrous evolved into spectacular . . . magical. As couples read the poem they gravitated together. Lone readers sighed wistfully. Some rushed out of the gallery, already on their cell phones to their lovers. Some just stood and stared, weeping silently at what was missing in their own lives. Some, like the sweaty-faced man, decided that if they just owned the piece then somehow, miraculously, love would find its way into their lives.

"It's what I want; what I have to have," the sweaty man said to no one in particular. "It has to be my story." He looked at Quentin one last time. "I really can't buy this?"

"No, you really can't."

The man's eyes moved back to the artwork. "But maybe I can get her to forgive me—ask her for a second chance." His eyes brightened and some of the desperate flush went out of his face. Quentin decided that he must be much more attractive when he wasn't so, well, sweaty and florid. "That's it! I'm going to ask her for a second chance!" He gripped Quentin's thin hand. "Thank you, Mr. Vlad! And thank the artist and the poet, too!" Then he rushed from the gallery.

Quentin grimaced and discreetly wiped his palm on his hand-tailored Italian suit. But like everyone in the room, his eyes were pulled unerringly back to the wall where the art was exhibited. The painting was almost life-sized. The medium was textured oil, so the nudes looked rich, their skin almost alive. Their bodies were twined together in an intimate embrace—erotic yet loving—sexual and sensual. Their faces were indistinct, and Quentin thought then, as he had the first time he'd seen the piece, about the brilliance of the artist. He'd created a painting that allowed each viewer to imagine his or her own face within the scene. But the woman's hair was distinctive—thick and long and blonde. The man in the painting fisted it in his desire as it cascaded around her shoulders. Quentin shivered. Even he was not immune to the passion in the piece. His eyes shifted to the poem and, again, he was captured in the poet's web as he read:

Second Chance

Remember when it went wrong,
When the fabric of our universe tore . . . frayed . . . dissolved?

But then you turned back time
and we escaped from the prison of withered desire
I flung my arms wide and embraced
passion newborn.

Because you turned back time
I dance naked, joyously teasing the fiery sun,
safe in the knowledge that even Apollo's
warmth cannot compare to
the heat of your caresses.

When you turned back time
I found the way to nurture
soft, sweet words
in my emerald meadow
I wound around you, a clear, cooling stream
soothing and nourishing,
helping you, in turn, to feel renewed.

And in that renewing
        found my own magic
        with you.

Beside the poem hung a placard that told about the artist and the poet. It read:

The medium of our work is not important. It varies from piece to piece. We do not focus on techniques or styles. We simply focus on the same thing we'd like you to focus on—the true magic of love, which will always transcend time and disbelief. May all of you live happily ever after. . . .

                                          —Justin and Candice Woods

DISDAINING TROUBLE

MaryJanice Davidson

This is for the girls, who know who they are (if you want to know who they are, check the dedication page from Mysteria*). They turn these projects into an awfully good time. Who said writing was work? Okay, my grandpa. And Jenny Hildebrandt. And Jessica Growette. And my sister. And my sister-in-law. And—well, I like it, anyway.*

ACKNOWLEDGMENTS

I owe many people thanks for this story, primarily all the readers who bought *Mysteria* without which, natch, there would be no sequel. So thanks for unlimbering the credit cards, y'all!

Thanks also are due to my long-suffering editor, Cindy Hwang, and my agent, Ethan Ellenberg, who really didn't suffer much at all.

Triplet: One of three children born at one birth.
                —The American Heritage Dictionary of the English Language

Too good for mere wit. It contains a deep practical truth, this triplet.
                —Herbert J. C. Grierson, The Good Morrow

Prologue

When the Desdaine triplets were born on a frigid February night (Withering came first, then Derisive, then Scornful, all sunny-side up and staring with big blue eyes at the ceiling), the doctor and attending nurse screamed and screamed. This startled Mrs. Desdaine, who started doing quite a bit of screaming herself, despite the epidural. Two other nurses and a resident also came running, and so did a custodian, wielding a mop like a lance.

The doctor was screaming because the nurse had dropped a tray full of sterilized instruments on his foot, and a scalpel was sticking out of his little toe. The nurse was screaming because he knew his clumsiness was going to cost him his job. Derisive, Scornful, and Withering just stared at the hysteria greeting their first moments out of the womb, then obligingly yowled when the cold air bit their fair skin and they were poked and prodded and (finally) swaddled in warm blankets. (The janitor went away, presumably to mop something; ditto the superfluous personnel.)

Of course, even in a town like Mysteria, natural triplets (that is, triplets born without the aid of artificial means like IVF or a really good splitting spell) were rare, and triplets that brought about screaming fits from qualified medical personnel were rarer still.

So it wasn't long before stories began to spring up about the Desdaine triplets. The why behind the stories became blurred over time, but the plain truth behind the stories—the triplets were weird—never shaded much one way or the other.

On their second birthday, the girls discovered they could do magic.

On their third birthday, they discovered if they cooperated, they could do *more* magic.

On their fifth birthday, they decided being good guys was for suckers.

And on their sixth, they decided they could count on no one but themselves, but that was perfectly all right. Mom was scolding and loving and superb at not noticing things; Dad had died a month before they were born.

And so time passed, probably the only magic those who don't live in Mysteria are aware of or care about. And the triplets grew older, but not fast enough to suit them or their mother.

One

"Ho-ho," Derisive chortled. "Here he comes."

The triplets were sunning themselves by the wishing well, a charming stone well shaded by trees in the center of town. They had chased the night mare away for the sixth night in a row with a combination of charms and spit spells and were celebrating by torturing the mailman, who was a drunk, a kicker of cats, and unpleasant besides.

The girls, who were beautiful and knew it (bad) but attached no importance to it (not so bad), were identically dressed in denim shorts, red tank tops, and white flip-flops. Although most twins and triplets outgrew the dressing-in-the-same-outfit stage by, oh, sixteen months, the Desdaines liked it. The better to fool you with, my dear.

"Mom alert?" Withering asked, squinting. Their mother, thank all the devils, was nowhere in sight.

Scornful waved her hand in the direction of the Begorra Irish Emporium. "Still looking at those tacky little leprechauns."

"Not so tacky," Withering reminded her sister. "They do grant one wish."

"Yawn," Scornful replied. "Little silly wishes, like not overdoing the turkey. Nothing significant."

"Do-gooder alert?"

Derisive also waved a hand. "Do-gooder" encompassed three-fourths of the town; there were so few really *evil* people around these days. That would change when they grew up. As it was, at fourteen, they were formidable. If a Mysteria resident wasn't a do-gooder, they were neutral, and stayed out of things. This suited the triplets fine. "No problems. Everybody's at lunch."

"Here he comes," Withering said, her nails sinking into Scornful's arm like talons. She ignored her sister's yelp of pain. Her conscience was clear, but then, it usually was. Besides, Mr. Raggle, the postal carrier, wouldn't be the focus of their wrath if he hadn't called their mother That Name. And in front of the whole pizza parlor, too. "Jerkweed," she added.

"Now," Derisive said, and all three girls made the sign of a V with their fingers, spat through the Vs, then stomped on the spit. They visualized Mr. Raggle coming to harm and, before the thought had barely formed in their treacherous teenaged minds—

"Hey! Help! Aaaagggghhh!"

"Scared of heights," Scornful said thoughtfully, eyeing the postal carrier who had been picked up by unseen forces and flung into the highest branch of the closest maple tree.

"Probably shouldn't have mentioned that where you could hear," Withering said, smiling with approval. She rarely smiled, and both her sisters took it as a gift, and not without astonishment.

"Teach him to call our mother names," Derisive added, and spat again for good measure.

"Girls!"

"Uh-oh."

Derisive craned to look. "Must have run out of leprechauns to look at."

"You girls!" Their mother was running toward them at full speed, black curly hair bobbing all over the place. The triplets knew they took after their late father; their mother was petite, while they already had two inches on her; she was dark-eyed, while their eyes were sky-colored; and they had straight blond hair that hardly moved in gale-force winds. "Girls! I swear, I can't turn my back on you for five seconds!"

"That's true," Withering said. "You can't."

"Get him down! Right . . . *now*!"

The triplets studied their mother, whom they loved but did not like, and tried to gauge the seriousness of her mood. A grounding, they did not need. Not with Halloween only three months away.

"Girls!" Panting, shoving her hair out of her eyes, even wheezing a little, Giselle Desdaine staggered up to her girls and glared at them so hard her eyeballs actually bulged. That was enough for the triplets, who, as one, made the V with their fingers, said, *"Extant,"* in unison, and spat.

Mr. Raggle shot out of the tree just as their mother said, "Why don't you just *grow up*?!?" He plowed into Withering, knocking them both back into the wishing well.

TWO

Thad Wilson was back in Mysteria, and not at all happy about it. Unfortunately, he had been born here, lived the first twelve years of his life here, and had taken fifteen years to realize that Mysteria got into your blood like a poison. The kind that wouldn't kill you but just kept you generally miserable.

An air force brat, his father had re-upped the spring he was in seventh grade (Thad, not his father), and around and around the country they went: Boston, Minot, Ellsworth, San Antonio, Vance, Nellis, Cannon. No wishing wells that really worked, no werewolves who disappeared during the full moon. No witches, no horses that brought nightmares. No wish-granting knickknacks. Just missile silos and PXs.

He'd been so bored he thought he'd puke. And as if bouncing around with his folks hadn't been enough, once he was of legal age, he'd moved to six cities in five years. Finally, he'd given up and come back to Mysteria. He'd had no doubts about finding it. Once you lived there, you could always get back.

As it happened, the local river nymph (what had her name been? Pat? Pit?) had sold the building, and he'd bought it, turning it into a pizza place. Living in Chicago and Boston had taught him what real pizza was supposed to taste like, and by God, he'd show the other Mysteria residents just what—

He heard shrieking, dropped the dough, and bolted out the door. Lettering in track in both high school and college stood him in good stead now; his long legs took him to the scene of the crime (because, since the Desdaine triplets were involved, what else could it be?) in no time.

"You girls!" Mrs. Desdaine was yelling. The girls—whom Thad had very studiously avoided since getting back to town, they just *reeked* of trouble and were way too cute for jailbait—looked uncomfortable and unrepentant. "Get him down right now! *Girls!*"

That's when he noticed the mailman, an unpleasant drunk named—what? Ragman? Raggle?—come sailing out of the tree and slam one of the triplets into the wishing well.

"Oh, shit," he said, screeching to a halt before he could topple into the well himself.

Three

Mrs. Desdaine had helped the wet and enraged postal employee out of the fountain, and the man had run off without so much as a thank-you, which surprised Thad not at all.

Almost immediately after that, a creature shockingly ugly popped up out of the fountain. It smelled, if possible, worse than it looked: like rotten eggs marinating in vomit. It was about five feet tall, squat, with four arms and a long, balancing tail. It was poison green and had what appeared to be a thousand teeth.

Then Thad noticed that the creature turned the exact same shade of gray as the blocks making up the well. Ugly as hell, and a chameleon, too. Terrific.

Mrs. Desdaine was screaming. The two (dry) triplets were screaming. People were starting to come out of their stores, much too slowly, and he put on speed.

He was, in the language of the fey, *naragai*, which literally translated to "no will."

What it actually meant was that he had inherited nothing from his fairy mother: not the immortality, not the strength, not the wings, not even the height (at six feet four inches, his mother was five inches taller than he was). Human genes, he had decided long ago, must be super dominant, because he took after his father in every way.

But he could run like a bastard, which he did now.

"Watch out, watch out!" he yelled, nearly toppling into the fountain himself as he tried to put on the brakes.

"That thing ate Withering!" one of the triplets wailed.

"My baby!" Mrs. Desdaine yowled.

The thing—it looked like a cross between a man and a velociraptor—climbed out of the fountain and stood on the brick walk, dripping and growling and slashing its tail back and forth like a whip.

Thad had no idea what he was going to do to it. Kick it? Breathe on it? Try to drown it without getting his face bitten off?

Then another figure rose from the water, this one a tall, luscious blonde dressed in tattered leathers and armed to the teeth; he counted two daggers and one sword, and those were just the ones he could immediately see.

"Wha?" was all he could manage.

She looked like she was in her early twenties, and he was amazed she'd come out of the fountain, which was only eighteen inches deep. Of course, the lizard man had come out of the fountain, too.

She smiled at Lizard Guy. "This will not end well for you."

Lizard Guy snapped and snarled and wiggled all four arms at her. Its thighs were as big as tree trunks.

The gorgeous blonde did something with her sword; she was so quick he didn't quite catch it. It was almost like she'd flipped it out of her back sheath and was now holding it easily in her left hand. She saluted the monster with it, smiling a little. *Great* smile.

"*Dakan eei verdant,*" she said, trilling her *r*. "*Compara denara.*"

Lizard Guy lunged at her. She ducked easily under the swing and parried with one of her own. "I've chased you across three worlds and ten years," she said, almost conversationally. "Did you think I would let you get away now?"

Thad wasn't sure if this was in addition to what she had said, or if she was translating what she had said. What was interesting was that she wasn't out of breath, didn't look excited or flushed . . . just businesslike.

Her backswing lopped off Lizard Guy's head.

"*Cantaka et nu,*" she said, saluting the headless (gushing . . . purple blood, ech!) body. "*Deren va.*"

The other two girls had stopped screaming, and Scornful (or was it Derisive?) kicked Lizard Guy's head out of the way. Thad had to give her props for her rapid recovery. He was still having trouble following the events of the last forty seconds.

"Are you—are you Withering?" Scornful asked in a tentative voice Thad would not have believed any of the triplets capable of.

The grown woman looked around and frowned. "*Cander va iee*—I just left, did I not?"

"I—I wished you'd grow up," Mrs. Desdaine said faintly, looking like she might swoon into the water. "And then you were gone. But you came right back."

At once the woman went to Mrs. Desdaine and knelt, the point of her sword hitting the bricks with a clunk and actually chipping off a piece. "O my mother, when this woman was a girl, she caused you many trials. This woman would ask forgiveness and would spend her life making things right for thee."

"What?" the other three Desdaines gasped in unison.

"Please, this woman asks most humbly," the tall blonde said, her gaze fixed on the bricks.

"That's not Withering," the other two said in unison.

"This woman certainly is."

"Honey, get up off the ground," Mrs. Desdaine said, pushing back matted dark curls. "It's fine, everything's fine. I'm just glad you're—you're back." She choked a bit on that last, but Thad thought she did a fine job of pretending she didn't mind missing the entire adolescence of one of her children.

"Hi," Thad said, utterly dazzled. "I'm Thad Wilson; I run the pizza place across the street."

Slowly, she rose until she was at exact eye level. Her blond hair was matted to her head, and she was dripping all over everything; her sword was stained purple, and he still couldn't take his eyes off her. "Sir, this woman is pleased to meet you."

"Look at you!" Derisive (or was it Scornful?) said, circling the woman. "You're all grown-up and bulgy. And you're talking with a seriously weird accent."

"It took many years to find my way back."

"Let's talk about it," Thad suggested, "over a pizza."

The woman—Withering—cracked a grin. "This woman has not had a pizza in some time. This woman would be delighted."

And so they trooped across the street.

Four

Withering ate as if someone was going to take it away from her. Given the state of her clothing (clearly homemade from animal skins) and the way her collarbones jutted, Thad guessed her meals were hard to come by.

And where had she been in the five seconds—fifteen years?—she'd been gone? Someplace demanding . . . even unforgiving.

Scornful and Derisive weren't at all happy with the new development, it was obvious to see. Normally you couldn't shut them up. But now the girls picked at their lunch and couldn't stop staring at their sister, then at each other, then at Withering.

Thad couldn't help staring at Withering, either, but for an entirely different reason.

"Honey, I'm so sorry," Mrs. Desdaine was saying, mournfully sprinkling red pepper flakes on her pizza slice. "I never should have said something like that around the wishing well. I've lived in this town my entire life, and I can't believe I was so careless—and at my own daughter's expense!"

"You meant no harm. And, if this woman's memory is correct, we were causing trouble in the first place."

"Traitor," Scornful muttered, picking another slice of pepperoni off her pizza.

"Wicked tall traitor," Derisive added, pushing her plate away.

"I don't care!" their mother cried. "You obviously were sent somewhere awful and forced to grow up there. Your clothes—and your weapons—and you're so *thin*."

Withering looked surprised, as if she wasn't used to anyone worrying about her. Probably she wasn't. "This woman adapted."

"Can you use some pronouns now?" Derisive snapped. "The whole 'this woman' bit is getting real old."

"You shush, Derisive," their mother ordered. "Tell me, Withering, dear. How long were you—were you wherever you were?"

Withering shrugged. "This wom—I didn't keep count. Long enough to survive and take over the realm."

"Realm?" Thad said, speaking for the first time.

"The demonic realm I fell into. I learned to fight by killing demons. And when the time was right, I killed the leader and took over. The one you saw in the water—that was someone trying to snatch back the crown."

"So you're like a queen in that other place?" Scornful said, finally sounding a little—just a little—impressed.

Withering shrugged. "I lead. But now . . ." She looked around the nearly deserted pizza parlor. "I know not where my place is."

"It's with your family, of course," her mother said firmly.

"Perhaps, O my mother," she replied, but she looked doubtful.

"Well, why not?" Thad asked.

Withering looked uncomfortable. "It may not be . . . safe. For me to remain here."

"Of course you're going to remain here," her mother said sharply.

"Yes," Scornful added, then giggled. "This woman will stay."

"You don't have to decide anything right this minute," Thad pointed out and was rewarded with one of her rare, rich smiles.

Five

Withering landed in black dust with a skull-rattling thud. The breath whooshed out of her lungs, and for a moment she just lay there, gasping and inhaling that strange dust.

She painfully climbed to her feet, looking around in bewilderment. She was in an utterly strange, utterly *alien* place. The colors and textures were all wrong; they actually hurt her eyes. She was in a large circle of black dust, beyond which was bright blue grass. It appeared to be an oasis of some kind, because beyond the grass was a waterfall gushing purple water over green rocks.

What had happened? Where the hell was she?

She remembered her mother shouting, she remembered that nasty postal worker knocking her into the—

Oh, no.

No, no, no.

"Mother! Please come get me!" In her extremity of terror, she was screaming. "Please don't *leave* me here!"

"This man . . . is pleased . . . to see this girl."

Her head snapped around, and she saw a grievously wounded man lying about ten feet away, on the edge of the blue grass. He had blood all over him, and every time he gasped for breath, blood bubbles foamed across his lips.

She scrambled over to him. "Where am I? What happened to you?"

His pupils were blown, actually bleeding into the whites of his eyes. She was awfully afraid she was going to barf. Never had she seen someone so hurt. And everything was happening so *fast*, she couldn't—

"Kellmannd Dimension," he groaned. "Demons . . . this man is done. This girl will take over."

"I don't understand. Do you know how I can get back?"

"Nobody gets back. We . . . fight. And die. And someone new comes."

"Fight? Fight who?"

The man managed a nod over her shoulder and coughed. She spared a glance . . . and nearly screamed. The ugliest creature she had ever seen was inching toward her, making its way across the blue grass, thick tail dragging, wrathful growls ripping out of its lungs.

"Take these." He pulled a knife and a sword from somewhere and handed them to her; they were so slick with gore she nearly dropped them. "And fight. Do not . . . fear. We are . . . the forces for good."

Withering had been called many things in her fourteen years, but a force for good wasn't one of them.

"Find . . . the others . . . of this man's kind. And . . . lead."

"But I don't—"

"Behind . . . you . . ."

She stood, holding the sword straight out, and the monster, which had been coming fast, couldn't slow in time and impaled itself on the point.

Not too bright, then. That's something.

She yanked the sword free, gagging at all the purple gore, and neatly sidestepped as the thing fell to the ground. She turned back to the man and discovered he had died during the brief fight.

She stood, looking around the odd landscape, sword dripping, panting slightly from the adrenaline rush. For good or ill, she was stuck here indefinitely. Apparently strangers dropping in out of nowhere was quite the common occurrence around here.

So. She would fight. She would defend.

She would *live.*

Oh, but her mother and her sisters . . . how could she turn her back on her family? It was too awful, resigning herself to never seeing them again. She'd give anything—anything—to hear her mother scolding her again.

She resolved to put them out of her mind and to keep them there.

A solitary tear trickled down one cheek; she wiped her face, wiped the sword on the grass, and went to look for other people.

≈

Six

MYSTERIA, SECONDARY EARTH
NOW

Withering obediently followed her mother and sisters out of the food place (restaurant? Gods and devils, how long since she had been in a restaurant?), leaving Thad behind to make more pizza pies. She was still having trouble following the events of the last hour. One minute she'd been chasing that horrid Katai, the next there was a crash of light and sound and *normal*-colored water (except the clear water seemed wrong to her, after all the years of purple water) and she was back with her honored mother and sisters.

And that strange man! Thick dark hair, wonderful chocolate (ahhh, chocolate! How long since she'd had some?) colored eyes. Lean, muscular body, and very quick on his feet. Spookily quick.

She had been impressed at how he had rushed over to help; she could sense no magic in him, nothing especially extraordinary. And yet he had jumped into the fray without hesitation.

And how long since she had looked at a man as a potential mate instead of a fighting partner? Back in the demonic realm, her couplings had been quick and very nearly emotionless; two people trying to snatch a little warmth because one or both would very likely die the next day. Now that she was back, perhaps there would be time for . . .

No. She had responsibilities. She had to keep the portal between Earth Prime and Secondary Earth closed; Mysteria was a wonderful place and did not deserve demonic infestation. She had to get back, and quickly.

But why? It isn't fair! I'm home now, I belong here, not Earth Prime.

But did she? Did she really? She knew now, as she had not many years ago, that special people fell into the demonic realm every few years, that they were charged with keeping the demons in their place.

She had been the first to wrest power from the demons and take over the entire realm. But her position would always be precarious; the demons wouldn't stand for her leadership. Now that she was back—now that her mother's wish had been granted—did that mean she had to put aside any chance for happiness?

She did not know.

"And you remember the home place, Withering, dear." Her mother was leading her into the old house. Strange how small everything looked! "And we'll just—ah—your bedroom is—you remember."

She did. She looked around the master bedroom (her mother had taken the guest room and had given the triplets the largest bedroom), eyeing the bunk beds and the twin bed against the opposite wall. She looked at the dressers and closet, which would be filled with clothes that were too small, not to mention age-inappropriate.

Her sisters said nothing, only watched her.

And suddenly, she felt like crying.

Seven

Janameides knocked on the door of the red house with black shingles. He was on a mission from his queen, Potameides, a river nymph whose territory encompassed the entire Mississippi River.

After a moment, the door opened, and a short, chubby brunette stood in the doorway.

"Hey!" she said by way of greeting. "You look like my friend Pot!"

"It is my honor," he said, "to be her subject. I am Janameides."

"Well, come in, come in. My husband's not here right now, but I—"

"I am here to see you, madam."

"Okeydokey." She stepped back and let him in. The house was all right (he preferred open water), with wooden floors and cream-colored walls.

"Who the hell is that?" a rude voice said out of nowhere.

"It's Janameides. He's a friend of Pot's."

"Well, what the hell is he doing here?"

"I dunno. I'm Charlene," she said to him, "but I imagine you knew that."

"Yes, ma'am. Is that the ghost?" he asked in a near whisper.

"I can hear you," the ghost snapped.

"Sorry. Who is she?"

"I can *still* hear you. If you must know, I was a roofer and got my stupid self killed patching a hole."

"And had the bad manners to stick around," Charlene said cheerfully. "Now. What can we do for you, Janameides?"

"My queen asked me to check on her friends. As you may know, she became very attached to some of Mysteria's residents during her exile here."

Charlene nodded. Pot—Potameides—had been exiled from her beloved river and had only been able to go back last year, when a coup returned her to power. Since then, there hadn't been a word.

"You know my name, ma'am," Janameides said politely to the ghost. "Might I have yours?"

"Mind your own damned business."

"It's Rae," Charlene said helpfully.

"Traitor!"

"Oh, hush up." She turned back to a bemused Janameides. "As you can see, we're doing just fine. Please give Pot our warmest regards."

"Don't give her my regards," Rae bitched. "She took off, so she's dead to me."

"Says the dead woman," Charlene muttered.

"I heard that!"

"What are you still doing here, Rae?" Janameides asked.

"Why do you care?"

"I do not know," he admitted. His queen had told him about the ghost, not glossing over her unpleasant personality, but he was intrigued despite his queen's well-meant warning. He felt sorry for Rae, stuck in this house for almost a century. "But I am interested."

"I'm the handyman."

"It's true," Charlene piped up. "She keeps the furnace running, she keeps everything up to code. I never have to so much as call a plumber."

"Flattery will get you nowhere," the ghost said sourly.

"But do you not wish to—to move on?"

"Move on *where*?"

"Wherever people go when they die."

"Rae will never admit it," Charlene said, "but she loves it here. And she loved Potameides."

"Didn't!"

"Without a house to take care of and my husband and me to nag, she'd be lost."

"Lies!"

From down the hall, they heard a baby start to cry. "Oh, nice going," Charlene said, exasperated. "You woke the baby."

"Oh, like that's a big trick. That thing doesn't sleep; it catnaps for thirty seconds at a time."

"That thing," she said sternly, "is my daughter, and that's quite enough of your attitude, miss."

"Mmmph," the ghost said.

"Excuse me," Charlene said, and hurried out of the room.

"So, Jan," the ghost said, "anybody ever tell you, you smell like the deep end of a swimming pool?"

"No."

"Not that it's a bad smell," she added hastily. "It's just different. Pot smelled the same way, that abandoning cow."

"I must ask you not to speak so about my queen."

"Ask away, pal, and see where that gets you."

"She did warn me about you," he admitted.

"What? That jerk was talking about me? What'd she say? Ooooh, I'll kill her!"

"How can you, if you're discorporated?"

"Just never mind. What'd she say?"

"She said you were unpleasant and rude as a defensive mechanism because you're really quite lonely."

"Lies!"

"Well," he said, drumming his long fingers on the kitchen table, "perhaps we can discuss that."

Eight

Thad managed to stay away from Withering Desdaine for a whole day, until he gave in and brought a pizza to her house. He was knocking on the door when he felt cold steel slip around his throat. This was disconcerting, to put it mildly.

"Uh . . ." He coughed. Cripes, he hadn't heard her move, much less get the drop on him. "Lunch?"

"Oh! This woman apologizes. Old habits, you know." He turned and saw Withering sheathe her knife. She had obviously been taken shopping, because she was wearing jeans and a T-shirt, both of which fit snugly. Also, she had on her sword and both knives. It was startlingly sexy.

"And you brought food!" She greedily snatched the pizza box from him. "This woman is so grateful."

"This man says it's no sweat. Invite me in?"

She blinked at him with those big baby blues. "Why?"

"Uh . . . so we can share the pizza?"

"Oh. Oh! Of course. Yes, indeed, please come in. My honored mother is at her job, but my sisters are here."

"Terrific," he muttered, following her inside.

"Oh," Scornful said, eyeing him in a distinctly unfriendly way. "It's you."

"It's me," he agreed. "Want some pizza?"

"No."

"Please excuse me for a moment," Withering said. "I was just about to urinate when you came."

"Oh. No problem."

Withering was barely out of the room when Scornful started in. "Look, pal, I know what you're up to."

"You do?" It was downright unnerving, looking at a much younger version of Withering. Same blond hair, same riveting blue eyes. "Odd, because I hardly know myself."

"You're sniffing around my sister like some kind of speed freak dog."

"A speed freak d—?"

"Leave her alone! She's still adjusting to being back. And we're still adjusting to her being—ugh—a grown-up."

"It's just a pizza," he huffed, offended.

"Suuuuuure, McHorny, whatever you say." She was seated at the kitchen table, flipping through a book that was not written in English but instead covered in runes and various squigglings. She slammed the book shut and added, "Look, you think we don't know she's a knock-out? That whole polite/tough/vulnerable thing prob'ly works on you like a hormone shot."

"We are not," he decided, "having this conversation."

"Look, we get it. But she's got enough on her mind right now. Not to mention she's trying to find a way *back*. Or, at least, we think she is," Scornful added in a barely audible mutter. "It's hard for us to tell *what* she's up to; she sure keeps her cards close to the vest."

"Wants to go back? Why in the hell—"

"We don't know, nimrod! She's not talking."

"All right, calm down, don't have a stroke and *don't* cast a spell on me. I hate that shit. Can't she just hop back in the wishing well?"

"You know how capricious that thing is. There's no guarantee she'd end up exactly where she wanted to be."

"Why would she even want to—" He shut up as Withering entered the room. "Have a slice of pepperoni?" he finished.

Scornful looked amused but said nothing.

"Do you think Derisive would like some food?" Withering asked.

"No. She's deep in the Web right now, trying to research your weirdo demon kingdom."

"She's in a web?" Withering looked alarmed. "That doesn't sound safe at all."

Scornful stifled a groan. "Never mind."

"How could she search for another dimension on our Web?" Thad asked.

"Magic, dummy."

"Scornful," Withering said sharply.

"Hey, you're technically the same age as me, so back off."

"I certainly am not; I am your elder, if not necessarily your better, and you will treat our honored guest with respect."

Scornful made a retching sound. "Honored guest? Withering, what the Christ *happened* to you over there?"

"Several things," Withering said dryly. "Watch your language. Now eat, dear one, or begone."

"Can't I do both?" she griped, snatching a piece and flouncing out of the room, her book of runes tucked under one arm.

"I trust you will overlook my dear sister's rudeness. This is a difficult time for her."

"For *her*?" He couldn't believe the mature, supercool Withering was sticking up for *that* brat. If nothing else, being stuck in that hell dimension had sure improved her people skills. He guessed fighting for her life most days and eventually taking over as queen of all demons was almost as good as charm school. "How about for you?"

Withering shrugged, took her own piece, and chewed. "It is . . . difficult for my family. Seeing me as a grown woman after being gone— how long was I gone?"

"About five seconds our time."

"Interesting. And yet it explains much. You can imagine their difficulty."

"Actually, I was a lot more worried about yours."

Withering shrugged again.

"What's this I hear about you going back?"

"That, good sir, is none of yours and all of mine."

Thad mulled that one over for a moment. "Listen. I normally don't thrust myself into other people's lives—"

She nearly choked on her pizza. "No?"

"—but I made an exception in your case. You must have missed your family all these years. Now you're back. Why the hell would you leave again?"

Withering stared at her pizza slice, then put it down as if she had suddenly lost her appetite. "It's complicated, good sir."

"Thad."

"Yes. Thad. I have many responsibilities. And it is not in me to hide in this lovely town while—while things happen that I must prevent."

"Don't you at least deserve a vacation?"

"Vacation?" she asked blankly.

"Or a date?"

"Date?" she asked, just as mystified.

"Do you like bowling?"

"I—I don't quite remember what that is. Is it like hunting?"

"Sure, except with balls and pins instead of swords and slings."

She brightened. "Then I might be good at it!"

"So. We'll go. Tonight. Hey, if you have to go back, I respect that—and like you said, it's none of my business." This was a rather large lie, as he felt (unreasonably, he knew) everything about Withering was his business. Was there another woman in the world—worlds—like her? He thought not. Was he going to let her go so easily? No damned way. "But before you take off, don't you deserve some fun?"

"I—I did not consider that."

"So. I'll pick you up tonight."

"You didn't listen," Scornful yelled from the living room, "to a word I said, McHorny!"

Withering glanced in that direction and frowned. "Please overlook my sister's rudeness."

"I could care less about *that* sister."

"Eh?"

"So," he added brightly. "Pick you up at seven?"

Nine

The late Rae Camille, former roofer and current spirit, watched with interest as Jan the river guy poked around the outside of the house. First he'd knocked on the front door for a good five minutes, but he was shit out of luck. Charlene had taken her smelly baby to a playdate with another drooling, incontinent infant and wouldn't be back until three. And Char's werewolf husband was visiting the Cape on Pack business.

Now he was futzing around in the back garden, and now he was trying the back door. What the hell? Was he some sort of river-nymph thief guy? Yeek.

Now he was—was he? Yes! He was actually kicking the back door with his long, squishy, pale feet. In fact, he looked a great deal like her old friend Pot, Jan's queen: ridiculously tall and too thin.

She could see the skull beneath his face, see the bones stretching through all the limbs. His hair was a sort of greenish blond, like he spent too much time in a chlorinated pool (which, for all she knew, he did). And his eyes were a pale, swimmy green, like a summer pond filled with algae. His eyebrows and lashes were so pale, they actually seemed to disappear. His fingers and toes were weirdly long; his voice low and bubbling, like he was always speaking through water. It should have been creepy, but it was sort of—what? Interesting? Yeah. Even soothing.

"Rae?" he called in that odd, bubbling voice. "Rae? May I enter?"

He was here to see *her*? Yeesh, when was the last time *that* happened?

She made the back door unlock itself, and in he came.

"Hello, Rae," he burbled cheerfully.

"Hello yourself, you big, wet weirdo. What's on your squishy mind today?"

"You," he said baldly.

She laughed, the sound echoing throughout the empty (well, not anymore) house. "Then you got problems, squishy."

"Perhaps. How may you be released?"

"Eh?"

He was pacing in the kitchen, every step a squish. Charlene was going to *freak* when she saw the mess. "Released. Freed from this prison of a house."

"Hey, this *prison* has a fixed mortgage rate of six point nine. Not to mention authentic hardwood floors and all the original woodwork. And, if I do say so myself, the place runs like a frickin' top."

"But your immortal soul is trapped on this plane. We must release you."

"'We,' huh? Why all the weird, creepy concern, Jan, Jan, the river man?"

"I have never met anyone like you before," he said simply. "It distresses me to think of your imprisonment."

"Imprisonment!" she hooted. "Ho-ho! Let me explain something about the afterlife to you, chumly. It's all about free will. Sure, you see the bright light and all, you see Grandma and your dog Ralph—"

"I never had a dog named—"

"—you feel like reaching out to it and being warm forever and ever. But you don't *have* to go. Especially if you feel bad because you left the house a mess."

"Left the house a—?"

"Stop interrupting, squishy! So, like I said. You don't have to follow the light. Especially if you like the town you've been in and want to find out—oh, I dunno. It's like walking out in the middle of a great movie. You feel cheated. You want to see how it ends."

"And have you seen how it ends, Rae?"

"Here? In *this* town? Not even close, chumly. Not even a little bit close." She paused. What came next went against her nature, and she could hardly believe she was thinking it, much less saying it. "But it's really nice of you to be concerned. I, uh—" She was struck with a sudden coughing fit, recovered, and finished, "I appreciate it."

"But you cannot remain stuck here for—for a lifetime!"

"Says the guy whose people live for centuries. You ever thought about what it's like to be human? With a life span of maybe sixty years? Well. It was sixty years in my day. It's more like eighty-some now."

"At eighty-some," he admitted, "we have barely attained maturity."

"Right. So why would I want to check out early? Huh? Huh?"

"But are you not lonely? Do not lie. I know you are."

"You don't know shit, chumly."

"I do indeed know shit, Rae."

"How so?"

"Because," he replied, "I am lonely, also."

"You?" She couldn't hide her surprise. Also her irritation at his incessant probing. "But you've got a zillion river nymphs to hang out with. You've got your queen back after she was exiled here for—what? A hundred years? You've got the whole Mississippi River to run around in. And you're *lonely*?"

"Yes," he said simply.

"Well, jeez." She paused, chewing on that one. "That's the saddest damned thing I've ever heard. And I saw the Depression."

Ten

Withering whipped the ball down the lane, envisioning the pins as a pack of Daniir demons, and watched with total satisfaction as they scattered and disappeared. She threw her arms over her head in triumph. "Die! Die, you filthy, unearthly scum! Die, die, *die*! Yessssss!"

"Uh, okay, that's another strike." Thad was eyeing the other bowlers, who were eyeing Withering. "Just simmer down, okay?"

"This is a battle like any other," she said grimly, snatching up another ball, testing its heft, and readying herself to hurl it down the lane. All strength, no finesse—which had always worked fine for her. "And I will win it."

"That's the spirit," he muttered, marking down her score.

"Although I detest wearing group shoes."

"Hey, they spray 'em every night with a disinfectant."

"This woman is not comforted."

"This woman," he sighed, "is kicking my ass at a game she barely remembered and has never played before. If I can put up with that humiliation, you can wear the bowling shoes without bitching."

"The man has a point." Kuh-clank, *Bam!* "Die, die, *die*! Arrrrghh! There's one still alive."

"It's a pin, Withering. It's never been alive, not once."

Hmph. Although she found him disturbingly attractive, *distractingly* attractive, he didn't have much in the way of a competitive spirit. Did the man not know that everything, every single thing, must be won? No matter how long it took, no matter the cost? Even a silly game of pins and balls? You could never know who was watching, weighing, judging. Deciding the manner of attack based on her most recent actions.

"I think," he was blathering, "you could stand to, uh, lighten up a little bit. You're not fighting demons tonight. Tonight is about taking a break, remember?"

"This woman does not understand this man."

"Well, that makes two of us," he said, and got up for his turn. Without hardly looking, he tossed the ball down the lane, and it went into the small alley—what was it called? Gutterball. A shameful, humiliating gutterball.

He cheerfully marked down a zero—how could he stand it? He hadn't even tried. He didn't even care. "Like we were talking about earlier," he continued. "You deserve a break. You've spent as much time at war as you spent in Mysteria raising hell with your sisters. I can't think of anyone who deserves a break more than you."

"It is difficult—and unworthy—to take a break from one's responsibilities. It pleases some on Earth Prime," she admitted, "to call me queen. But does a queen ever get a vacation from royalty?"

"But you're not on Earth Prime. You're back home. And while we're on the subject, I think *this* ought to be Earth Prime. What'd you say this was? Secondary Earth? Jeez. How many are there?"

"Thousands," she replied simply.

"Well, from what you've told me, Earth Prime is all weird grass and demons and only a few humans. *This* Earth has Mysteria and tons of humans and almost no demons. Ergo, we're Prime."

"I," she said, amused, "did not name the parallel universes."

"No, you only rule one."

"Hardly that," she said, laughing a little to hide her discomfort. Why was he looking at her like that? So intently, as if everything she said was exceedingly important? "This woman keeps it safe for those who cannot protect themselves. If it pleases some to call this woman queen, this woman has other things to worry about."

"See, see?" He threw another gutter ball, ignoring her groan. "This is what I'm talking about. You won't even take the spoils of war—a royal title! It's just kill, kill, kill and work, work, work with you."

"And bowl, bowl, bowl," she said, snatching up another ball. "Now watch this, Thad. You have to *look* at where the ball goes. Visualize the enemy lying dead and bloody. Then throw." She hurled the ball; the pins split apart so hard, one actually flew into the next lane. "Then, victory."

"Psycho," he sang under his breath, marking down her score.

"This woman is unfamiliar with that word."

"It means terrifying warrior queen."

She narrowed her eyes at him. "Your face does not match your words; this woman thinks you lie."

"Well, you're a pretty smart psycho. We'll add that to the list of your very fine qualities."

"You seem oddly cheerful."

"Why not? I'm on a date with a gorgeous warrior queen who bowls like a fiend and can eat half a large pizza by herself."

She laughed in spite of herself. "You may blame yourself for that last, sir; you make an excellent pizza pie."

"It's true," he said without a trace of modesty. "I do."

"But you cannot bowl," she teased, then remembered one of Scornful's favorite epithets, "for shit."

"Ouch, nasty! Gorgeous, there's hope for you yet."

Eleven

They walked outside the bowling alley, to Thad's serial killer gray van (which his employees occasionally used for deliveries; thus, the logo WILSON'S PIES: YOU COULD DO BETTER, BUT WHY BOTHER? plastered on the sides in bright red paint). Thad was still fumbling with his seat belt when Withering seized him by the shirt and hauled him toward her. His elbow hit the horn, which let out a resonant *brronk!* and then her mouth was on his.

"What am I?" he asked, managing to wrench free and gasp for breath, "the spoils of war?"

"No. I wish to mate. Right now."

"Well, I'm sorry," he huffed, straightening his shirt and hair, "but I'm not that kind of guy. I need wooing and romance. I need flowers and dinner. I—oh, fuck it, come back here."

They climbed into the back of the van, which was empty, carpeted, and smelled strongly of garlic and pizza sauce. They rolled around the strong-smelling floor, tugging and yanking at each other's clothes, Thad marveling at her smoothly muscled body: not an ounce of fat anywhere, but my God, the scars!

They didn't detract from her beauty; they deepened it, made her seem more like a real woman and less like a goddess. The one arcing across her abdomen was so long and twisted, he wondered how she'd survived the original wound.

She wrapped her legs around his waist and urged him forward—well, yanked him forward was more like it. He was concerned; he normally liked to give a partner more than eight seconds of foreplay. But she was having none of it, pulling him forward, her fingers digging into his shoulders, her hips rising off the carpet to meet his.

"I don't want to hur—whoa!" Sex with Withering wasn't unlike being caught in a rowing machine. A hot, limber, blond rowing machine. Used to being the aggressor in sex, Thad just closed his eyes and tried to hang on for the ride. In less than a minute he was spasming inside her and shaking so hard he wondered if the van was rocking.

"Gah," he said as she gently pushed him off her. He flopped on his side next to her, trying to catch his breath. "Well. That. Ah. That was—"

"Very quick," she said, sounding indecently satisfied. She was rapidly rearranging her clothes, tying her long hair back with a ponytail holder. "Thank you."

"I guess it's all right," he said slowly, "that swiftness impresses you."

"How else would you do it? This way we can clothe ourselves and be ready to face danger."

Oh my God.

"Uh. There are lots of other ways to 'do it.' In fact—"

"Oh, no. No, no, no. Much too dangerous."

"But did you even come?"

"Come where?"

Oh my God. Please let me teach her the many ways two people can pleasure each other. Please let her stay so I can teach her, please God.

"I guess," he said slowly, buckling his belt, "I'd better drive you home."

Twelve

He dropped a cheerful Withering at her front door and began the walk back to the van, when suddenly the sidewalk turned to glue (or so it felt) and he was stuck fast.

"Cut it out, you two!" he said loudly, struggling to extricate himself.

Scornful and Derisive peered down at him from their tree house. The town knew the girls were too old for it, as they also knew that was where the triplets (when they *were* triplets) retreated to work on their more diabolical plans.

"You'd better explain," Scornful said.

"And right now, before the sidewalk ends up over your head."

"Unnnf!" he replied. "Nnnnnfff! Mmmmmff!" One foot moved a whole inch.

"So talk," Derisive added.

"Mind—nnf!—your own—mmfff!—damned—argh!—business," he panted.

"Our sister *is* our business. She might look like a hottie grown-up, but she's a little naive in some areas, like you haven't noticed."

His feet were moving slightly easier. "You can't—nnff!—do the magic—rrggh!—you could when—mrrgg!—you were the Desdaine triplets."

"We can do enough," Scornful said shortly, and he knew he had touched on a sore spot. He wondered what had happened to Withering's magic. Out of practice, probably, from the years of fighting. "So what are you doing with her?"

"None of your damned—ha!—business." One foot was free. He set to work on the other.

"It is, too! Is this why you came back to Mysteria? To score on the new girl?"

"No. And *that* is none of *your* business."

"We can do a lot more than stick you in cement up to your ankles," Derisive threatened.

"Think I don't know? But what's between your sister and me is private."

"Guess he doesn't kiss and tell," Scornful said to her sister.

"Prob'ly just as well; who needs to puke after that good supper Mom cooked?"

He knelt to get better leverage as he tugged on his left foot. "You two are a menace!"

"Tell us something we haven't heard since we were two. Look, all we want to know is, are you sticking around this time?"

"This time?"

"We looked you up in the archives. Your whole family picked up and left when you were a kid. Now you're back, and you're sniffing around our sister. So are you in it for the long haul, or just a slap and tickle before you vanish?"

"I'm—never—leaving—again. God *damn* it, what'd you turn the sidewalk into, rubber cement?"

"Oh."

"Huh," Scornful added. "Never leaving again?"

He temporarily abandoned his efforts to escape. "I came back because I thought Mysteria had gotten into my blood. There's nowhere else like it in the world, kids, but I guess you know that."

"So?" they asked in unison.

"So. Your sister grew up in five seconds, and now I'm here for her. I'll always be here for her. I'm trying to get her to stay. I'm trying to get her to relax and not be ready to fight all the time. Now get me out of this shit!"

The girls made identical gestures, as if they were pulling invisible taffy, and his foot popped free, and the sidewalk was solid again. He nearly toppled backward but righted himself in time.

"I guess that's all right, then," Scornful said.

"We can't watch her twenty-four/seven," Derisive added.

"So nice to have your permission," he snapped.

"Don't kid yourself, Thad. You did need our permission. Unless you like the idea of getting stuck in every sidewalk, driveway, and linoleum floor between here and the shooting range."

"Oh, and Thad?" Scornful added sweetly as he stomped down the sidewalk. "Break her heart, and we'll break your spine."

"Among other things," Derisive added.

Great, he thought, climbing into his van, *teenage mob enforcers.* Just what the town needed.

Thirteen

"Pardon me," Janameides said politely, "but do any of you know where I might find an exorcist?"

He was standing in the Desdaine living room, having been ushered in by Mrs. Desdaine, who had been headed out the door for work. Shrugging at the sight of the river nymph (but not at all worried for her daughters' safety—she hadn't been *before* Withering grew up in an alternate dimension)—Mrs. Desdaine had made herself scarce.

"This woman would know why the—the man needs an exorcist," Withering said. She was the only one fully dressed at 7:45 a.m.; the other two girls were in the shorts and T-shirt sets they used as pajamas.

"Yes, what *are* you?" Scornful asked. "You look like Pot . . . she's the lady who used to—"

"She is my queen. I am her subject."

"River nymph!" Derisive said, snapping her fingers and pointing at him.

"Just so. And I require an exorcist, please. I was told you three might help." Jan frowned, the expression much more dour than it could be on a human face. "I was also told you are the same age."

"Technically, we are," Derisive said.

"But it's a long story," Scornful added.

"Actually, it's not," Derisive said, "but who cares? What's the exorcist for?"

"A haunted house. But perhaps the three of you could handle the task. I was told your power as triplets—"

"Is no longer a resource to be tapped," Withering said.

Scornful turned to her tall sister. "Yeah? And why is that? Did you forget the spells? Because we can get you books and stuff."

"I did not forget. I merely submerged my share of our magic into my fighting skills, an essential component to my survival. As such, I am faster and stronger than most; I also heal from wounds very quickly."

"So, you made yourself bionic?" Scornful snorted.

"I did what I had to," Withering said simply, "to live."

The two girls were, shockingly, shamed into silence. It was only temporary, though. "I think we can help you," Derisive said. She turned to her younger sister. "The new guy? Not Thad, the other new guy."

"The witch doctor?"

"You're only assuming that because he's Jamaican."

"Yeah, but he might—"

"He might."

"So we should—"

"We should."

"What my sisters are saying," Withering explained to an increasingly bewildered Jan, "is that we may be able to assist you. If you will come with us, please?"

"This has nothing to do with you, gigantic big sister."

"This woman will see the girls safe."

"Oh, barf," Scornful said, stomping toward her bedroom to get dressed.

Fourteen

The witch doctor shook various homemade implements at various appliances in the kitchen. He had multiple piercings (including four gold rings in each eyebrow), but was dressed in street clothes and carried a blue backpack, from which he pulled various odd things.

He refused to tell them his name, so Scornful christened him Dr. Demento. As in, "Hey, Dr. Demento! You gonna keep shaking stuff at the toaster, or are we actually going to get to work, here?"

"Dis house, she's evil, mahn."

"Evil, my big butt," the ghost said out of nowhere. The two younger girls jumped; Withering had her knife in her hand by the word *my*. The witch doctor shook harder. "You realize, I only let you idiots in because nobody's home, and I'm bored out of my tits. Right?"

"Now, Rae," Jan said in his bubbling, oddly soothing voice, "just cooperate, and soon your essence will be set free."

"Sounds nauseating. I think I'll stay put."

Dr. Demento reached into his backpack and withdrew a second mysterious object (a good trick, with the backpack strapped behind him as it was), and shook both at the fridge.

"I can't believe we've never been here before," Scornful whispered to her younger sister.

"I heard that, you little brat. And you don't have to get your perky little noses into *everything* in this town."

"You do not belong here, ghost," Withering said, the knife point never wavering. "Begone at once."

"Look who's talking! Don't you have a demonic realm to be ruling? Instead, you're nosing around in *my* house and poking around in *my* business."

"How did you—"

"Ha! The whole damned town is talking about it, that's how I knew."

"Then if this woman may so inquire, what is it like to be displaced?"

"If I didn't like it, I wouldn't be here, get it? So buzz off, and take the witch doctor with you. Better than him have tried and failed."

Jan protested as Withering sheathed her knife. "But he will set you free, Rae!"

"Aw, that's super. No sale."

"Hey, Dr. Demento. Can I shake something at the television?" Scornful tried to get at his backpack, but he whirled and backed away from her, still shaking various homemade tools. "Aw, come on. How come you get to have all the fun?"

"You call this fun?" Rae grumped. "Will you people get lost before the fridge accidentally falls on one of you? Two or three times?"

"Yeesh," Derisive said.

"You say it's been tried before? Was that John Harding, by any chance?"

"Sure."

"But he was alive when *you* were alive. The way I heard it, his heart wasn't in it, and that's why he couldn't banish you. Dr. Demento here doesn't care how you got here or where you go."

"Jan, you got a lot of nerve, bringing the psycho triplets and a witch doctor—a *witch doctor* of all things!—into this house."

"But Rae, I wish only to—"

"—be an enormous pain in my ass. At which you're succeeding beautifully."

"There is little we can do here," Withering told her sisters. "I suggest we take our leave."

"And take Dr. Demento with you!" Rae called.

"No." Jan actually stomped his foot, which squished. "He will set you free, and you will no longer be imprisoned."

The refrigerator slid all the way across the room, the yanked plug trailing behind it like a tail.

"We're out of here," the younger girls said in unison as Withering grabbed the witch doctor by the elbow and started hauling him toward the front door.

"I'd vamoose, too, if I were you, River Nymph."

"That's good advice from the kid," Rae warned. "Whichever one it was."

"Thank you," Jan called as all four made their way to the doorway, "for your assistance."

"Yeah, and next time, take your damned shoes off in the entryway!" Rae hollered as the front door slammed.

Fifteen

"You tried to get rid of me!"

Jan ducked as the toaster sailed over his head. "It was my dearest wish to see you free, yes."

"Tossing me like a dead Easter chick!" The small board that normally held car keys soared toward him; he backpedaled on his long feet and handily avoided it.

"Rae, you are reading this entirely the wrong way."

"If *I* showed up in the Mississippi River with antinymph spray, how would *you* take it?"

"Anti what?"

"Oh, never mind. Just get out of here."

"I will not." He stood his ground stubbornly, even when Stephen King's *The Stand* (hardcover edition, which weighed approximately twenty-seven pounds) hit him in the chest. "You need my help, and I will not leave until you have it."

"I'll bet Pot will have something to say about that, Squishy."

"My queen has given me leave to stay. In fact, she was pleased that one of her people will watch over the town she so loves."

"Pot said torturing me with witch doctors who wear Dockers is okay? What the blue hell is the world coming to?"

"I do not know. I do know I cannot bear to see you trapped when I have unlimited freedom of movement."

"But Jan—" Rae's tone softened, and he tried not to display his surprise. "Jan, by staying here, you're restricting your own movement. You said it yourself, your home is a long way away from here."

"My home," he said firmly, "is wherever you are."

There was a long, long silence. When she broke it, it sounded like—but of course he must be mistaken—but it sounded like she was crying softly. "You mean it? You want to stay here with me?"

"Yes. I never lie, Rae, and I certainly would not start with you, even if I did."

"But why?"

"I do not know," he said simply.

"Because if it's because you feel sorry for me, I'll throw the door at your head right now."

"I did at first pity you. But even in my pity, I greatly admired your fortitude in a difficult situation. And when my queen's business was finished, I was unable to leave town. Because of you, Rae, I was unable to go back to my people. That is not pity. That is—something else."

"Something else," she mused.

"If you will not leave this silly red house and move to the next plane, I have no choice but to also remain."

"I could build an extension," she said eagerly. "I could give you your own bathroom and everything. A *big* hot tub for you to soak in whenever you want!"

"So you do not mind if I remain?"

"Like I can do anything about it?"

"You cannot," he said smugly.

"Char and her husband might have something to say about it—oh, who am I kidding? They're always looking for babysitters for the Thing That Poops. And they've been reaping the benefits of my free handiwork for ages. Okay, for a few months. But I'll ramp up the value of the house if I build on another bed and bath. Of course, they'll have to buy the supplies, but it's still cheaper than—"

"Rae, do be quiet."

"Better get used to it, pal. Anybody nutty enough to fall for a ghost—*my* ghost—and give up his river for Mysteria had better be resigned to everyday chatter. But I'm betting there are compensations."

"Compensations?" he asked, then gasped as he felt her essence rush through him like a cool wind, raising goose bumps on his arms and causing him to rock backward on his heels. He could feel cool, ghostly hands on him, touching, caressing, stroking, and oh, the sensation was delightful, the coolness was delightful; living humans were just too *warm*.

He heard her laugh in his ear, and that raised more pleasurable goose bumps, heard her sigh and felt her grip tighten, except it seemed as though she had four hands, ten, a dozen, and they were everywhere, everywhere, touching and cuddling and making him hard and making him shudder and making him spasm all over until he realized he was flat on his back on the kitchen tile.

"Oh," he gasped, thinking he needed five or six bottles of water. Right now.

"Hmmm," Rae replied, sounding like she was lying beside him.

"That was—that was—" What? Supremely satisfying? Sublime? Out of this world?

"Fun!"

"For you as well?" He was unable to hide his surprise.

"Whoo, yeah! First orgasm I've had in—what century is this again? Never mind. When I went into your body, I could feel everything you were feeling, which made me feel even better, which I projected onto you, which made me feel better—you get the picture."

"Oh, my," he gasped. "So you can do that whenever you wish?"

"Apparently so."

"I may never walk again."

"So who's asking you to?" she said and laughed in his ear, the sound a warm caress.

Sixteen

It came from the wishing well and found it was dark in this place; the moon was high, and the stars were bright—and the stars were wrong. It followed the hated woman's scent through the small park, down the oddly flat lane (the blacktop felt strange beneath its feet and claws) and toward the small red house, her scent getting stronger with every step.

And with every step, it became angrier.

It would find the usurper, the dire queen, and pull her throat out with its teeth until it was gulping her blood and picking its teeth with her vertebrae. Then the land would once again belong to its people, the Krakeen, and this land, too, this ridiculous land of soft pink things. This land with no demons, this land that had spawned the dire queen and foisted her on its people.

It charged up the walk, already drooling at the prospect of chewing on the usurper, and easily pushed down the door, barely noticing the astounding crash the wood made as it hit the floor.

It walked into the house, still following the trail, which was stronger here; she had spent some time here, at any rate. But one of the soft pink things wasn't so soft, because it was standing protectively in front of a female and a baby, and it was baring its teeth at the demon.

"Cole, don't!" someone without a scent said. "Get Char and get the baby and get the hell out of here!"

The man paid no notice; the man growled and came closer, his eyes seemed almost lit from within, and the Krakeen licked its lips and wondered how the man's liver might taste.

"Cole!" the voice screamed. "Get your wife and get your kid and *get the fuck out of here*! Find Withering! Go now!"

The voice seemed to penetrate this time; the man remembered his responsibilities and fled with the female and infant. The Krakeen let them; they were not its rightful prey. This time. Instead, it looked around for the voice—and staggered as some strange, hard object smashed into the back of its head, followed by a rain of smaller objects.

"There's more drawers, and there's more silverware," the voice warned him, "so get lost."

It growled, dribbling saliva on the floor, and swiped at the air, reaching for the voice.

"Not the brightest bulb, are you?" the voice said, this time from behind him. It whirled in time to catch another heavy object in the face, and it staggered. "How'd the toaster taste? Hey, stand still, so I can crush you underneath the washing machine."

It roared, infuriated at something it could not see or smell, still wanting the dire queen's blood but not at all happy at shedding its own—*its* blood, for like all Krakeen, it had both male and female genitalia.

"Boy, did *you* pick the wrong house," the voice remarked, and something smashed into the back of its head and shattered, something that smelled sweet and crumbly.

"Char's gonna kill me; she made that stupid cookie jar in her pottery class. Eh, easy come, easy smash."

It stepped across the shards, its hide far too tough to be cut or even scratched. The dread queen's scent was strong here, but then seemed to backtrack, so he followed it toward the door, staggering as the voice hurled something yet again, something that felt like a rock with hard corners.

"Damn it! With no blender, I guess it's bye-bye Margarita Saturdays."

Nearing the doorway, it saw the usurper standing on the wooden thing it had knocked down, standing on it with her sword drawn.

"Krakeen demon, this woman will make the demon pay for daring to come here."

It roared a challenge; it hungered for her blood, her blood for its people, for its land, for the crown she had wrongfully stolen—stolen and then fled!

"You dare come to this land, my town? You dare pollute this place with the stench of your hide? This woman cannot even make clothing out of your skin, you stink so badly."

It gnashed its teeth and rushed at her, ducking under her swing and slashing at her. She wrenched herself back, and all it could do was scratch her, not gut her as it had intended.

"He shoots and he misses and, oh, ladies and gentlemen, have you ever *seen* such humiliation?"

Yes, it would kill the dread queen, and then it would hunt down that bedamned voice and kill it, too!

It followed up, swinging its long arms, each finger tipped with a razor-sharp claw an inch and a half long, and she had to backpedal out the doorway to avoid getting cut again. It ducked as she swung, but not quite fast enough, and it lost an ear.

"Oh, man! She's cutting pieces off you! And you're the best of the bunch? How embarrassing is *that*?"

"A fine point, Krakeen," the usurper said and bared her teeth at him in what the soft pink things called a "smile." "Rae, remind this woman never to anger you."

"D'you know how long it's going to take me to fix this door?" the voice griped in response.

The Krakeen kicked, its powerful feet also tipped with sharp claws, and the dire queen backflipped out of the way, catching it on the underside of its chin as she did. It shook its head and went after her again, only to find its feet were stuck in the hard walk outside the house. It wrenched itself free easily enough and stepped onto the grass, where it caught the usurper's sword with one hand as the blade descended.

Got you now, dread queen! Your guts will feed my young! Ignoring the blood pouring from its hand, it held the blade away from itself, readying its other paw for the killing blow, when she abruptly let go of the sword. As it staggered in surprise, it felt something hot slide into its throat.

Hot, and then very, very cold. And something was wrong with its throat. It was getting its chest wet. It was getting dizzy. It tried to swing at the dread queen and missed by too much, missed, and then the odd colored grass was rushing up to its face, and the Krakeen demon knew no more.

Seventeen

Withering stepped back, neatly avoiding the splash, and coldly watched the Krakeen fall facedown onto Charlene Hautenan's lawn. Then she looked up into the nearest oak tree.

"This woman would ask her sisters to come down."

"Why? We helped, didn't we?"

"There may be more, dear ones, and this woman would not see you hurt. It is bad enough," she added sternly, "that you disobeyed me in the manner of following me here."

"Point," Scornful replied, and they both climbed down with the speed of monkeys on crack. Then they stood over the body of the dead demon, which was bleeding black all over the grass. "Guh-ross!" she continued. "Those things come from where you used to live? This one's even nastier-looking than the other one. It's a miracle you made it out alive!"

"Mom's gonna freak," Derisive added.

"Only if you tell the good lady," Withering said, squatting to wipe her blade on the grass, retrieving her sword, then standing in time to see Thad's pizza van drive over the curb and straight up to the house, ruining more grass. He leaped out, leaving the engine running, and nearly fell onto the corpse.

"Are you okay? I got your sister's message. One of your sisters. I don't know which. Are you okay?" He took her into his arms, feeling her for injuries. "Withering, you nut, you shouldn't have tackled that thing by yourself!"

"Why?" she asked, honestly puzzled. "Who else should have 'tackled' it?"

"You dope! You could have been sliced! Chewed! Skinned! Gutted!"

"Indeed, the Krakeen would have seen to all those things if it could."

Thad actually staggered. "That statement did not make me feel better. At all."

"But it did not, and will not, ever." She gently divested herself of his frantic grip and slid her foot under the body.

"Careful," Scornful warned. "In the horror movies, this is where it leaps up for one last scare."

"Not once my knife has been in its throat." She flipped the body over and examined it carefully. Finally, straightening, she said with surprise, "It *is* a Krakeen."

"Yeah, you said that. You called it that. You also mentioned it would have gutted and stabbed and mangled and mutilated you. So?"

"So. Krakeens inhabit the other side of the planet. It once took me the better part of my sixteenth year to reach their territory. This one could have been nowhere near the thin spot where I fell through and, later, returned. That means—"

"I don't care what it means!" Thad shouted. "You're not leaving me—or Mysteria! This is your home, and nobody made you killer of demons and giver-upper of a social life."

She squinted at him. "That doesn't make any—"

"I don't care if this thing was from halfway round the planet or the house next door; *you're staying*."

"What he said," Derisive said.

"Yeah, except without that weird 'giver-upper' line," Scornful added.

"As *I* was saying," Withering continued gently, "it would appear the wishing well is now a conduit between Earth Prime and Secondary Earth."

"Sorry if you've heard this before: So?"

"That means a demon from anywhere on Earth Prime might find its way here."

"Gross," Scornful commented.

"Not to mention inconvenient," Derisive added.

"And unless I am here, in Mysteria, to protect its citizens, that could be disastrous. I cannot leave my dear mother and dear sisters to defend themselves against such creatures, nor any citizen of the land."

"So . . ." Thad held his breath and then, because the stress appeared to be too much, let it out in an explosive sigh. "So you're staying."

"Yes. I must. I do not understand why I did not see it before."

"Because you were too busy jumping Thad's bones?" Scornful suggested.

"And learning how to pick up a spare?" Derisive added.

"I suspect," she said, kindly enough, "it is because I was confused about exactly where my responsibilities lie. But I can no longer return to Earth Prime, no matter how noble my intentions, if it means leaving my town exposed to any demon with a whim to take the crown."

"Where'd Char and the baby go?" Thad asked, seeming to realize their absence all of a sudden.

"To our house, where they remain."

"You better go tell them they can come back, that Withering took care of their little infestation problem."

"*Little?*" Scornful snorted as they started down the street.

"Oh, he just wants to mack on her in private."

"Perv."

"Double perv."

"I can hear you!" Thad called after them. Then he turned to Withering. "Although they have a point."

"That you are a double perv?"

"No. That I want to do this." And he took her in his arms, no pretense of looking for injury *this* time, no indeed, and kissed her, a long, bruising, possessive kiss.

When they came up for air, Thad said, "Don't even think about leaving this town without me."

"I won't even think of leaving this town, if you find that helpful."

"My front door!" someone wailed, and they turned to see Char and her husband coming up the sidewalk. The baby, Withering presumed, had been left in Mrs. Desdaine's care. "All smashed up!"

"Wait till you see the inside!" Rae called, though it was difficult to hear her outside the house. "Also, I've taken a lover, and he'll be moving in as soon as I get an extension built."

"Fine, Rae, fine." Char and her husband were staring at the corpse on their front lawn. "That'll be—wait. *What?*"

"Oh, like you two aren't doing it every half hour of every day," Rae snapped. "Don't judge *me*, honey!"

"I wasn't. I just—" Charlene gestured vaguely: at the corpse, at the van parked in her begonias. "This is a lot to take in at once."

"Welcome," Withering said dryly, "to Mysteria."

THE NANNY
FROM HELL

Susan Grant

For three amazing, talented women:
MaryJanice, P. C., and Gena.
What an absolute pleasure to revisit
Mysteria with you all.

Prologue

Once upon a time there lived a demon
with a secret wish to be human.
It made Satan very, very unhappy . . .

CIRCUS MAXIMUS, ANCIENT ROME

One hundred and fifty thousand spectators lunged to their feet, cheering as the chariots flew out of the starting gate. Everyone from the lowliest slave to the emperor himself added to the deafening applause. The attention, the excitement, the anticipation: Shay reveled in it, savoring every aspect of the races from the dust churned up by chariot wheels to the dizzying sensation of sheer speed. Most racers conserved energy in the early laps in order to give it their all in the final stretches. Bah! Rules were for mortals. Full speed ahead!

Four powerful horses tugged on the reins wrapped around Shay's fist and down her arm to her waist. If she were to crash, she doubted she'd have time to cut free with her dagger before being trampled or dragged to her death. Not that she worried about such frivolous things as dying.

Shay threw back her head and laughed. Dust billowed into the air and settled like fine powder over her toned, slender arms and her black racing colors. The fabric fluttered around her breasts, barely concealing them. She heard shouts of surprise. "A woman!" they cried.

"A she-demon, actually," she murmured smugly. Not that they'd care. Men never seemed to mind as long as they thought they were getting what they wanted from her.

In particular, she noted the emperor's hot, interested gaze, dismissing it as a mere annoyance. Warlords were sometimes diverting, yes; chieftains, too. But emperors? All pomp and little circumstance. She wouldn't bother with this one unless she was very, very bored. And she doubted she'd be bored today. There was much to be done.

A blink of her eyes, and two chariots collided. Spectacular! Ooh, and a trampling, too. Score!

Shay couldn't remember the last time she had so much fun. She was sent by Lucifer all over the world—a plague here, a fire there—but she'd rather be here. Something about racing made her feel so *alive*. So . . . real.

She cringed. *Cease that drivel!* If the Dark Lord ever got wind of her addiction to earthly life, he'd snuff out her existence like a boot crushed a flickering ash. He'd told her as much, countless centuries ago when he'd suspected she was hanging around an Ice Age settlement because she'd taken a fancy to nights spent cuddling in the furs with one of its hunters, Swift River. Master had been right, of course. With the fear of permanent extermination hanging over her head, she ended the affair with a good-bye kiss and an avalanche and went on her way.

Shay pushed the painful memory away. Her job was to break hearts and tear families apart, not to pretend she was human. Not to pretend *love*. Especially not at the risk of her own existence. Something about ceasing *to be* frightened her. She'd do everything she could to avoid that fate.

Snarling, Shay punched her fist to the side. The horses pulling the chariot next to hers went wild, yanking their rider toward the wall with a snapping of wood and the scraping of metal. The champion's scream was cut short. "Buh-bye, Scorpus." He'd won far too many races, anyway. It was time he retired.

Dust rose from the wrecks as the remaining racers plunged down the straightaway. Easily, Shay commanded the lead. Only one other racer had the stamina to keep her pace. Aquila. The shaggy-haired up-and-coming champion seemed to have it all: looks, youth, a beautiful wife and child, and all of Rome at his feet. Sensing she was pulling ahead, Aquila slid his narrowed eyes in her direction, sizing up her chariot, her horses, and her technique. Roman sunshine gleamed on his sweating skin. My, but he was nicely muscled. She could tell by his glance that he saw her as simply another competitor and not a potential lover. Probably because of his pretty little wife and baby. Aw, he was in love. How easy that would be to change. In fact, she'd keep him alive just to prove the point!

Laughing, Shay urged her horses on ahead, just like she'd urge on Aquila in bed after the race. Feeling generous, she'd even let him win. What did it matter? He'd lose later. They always did.

Neck and neck, they careened around the last turn. Who would win? Who would lose? In those final, breathless, exhilarating moments, Shay allowed him to drift into the lead. He beat her by a length. The crowd's applause was thunderous. They had a new champion!

Magnificent in his crimson racing colors, Aquila beamed as he received his palm branch and wreath from the magistrate. Shay shook out her hair as she jumped down from her chariot. As the silly Romans fawned over him, she undulated her hips as she sashayed past, brushing her finger down his arm. In his mind was planted a vivid image of her moaning and naked, submitting to his every desire. His dark eyes flashed with sudden awareness. It was done.

Away from the circus, she'd barely breezed into her tent when he came striding after her, stripping her out of her clothes before she reached the bed. He threw her on her back, impaling her with his body, pumping with sweaty, dusty, postvictory vigor. Mentally, she took control, making him believe it was the best sex he'd ever had, and that she was first in his heart. *You'll love me to the end of time, Aquila.*

"To the end of time . . ." he breathed in her ear.

Stupid mortal.

The tent flap eased open, and a woman stepped in. A babe on her hip, she took a moment to let her eyes adjust to the shade and to the sight of Aquila's pumping bottom. Then she met Shay's amused gaze.

He loves me. Shay planted the realization in the woman's mind. One startled sob, and the wife was gone.

Shay vanished herself—at the very moment of Aquila's release. He spilled his seed on an empty bed, not knowing what had happened to her, to him—or to his little wife when he returned to an empty house later.

Love, Shay thought with disdain. It was her mission to destroy it. It was her entire reason for existence. When all was said and done, she had to say she was very, very good at her job.

One

Wanted: Loving, live-in nanny to care for working couple's only child. Must be willing to relocate to Mysteria. Private bedroom in home. Call for salary and details.

"Demon!" Lucifer bellowed loud enough to shake the depths of Hell. Molten rocks fell from the walls, sending shrieking banshees into the shadows and waking every manner of dark creature.

Head bowed, her hands clasped in submission, Shay scurried forward to answer her master's bidding.

"You're late!" Lucifer tugged on his black goatee. "What's your excuse this time?"

"This demon offers exquisite apologies, my lord. This demon had a raft full of orphans to set adrift in shark-infested waters."

"And did you?"

"Yes, Master." She chanced a peek at him. "Is something amiss, Master?"

His horns pulsed as he sank his pitchfork into solid rock and bellowed once more in rage. It was clear that something had made him very, very angry. Shay hoped it wasn't anything she'd done. How quickly he could change her back into what she was at the beginning of time: nothing. "I will never surrender to the spawn of a demon whose ass I fired for committing random acts of kindness!" He jerked a claw at the cave wall. The stones shimmered and opened up to a view of a charming town.

A tall man of dark good looks strode down a road leading to a cottage and a small church. "Damon of Mysteria . . ." Shay narrowed her eyes, scanning the scene with slitted pupils. She was starting to understand the reason for her summons. For ten centuries Damon had served as Lucifer's Demon High Lord of Self-Doubt and Second Thoughts . . . until he was caught, red-handed, committing random acts of kindness. After a couple of hundred years of torture, Lucifer made him mortal, sentencing him to live out his days in Mysteria, the very town he'd saved hundreds of years before. Such a mundane, pitiful existence was every demon's worst nightmare.

Except that Damon didn't seem to be suffering at all. He'd fallen in love, not only with his sorry life but with a human woman. A woman of God, no less: Harmony Faithfull, who presided over Mysteria's silly little house of worship.

Not that Lucifer had taken it sitting down. Rumors circulating around the lava pools reported that the Devil had been acting downright petulant about Damon's—dare she say it?—*contentment*. The Dark Lord had sent wave after wave of subdemons and other obnoxious creatures up through the gates of Hell to torment Damon and his new wife, along with the residents of Mysteria, many of whom were undead themselves. Each time, the town fought back. No one was quite sure how or even why they could, but the matter was being investigated.

Now the couple was married. Harmony was said to adore the former demon beyond all reason. Shay snorted. No man was worth that kind of dreamy, addle-brained worship. If that wasn't bad enough, they'd spawned a child.

It was all so revolting! Shay made a face. Clearly, Lucifer wanted the family broken apart. "I'll bed him as soon as I arrive there, Master. Or, perhaps, her. I can do them both."

"No, you stupid creature!" He hoisted her off her feet. "I do not want you to bed them. I want you to destroy their child!"

Shay hung, trembling, from her master's clawed hands. His crimson eyes were whirlpools of lava, threatening to suck her in, luring her deeper and deeper. If she lost herself in those eyes, she'd be trapped, unable to free herself. She would . . . end.

A slow smile revealed his glittering fangs. "You fear the end of your existence."

He knows.

Of course, he did. Did she think she could keep her deepest fears secret? "Answer me, Demon!" He shook her hard. Goblins and gargoyles somersaulted through the shadows, fleeing the chamber and Lucifer's wrath.

"Yes," she wheezed in his grip. "This humble demon fears being no more."

His fanged smile widened. His glowing eyes sparked with malice. "Then you will not fail me."

"No, Master."

"Win their trust so they let you near the child."

"Yes, Master."

"And stay away from the fountain," he growled.

"What fountain?"

"What fountain?" He shook her, fire erupting in his eyes. "If only you were as smart as you are evil! Mysteria's fountain, stupid demon. The wishing fountain. Do not go near it."

"Why?" Even as she asked, she knew it was a mistake to do so.

He shook her so hard that her ears rang. "My word is law! It is not to be questioned. Go earthward and win the trust of the family. Then kill the child and bring its bones back to me. Fail and . . ." He brought her face-to-face with him. "I will erase you, eradicate you, stamp you out—for all eternity!" His roar shook the entire cave. "No matter where you run, no matter where you hide, I will find you, and *end you.* You will never escape your fate."

Sputtering, he threw her to the ground. She scrabbled backward to her feet, stumbling away from his threat: *"I will find you, and end you."* Humans had their Heaven (or Hell). Angels, also, could look forward to Heaven. As well, all matter of undead creatures had a future ahead of them, whether they were vampires, shape-shifters, or even ghosts. But for a ruined demon, eternity meant nothing, zero, zilch. She simply would no longer *be.*

The prospect frightened Shay more than anything else. She would find the child and kill it. There was no other choice. Failure was simply not an option.

* * *

Damon, new father and ex-demon, climbed the porch stairs to the home he shared with his wife, Harmony, Mysteria's minister. Their black Lab Bubba bounced around his heels, barking happily. Before Damon reached the top of the stairs, Dr. Fogg burst out, juggling his black medical bag and his ever-present BlackBerry as he pushed his glasses up his nose.

Damon's heart rolled over. His wife, his babe—he couldn't bear the thought of any harm coming to them. "Is everything all right, Doctor?"

"In your house, yes. My visit with your wife was interrupted. They need me at the high school. Fighting Fairies practice was a little rougher than usual today."

"I do like American football," Damon admitted.

"Football? It was the cheerleaders." Fogg ran a finger around the inside of his collar as he trotted the rest of the way down the stairs.

Despite his intellectual outward appearance, Fogg had taken a wild-elf princess as a wife. Wild-elves lived outside Mysteria and outside the law. When they mated with humans it was usually by force. A month into the surprise marriage, the elf left him. The mild-mannered doctor had referred himself to Harmony for spiritual counseling. Today had been the first session.

Harmony stood in the doorway. "Well," she said with a sigh, "that was interesting."

Damon lifted a brow at his worried-looking wife. "He doesn't look well, lass."

"He's not, the poor man. He's been through a hard time. I think today helped—a lot. He'll be back. As for you, come here, honey. I need a kiss."

The lass knew how to do things with her mouth no woman of God should know how to do, but he was glad of it. He took a moment to hold her close, cupping her sweet face in his hand, savoring the feel of her skin and the love shining in her eyes as she smiled up at him. He'd existed ten thousand years before Harmony. In his mind, life had only just begun.

He brushed one more kiss across her lips and took her hand. "Damon Junior misses his daddy," she said, leading him inside.

In the kitchen, little Damon sat in his highchair. He squealed in delight, seeing his father. "Papa!" The vase of flowers on the kitchen table jumped, took two hops, and stopped.

"Omigosh," Harmony cried, running for a dish towel to mop up the spill as Damon said sternly, "Son, I told you no moving furniture—or any other items—without my or your mother's permission."

Harmony paled, the damp cloth dangling from her hand. "Are you saying little Damon moved that vase?"

"Aye. I saw him do it for the first time the other day. When you came home from the store and the lamp fell."

"That was the wind."

"Nay," he said quietly.

"You mean our baby has . . . *powers*?" she practically squeaked.

He tried to reach for her hand, but she'd shoved it through her hair. "We talked about that possibility when you were pregnant, love."

"I know, but . . ." She sighed. "We thought the chance of your demon powers being passed on in your DNA was remote if not impossible."

"Impossible is a woman of God falling in love with an ex-demon," he said tenderly. "Impossible is a former minion of Lucifer finding out he has a soul. And yet, both happened. Aye, love, who are we to say what is possible and what is not? Besides, I'm not the only one with powers in this relationship." Harmony was a powerful seer, a talent she'd inherited from her great-grandmother. She hadn't yet fully come to terms with what she was. He wasn't surprised she'd "forgotten" that he wasn't the only one supplying their offspring's supernatural genes.

The vase jumped again. Harmony turned to their son, shaking her finger at him. "Damon Junior! You heard your father, no . . . no *telekinesis*!" She made a face. "I can't believe I just said that."

The babe flashed a blinding grin, and Harmony melted. "The little charmer. He has your smile, honey. I'm going to have to become immune to it if I'm ever going to effectively discipline this kid. Oh, Damon, what are we going to do?"

"He's only a year old, lass. In time he'll learn to control his powers." Powers that Damon predicted would grow even stronger as he aged. "It's of utmost importance that we keep his abilities secret from Lucifer."

"I don't think that'll be a problem, seeing that I haven't talked to your former boss in"—Harmony pretended to concentrate—"ages. Our paths just never seem to cross," she quipped sarcastically. Then she noticed how serious he was, and her eyes opened wide. "Will Satan be able to sense him? Will he know what our baby can do? Oh, Lord, Damon, will he try to hurt our child?"

Fear gripped Damon. Anger, too. "We'll do everything in our power to ensure that never happens, lass. But one day the boy will rise as a powerful rival to the Devil."

Little Damon giggled, and the ice cubes in the pitcher of ice tea rattled. "Damon Junior!" Harmony scolded in unison with Damon. Then she whirled on him, eyes ablaze. "As for your last comment, Damon of Mysteria, don't think I didn't notice you sneaked that in. There will be no ultimate showdowns between our baby and the Devil. Do you hear me? I forbid it."

Outside, thunder rumbled as Harmony took a seat at the table. She mumbled grace before serving lunch, which they ate awed into silence by the prospect of epic battles of good and evil. A few moments later, the first raindrops began to fall.

The doors to Hell opened with a belch of heat, expelling a single demon before slamming closed again. The forest sang with the squeaks and scrabbling of the few winged subdemons and goblins released when the hellhole opened. The lesser beasts scattered into the mist, off to their wanton mischief, but the demon, experienced and centuries-old, scurried with purpose through the rain. There were miles yet to cover before reaching the hamlet of Mysteria.

Mindful was the demon of keeping out of the sight of humans. It could not be interrupted, stymied, or sidetracked. It had a job to do. Find the child. Kill it before it grew to adulthood and challenged Lucifer himself.

"Fail, and I will erase you, eradicate you, stamp you out—for all eternity! No matter where you run, no matter where you hide, I will find you, and end you."

The she-demon cowered and hissed, crouching out of sight as she took on her traditional human form. Her coarse red hide fell away, replaced by smooth, creamy flesh. Cloven hooves elongated into two feet, complete with ten perfect shell-pink toenails. Gone were the horns sprouting from her skull; in their place were jaw-length waves in rich, reddish brown. Slits no longer dominated her copper-colored eyes. They were rimmed with dark lashes, appearing completely human. No one would be able to tell what she was and what she'd come here to do.

Kill. The wind howled and shook the canopy of rain-drenched trees. Under the cloak of low-hanging clouds, Shay lurched forward and down the hillside, knowing *exactly* where to go.

Two

"Can you really smell a demon a mile away?"

Quel Laredo stood in front of Mysteria's wishing fountain, surveying the town square. A breeze whipped his duster around his long, denim-clad legs. Water from the fountain sent mist into the dry, Rocky Mountain air. Sniffing, his eyes in a perpetual squint, he sampled that air, tasting it. The storm had passed, allowing the sunset to break through, but something wasn't quite right about this twilight. He couldn't figure out what.

"Can you, Mr. Laredo?"

"Yeah." The wide-eyed boy was one of the O'Cleary grandchildren, he guessed. He'd lost count of them all. They weren't a family; they were a herd. "Two miles if the wind is right."

"Like now?" the boy breathed in fearful wonder.

Nodding, Quel peered into the deepening shadows in the woods at the edge of town. The scent of evil was growing stronger. There was definitely something out there.

"Hey, Laredo, do you want to buy me a drink? Come on, you know you do." A comely enchantress brushed her hand along his arm as she passed by with her female friends. "We'll be at Knight Caps. Afterward, I'm free."

"I'm working."

"Late?"

"Late."

"Shame." Her voice turned husky. "All work and no play makes Quel a dull boy." In the face of his silence, she tried to recant. "I mean, not that I find you dull. Not at all. It's just a saying."

He tipped his hat. "That's all right."

Smiling, she backed up, almost stumbling on her high heels before hurrying away to join her friends.

Her lush little ass swayed as she shimmied away. A nice piece, but Quel didn't feel much like company. There was something about the air tonight. It was different from anything he'd detected before. Something very old and very dark had been unleashed, and he wouldn't let down his guard until he figured out what it was.

Making snuffling sounds, the boy screwed up his face. "You smell anything yet, Mr. Laredo? I don't."

"Hurry on home, boy. Your mama's going to be worried."

Half in awe, half-terrified, the boy ran off. Not all that different of a reaction from the women in town, Quel thought. Not that he blamed others for the way they acted around him. He'd grown up tough, eight foster families in ten years, but that wasn't it, entirely. It was what people saw in his eyes that scared them away. His eyes reflected what he'd seen—and continued to see: demons.

Growing up, he thought demons were make-believe. Now he knew more about them than he wanted to know. The first time he'd laid eyes on a demon was on a battlefield in Iraq. He'd woken up bleeding from his head and chest after a roadside bomb had taken out the convoy he was escorting. He'd been working private security for Blackstone, he was experienced and sought out for it, but this time the terrorists had been kids—nothing but damn kids, no more than fourteen, fifteen years old. They did what few others had ever been able to pull off: they caught Quel Laredo by surprise. The attack was quick and on target. He'd woken to see a gangly, leather-skinned monster crouched next to one of the wounded soldiers. At the time, Quel was sure he was hallucinating. "You see that?" he croaked to his buddy, Hauser, who'd dragged him out of the hot sun.

"We're gonna get you patched up, Laredo. Hang in there."

Hang in there? As clear as day, Quel saw a medic fighting to save the soldier, pumping his heart even as the demon drained his soul. "I'm losing him," the frustrated rescuer shouted, oblivious of the demon.

Quel fought off Hauser. "Get it the fuck away from him!" The soldier would die if they didn't. Quel got to his hands and knees and dragged himself to the dying man, shoving the demon off his chest. The monster came back—this time for him. *Don't look at its eyes.* Quel remembered thinking that. The whirling red balls sucked his strength, his very life, leaving despair and terror in its place. *No!*

They rolled over the sand, grabbing for each other's throats. Then, remembering every last horror movie he'd ever seen, Quel stabbed him with the cross his mother had given him before she died.

Quel wasn't religious—he didn't follow much of anything—but the necklace was the only link he allowed to his past. The silver sank between the demon's ribs, sizzling as the creature convulsed, shrieking. By the time the surviving guys on his team got him wrestled to the ground, the damn thing was dead.

Everyone assumed he'd suffered a hallucination. So did Quel, until he started seeing demons all across Iraq. No wonder there was a damned war going on. Evil fueled it.

He put in his papers and left the Gulf. After a few months kicking around a friend's ranch in Montana, dogged by restlessness and too many memories, he ran into more demons. This time he knew what to do. People were more grateful than they were skeptical, and now even more afraid of him, but he was used to that. Might as well use his ability to see demons to make a living. Now he was Quel Laredo, demon hunter. It kept him on the move. Moving was good. It gave him less time to think. As a demon hunter, he could do some good, and he didn't have to face his past. A win-win situation, in his mind.

He had a lot to learn at first, and there was no shortage of people wanting to help him. Over the years, he'd studied with everyone from ninjas to witches. He learned that some demons were obvious to the human eye and that others preferred to be invisible, either by disguising themselves as humans or by using dark magic to remain unseen. Quel grabbed freelance demon-hunting jobs where he could find them, never staying long in one place or with any one person. He was like a swift river, sure and cold, always moving on. When Mysteria was hiring, he took the job—just for the winter, he'd thought—but he ended up staying. It had been a year now. He liked it. Maybe he just felt at home with the collection of other lost souls there.

The lost souls he'd sworn to protect.

Quel checked for his rifle, pistols, ammo, silver BBs for the smaller creatures, garlic, and the cross hanging from his neck as he paced in front of the fountain that was the centerpiece of Mysteria's town square. The water bubbled, sending up spray. The townspeople insisted the fountain was magic, that wishes made there would come true. Hell, he wouldn't mind the help. He'd find his demon that much sooner.

Frowning, he tasted the air again. Yeah, definitely demon. It was getting stronger, too—the scent of demon mixed with something sweeter, almost distracting. He didn't like that. No one distracted Quel Laredo.

He pulled on the brim of his hat and kept walking. There was a demon about, and he'd find it before sunrise . . . like he always did.

The night had cleared. Stars had come out. In the moonlight, Shay followed the road leading into Mysteria. She attracted less attention now that she was no longer naked—thanks to the generosity of some campers. Oh, they were startled to see her waltzing into their campsite wearing nothing but her bare curves. A well-placed thought, a blink of her eyes, and they let her take what she needed, convinced they'd done a good deed. Shay liked to leave mortals believing they'd done good, even when they helped her do things that were very, very bad. Yes, she was like the Good Samaritan except with ulterior motives.

The jeans were a little tight in the butt, but the T-shirt was just perfect, snug and smooth. ANGEL, it said, BY VICTORIA'S SECRET. Well, Shay had a secret, too: she was no angel. Her laughter floated in the damp, chill air of the mountains as she smoothed her hands over the outfit. She enjoyed showing off her assets. This body was her favorite. It had served her well for most of the last few thousand of years. Why not showcase it—to Damon's downfall? *You're not to bed him. You're to kill the child.* Yes, she must remember, no sleeping with Damon. She must keep focused on her mission, even at the temporary expense of fashion. Lucifer wanted no delays.

Eventually she came upon what looked to be an inn. Inside, several couples shared a table as they ate dinner. She sashayed past the line of parked cars, brushing her fingers over the hoods, and paused next to a little red sports car. Her driving had never been as good as her chariot skills, but then she'd not had as many centuries to practice. Still, how could she walk away from this sweet little Porsche, irresistible in devil red? She had a job to do, yes. No one said she couldn't have some fun while doing it.

A blink of her eyes, and the locks popped open. The diners behind the restaurant window glanced her way, alarmed. Shay blinked, placed the thought: *You see my taking the car as a favor. You want me to have it. Think of it as a little gift. Your generosity makes you feel good.*

They went back to their meal. Smug, Shay slid in behind the wheel and started up the car. A blink of her eyes, and the license plates and registration reflected her human alter ego: Shay d'Mon. She giggled. Oh, how she enjoyed a good play on words. Yes, Miss d'Mon, single, white, twenty-five years old, complete with no living family and a teaching degree. With the engine purring, she smiled and pulled onto the highway and shoved the gas pedal to the floor. "Full speed ahead."

A pair of headlights appeared on the road that wound down through the hills into town. Someone was driving way too fast. Outsider, Quel thought, testing the air. Demon. He smelled demon. Yeah, demon and that sweet hint of something delicious underneath that somehow didn't belong.

Maybe the car had come in contact with the demon and didn't contain the creature itself. He'd never known demons to drive, but they were crafty; they adapted. He wouldn't know until it got closer. Quel cradled his rifle in his arms and waited.

The car sped toward town, barely staying on the rain-slick road as it made the switchback turns. It was either a demon without a driver's license or a dumb-ass city boy playing NASCAR.

A pack of werewolves scampered across the square, headed toward the woods. They'd have to cross the road to do that. Quel glanced at the rising full moon and swore. They'd be too crazed by their hormones to see the danger careening toward them.

"Watch out," Quel shouted as the car sped toward them. The sound of brakes being applied shrieked in the night. Werewolves scattered. The car fishtailed and spun. A rear wheel clipped the shoulder of the road, flipping the vehicle over. It rolled all the way down the embankment and landed right side up in the center of the fountain with one helluva splash.

Now he'd seen everything. Quel cocked his rifle and headed that way. Whoever—or whatever—was driving that car sure knew how to make an entrance.

Three

Satan's stones! One minute Shay was swerving to avoid hitting what looked like a dog pack, and the next she was submerged up to her neck in cold water that smelled like a stale pond. Her legs were pinned by the crushed front end of the car, while the rest of her was being crushed by something that felt like a giant balloon.

Cursed air bags. Safety devices were for cowards and mortals with finite life spans.

It took a few seconds to register, but the water was rising—and rising fast. It bubbled over her chest to her shoulders, creeping toward her neck. She couldn't kick free; her feet were wedged in too tightly. Her hands hunted for something to hold onto, flailing and splashing. Hell's bells, she felt like a landed trout!

More like a landed piranha. She was that angry—at herself. She liked attention—adored it, actually—but not this much attention. The crash would wake everyone in town and maybe put them on guard against her. She was a stranger on a secret mission. *Win their trust,* Lucifer had advised her. Escapades like this were not going to get her closer to the child.

The rising water now sloshed at chin level. She sputtered, swearing. Instead of succumbing to panic, she followed the pull of a new and all-encompassing urge—the will to *survive*—and tried to claw her way out of the air bag.

Something banged on the outside of the car. A shadowy form moved outside the shattered windshield. "Here," she called. Fires of hell, *here*. Never had she been so happy to see a mortal, a silly, selfless human who'd come to save her. She couldn't afford to drown.

If she destroyed this body, she'd have to return to Hell and get a new one, starting all over again. What would the Dark Master think of that? Not much. She could picture him now, pacing and spitting in fury. Not a day into this mission, and she'd already faltered. *"I will erase you, eradicate you, stamp you out—for all eternity!"*

The human was pounding on the door now, mere inches away. *Please,* she thought. *Please?* Since when did Shay beg for anything— or anyone?

"Snap out of it, Shay," she muttered through gritted teeth. She used to be resourceful. She tried to reach the door handle herself, but her legs were pinned, wouldn't let her stretch far enough.

The urge to survive expanded, filling her chest, growing more powerful with each beat of her heart, as if she were indeed truly alive and not pretending. She'd long wanted to know what that felt like. Now she never would.

Oh, how she wished otherwise. Over the centuries she'd barely touched what it meant to live, to feel, always wanting more depth of emotion, craving it, but unable to cross the line separating her from what she was and what she'd secretly yearned to be. Always, Lucifer would figure out what she loved most and take it away: Circus Maximus and chariot racing, cuddling in the furs with Swift River on glacial, star-filled nights. He took them all. The poignancy of loss sliced deep— that which was dealt her and that which she'd caused.

She'd inflicted much pain. She'd never cared before. Now the knowledge of her deeds hurt in a way she'd never thought imaginable. She regretted not only her recent misdeeds but every evil act she'd ever accomplished.

You shouldn't have sent those orphans on a one-way voyage into the sea. Or bedded Aquila the day after his wife told him they were going to have another child.

She even regretted stealing the red sports car and wrecking it. Remorse and shame flooded her, choking her. *I'm sorry . . . Truly sorry.*

She was evil. She deserved to die.

No, only living creatures died. *Monsters like you cease to be.*

Shay tipped her chin up and stole a few last breaths before the water caught up, rising over her eyes, her forehead, and submerging her fully. In no time she'd be waking up back in Hell with Lucifer kicking her ass.

Instead, a soft, white cushion enveloped her, something she'd never remembered experiencing after her previous accidents. She went from acute remorse to utter serenity and did not question it. The roll bar slipped from her hands, but somehow she knew everything was going to be okay. The feeling of trust was instinctive, all-encompassing.

For the first time in her life she felt at peace.

It was no longer dark. Shay looked around in wonder. A field of endless soft snow surrounded her . . . so white, so beautiful. And there, across the way, Swift River waited, dressed in furs, his hair flowing in a wind she couldn't feel. He opened his arms. Smiling, she took the first step toward him.

*   *   *

"Goddamn it, *breathe*."

Reality returned in jagged slices. Someone pushing on her chest. A warm mouth sealed over hers. Air swelling her lungs. The scents of sweat and leather, dust and man filling her nostrils. Then she was coughing, her lungs on fire.

Another flash: her eyes opening, a face looming inches from hers. "About damn time," the male voice muttered. He cushioned her skull from the ground with a hand buried in her soaked hair. Water fell nearby, misting, gurgling, soothing in contrast to the agony hammering inside her skull. "Thought I was going to have to call the coroner," he growled. "You saved me the trouble, but don't get me wrong, lady, you're still a pain in the ass."

Her vision cleared, and the face came into focus: handsome, raw-featured, and eyes so blue it hurt to look at them. *The color of cold, deep water that all but begged a probing of their bottomless depths.* She knew that face and those eyes. "Swift River . . ."

"River?" His laugh was quick, derisive. "You landed in the damn fountain."

She tried to make sense of his modern speech. And his apparent anger. "What happened to the snow?" Her speech sounded a bit slurred to her ears. "All the pretty white snow . . ."

He muttered what sounded like an exasperated curse. "You damn well better not go into hypothermic shock. That'll really piss me off. Here, put this on." She was as limp as a rag as he jostled her, lifting her gently to wrap her in a coat—his coat. That's when she realized she was shivering, her teeth clattering together.

"It's b-been so long." She soaked in the sight of the man she never thought she'd see again. Centuries hadn't erased the memory of his eyes that could alternately turn dark with passion or shine with intelligence, cruelty, or mischief. *Lucifer took you from me. He made me hurt you.*

How could she have done what she did? Her throat ached. Tears welled up in her eyes. Real tears, not the ones she was so good at simulating. "I made the avalanche," she confessed in a whisper. "I buried you. I destroyed the settlement."

Swift River bent forward, coming closer. To kiss her, she thought.

She hungered for the touch of his lips. Her entire aching body strained upward to meet him halfway.

He didn't kiss her. He didn't even touch her. He sniffed the air as if trying to detect an odor.

"I like your smell, woman," Swift River used to tell her. He told her so many things; *"I love you,"* even, although she'd implanted that thought in his mind. Still, a part of her sensed, *hoped*, he may have meant it.

She brushed her fingers across his warm jaw. "I'm so sorry . . ."

Sighing, he took hold of her hand, removing it from his face. For a second, she thought there might have been a softening of his hard expression; then he spoke, spoiling the illusion. "I'd be sorry, too, lady. Someone's going to be mighty pissed you wrecked their pretty red Porsche."

A siren wailed in the background, piercing her head with pain and bringing her back to her senses. The snow was gone. People had gathered around, murmuring in hushed, concerned voices. The man crouched next to her wasn't Swift River, though the resemblance was strong. This wasn't the Ice Age; this was Mysteria, and this angry, modern-day man wasn't her lover. Not even close. By now Swift River would have had her out of her clothes and under the furs with him, hot skin, cold nights. Bliss.

The blue-eyed stranger observed her with a curious expression on his face. He shifted his weight, his boots creaking, his narrowed eyes darker. Had he guessed the direction of her thoughts?

"I thought you were someone else," she explained.

He gave the air another sniff. "That makes two of us, sweetheart."

Sweetheart. An endearment, but spoken without any obvious tenderness.

You love me. You adore me. She planted the thought in his mind. She'd rather face a simpering love slave than this man's indifference. His expression, however, remained unchanged.

What, was he immune to her powers of persuasion? She didn't sense dark powers in him. Bat bugger, she didn't sense anything at all. Something wasn't right. An uneasy glance around made her aware of the gathering crowd. Why was she still here in the human's world, anyway? It made no sense. She'd died—or at least she'd experienced a demon's version of dying. *Except for the haunting vision of the snow, and all the white light.*

It was so beautiful . . .

Shay gave her head a small shake. Mistake—the sharp pain nearly blinded her. She moaned. Maybe she *was* back in Hell, and Lucifer was playing with her, teasing her with images of her Ice Age lover. More than any other demon, Lucifer liked to torment her. She'd eventually learned never to reveal partiality to anything—or anyone—because he'd force her to give them up.

The blue-eyed man stood as the ambulance pulled up and stopped. Doors slammed. A man with tousled brown hair and glasses, a wrinkled shirt, and loosened tie elbowed his way to where she lay on the pavement.

"I'm Dr. Fogg," he greeted. He immediately took out a flashlight and shined it in her eyes. Grumbling, she tried to turn away, but he wouldn't let her. If she hadn't been hurting as much as she was, she would have gotten up and left the scene, leaving them to practice their mortal medicine on someone else.

The blue-eyed man watched the doctor's every action—and hers. His glare was intent, unwavering. A rifle hung from one hand. "You'd better take a good look at her, Doc. She's been babbling. She thinks it's snowing."

Babbling? Suck a frog, mortal. She shot him a glare, but it made her head spin. He seemed to notice, his mouth twitching ever so slightly in amusement, almost as if he'd provoked her on purpose. Then he sobered, sniffing the air again and frowning. She was tempted to conjure up some exotic perfume—the Egyptians were quite good at crafting it—but she didn't want to call notice to her identity. She was here undercover.

A dark-haired woman wearing a khaki uniform and a star pinned to her chest showed up, jotting notes on a pad. She had a pretty face and a boyish way about her. "Sheriff," the blue-eyed man said, nodding.

"Laredo," she greeted back. Surveying the Porsche with its front end submerged in the fountain, she sent Shay a withering look. "A dead-on dunk by a drop-down drunk. Now, this is a new one on me."

"I'm not drunk," Shay said.

"High, then."

"No."

The sheriff made a quiet snort. "Miss, how fast were you going? Was there a reason you were in such a hurry?"

The doctor removed his glasses to frown at the sheriff. "She's in shock and probably has a concussion. Save your strong-arm tactics. I'll give her a blood test at the hospital. In the meantime, no more questioning until she's stabilized."

That suited Shay just fine. With her powers of persuasion apparently on the fritz, she'd be forced to make up a story. Mortals were basically smart; they wouldn't believe just anything. Whatever she fabricated had to be convincing.

"Can you touch your right finger to your nose?" the doctor requested.

"Of course." Shay's finger landed on her upper lip.

"Must be that alcohol she's not drinking, or the drugs she's not taking," the sheriff muttered.

Blue eyes—Laredo—chuckled. Shay's temper burned. No one laughed at her. She'd show him the consequences of his error. *You fall to your knees, sobbing as you beg forgiveness.* She blinked, implanting the thought. Nothing. It bounced right off his mind. Fuming, she turned to the sheriff. *You itch terribly between your legs.*

The woman continued to scribble notes on her notepad. Shay felt the first tingles of fear. What had happened to her powers? She felt as disoriented and defenseless as a gladiator standing in the middle of the arena who just realized he'd left his weapons behind.

"Hey, Laredo," the sheriff said. "Doc Fogg says you pulled her out of the wreck and resuscitated her. That's hero stuff."

Laredo shrugged off the sheriff's compliment.

"Just doing your job, I know. Consider me impressed. When I hired a demon hunter, I thought I was getting a killer not a lifesaver."

Shay's gaze whipped back to Laredo. Satan's stones! He was a demon hunter? How could she have let him get this close without sensing what he was? Then it hit her that he didn't recognize what she was, either. If he had, he would have killed her, not revived her.

He wasn't completely fooled, though. He acted suspicious but not certain—but to a demon hunter, a demon of her caliber should have been obvious. It was clear something had neutralized her dark powers.

"You landed in the damn fountain."

She remembered Laredo's words with sudden unease. Lucifer had warned her to stay away from Mysteria's wishing fountain. *This* was why. The "damn fountain" had stolen her powers and rendered her helpless. Well, if not quite helpless then very much human.

Human . . . Something inside her leaped at the thought. All her long existence had she not fantasized about being human? *Mortal.* Craved the thrill of feeling real emotion, of knowing she walked along a finite road of destiny under the constant threat of death? How exhilarating it was to pretend; doing it for real was another thing entirely. The vulnerability was breathtaking.

Terrifying.

And most certainly terminal.

"I will find you, and end you." Lucifer's threat strangled her silly daydreams and dragged her back to her senses. *"You cannot hide."* Panic gnawed away at her composure, worsening her all-too-human headache. This condition had better be transitory, or she was history. Literally. How could she complete her mission if she was weak and had—she cringed—emotions? Hell's bells, she'd been bawling only moments ago, thinking Laredo was Swift River. Ugh—how weak! How human. Even now her heart—or what passed for a heart—leaped every time their eyes met. Which was every damn time she glanced his way.

Even as she formed the thought, Laredo was watching her, hard—and not because his heart was leaping (or any other part of him) with the sight of her, she'd bet. He wanted to kill her, not kiss her, and wouldn't hesitate if she gave any hint of being a demon. In her weakened state, he might very well finish the job.

A woman squeezed past the people surrounding the scene. "Hello, honey." The woman dropped to a crouch next to Shay and took her hand in hers. She had creamy brown skin, black curly hair shot through with copper highlights, and a smile that could melt glaciers. "I'm Reverend Harmony Faithfull. How can I help?"

Shay's gloom vanished in a *poof*. Harmony Faithfull. The mother of the child Lucifer wanted destroyed had walked right into her clutches. What a stroke of devil's fortune, she thought with a slow smile. Suddenly, things were not as bleak as they seemed. "You already have helped, Reverend. More than you know." Yet, the thought of hurting Harmony or anyone else gathered around left her feeling sick to her stomach.

Once she got away from the damn fountain, she'd be fine. By morning she'd be able to commence her mission.

As the doctor checked Shay's blood pressure and other vital signs, Harmony took out a cell phone. "Is there someone I can call for you? Your family? A husband?"

At the mention of a husband, Shay felt Laredo's stare sharpen. Jealous, was he? She ignored him, trying to project instead a quiet sadness as she shook her head. She needed to throw her whole being and many millennia of lying into convincing Harmony to trust her around the babe. The thought made her stomach clench and her mouth go dry.

Before she had a chance to answer, the sheriff returned. "I ran your plates, Miss Shay d'Mon." Shay cringed at the surname she'd chosen. It had seemed a good idea at the time. Now she regretted it. Laredo's suspicious stare was fierce. She didn't want that man making any connections between her and the underworld, especially not while her demon powers were down. "Your record's clean. Nothing on you at all. Yet, here's your car, swimming in our fountain. What did you do? Fall asleep at the wheel?"

Shay's gaze shot to Harmony's. She couldn't have the woman thinking she was irresponsible. *I'm hardworking, honest. I'm the perfect woman to trust around your son.* She blinked, planting the thought in Harmony's head.

The minister's expression remained exactly the same. Serpent's breath! Without her legendary powers of mental persuasion, she'd have to rely on her wits. She was sure she had some; she'd just never had to rely on them before.

"Aw, honey. It'll be all right." Harmony took her hand, squeezing it. Her gaze intensified as she held fast to Shay's fingers, conjuring the unsettling feeling that the minister saw much more than she let on. Shay's instinct was to pull her hand away, yet there was something so compelling about the reverend's regard that it kept Shay in place. In Harmony's gaze, she felt accepted, forgiven . . . *good*. Yes, good. In that breathless moment that seemed to hang still in time, Shay was no longer evil.

No longer a monster.

Then Harmony patted her hand, breaking the spell. Her eyes were moist; a sheen of perspiration shone on her forehead. She appeared almost as unsettled as Shay. "You have a soul," she murmured. "A good and sweet soul."

Shay covered her appalled snort with a fake coughing attack.

"Leave her be, Reverend Faithfull," Dr. Fogg scolded. "This young woman needs to rest. She's in shock."

If she wasn't in shock before, she sure was now. Shay hoped Lucifer wasn't eavesdropping on any of this. Withering warts, a soul! And not just any soul, a "good and sweet" soul. Bat bugger. She hoped to hell the condition wasn't permanent, merely a trick of the fountain.

Some trick. If it could implant souls in demons, the fountain was more dangerous than she'd thought. Lucifer should have been more specific. *Unless he didn't know.* If he didn't, and these mortals did, it could prove the undoing of the entire dark empire.

Well, no matter. If a soul got in, she could get it out. She'd worry about that tomorrow. As long as her master didn't know anything was wrong, she was fine.

Harmony stood. "I'll be out of the good doctor's hair now, but if you need anything, call." She smiled once more before disappearing in the crowd.

At the doctor's direction, the ambulance crew transferred Shay to a stretcher. Going to a hospital was a delay she couldn't afford. What choice did she have? She didn't know how severe her injuries were. Without her demon powers, she'd have to rely on the mortals to repair her. Then again, Harmony Faithfull was coming to her hospital room in the morning to see how she was doing. Shay didn't have to lift a finger to lure her there.

A soul, a good and sweet soul. The woman's pronouncement haunted her. On the bright side, a soul would throw Laredo off her scent. She stole another glance at the man working so hard to figure her out. Her heart gave another little leap.

He walked alongside the stretcher as they wheeled her to the ambulance. His gait was deceptively casual. There was banked power in that walk. Killing power. He was impressively built, though his frame tended toward leanness rather than bulk. She imagined he hadn't an ounce of fat on that body. He didn't seem to be a man who tolerated overindulgence in himself or in anyone else. Shay, on the other hand, loved to indulge, which, of course, underscored the fact that they'd never get along.

Much to her annoyance, Laredo stayed close as she was loaded into the rear of the ambulance. Was he that worried she'd escape? She could hardly lift her aching head much less sit up or walk.

With his rifle cradled in his arms, the demon hunter waited in silence until the doctor and medics had settled her in. "Your coat, Mr. Laredo." A medic handed Laredo the coat he'd draped over her. It left her top half uncovered. Her soaking-wet pink T-shirt was molded to every curve and contour of her breasts.

Laredo read the slogan scrawled across her chest. "Angel?" His smile was slow, feral. "We'll see about that, Miss d'Mon." To her disgust, her heart leaped with the heat and the challenge of his dark stare. Slamming the door closed, he walked away, shoving his rifle back in his holster.

Shay glowered after him. Let him see if he was as arrogant once her powers of persuasion returned!

Four

The morning Shay d'Mon was released from Mysteria General, Quel blended in with the crowd gathered in the town square for the weekly farmers' market. He bought an apple from a vendor and leaned back against a light post, biting into the fruit while keeping an eye on the Faithfull family: Harmony, Damon, and their boy. The couple had picked up Shay the moment she was discharged. Now, after taking her to lunch, they were giving her the grand tour, including introducing her to what townspeople hadn't witnessed her infamous crash into the fountain.

They exited an ice cream shop. Shay ran a pointed tongue around the base of the ice cream. It was just a damn ice cream cone, but the woman put her whole focus into indulging in it . . . licking . . . savoring. It was probably the thousandth time she'd eaten ice cream, but she made it look like it was the first time and the best damn thing she'd ever tasted. Swearing, he forced his eyes away from that mouth. He'd been all about resuscitating her the night of the crash, but he hadn't forgotten the way those lips felt. She was dressed in the same clothes. Laundered, they fit just right on her tight, toned little body. "Angel," he muttered, shaking his head as he read that damn pink shirt of hers. "We'll see . . ."

As if she'd sensed his attention, Shay turned his way. Quel touched the brim of his hat and nodded. *Yeah, darlin', I'm keeping an eye on you.* There it was again, always that look of surprise chased by sadness and unmistakable heat. Just like the other night, it got to him, and he didn't like it, not one frickin' bit. If he didn't know better, he'd say she missed him. But, hell, she didn't know him—and probably didn't want to, based on his record with women. He probably reminded her of someone who'd done her wrong. Or maybe his little "angel" had done the man wrong.

Then she was whisked away by the Faithfulls without another glance in his direction. Quel narrowed his eyes and took a sniff. One taste of the air brought the unmistakable scent of *her*.

Not, he acceded stubbornly, a demon.

Bullshit. He took a brutal bite of the apple, frowning as he chewed. He'd smelled that she-demon the moment it came down the hill. If it wasn't Shay, then somewhere, somehow, a demon had done a bait and switch. All he could do was lay in wait for it to make a mistake.

"Take him," Harmony said, grinning as she dropped a wriggling little boy in Shay's arms, drawing Shay's attention away from the enigmatic demon hunter who'd been shadowing their tour of the town. If only Quel Laredo would go away and stop reminding her of what she was—and what she could never be.

Awkwardly, Shay juggled the squirming weight in her arms. Satan's stones—here she was, pretending to be a child-care provider, and she'd never once held a child. She'd never wanted to. Harmony, thank the Dark Lord, didn't seem to notice. "He's a handful, isn't he?"

Shay swallowed hard. It wasn't her intent or desire to get to know the boy. Especially since she was going to have to—

"Park!" The boy strained in the direction of the lawn and play area across the street. Other children played, their mothers watching, smiling as if their offspring were the cutest things on earth.

To Shay's shock, disgust didn't fill her as she'd expected. Nor, however, did she want to join the group. It was too far outside her experience—and interests. *It's a chance to get the babe alone.* Yes, but she couldn't kill it here, not in front of everyone. The thought of killing it at all was growing increasingly repulsive. As soon as she recovered, her reservations—*her conscience*—would pass, she was certain. Meanwhile, she'd better role-play and strengthen the family's trust in her.

"Take him to the swings, if you like," Harmony coaxed. "Damon and I will stay here. It'll give you two a little time to become acquainted."

Forcing a smile, Shay hoisted little Damon higher on her hip. "Let's play while your mama and papa finish their ice cream." She remembered to look both ways before crossing the street—pretending to be mortal required so many little details—and headed toward the park.

The babe brought a warm sticky hand to her cheek, holding her gaze in a direct, quite disconcerting way, much like his mother. "Shay good."

A low laugh escaped her. "I wouldn't jump to conclusions."

"Good Shay," he insisted.

Wincing, Shay took the babe's hand, holding it in hers as she lowered it. She wasn't good. Not at all. She was a monster of the worst kind. Soon, very soon, the babe would learn the truth about her.

"Hey, Laredo, what do you think of the Faithfull's new nanny and Mysteria's newest citizen, Shay d'Mon?"

Quel almost choked on the cup of coffee he was about to gulp. "What?"

Jeanie, the sheriff, slid onto a stool next to him in the coffee shop. "Yup, our little fountain splasher. Hired. Yesterday. I'll take the special, Elvira," she called to the waitress.

Quel drained his coffee cup and rammed it down to the counter. He grabbed his hat and coat, grumbling, "See you, Sheriff."

"Where you going?"

"To talk some sense into those folks."

"Harmony and Damon? They know what they're doing."

He snorted. "Doesn't much sound like it. Look, you hired me to look after the people here, and that's what I'm going to do."

"I appreciate that, Laredo. You know I do. But her background check came back clean."

"As clean as an unemployed, midwestern schoolteacher who crashes sports cars willed to them by their deceased parents can be, I guess." If Shay had relayed that information with her own lips, Quel would have laughed it off as lies. But the woman didn't have to say a thing. Jeanie had found it all using the info from Shay's license and registration. "A sweet smile or two, a pure-as-driven-snow background as a kindergarten teacher, and she goes and gets herself hired as their nanny? Do they have any idea who—or what—she might be?"

"Like you just said, a small-town teacher with a spotless record. Not even a traffic ticket. Well, before last Tuesday."

"You gave her a ticket? Well. There's justice in this town, after all."

"Shay owes me community service in lieu of a fine."

"Let me guess—at the car wash." Quel threw the tip on the counter and headed for the exit. "Now, if you'll excuse me, I'm paying the Faithfulls a visit."

"Or maybe it's just an excuse to say hello to Miss d'Mon. There's more than a little electricity going back and forth between you two. I'm not the only one who's noticed."

Quel stopped short, his back aimed at the sheriff. *Electricity?* He removed a toothpick from his pocket and slipped it between his lips. "The only thing going back and forth is my investigation and Miss d'Mon not liking it."

Then he pushed out the swinging door into the sunshine, scowling as he did so. Since when had he become such a rotten liar?

In the cottage that Reverend Faithfull shared with her husband Damon, Quel stalked past a kitchen table topped with brownies and milk. His boots scuffed over the hardwood floor. His silver-bullet-loaded revolver rubbed against his hip. "Reverend Faithfull—"

"Harmony," she corrected with her usual bright smile.

"Harmony. Jeanie tells me you're thinking of hiring Miss d'Mon as your new nanny."

"We already did."

"Because you think she has a good soul," he said, skeptical about the minister's purported talent as a seer that the entire town took for granted—except him. "How do you know for sure?"

"It's my job to know." The reverend wore her pastor's face that tried to get him to feel guilty about never setting foot in her church. Thing was, he had more things to blame God for than to thank him for. Since church was for praying and thanking, and not blaming, he never showed. The way he saw it, he killed demons for the Big Man. That should be enough. "And," she said, blushing, "I can see things other people can't, Mr. Laredo, just like you can sense demons. Shay has a good soul. I saw it. I *felt* it."

"It's a demon trick. That's what they do. Your guard goes down, and they get you. Or, in this case, your kid."

Her husband spoke up. "Demons can do many things, aye, but they can't replicate a mortal soul." Damon was a former demon high lord. If anyone knew about demons, it was this man.

"All I know is that I never sensed anything that powerful. Whatever came down that mountain was old as shit. I had one thing on my mind: get it out of the car and kill it before it killed any of us."

Harmony lifted a brow. "Glad you took a moment to access the situation."

"That's the thing. I didn't. By the time I got to the wreck, it didn't smell like demon anymore. It didn't smell like anything I've ever come across, either." Not exactly demon, not exactly human.

But 100 percent woman. A damned sexy woman, too, with all the right curves and attitude to spare. He couldn't stop thinking about how the hell stench had morphed into a hot little thing with an innocence about her that didn't fit the heat in her eyes. His senses blasted on high alert whenever their eyes met. No one had ever looked at him with that much hunger, that much longing. Even if she did admit she'd mixed him up with someone else, it was damn unnerving. Damn arousing. *Laredo, focus. You gotta think with your head not your cock.* Hell and damn. Since when did he ever have trouble keeping the two apart? It was all jumbled up. He was all jumbled up.

"Shay has no defenses, Quel, none," Harmony assured him, clearly trying to sway his opinion. "I can see right through her. There's goodness there. She's also conflicted, lonely. Afraid."

He remembered Shay's tears. Yeah, they'd looked pretty frickin' genuine. Damn lucky he came to his senses before he wiped them off her cheek with his knuckle like he wanted to. He frowned. Quel Laredo didn't wipe away tears. He didn't know how. Yet she had him wanting to learn. She'd gotten under his skin, skin so thick he'd long since assumed it was impenetrable. Maybe Shay *was* an angel, and he was all wrong. Maybe he'd been around the wrong kind of woman for so long he didn't know how to recognize the right kind.

Quel glanced out the kitchen window and into the backyard where the couple had told him Shay was spending time with the boy. Standing by the pond near the barn, she held the child in her arms, handing him bread crusts to throw to the ducks. The breeze lifted and tossed her curls around her neck and jaw. Suddenly, she looked sweet and vulnerable, like a young mother. Was this the monster he thought he'd find in the sports car? A woman with the face of an angel, the shirt of an angel, and the devil in her eyes. Damon and Harmony trusted her. Was he wrong not to?

Exhaling, Quel tiredly rubbed his face. He hadn't shaved. He'd hardly slept. "I know what I sensed that night, Damon. As clear as day I know. My gut's telling me whatever came down that hill didn't up and disappear. Yeah, maybe it's not Shay, maybe it's not in Mysteria at all, but I won't ignore my instincts. I did, once, and half my convoy got taken out in Iraq. Now I pay attention. I'm not letting down my guard. I advise you don't, either."

"I trust my wife's instincts. I'll take yours into account, as well."

Quel nodded. His attention drifted outside again, where Shay hugged the boy close as if he were her own. Quel had a fleeting memory of being hugged by his mother in the early years before she left. After that he adopted such a fierce outside shell that few risked reaching out. He never made it worth their while. Though if they'd tried a little harder, tried more than once, he might have let them in. No one ever did. He didn't need cowards in his life then or now. He'd raised himself and was proud of it. Yet he had to wonder what he'd missed with the absence of any softness in his life.

With the child in her arms, Shay disappeared behind the barn. A chill washed over him. It was as if the sun had gone behind a cloud. He made fists, trying to resist the urge to follow—to chase down the sun. Impossible, he realized, and grabbed for an excuse to see her again. To see the pining in her eyes again. Hey, so he was being soft. So what? Sue him. If he liked the way a woman looked at him, no one needed to know. "Now that she's going to be staying here, I'd better go and reintroduce myself."

Harmony frowned at him. "It took us weeks to find a nanny. If you scare her away, Laredo . . ."

"I'll be good. I promise."

The couple sitting at the table didn't look convinced. Damn, his reputation was worse than he'd thought. No one, not even the town pastor, wanted him near the woman. "I'll play nice. I do know how." So he was a little out of practice. No one needed to know that. In the meantime, it wouldn't hurt to get to know Miss d'Mon a little better, angel . . . or not.

⚘

Five

If ever the moment to strike was right, it was this one. Here she was, alone with the babe, unwatched. Now was her chance.

Pink-cheeked, little Damon sat perched on Shay's hip, giggling at the ducks. The idea of murdering the child and taking its bones to Lucifer threatened to make her violently ill. She'd killed men with a blink of her eyes. Now she was paralyzed by guilt and disgust at the thought of betraying the mortals who trusted her. The sensation had gotten worse over the past few days, not better.

Bat bugger. It was the blasted soul. *Out, out,* she chanted in her mind. Ever since she rode the ambulance to the hospital, she'd been willing the soul to leave her body, begging it to go away throughout her treatment by humans who seemed to care for her despite her sloppy entrance into town, despite her being a stranger. No matter how hard she tried, she couldn't get rid of it. Worse, kindness was feeling pretty good when it used to make her sick. How much longer could she fool Lucifer into thinking she was doing her job? If he found out what had happened, she was toast. And if the Faithfull family learned of her true mission . . . well, she was still toast.

Think of something, Shay. Think!

No plan beyond hiding out came to her. No ideas. No strategy. Where were those wits she was so sure she possessed? *"You stupid creature."* She squeezed her eyes shut, remembering Lucifer's tirade before he sent her from Hell. He made no secret that he thought her stupid. Vile, yes, but lacking in the wits department. Anger lanced through her, and she opened her eyes, glaring at the pond. She was smarter than her master thought, and she'd prove it. How, she didn't yet know, but it would come to her; surely it would.

By now, Lucifer would be wondering why she hadn't reported in with her status. Soon she had to send word of her progress, or he'd grow suspicious. Her master knew her weaknesses. Even now he might be watching her holding little Damon, the scene projected on the molten walls of his lair.

"More!"

She pressed more bread into Damon's outstretched hand. His baby fragrance drifted to her. Babies mystified her; she knew little about them and wasn't interested in learning more, yet there was an innocence about them, a goodness, that she'd never really noticed before. *Perhaps you were not capable of noticing.* Glancing around to make sure no one was watching, least of all Lucifer, she touched her lips to the top of little Damon's head, her favorite spot. Soft, warm skin, silken curls. Her hand drifted lower, down to the babe's fragile neck, so easily snapped . . .

No.

Gasping, she snatched back her hand. Assassinating the babe ensured her master's future. Letting it live assured her master's end. Kill or spare the child: each of her potential actions contradicted the other. She'd seen people tortured on the rack during the Middle Ages, pulled apart by opposing forces. Torn between good and evil, between conscience and duty, she decided the rack could not have been any worse than this.

Tiny fingers landed on her cheek, turning her head to bring her eye to eye with the child she was supposed to kill. Those gray blue eyes searched hers, deeply and with disarming intensity. Swallowing, Shay turned her eyes away, lest the little one see her purpose and her true nature.

The boy's sticky hand pressed on her chin, forcing her gaze back to his. A year-old babe imposing his will on an ancient demon! No wonder her lord wanted the child dead.

"Shay . . . good," the child said. "Good Shay."

Choked with guilt, she hugged him close, burying her nose in that pile of curls. "You know I'm not good," she whispered. "I'm a monster. But I can't do it." *Yet.* "You're safe." *For now.*

The only certainty was her demise. No matter what her decision, it would bring about the end of her existence.

"Birdie!" Shay lifted her head at little Damon's cry. With the child cradled close, she turned around. A raven had landed in one of the surrounding trees. Even without her demon powers, she sensed something amiss in its presence. Was it Lucifer's minion, here to check on her? Or was she just being paranoid, hindered by her new, humanlike weakness?

"More birdies!"

Several other ravens flew into the trees, ruffling their shiny black feathers as they settled in to watch her. Their small, obsidian eyes followed her every step.

The sound of more approaching ravens came from behind her. A pinpoint of red glowed in their eyes now. Subdemons. Her pulse quickened. *Don't act afraid.* Lucifer will sense it. Shadows flew all around them, swooping uncomfortably close. She glanced wildly in the direction of the house. The more mortals to stand against subdemons, the better the chances of success. Even Lucifer accepted that. It was why he sent the inferior creatures in large numbers. She opened her mouth to call for help.

And stopped before she uttered a cry. To call attention to the sudden interest of the subdemons in her and the babe was to risk raising suspicion as to what she was and why she was here. She could—and would—handle this on her own.

She kept her voice calm. "Shall we go inside, little Damon? I will feed you one of your mother's brownies." A confection Shay had quickly become addicted to, she was happy to say. She deposited the babe in the stroller and gave the contraption a shove. It might not be a chariot, but she could steer it like one if she had to.

The ravens cawed, as if calling her back. *Speak with us.* The command rang in her head. She ignored them. *The Dark Lord wants an answer.*

"Shove it up your arses," she muttered.

"Arses!" the babe repeated.

"I will complete this mission in my own time," she sneered at the demons. "I will not be rushed. Do you hear? Tell your master to leave me be, or the trust I have gained with the family will be for naught." She jogged away from the pond, pushing the stroller along a dirt path. "Don't say *arses*," she told the babe. "It's not a nice word."

The cottage came into sight. Seeing it, she almost sobbed with relief. Then a deep, threatening growl brought her to a halt.

Damon and Harmony kept several goats. One of them stood in the middle of the path ahead. Its eyes were unnaturally bright—bright red. It should have been calling "Maaah." Instead it was growling like a wolf, its lips drawn back over yellowed fangs.

Little Damon pouted. "Bad doggie."

Shay grabbed a fallen stick and turned to face the new subdemon. "Go! I gave you my answer—go *now*."

With a breathtaking purpose, it clawed at the dirt with a cloven hoof and advanced on them. Shay stood between the stroller and the creature. It would have to kill her, or at least hurt her badly, to get past. She didn't want to think about that right now. *Keep positive*, she told herself in disgustingly optimistic mortal fashion as she held the stick out in front of her. Without powers, it was all about appearances, she realized. She put all the menace she could muster in her face and body and assumed the stance of a warrior.

The goat leaped. Shay raised the stick, gladiator-style. A loud pop tore through the silence. A second later, the goat was lying still on the path many feet from the reach of her stick. How?

Several smaller pops followed. Dark feathers and silver pellets rained down. One by one, the ravens disappeared from the trees. Then, like a vision of vengeance, Quel Laredo strode out of the woods, a weapon in each hand.

"Hello, angel," he said. "We're gonna have to talk about the company you keep."

Six

"My, aren't we the center of attention," Quel said as he sauntered toward Shay.

She stared at him, her lips parted in surprise, the stick still gripped in her fists. This time there was more tenderness in her gaze than heat, more apology than anger. For a second he thought she'd run headlong into his arms. A kiss of gratitude with the promise of more to come would hit the spot. No such luck. He knew what he looked like: his narrowed, mistrustful eyes and guarded expression kept her rooted to the path. "Any reason I should know about for why there are suddenly so many subdemons, Miss d'Mon? The town's been clear of them for months."

"I don't know. You're the demon hunter, not me."

"Any prior experience with demons?"

"That's irrelevant."

"I don't think so."

"If you feel the need to interrogate me, call the sheriff and make it official." She looked him square in the eye when they spoke, and she spoke what was on her mind, holding nothing back. She seemed afraid at times, just like Harmony said she was, but not afraid *of him*. Not one frickin' bit. She held her ground, didn't let him intimidate her. It had him aching to get her into bed. To see how she looked at him then. To see if she maintained eye contact when he made her come. When he made her beg for more. Yeah, that'd be something.

She reached for the child, lifting him out of the stroller. Her voice lost its edge. "Thank you for saving us."

"That's what they pay me for, ma'am." His hunter senses were turned on so damn high that he could feel the surge of heat in her body as he took another step closer. Longing and hunger flashed in her eyes. Her scent washed all around him. It was a frickin' aphrodisiac.

"Stop it," she whispered.

"Ma'am?"

"The way you look at me, it drives me crazy."

"Nice to hear it's mutual."

"Shay! Damon Junior!"

The boy squealed at the sight of Damon and Harmony jogging toward them. "Mama! Papa!"

The reverend reacted in obvious terror, seeing the dead goat, the fallen ravens, and scattered feathers. "Subdemons."

"Aye," Damon said, grim. His wife gently took the boy from Shay.

"You okay, honey?" Harmony murmured to Shay.

"Fine!" Her voice was overly perky. A sign of guilt, but she'd done nothing to warrant it. It added to the mystery Quel was determined to figure out.

"Miss d'Mon was no mere observer," Quel told them. "She was fighting them back with a stick when I got here. Defending your little boy."

His compliment drew praise from Harmony and Damon yet seemed to make Shay uneasy. In fact, her obvious embarrassment told him she'd prefer the topic to go away completely. Why?

Damon's hand fell on Quel's shoulder. "You protected my son— both of you," the former demon said, his voice deep with emotion, with accent thicker. "You have my loyalty and my gratitude." He gave Quel's shoulder a hearty squeeze before turning back toward the cottage with his wife.

"Would you like a second chance at those brownies, Mr. Laredo?" Harmony called over her shoulder.

"No thanks, Reverend." He wanted a second chance at Shay d'Mon.

She started to follow the couple. Quel cleared his throat. She stopped, glancing over her shoulder. "Woman, you ought to take credit where credit is due. You did a damn fine job with those subdemons."

"The credit's yours. You killed them."

"You're no coward. That's something to be proud of, not ashamed of."

She sighed in exasperation. "I don't want to talk about it." She started walking away.

"You want to get a drink?"

She halted. "What?"

"A drink. On me. At Knight Caps, the bar on Main."

The breeze tossed her curls and the hem of her soft shirt. Her silence made him feel like an idiot for asking her out.

Since when had he ever cared whether a woman took him up on an invitation or not? When they said no, he'd call it their loss. Hell, usually he wasn't ever doing the asking; he didn't need to. Women were buying him the drinks, not the other way around. That's not how he wanted it with Shay. Suddenly it became pretty damn important that she said yes. "When's your night off?" he persisted.

"Tomorrow. I'm off at six. Six until . . . until dawn."

He lifted a brow, waiting. As much expectancy as reluctance filled the new silence. Maybe she was in as much doubt about him as she was her. He didn't blame her.

"Knight Caps," she said finally. "Tomorrow, six o'clock."

He touched a hand to the brim of his hat. "Yes, ma'am. Six works." The "until dawn," he figured, was still negotiable.

Laredo walked her all the way back to the house. Thunder rumbled distantly. The scent of rain was acrid in the air. Then the first drops fell, wetting her skin. An image of stripping Laredo out of his clothes and making love on the wet lawn filled her mind with vividly erotic images. She sucked in a quiet breath, trying to control this new body that seemed to have a will of its own. Her arousal added to the many sensations, internal and external, colliding in a vivid, exhilarating storm. All these long centuries, she thought she knew what it was like to be alive. She hadn't known squat.

The demon hunter stopped at the base of the porch steps, turning up his collar against the rain. His right cheekbone had a small scar. A bump on the bridge of his nose hinted at a long-ago break. He hadn't lived an easy life or even a happy life; even without her demon mental powers, she could tell.

It made her want to make it all better.

Stop! It was bad enough he hunted demons. Why did he have to look like the only mortal she ever cared about and would have lost her heart to, had she a heart to lose? Acquiring a temporary soul may have heightened her ability to feel emotion, but she sure as snake's scales wasn't going to let it turn her into a simpering, lovesick fool. Her weakened state was humiliating as it was. No need to make it any worse.

"Before I go, since you have such a nasty habit of attracting subdemons"—he lifted his silver cross off his neck—"use my talisman to ward them off." He dropped the chain over her head.

Cool and smooth, the cross dangled between her breasts. She gasped, half expecting some sort of sizzling to begin, the silver burning her demon flesh, the cross shredding her, but her skin didn't react. In wonder, she fingered the cross. This body of hers was unlike any other she'd inhabited. "It protects you?" she asked, trying to hide her shock.

"I'm still here, aren't I?"

That had more to do with the fact she'd been avoiding him, fearing Lucifer would sense her attraction to the mortal. Now she'd gone and agreed to meet him—at a bar, no less—like a common human.

"Well, I'd better get going, Miss d'Mon."

"I guess so," she said.

Hesitating, he acted as if he wanted to say more. She knew *she* did. The intensity between them made no sense, considering they hardly knew each other. Their inexplicable connection seemed to prove what she already sensed herself. They went back, *way* back. Fifteen thousand years and counting. Call it reincarnation, whatever, but they'd been down this road before: Laredo as a doomed Ice Age hunter and she as an inexperienced demon who thought she could live as a human. With deadly consequences.

Then why was she heading down this same road again, knowing where it ended? *This time, you won't let it get that far.*

Laredo tipped his hat. "Good day, ma'am." Swinging his rifle from his hand, he walked away, his long legs carrying him swiftly out of sight.

Sipping a scotch, Quel waited for Shay the next day in Knight Caps. The bar was filling up. The music was loud. The fairy-goths were stirring up the usual trouble, and a trio of witches near the back were having themselves quite the party with a sullen-looking vampire. Quel had saved the stool next to him. It had taken some work keeping it empty of the shapely asses of the women he didn't want sitting there, which was every other female in this bar.

He glanced at his watch. It was almost seven, an hour past the time Shay said she'd meet him. What had he been thinking, giving her the cross? It was his mother's cross. Shay was a stranger. *No, she's more than that.* He damn well couldn't figure out what, though.

Frowning into his drink, he pushed his thumbs impatiently around the rim of his glass. Then he downed the drink he'd been nursing for an hour. He'd wanted to be sober when she got here. Guess it didn't matter anymore. He flicked a finger at the empty glass. The bartender, Falon, poured another scotch—straight up, no ice, no water.

Then a woman's voice: "Nothing gets in the way of you and your scotch, I see."

She came. He slid around on the stool to face her. Shay wore a black tank top cut low enough to show off the rounded tops of those amazing tits, a pair of faded jeans, and stilettos with heels high enough to give someone a nosebleed. Her tanned skin sparkled like the cross she wore around her neck. She'd glazed her skin with some kind of lotion. *Everywhere?* He couldn't help wondering. This wasn't the timid schoolteacher-nanny; this was the crazy girl who'd driven that Porsche. "I like my scotch the way I like a woman," he drawled. "Real, undiluted, nothing in between me and her."

There it was: that flash of heat again. He wanted to press his lips to her neck where those hoop earrings glittered in her soft halo of curls. He wanted to grab her thighs and haul her legs over his hips, right here in the bar. No, he wanted her in private, hard and up against the wall in his small room. Then, when he'd slaked the fire burning in him all damn week, he'd take her nice and slow.

Shit. He hadn't moved, and he'd already worked up a sweat, not to mention one helluva hard-on. He motioned to the bartender. "Give me a couple of cubes." Ice splashed into his drink.

"What happened to undiluted?"

"You showed up, Miss d'Mon." He turned the stool to face her. They sat, jeans to jeans, knees almost touching. "Woman, you got a way of looking at me that . . ." He let his words trail off, shifting his focus to the drink. He wasn't used to this kind of frank talk. Revealing talk. Telling people his feelings.

"That . . . *what*?"

He shook his head. "Who do you think of when you look at me?"

This time she glanced away. "Wine," she told the bartender.

"Red or white?"

"Roman."

The bartender glanced at Quel for enlightenment.

"Italian," Shay corrected.

"We've got Californian." The wall behind the bar was filled with wine bottles.

Shay pursed her lips and pointed to one, seemingly at random. "I'll have the red."

Her first sip was a hearty one. Shay d'Mon definitely attacked life with gusto. He liked that. Careful women bored him. "You never answered my question," he said, low in her ear. "Who are you thinking of when you—?"

She sealed her mouth over his. He almost fell off the stool. Two heartbeats: that's all his surprise lasted. Then he took hold of her soft hair and kissed her back. The soft little sound of pleasure she made drove him crazy. His hand fell to the side of her throat, resting on her throbbing pulse. The scent of her skin and her perfume filled his nostrils along with another scent that threatened to make him drunker than the scotch: he couldn't make sense of it; he only reacted to it, as he had the night she'd driven down the mountain. It seemed like a scent that he already knew—deep down, a memory he'd always carried without realizing it, just like he felt he'd kissed her before. It was impossible. No way would Shay have entered his life and sneaked out of it without him noticing. And she definitely wasn't sneaking out now. No damn way. He suckled her tongue, devouring her lips like she was the best damn bite of candy he'd ever tasted in a life of savoring every last piece thrown his way.

He became aware of a roar. Not the one in his head. The crowd in the bar was cheering.

Shay pulled back. "You," she said. "I think of you."

"Liar."

She blushed. "You can tell?"

"Yeah, I can tell." He reached for her, needing to touch her again. His fingers trailed up and down her back, following the bumps of her spine. He liked the goose bumps his caress raised on her bare arms. "That will come in very useful, too, angel, knowing how bad of a liar you are."

She shot him a panicked glance. "Because," he brought his lips to her ear, "when I kiss you again, I'm going to ask that same question. You're going to tell the truth this time, and the answer had better be me."

He saw her throat move before she glanced away. The song that had been playing ended, and a slower tune came on. "I'm thinking you dance as good as you kiss," he said.

"Maybe . . ."

"Let's get out there, and you can show me." What was with him? He never wanted to dance.

She sent a look of longing to the dance floor. "I used to like dancing."

"With so-and-so?"

Lifting one reddish brow, she shot him a confused look.

"The guy you think of when you look at me."

She shook her head. "We never danced."

It had Quel wondering what they did do that had been so memorable. He took her hand. "It's been a while," she warned.

"We can fix that."

He sensed only a moment's resistance before she let him lead her to the dance floor. He found a place in the middle of the swaying couples before sliding his hands over the body he'd been aching to touch all damn week. She melted against him, threading her fingers in his hair. It was like coming home. She fit him; he fit her. Déjà vu. He could almost believe he'd done this before and knew just how to hold her. Call it schmaltzy, but there it was.

Shay's body was toned and firm in all the right places, and soft where it counted. He, on the other hand, was hard where it counted, almost to the point of pain. Even harder was his ability to remain a gentleman, but he did, keeping his hips from pressing too hard against hers and giving away just how eager he was to have her.

The music stopped. They stayed there, holding each other, his lips resting on her hair. Her shirt was so thin he could feel the heat of her skin burning his palms. He didn't know what possessed him, and he kept thinking she'd chicken out, but he took her hand, steering her out of the bar. He led her around to the back alley and up the dark, narrow staircase to his room, shoving the door closed with his boot.

❦

Seven

Shay still hadn't come to terms with the fact that she'd showed up at the bar at all, and here she was, in his room. They were kissing before the door slammed shut, the kind of deep, thorough, wet kisses she'd always loved and that too few men knew how to do right—and as skillfully as Quel Laredo. *You desire me. You can't get enough of me.* Shay instinctively sent the thoughts. Then she remembered there were no powers of persuasion to back them up. She was on her own. Nothing but chemistry fueled this seduction. She knew little of making love as a powerless being. There was no dark magic holding Quel here. There was no reason other than chemistry to make him want her. To desire her. How did humans manage it? How did they overcome the fear and doubt?

The kiss turned even hotter. Then he was pulling off her shirt and smoothing his hands over her breasts. She unhooked the bra. He threw it out of the way. His pants dropped, then hers. And he reached for a bedside box. *Protection*, she thought, dazed.

They were frantic now as he backed her up against the wall. It was a blur of sensation, uncontrollable need. Kissing wasn't the only thing that was going to be good with Quel Laredo. Of that she was absolutely sure.

He lifted one thigh over his hip. "Quel . . ." she moaned. She thought she saw a shadow of a smile as he hoisted her other leg off the floor. Then he plunged deep.

A flash of pain, a swift intake of breath. In the next breath the stinging dissolved into sheer pleasure.

"Who are you thinking of now?" he demanded. "Me or him?" He was thrusting slow, swaying just right. His eyes were dark, burning into hers.

"You," she whispered. Dark satisfaction, even triumph glimmered in Quel's gaze as he crushed his mouth to hers. Perhaps he read the earnestness there that she hadn't revealed before, perhaps, too, a glimpse of her surrender, yet she felt nothing that smacked of defeat. She'd simply told the truth, a new habit for her, but one that felt exquisitely freeing.

She clung to him as he rocked inside her, her fingers grasping for purchase on his hard, slick body. No words now, only her sighs and his groans, his scent mingling with hers. Her human body was a gift. The pleasure it brought her was intense. Sex had always been good but never like this. Never like—

"Oh!" She came apart, crying out as she writhed against him.

"Angel," he hissed, pressing his teeth to her shoulder as he thrust into her body. His peak came soon after, crashing over them both like an earthquake before subsiding into trembling aftershocks.

He swept her away from the wall and tossed her onto the bed, kissing his way down her body to where she still throbbed for him. When his lips touched her between her thighs, her body made no secret of how he affected her. She moaned, arching her back. He chuckled smugly. "Angel, we're gonna have a good night tonight."

They kissed and stroked each other until Quel pushed up, frowning down at the tangled sheets. "You're bleeding."

"I am?" She squinted in the dim light but couldn't make out much.

"Did I hurt you?"

"No." Then she remembered the pain. "Just for a minute."

He stretched out next to her, his head propped on one hand, his other flattened on her stomach. The heat of his palm, the male possessiveness in his touch, made her shiver. "It's not your period?"

"I . . . don't think so." Could this body menstruate? The other bodies hadn't.

"Shay?"

"Yes?"

One, two moments of silence ticked by before he asked, "Were you a virgin?"

Hades. That was it. She hadn't even thought about the issue of virginity. She'd been so hot for Quel that she'd forgotten all about her cover. Her demon self was no virgin, but her physical body was—as innocent and untouched as . . . that damn soul she was stuck with. "I should have thought to say something."

"Hell yeah, you should have." His gaze had changed. It was oddly soft, as was his voice. "Jesus, Shay. Why didn't you?"

"Would it have mattered?" She honestly wanted to know.

"Damn right, it would have. I would have done things differently."

Curiosity burned. She'd never experienced lovemaking where the act had been entirely voluntary—a fact best kept secret, though. "How so?"

His mouth, tipped in that half smile of his, filled her vision as he moved closer. "Give me a second to recover," he said low in her ear, "and then I'll show you."

Toward dawn, Quel gently roused her from a doze of pure exhaustion. Her human body tired as quickly as it surrendered to pleasure. The trade-off was worth it. "I knew your ass looked great in jeans." Quel nibbled and kissed his way down from her neck to the ticklish spot between her shoulder blades and lower. His heavy erection brushed against her thigh. The man was insatiable. She quite liked that. "Though I've got to say it looks a hell of a lot better without them." On all fours, he playfully bit her left cheek.

She laughed then winced as she rolled over. Her body continued to remind her that tonight was its first time making love.

As did Quel. "Sore?" He sounded slightly more smug than sorry.

"Yes. A bath sounds lovely right now."

"Sorry, angel. I've got a shower, no tub. There's a new motel in town. Nice place. Maybe on your next night off we'll check in and have ourselves a party in one of those in-room Jacuzzis."

His words shattered the lovely spell she'd been under all evening. There wouldn't be a next time.

Bat bugger. What had she been thinking, coming here tonight? She should have said no to the drink, she should have stayed close to the Faithfulls' home. She'd put Quel at risk by spending the night with him. It was a selfish risk, even if she hadn't planned on it going this far. Lucifer was all too good at discovering her affinity for anyone and anything—and taking it away.

She wriggled out from under Quel's weight. "It's nearly dawn. I've got to go." She hurried around the room, snatching her clothes off the floor, blaming her mistake on her addiction to feeling alive—and her curiosity and attraction to Quel. *In coming here, you may have just signed his death warrant.* Her tenderness with the babe could be explained away as winning the family's trust, but what of the others she'd met here? She couldn't afford to get close to any of them. She had to keep her distance or risk the unthinkable. She mustn't become attached to Quel, to the babe, or to anyone. Mortals were off-limits. Starting now.

She was going to miss him. She was going to miss this life. More so than the others, this one had felt . . . real. Her body did, too, she thought with another wince. Her other bodies had all been virginal. Why hadn't they stung like this one did? Maybe it, too, like this life, was real.

The realization froze her in place. Did the soul mean she was no longer a demon? No, that was impossible.

Jeans, bra, blouse . . . one shoe, then two. Frantically she tore through the fallen garments. "Did you see my—?"

"Panties?" Propped up on one elbow in bed, glorious in his unself-conscious nakedness, he twirled her tiny undergarment on his finger. "Come and get 'em, angel." His blue eyes danced with devilish mischief of the sexual sort, reminding her all too much of Swift River the last time she saw him. The night he died. *At your hand, Shay.*

Lucifer would make her kill Quel, too. She thrust out her hand. "I have to go, Laredo."

In a move so swift she hadn't time to react, he caught her hand, yanking her across his body. She batted at him, pushing him away as he kissed her . . . kissing her until she'd melted into the embrace. It didn't take long at all to thaw her. She could almost taste the smile she was certain curved that self-satisfied mouth, a smile she sensed faded as he rolled her under his body to give her a kiss as tender as any she'd ever experienced.

When he finally lifted his head, cradling her face in his hands, she was reluctant for their lips to part. No one, not even the men she'd persuaded to love her, had ever kissed her quite like that. "That's my parting gift to you, angel," he said quietly. "A little something to remember me by."

"I will remember you." With that vow, a shiver ran through her. "Always."

Suddenly gruff, he pushed her waded-up panties into her hand. "Shower. Get dressed. Whatever you need to do, Cinderella. I'll walk you home."

"Cinderella?"

"Yeah. I gotta get you home before your coach turns into a pumpkin. As long as you leave a glass slipper behind, we're cool."

"And you accused me of babbling?"

"Hey, you're the teacher. You know your fairy tales better than I do."

Actually, she didn't. "Of course. Cinderella. The glass coach."

He gave her a strange look. "Slipper."

"Right." She bit her lip before she revealed more of her ignorance.

There were many details of being a modern human that she didn't know. She'd never thought she'd be staying here as long as she had. She hadn't banked on meeting Quel Laredo.

He shook his head at her. "If it takes me the rest of my days, I'm going to figure you out."

She was going to use the rest of her days to make sure he didn't. Not that she had many days left.

The fountain was the centerpiece of the town square. This time of night the area was deserted. The sky was growing light already. If she'd been human, she'd be greeting the sunrise with all the excitement of having spent the first night with a lover she wanted to see again and again. Instead, the coming dawn brought a feeling of dread.

Oblivious, Quel wrapped his arm over her shoulders, holding her close as they walked. "That was one hell of a night. I'd like to see you again. Though if the good reverend figures out you're no longer a virgin after one date with me, she might not let you."

"That might not be such a bad thing, Quel."

His steps slowed as her heart banged hard in her throat. "What the hell is that supposed to mean?"

"I don't know if seeing each other is a good idea."

Now he stopped, holding on to her hand as he searched her face in disbelief. "Are you giving me the brush-off?"

"I can't see you anymore," she blurted out. She had to sever ties with Quel before Lucifer discovered her attachment. It was what she'd failed to do all those thousands of years ago with Swift River. Then, she'd made the one, unforgivable mistake: she'd underestimated Satan. She might not be the smartest demon, but she did have a learning curve, and she was going to prove it tonight. She'd put Quel's welfare over her own desires. "It's over. I'm sorry."

Quel swore under his breath. "I don't frickin' believe this. Shay—"

He'd stopped speaking midsentence. Reaching for his pistol, he peered into the shadows, his nostrils flaring. "Hell stench."

The thunder of small hooves drew their attention to the far side of the square. A herd of billy goats trotted toward them. Fluffy and white, they looked like the ones in Harmony and Damon's pen. Glowing red eyes gave away their origins.

"Subdemons," Quel growled. He sprayed silver BBs into the herd, decimating it. The goats sizzled and popped, dissolving before their eyes.

A shriek sounded overhead. Something whooshed past, blowing Shay's hair. Quel took a shot. An owl fell to earth, its red eyes fading as it flapped at their feet. Even as it vaporized, the sky filled with other creatures, hundreds of them. Their flapping wings rustled like dry leaves. "Bats this time," she said. The subdemons swooped and squeaked.

Quel hauled her close, letting her bury her head against his chest as he blasted away at the beasties. More varieties appeared to replace what he destroyed. Evil soaked the very air. Malevolence, she could feel it.

And so it begins . . . Lucifer's patience had run out. Her time of freedom was up. The time to act was upon her. She twisted around. "Quel, protect yourself before me. When the time comes, you cannot hesitate. You must save yourself."

He jerked back. "Woman, you're definitely babbling now."

"Promise me you'll do it." She gripped his arms. His eyes were wide with denial. He'd rather die himself than hurt her, she knew. There was only one way to get him to do as she said, and that was to tell him what she was. "I'm a monster, Quel. A demon. Your instincts were right about me."

"Bullshit," he growled. His blue eyes were blacker now. He was angry.

"I came to kill the Faithfulls' baby. Lucifer ordered me here. He thinks the child will grow up to rival him, even defeat him. He sent me to make sure that doesn't happen."

"And you couldn't do it."

Her throat constricted. "No," she whispered. "I can't."

"You're human, that's why." Quel grabbed the cross hanging from her neck, pulling the chain taut. "A demon couldn't wear this. You can. You're mortal, Shay. You're one of us, not them. You're human."

Human . . . could it be? Yes. She was already halfway to believing it. Quel's conviction pushed her the rest of the way. Her soul, her immunity to silver, her virginity, it was obvious. "I crashed into that wishing fountain and came out mortal."

"You wished to be mortal, to have a soul, and it gave you what you wanted."

A soul. The chance to really live. For a finite period, she realized. "I'm no longer immortal."

"Quality over quantity, we humans always say."

She laughed at that until reality returned. Her new status meant she was even weaker than she'd thought. She had no powers at all to fight anything Lucifer threw at her. And these subdemons were only the tip of the iceberg.

"Go, Quel." She shoved at him. It was like trying to move a brick wall. "Get out of here. It doesn't matter what I am now; Lucifer will kill you if he finds out I love you."

For all his hardness, he gave her the classic double take.

"Yes, I love you. We go back, Quel, *way* back. It was during the Ice Age. You were a hunter, even then. I was a demon, but I fell for you. Lucifer didn't like it. He had me kill you. He'll do it again—"

"Hold on. I smell a demon." His voice sounded a little too calm, a little too steady. A glance at his face revealed alarm. Damnation, the demon hunter was nervous. Not a good sign. Whatever was on the way frightened him. "It's powerful, Shay. Ancient."

Who was it? She glared into the shadows. The oldest demons were few; she knew them all. "See? You've got to get out of here." Why couldn't he understand? She knew! She'd lived this all before. "Forget all that crap about protecting me. Go. You're in over your head."

"You got the wrong man if you think I'm going to cut and run, angel."

"I'm not an angel," she screamed in frustration.

"You are to me." Quel made a stifled groan and hauled her closer, crushing her against him. Sliding her hands under his coat, she soaked in his body heat. It didn't help her shivering. It was like the night of the crash all over again. "It doesn't matter what you were," he said in her hair. "I don't frickin' care."

A quiet laugh interrupted. "I'm jealous, Shay. I've missed you down in Hell, and here you are, once again keeping company with mortal men. What do they have that I don't? *Feelings?*"

The familiar deep, lilting voice chilled her to the core. Nevin, she thought. Lucifer hadn't sent just any demon after her. He'd sent the most feared high demon lord of them all.

Eight

With a tornado of bats spinning overhead, Nevin advanced on them, his eyes glowing red. "Down!" Quel shoved her to the ground and took aim.

Nevin flicked his wrist. A burst of black energy sent Quel flying backward. He hit the ground hard, his boots scraping over the dirt.

"Quel!" She bit her lip. Too late. She'd revealed her feelings.

Nevin appeared absolutely delighted by her outburst. "Master wanted me to see what was taking you so long. How quickly I found my answer. Our little mortal wannabe has found herself another man. Is she *in love?*"

"He's nothing but a bit of sport, Nevin. You know how much I enjoy sex."

"That I do." Nevin was heartbreakingly handsome. When he smiled, broad and perfect, he could bring a woman to tears. And he had, many times; she'd been witness. "You always did prefer me to the humans, dear Shay, didn't you? A real lover. A dark lover." *You want me, Shay. You desire me above all others.* His commands rang in her mind. *Take off your pants and beg me to fuck you in front of him.*

Gasping in shame, she shook her head even as her fingers tangled with the top button on her jeans. *Fight it,* she told herself.

You desire me above all others. You can't help it.

No! The compulsion to please Nevin warred with her drive not to give in. Crying out, she rolled her fingers into fists.

Nevin howled with irritation. "How do you defy my commands? You are human, weak." He blinked, sending another wave of persuasion. *Undress.*

"No." Her voice sounded guttural and surprisingly strong. How? Residual power? Sheer will?

This crazy town?

Nevin grabbed her wrist, spinning her around. He lifted his hand as if to rip off her blouse but recoiled at the sight of the cross. A shot rang out. The demon staggered backward, roaring in fury as he centered the forgotten Quel in his sights, his eyes glowing fiercely. Although obviously hurting, Quel had staggered to his feet, a pistol in each hand. The weapons and his eyes appeared preternaturally bright against the backdrop of the fountain. Did the demon hunter have powers of his own?

If so, they were not enough to go up against Nevin. The demon hurled another pulse of energy, and Quel staggered backward. Quel uttered a harsh sob and pressed a fist to his forehead. His struggle to fight off the nightmares the demon had implanted in his head tore at her heart. The emotional turmoil a demon could inflict was truly horrible. Another attack of Nevin's sent Quel plunging to his knees.

"Stop it!" she shouted at the demon.

Nevin sneered, turning back to her. *Remove the cross.*

"No."

I will take you, and you will like it. You will cry out in pleasure for him to hear.

"Fuck you, Nevin."

"Actually, I was hoping you would do that. You were always so good at it." His arm slid over her shoulders. He kept his chest away from the cross, she noticed. "Down in Hell, you were the butt of all the jokes. The demon who dreamed of being human." His laugh rang out in the square. "It's why Master never gave you the rank of high demon lord. He knew he couldn't trust you. He was right, of course. Look at you: weak, powerless. Pitiful. It seems you finally got your wish."

She took the cross and plunged it into his chest. It glanced off his ribs but sank deep enough. An unearthly shriek filled her ears. He hurled her to the ground, his hand pressed against the bubbling, ruined flesh.

"Mistake," he hissed, leveling an arm at Quel. Wave after wave of persuasion and dark energy flew in Quel's direction until the demon hunter writhed in agony.

"Stop it, Nevin!" Quel was suffering, and she was weeping. She couldn't bear to watch. Then again, Nevin knew that. He was torturing Quel for her benefit. He'd kill Quel, then her, but before he did, he intended to thoroughly enjoy the moment. With feline delight, he'd toy with his prey.

"Nevin, please." Choking on a sob, Shay reached for the hem of her blouse and lifted it. "I'll do it."

"Pretty water!" From across the square, a little figure in *Transformers* pajamas appeared. Dread pierced Shay at the sight of Damon Junior toddling toward the fountain, dragging his beloved "binkie" blanket behind him.

Nine

Little Damon stumbled once, landing on his padded bottom before righting himself. The town square looked like a battleground. The babe gave the remains of the subdemons little more than a passing glance. "Bad doggies," he muttered.

Nevin followed her horrified gaze. His lips slid back over his perfect teeth. It wasn't a smile as much as it was a snarl. "What is this?"

Pure, cold terror plunged down Shay's spine and slowed down her racing thoughts. Slowed down everything. *Protect the boy.* As if she were under water, she was flinging off her heels, tossing the pumps over her head. She was glancing in Quel's direction, seeing him pushing to his feet with shaking hands, his face pain-ridden but determined. Turning, she ran as Nevin lifted his arm to fire.

"No . . . !" Her voice was deep, drawn-out, as was each long stride that carried her ever so slowly away from Nevin and toward the approaching child.

Her focus had narrowed to one goal: reach the babe before Nevin attacked. *"No matter where you run, no matter where you hide, I will find you, and end you. You will never escape your fate."* Even as Lucifer's awful threat echoed in her mind, she focused outside herself, shoved aside her qualms. She did in fact no longer matter; what happened to her was irrelevant. Instead of the idea being frightening and terrible, it was freeing and wonderful. This was bigger than her, far bigger. Bigger than any of them. This little boy would save the world, and she would save him.

One last straining leap brought her to the boy. Sweeping him off the ground, she whirled, dancing on bare feet as she came face-to-face with Nevin. The demon's glowing eyes had narrowed, both of his arms rising, weapons to be used on her and the babe.

"Shay," the child said calmly, patting her arm. "Shay, good."

She'd already turned away from the imminent threat of Nevin, intending to flee across the square. Caught in the odd time warp of slow motion, she knew what she had to do. *Save the boy. At all cost, save him.*

"Bad man." Little Damon peered over her shoulder. His cherub mouth had screwed up into a frown. He pointed a chubby finger in Nevin's direction. "Bad man!"

Energy crackled, lifting her hair and blowing it in front of her eyes. It gathered strength and released in a resounding boom. Then a shout of outrage and pain came from Nevin's direction.

Shay turned to see what had happened, shoving tangled curls out of her eyes. Nevin clutched his chest with one hand, his other arm coming back up. Quel had risen to his feet behind him, raising his rifle as if it weighed hundreds of pounds.

Giggling, Little Damon clapped his hands together. "More!" Another pulse of energy lit up the night.

"More!" Lightning arced out from the babe's outstretched hand.

Nevin lurched backward. Quel took aim and fired. The demon's eyes dimmed and grew bright again, like dying coals.

"Bad man!" Again and again the babe attacked, until Nevin's last cry drowned in a resounding splash. Then, it was silent, utterly silent.

Shay let out a startled sob. "Good Shay," she heard the boy soothe as he stroked her cheek. Everything seemed to speed up, the world returning to normal. Nevin was in the fountain, his feet hanging over the edge. Limping, Quel and now the town sheriff ran toward him.

Shouts sounded all around them. Drawn by the commotion, what looked like the entire town converged on the square.

Quel vaulted into the fountain and yanked the demon out of the water. With Quel's arm locked around Nevin's elegant neck, he wrenched him backward as Jeanie secured his hands behind his back with handcuffs.

"Damon Junior!"

"Mama!" Little Damon twisted in Shay's arms, straining to reach Harmony.

Shay was drawn into the family embrace, submitting to the hugs and kisses as the child was lifted from her arms. "He is an amazing boy," Shay said, breathless. "He saved my life, and Quel's. He defeated a demon lord. He's more powerful than we ever imagined." The estimations of her former master, Lucifer, included.

A familiar, foul odor filled the air. Harmony wrinkled her nose at the dirty diaper. "A shame my heroic son's superpowers don't extend any . . . lower."

They shared a teary laugh. "There's a lot more to tell you, Harmony," Shay confessed.

"I know." The woman's eyes revealed that she did indeed know. "For now, you belong somewhere else."

"With Quel . . ."

"Yes, honey." She smiled her knowing, enigmatic smile, the one that revealed her powers that she kept so well hidden. "Not everyone gets a second chance, Shay. Take it, and do not squander it."

"I won't," she whispered. It looked like Harmony would have to run another ad in the newspaper.

"Shay!" Quel was striding in her direction. Blood trickled from a cut above his right eye; bruises and dirty scrapes marred his knuckles. Their embrace was long and heartfelt. She breathed in his scent, willing it to stay inside her forever.

"Nevin?" she asked when they separated.

"He's being read his rights."

Sitting near the fountain, Nevin appeared decidedly unhappy as the sheriff angrily recited something to him. "Now I'm hauling your ass off to jail," Jeanie declared. "Get up and walk, pretty boy."

"I was sure you'd kill him."

"I thought about it." Quel's eyes narrowed at the departing demon. "Then I realized fate cooked up a worse punishment for the man."

"*Man?* You mean he's turned mortal, too?" The magic wishing fountain, she realized. Like her, Nevin had fallen in and come out with a soul. Unlike her, he'd never wished to be mortal. Or so she'd thought. "Just when you think you know someone . . ."

"My son Damon made that decision for him," Harmony said. "He wished it on the demon, not the other way around."

"Ha. Poor Nevin." Shay grinned and threw up her hands. Her giddiness reminded her of the postrace celebrations at Circus Maximus. "To Damon Junior, the new champion!" Everyone around them applauded and cheered. This was one victory she'd savor. Two ancient demons lost in the space of a week: Lucifer wouldn't be so eager to send another for quite some time to come.

"Now, I'd like to see you alone, Miss d'Mon." Quel grabbed her by the elbow, steering her away from the crowd.

"Both of you need medical attention," Dr. Fogg called out after them.

"Will do, Doc." Then Quel brought his mouth to her ear. "But first, we're gonna talk."

"I didn't mean it about not wanting to see you anymore." She assumed that's what he wanted to know. "I feared for your safety. I feared for your life."

"I hope you learned your lesson. I can take care of myself. And I can take care of you." His expression was fierce as he tugged on her hand. He found a quiet spot under a stand of fragrant conifers. There he stopped and turned to her. "From the very beginning, I knew you were lying to me."

Shay's heart sank.

"From the night you showed up, I was dead set on uncovering your little ruse, even if it happened *under* the covers. One thing was pretty damn certain: I wasn't going to fall for you in the process. No way in hell."

Shay bowed her head.

"I asked you out for a drink on your night off for investigative purposes. Then there was our hot little hookup afterward. I'd say that was 100 percent investigative, too, but I'd be lying." He took her face in his hands, forcing her to look up at him. His eyes weren't angry, they were heartstoppingly tender. "The woman who started out as a she-demon turns out to be a virgin. Then she tells me we've got history I don't even remember but I sorta do, especially when we're kissing and I feel like I've been to that little corner of heaven before—so to speak."

"It *is* heaven," she whispered, imagining what God's domain would be like: all good, nothing bad.

"Shay, you've got me turned so inside out I can't think of anything else. I can't have that. No way. I'm a sixth-degree demon hunter, and I've got a job to do." He swept her into a passionate kiss. She could barely stand up when he was done. "How do you frickin' do that?" he said harshly against her mouth, sounding winded himself.

"Whatever it is, you do it to me, too."

"I'm thanking God it's mutual, because I wouldn't want to live knowing that it wasn't. I don't want to live without you at all. Angel, I know we're only getting to know each other again. I know you're just getting to live for the first time. What I need to know is if you wanna do it with me?" He pressed a finger to her mouth. "You're mortal now, so you have to think like one. That means waiting before you answer."

"Quel . . ." she mumbled, wanting to reply.

"Hear me out, woman. Life is short. That means you don't have to say yes to spending it with me." He stroked his knuckles down her check. "But you goddamn better."

"And I goddamn will." Smiling, she wept tears of joy that he gently wiped away.

Ten

The ring of a phone pierced the early morning silence. Shay's hand popped out from under a pile of blankets, hunting blindly for the contraption. For all she loved modern technology, there were times she despised its intrusions.

She found the phone and brought it to her ear. "Laredo and d'Mon," she answered. "Demon Hunters, Incorporated."

Quel's body was large and warm pressed to hers. His hand slid up her leg, then her thigh. Grinning, she stopped those clever fingers in their tracks so she could concentrate on the call. "Yes, we're available. Yes, we can fix your problem." Hanging up, she turned to scribble the information on a bedside memo pad.

"What do we have, angel?"

"Small town about a hundred miles north of here. Hellhole. Goblins have been disrupting the ski lifts."

"Sounds easy enough."

"Snow and goblins? I suppose. What I'd really prefer is another gargoyle-demon assignment. I loved New York City."

"Manhattan's better in the spring." He stroked his hand up and down her leg. "We don't need an assignment for me to take you there."

He was right. Business was good if mostly uneventful. Neither one of them complained about the lack of challenge in most of their assignments. Someday, Lucifer might try to hit them harder. For now, he'd taken his defeat, and they'd take the respite. It left her with energy to spare for her charitable work with children from poor areas in New Mexico, where Quel had experienced his rough upbringing. Shame over her past deeds had initially driven her to help innocents, although Harmony assured her she'd been forgiven by "the Big Guy upstairs."

The fact that she really did care about what happened to the kids had kept her involved ever since.

In Mysteria, she and Quel helped Harmony and Damon protect little Damon, planning to extend that assistance when the Faithfulls' second baby arrived in a few month's time. No one knew if the second child would have powers or if little Damon's amazing abilities were a fluke. The town's collective breath was held as everyone awaited the news.

Tossing aside the pen, Shay took refuge back under the covers in the rustic mountain cabin they rented every once in a while. Quel peered out the frosted-over windows. "It's a frickin' blizzard out there."

She sighed in bliss. "I know."

"You're crazy, woman, wanting to stay up here in a snowstorm. It may be why I love you."

She straddled him. "One of the reasons."

"I hear wind," he said. "And snow drifting up over my jeep. I hear my stomach growling for a cheeseburger and a beer, and my ass telling me it wants to be sitting on a warm couch watching the football game."

"I hoped you'd have a better time up here. I thought maybe it would jog your memory of when we used ride out the storms together. The first time."

"The first time," he muttered. "Angel, this is the first and definitely the last time we're camping in the middle of a blizzard—"

She silenced him with a kiss. "Swift River was never this cranky."

He slid his fingers behind his head as he sighed.

"Quel?" Shay asked, worried.

He sighed again and rubbed her back. "Look, Shay, I've never loved anyone—or anything—as much as you. Every day it gets better. But when you get to talking about our 'first time,' I get possessive, even though the man you're referring to is supposedly me."

"He is you . . ."

"No," Quel said. "He's not. I'm me."

In his voice and words, Shay sensed his disappointment and even jealousy. The mentions of Swift River had cast in doubt that what he shared with her was special between them, and only them. Shay ran guilty fingers over her lover's handsome face, hoping that what she felt in her newfound heart got through to him. "Quel, it's not like that. When I look at you, it's you I see. It's you I want. It's you I'm in love with."

"Yeah, I know." He smiled. That smile made her heart ache. He had the patience of a saint. She'd made a mistake waiting as long as she had to tell him those words. For as long as she'd walked the earth, she knew shockingly little of affairs of the heart. The past six months had been a learning experience for both her and Quel but most of all for her. She hadn't been capable of true emotions when she'd bedded Swift River. She was now, making her relationship with Quel a real one. Yes, there were moments she was sure Swift River and Quel Laredo were of the same, reincarnated soul, but the better she'd gotten to know Quel, the more the differences between the two men became apparent. For one, Swift River had been an open book, easy to read. Quel Laredo had been slow to give up his many secrets. Swift River had led a simple if not easy life, limited to the task of survival—his and that of his clan—whereas Quel's survival had been more complicated. His scars were mostly internal as opposed to Swift River's visible ones.

She shook her head. No more comparing. It was wrong. "I'm sorry, truly sorry. No more living in the past. From now on, I'm living for today and for however many tomorrows we're allowed to have." She poked him in the chest. "I intend to spend every last one of those days with you, Quel Laredo. In the future, when I ask you to camp in the snow, it's because I feel peace here and want to share it with you, not because of Swift River."

"Then we'll continue to come up here."

"Camping doesn't have to be," her voice thickened with mischief, "burger-less."

"What?"

"Or—" Eager to reveal her surprise, she hopped out from under the covers. From under the bed she pulled a large box, then a small satellite TV. "Football-less!"

He coughed out a laugh of pure surprise. "When did you bring that shit up here?"

She joined him in laughter. "A girl can have her secrets, Laredo."

Next, she pulled out a portable grill and a cooler full of chopped beef, all the fixings, buns, and beer.

Laughing, he watched her, love filling his eyes. Shay popped two of the cans, handing him one. "It's after five p.m. somewhere in the world," she reasoned, shrugging.

He raised his drink. "Here's to the good life."

"*This* life. The one we're going to concentrate on from now on."

Nodding, he touched the can to hers. "You got that right, angel. You got that right."

And so it was that the little demon
who'd always dreamed of being human
got her wish and lived happily ever after . . .

A TAWDRY AFFAIR

Gena Showalter

To P. C. Cast, Susan Grant, and MaryJanice Davidson. Or, as we would probably be named inside of Mysteria: P. C. Sweetbottoms, Susan Buttercup, and MaryJanice Sugarlips. (Maybe I'd be Gena Dinglehop—that's wait-and-see, though.) To Wendy McCurdy and Allison Brandau for putting up with me!

One

If Glory Tawdry discovered her sister, Evie, and Evie's vampire boy-friend going at it like wild cougars one more time—just one more!—she was going to throw up a lung, gouge out her eyes, and cut off her ears.

"You're disgusting," she grumbled, standing in Evie's *open* bed-room door. Her sister and Hunter must have severe discovery fanta-sies, because they always "forgot" to barricade themselves inside when things were getting heated.

They didn't even glance in her direction.

She coughed.

They continued.

Sadly, if Glory walked down the hallway of their modest little three-bedroom home, she'd probably hear her other sister, Godiva, going at it with *her* boyfriend, a werewolf shape-shifter. They, at least, liked privacy when they were screaming like hyenas.

Still. There was no peace to be found for Glory. Not even in town. Lately Mysteria, a place once known for its evil creature population, as well as a place she'd taken great pride in, had turned into a horrify-ing love fest of goo-goo eyes and butt pinching.

Except for me. No one makes goo-goo eyes at me. No one pinches my butt, even though there's enough for everyone to grab on to at the same time. She didn't care, though. Really.

Men and relationships were so not for her. Really.

"Hello," she said, trying again. "I'm right here. Can you stop for like a minute?"

Thankfully Evie and Hunter finished their show and collapsed side by side under the covers. Moonlight spilled from the beveled windows and onto the bed, painting them in gold. Both were panting, sweat glistening from their skin. Evie's dark hair was spread over the pillow and tangled under Hunter's arm. Vitality radiated from her.

Handsome Hunter looked exhausted and incapable of movement.

Score one for Evie, Glory supposed.

"Oh, Glory." Evie grinned, happiness sparkling in her hazel eyes. "I didn't see you there."

Ugh. Evie did everything happily now, and Glory was seriously embarrassed for her. Evie was the greatest vengeance witch ever to live in Mysteria. As such, she should scowl once in a while. *Glory* was the love witch, damn it, so *Glory* should be the happy one.

"Don't you know how to knock?" her sister asked.

Are you freaking kidding me? "Don't you know how to close a door? I mean, it's a difficult task to master, but with hard work and the proper training, I think you might be able to do it."

Hunter laughed, revealing long, sharp teeth.

"Ha-ha." Evie punched him on the shoulder.

When Evie said no more, Glory shook her head in disappointment. Used to, they would have argued and insulted each other, maybe yelled and thrown things. Now, she was lucky if Evie frowned at her.

A dysfunctional relationship it had been, but it had been *theirs*.

"I miss us!" she found herself saying. "You're a softie now, and it's killing my excitement levels."

Understanding dawned, and Evie scowled. Even pointed an accusing finger at her. "Seriously, what's up with you, little sis? Every day I think you can't possibly get any bitchier, and then you go and prove me wrong."

Much better! Life was suddenly worth living again. "Lookit, you show pony, I need your help."

"Yeah? With what?" Unable to retain the harsh expression, Evie gave her another smile.

As always, that satisfied smile caused a deep ache to sprout inside Glory's chest. *When will it be my turn to fall in love, have great sex, and sicken the people around me?* The moment the thought drifted through her mind, she blinked in shock and revulsion. *Whoa, girl. That line of BS has to stop. Like, now. Before you crave more.*

She was a love witch, yes, but *she* didn't want to fall in love. Ever. People became slobbering fools when they succumbed to the soft emotion. Look at Evie! Proof right there in all her glowing splendor.

"I'm waiting," Evie said.

Glory opened her mouth to say . . . something. What, she didn't know. Great Goddess, how should she begin? She could *not* allow Evie to turn her down.

"Seriously. I want to bask in the afterglow." Evie rubbed her leg up and down Hunter's lower torso. "Hurry this along."

"I'm thinking."

Evie sighed. And yes, she was still smiling. "Go think somewhere else."

"You left your door open, so no afterglow for you. One year," she said in her best "Soup Nazi" impersonation. Glory tangled a hand through her hair, surprised as always that it was cool to the touch. Every time she saw the flame red tresses in the mirror, she expected smoke. *I can do this.* "Remember a few months ago, when Hunter was ignoring you—again—and you promised me a favor if I helped you win his heart? I told you that in return for helping you, I wanted you to give me something to ruin Falon's life, and you said okay, so I gave you a potion and you—"

"I know what I did. Jeez." Nibbling on her lower lip, Evie moved her hazels to Hunter.

He knew the full story, but Glory suspected Evie didn't like to remind him. He'd died because of Evie, after all, killed by demons the lovesick fool had accidentally summoned. *Then* he'd been turned into a vampire—a species he'd once hoped to destroy. It had been difficult for him to adjust to the change.

"You want to ruin Falon's life? Why?" Hunter's vampire-pale arms tightened around Evie. Obviously no bad feelings remained on his part. But he did frown over at Glory as if she had sprouted a second head. With horns. Falon was his best friend and right-hand man.

At least, Glory thought Falon was a man. In Mysteria, it was sometimes hard to tell. He could have been a demon for all she knew. Now that made sense. "Just . . . because," she said, then squared her shoulders and raised her chin. She refused to say more about her reasoning. "Evie owes me. That should be enough."

Evie threw up her arms and let them fall heavily onto the bed. "Can't you drop this? I don't know what he did to you . . ." She paused, probably waiting for Glory to pipe up with the answer. When she didn't, Evie sighed again. "You live in Bizarro World, little sis. You're supposed to be the good witch, and *I'm* supposed to be wicked."

Glory arched a brow, her mind caught on the first part of Evie's speech. "No, I can't let this go." The bastard deserved to die. Slowly. Painfully. Eternally. "You reneging on me?"

Hot color bloomed in her sister's cheeks. "No. Of course not."

"Evie," Hunter said.

"I promised her, baby."

Glory anchored her hands on her hips. "If it makes you feel any better, Hunter, know that Falon brought this on himself. He hurt me."

Hunter's green gaze sharpened. "Hurt you? How?"

Once again, she raised her chin and pressed her lips together. She hadn't planned on admitting even that much.

Realizing she'd say no more, he scrubbed a hand down the harsh, rugged plains of his face. "You know I'll warn Falon, right? I'll tell him what's going on."

"Like that scares me." Glory *wanted* Falon know she was gunning for him. She wanted him to be scared, to tremble and jump at every snapping twig in the night. Hell, maybe she *was* a wicked witch, because she chuckled every time she thought of him dropping to the ground in a fetal ball and crying for his mother.

Sure, he was six feet four of solid—delicious—muscle. Sure, he'd kicked more ass in the few years he'd lived in Mysteria than the town's citizens were currently nailing. And sure, he probably made the creatures of the underworld pee their pants in fear of him. A girl could dream, though.

"Now." She rubbed her hands together. "Evie, my revenge, if you please. I've tried to bring it up several times, and you ignored me, ran from me, or let your boy toy sweep you off your feet. Literally. I'm not waiting anymore!"

"Whatever he did, I'll talk to him," Hunter said. "He'll apologize."

Glory shook her head, long hair slapping her across the face. It was too late for that. "*I'll* talk to him. Evie . . ."

"Fine." Frowning, Evie uncurled from her lover's body and rose from the bed, taking the sheet with her.

Cheeks heating, Glory quickly turned and faced the hallway. She so had not needed to see Hunter's crowning grandeur. Did she appreciate it? Yeah. Boy was blessed! Still. Her sister's boyfriend was not meant to be eye candy for her, and besides, she didn't need to add fuel to the fire of her constantly unsatisfied desires.

Behind her, she heard cloth rustling, the slide of a drawer, then things bumping together.

"Ah, here it is!" her sister said.

Footsteps sounded, then a delicate finger was tapping Glory on the shoulder. Heart pounding excitedly, she turned. Of course, her gaze flew to Hunter of its own accord hoping for another peek. He'd already tugged on a pair of jeans—jeans with a missing top button. Evie had probably bitten it off.

Glory's chest started hurting again.

Evie waved a black pen in front of her face. "Hello. You paying attention to me?"

Her gaze latched onto the pen, following its movements. Her frown returned. "You're giving me a pen? A *pen* to finally claim revenge against the man who savagely wronged me?"

"Yes. How did he wrong you?"

She ignored the question. "What, I'm supposed to draw a mustache on his picture? News flash. That's not going to leave him crying in his cornflakes."

"Why do you want him crying in his cornflakes?"

Grrr! "No matter how many times you ask, no matter how many ways, I'm not telling."

"Well, don't make him cry too hard. He's a good man and has always been nice to us."

Nice? Nice! Evie had no idea the cruelty that man was capable of. But revealing what he'd done to her would be more mortifying than, say, finding one of her sisters naked and in bed with a vampire, screaming his name as she climaxed.

"Pay attention, sister dear." Evie released the pen; it didn't fall. It hovered in the air between them, swirling, glitter falling like raindrops around it. "This little pen is magical."

"Rock on! What will it do?"

"Anything you write with it will come true."

Glory's eyes widened, the words sinking in. "*Anything* I write will come true?"

"Yes. Well, anything physical, nothing emotional. Just be careful. The more you write, the more ink you'll use, and there's no way to refill it. Also, the effects don't last forever, only for a few hours. For proper revenge, it's best to write about clothes disappearing right off a body in the middle of a crowd and—"

"Don't help her," Hunter growled.

"Yes, but *anything* I write comes true?" Glory asked again, just to be sure.

Evie rolled her eyes. "Physically, yes. I said so, didn't I?"

A laugh escaped her, her first true laugh in months. "Oh, this is classic. Truly perfect."

"I knew you'd appreciate the irony."

"What irony?" Hunter sat up and propped himself against the headboard.

"Can I tell him?" Evie asked her.

Why not? "Sure. He's almost family, and I've seen his goods."

"She's a novelist," Evie threw over her shoulder, "best known for bringing her heroes to their knees. Not always because they fall in love, but mostly because the villains always jack them up with a hammer to the tibia."

"Dear God," Hunter mumbled. "This is bad. Real bad."

Glory rubbed her hands together. Yes, it was. Falon the bastard was about to fall. Hard-core!

Two

Anticipation hummed through Glory for the rest of the night and the following day, possibilities rolling continually through her mind. She'd hoped Hunter would tell Falon what was going on, Falon would rush to her and beg her to forgive him, and she would get to slam a door in his face, causing him to toss and turn for hours in fear.

But he never showed up.

So when the sun finally descended on the second day, she padded to her bedroom, wading through clothes, shoes, and donut wrappers, grabbed a notebook, and climbed onto the bed.

It was time to test the pen's powers.

Ever since Falon had—*Do not think about that right now! You know better.* Already, with that tiny half thought, her pulse had kicked into overdrive, and her stomach had clenched, sickness churning inside of it.

Think about your revenge. For this to work, she needed to be strong, unemotional. Otherwise, she'd do something mean, Falon would look at her with those otherworldly violet eyes of his, and she'd cave. Maybe even apologize. *He deserves to suffer.*

How best to torture him?

She thought about what she knew about him. She'd never slept with him, but she knew what he looked like when he experienced ultimate pleasure. She knew how he tensed, knew his voice dripped harsh and raspy. Knew he roared with the last spasm, pounding his big, hard body into his lover's.

Uh, not helping. Breath burned in her lungs, and fire rushed through her veins, but she couldn't stop her mind from traveling that road. One night she'd stumbled upon Falon in the woods, making love to one of his many women. Or, as Glory liked to call them, one of his many hookers. Anyhoodles, she'd been unable to walk away. He'd been unnaturally beautiful and darkly seductive, whispering the most erotic nothings in the hooker's ear.

Glory had suddenly understood why Falon could fight vampires and demons for hours and hours without breaking a sweat. He was total strength, inexorable stamina. *Nothing* tired him.

That night, she'd developed a tiny—enormous—crush on him. Even though he was way out of her league. Glory was a wee bit on the pudgy side, while Falon personified perfection. She exercised by riding her bike into town to buy a bag of Doritos; he worked out slaying his enemies without thought or hesitation. Men ignored her; women flocked to him. She spent hours in front of a computer, living life in her mind; he actually lived. Inside other people's pants, but whatever.

Rumor was he knew what a female craved before even she knew, and anyone who experienced the bliss of his sometimes gentle, usually savage touch was never the same again. Watching him, Glory had begun to believe that.

She'd fallen completely under his spell, haunted for days by his mesmerizing image. She'd yearned to have him in her bed. In her shower. On her floor. Wherever. She hadn't been picky. She'd just wanted him. Desperately and unequivocally. She'd wanted him naked, slipping and sliding into *her*, no one else, wrapped around her, cherishing her. She'd wanted her name on his lips, his taste in her mouth. Until . . .

Her hands clenched into fists. *You aren't supposed to think about this!*

The memories flooded her, anyway. A few months ago, she'd overhead him tell Hunter that one woman was the same as any other, and love was for idiots. Since they shared the same mind-set—love sucked giant elephant balls!—and he didn't care who he slept with, she'd decided to go for it and throw herself at him.

Pleasure was seriously lacking in her life, and she would have given all of her powers—well, rather, all of *Evie's* powers—to have him look at her with desire. Just once. That's all she'd needed, all she'd wanted.

So she'd gone to his house in nothing but a trench coat and heels. And yeah, she'd flashed him.

He'd taken one look at her and laughed. Laughed!

"Go home, little girl," he'd said. "You don't know what you're playing at."

"I'm twenty-three, not jailbait, and I'm anything but little, as you can clearly see. I'm here for a few hours of fun, that's all."

"Okay, let me put this another way. Get lost. You're not welcome here."

"I'm—I'm not your type, then," she'd stammered, mortified to her very soul. In that moment, she'd understood. Even though he'd said any woman would do, he'd meant any *pretty* woman would do.

His gaze had become hard as it perused her. "No, you're not my type."

He could have spared the remaining tatters of her feminine pride, but another woman had walked up behind Glory. Kaycee, a girl who had graduated a few years ahead of Glory, had obviously craved the same thing as Glory, despite the fact that she'd come with a basket of fruit to "sell." Just as she'd been in school, Kaycee had been tall and thin and pretty. And Falon had allowed that pink-skinned *married* fairy hooker inside before shutting the door in Glory's red-hot face.

Remembering, Glory gnashed her teeth together. "I will destroy his male pride," she said, determined. "I will teach him what it's like to feel unwanted and ugly."

But she spent the next hour staring at the notebook, mind blank. Shit! How did a girl teach a man that kind of lesson?

Just write something. Anything! Pretend this is one of your novels and test the pen's powers. Let's see, let's see. Roman solider? No. Falon didn't deserve to carry a sword. But she saw all kinds of possibilities in that time period. Gladiator? Oh, yes, yes, yes. Gladiators were slaves, and she really liked the idea of Falon in chains.

Closing her eyes, she pictured Falon pacing the dirt floors of a barred cell, sweat rolling down the sculpted muscles of his bronzed stomach, pooling in his navel and dipping lower. Fresh from fighting, blood splattered him.

Licking her lips, Glory shifted against the covers. The scene continued to open up in her mind, painting her thoughts with its descriptions. She sucked in a deep breath and forced her hand to write what she saw . . .

Falon was lying in bed, cool, dry, staring at the ceiling of his bedroom one moment and inside a dirt-laden cell the next, pacing back and forth, sweat pouring from him. Shocked at the sudden change, he tried to stop. His feet kept moving as though they were no longer connected to his brain.

What the hell?

Moonlight slithered around him as he passed a crudely crafted bed, then an equally crude bench, kicking dirt with his sandals. *Sandals?* There was a metallic tang in air. The rustle of chains could be heard beyond the cell, as could moans of . . . injured men? Pleasured men?

Confusion slithered through him.

"Yo. Falon."

Hearing the husky female voice, he spun and faced the cell's farthest set of bars. A lone woman stood behind them, shadows covering her face. Glistening white cloth draped her, and gold flowers glinted from her left shoulder and hem. A chain belt circled her waist, cinching the drape around her and revealing slender curves. The scent of pampered, eager woman and desire drifted from her, sweet and exotic.

His body hardened in hated desire. Hated, because only one woman had that effect on him lately.

"Glory Tawdry," he said through clenched teeth. "I should have known."

"Great Goddess, it worked!" She clapped her hands, and he could easily imagine her smiling that sultry, white-toothed smile of hers. "I hope you don't mind, but I decided to write myself into the scene."

"Scene What scene?"

"This one." As she spoke, she stepped into a ribbon of that golden moonlight.

He couldn't help himself. He sucked in a heated breath and drank her in. Long, red hair framed her pretty face—the most sensual face he'd ever seen. Her eyes were large emeralds flecked with gold. Her nose was gently sloped, her cheeks pink and perfectly rounded. Her lips were luxuriant and red, utterly magnificent—but they would have looked better moving over his body.

You know better than to think like that, you walking penis! "What do you mean, you wrote yourself into the scene? What is this place? How did you get me here?"

Her sculpted brows rose. "Didn't Hunter tell you?"

"Tell me what? I haven't spoken to him in days." His friend had stopped coming to Knight Caps, the bar he owned and where Falon bartended, preferring instead to spend every moment with his revenge witch. Disgraceful, if you asked Falon.

"Evie must have distracted him," Glory said with a laugh. "Damn, but I do love my sister."

That laugh . . . God, it was magical. Almost melted his fury. Almost. His gaze circled the cell. "What have you done to me, Glory?"

"Nothing much. Yet. This is just a small taste of my revenge."

Revenge. He didn't have to ask why. The night she'd come to his house, flashed him every one of her spectacular curves, and nearly felled him, he'd resorted to the only thing capable of saving him: cruelty.

His gaze met hers, and something hot filled his veins. This time, it wasn't fury. She looked utterly pleased with herself, and the look was good on her. Good enough to eat. She must have sensed the direction of his thoughts because she backed up a step. A pause stretched between them, layered with awareness. Sizzling with need.

There was something about her that appealed to the beast inside him. Something dark, dangerous, and bone deep that awakened urges inside him he'd thought long dead. Tender urges, savage urges.

Do not think like that, idiot! He'd made the mistake of willingly dating a witch twice. Once because he'd wanted the woman, once because he'd needed the woman. Both experiences had scarred him for eternity. The relationship with the first, Frederica, had not ended well, and the damn woman had cursed him with impotence. And no amount of Viagra or stimulation had fixed the . . . limpness.

Falon had been forced to give up a year of his life acting as a slave to Penelope, the second witch, to win his freedom. In return, Penelope had challenged Frederica, who quickly lost and finally reversed her spell. Had the return of his manhood been worth it? He wasn't sure. Penelope had not been an easy mistress. He'd cooked, cleaned, run errands, supplied her with orgasms and massages, balanced her checkbook, punished her enemies, and fixed her TiVo. So yeah, he fucking hated witches! They always abused their powers.

That hadn't stopped him from wanting Glory, though—who was now in the process of abusing her goddamn powers! Yes, he'd hurt her all those months ago. But he'd had to push her away before he'd caved.

Still, he'd regretted it ever since and had even tried to make it up to her, acting as her protector on several occasions. "I don't desire this," he said.

"Yes, you do."

"No, the hell I don't! That night in the cemetery, I saved you from hungry corpses." He wasn't sure how or why, but since that night on his porch he always seemed to know when she was in trouble. A fierce surge of protectiveness would rise inside him, and the next thing he knew, he'd be rushing to get to her, wherever she was.

Maybe she'd cast a spell on him.

He bit the inside of his cheek until he tasted blood. That made sense. He should have realized it sooner, but he had been consumed with thoughts of her naked. He wanted to curse at her but held back the words. No need to provoke her. Yet. Damn, what should he do?

Before that fateful night, he'd always avoided looking at her and her witch sisters. Had left a building the moment they'd entered it. Because one glance at that sensual face of Glory's, and he nearly forgot his no witch rule.

Rejecting her that night on his porch had been one of the hardest things he'd ever done. Literally. She'd been naked. But he'd managed to do it—and he'd done nothing but dream about her ever since.

"What kind of spell is this?" he demanded.

"Don't you worry your pretty little head about that," she said with a sugar-sweet tone. "You worry about the pain and suffering I'm about to rain upon your life."

"Glory—" He pressed his lips together. *Do not antagonize her, or she'll make it worse. Duh.* He raked his gaze over her, trying to decide what to do. Wait. She looked . . . different. His head titled to the side as he frowned. "What did you do to yourself?"

"I wrote myself in as a glorious one hundred and twenty—" Now *she* frowned. A moment later, she disappeared as if she'd never been there.

"Glory?" He spun around, eyes roaming. Where the hell was she?

A moment later, she reappeared in front of the bars. And she looked even thinner, the robe bagging over her bony body. He didn't like it. He liked her curves and the lusciousness of her breasts, hips, and thighs. Even thinking of them caused his mouth to water. Was his tongue wagging?

She smiled. "I wrote myself in as a glorious one hundred and *fifteen* pounds."

"You're skin and bones."

"I know. Isn't it great?" She didn't wait for his answer but twirled, her smile never fading. Material danced at her ankles like snowflakes. When she stopped, her eyes narrowed on him, and she added tightly, "What do you think of me now?"

He decided to be honest. "I liked you better the other way," he said, crossing his arms over his sweaty, bloody chest—still having no idea how he'd become so sweaty or so bloody.

At first, Glory appeared stunned by his admission. Then her eyes narrowed even more, becoming tiny slits that hid those beautiful hazel irises completely. "Yeah. Right. I've seen your harem. You always pick the skinny ones."

Actually, the skinny ones always picked him, and after a year without being able to get Little Fal up, he'd taken what he could get, when he could get it. Except for Glory. Why'd she have to be witch?

"Where are we?" he asked.

Her lips curled into a slow, sensual grin, and his stomach tightened. "This is your prison."

He ran his tongue over his teeth. "Why?"

"We already covered this."

Yeah, they had. "Look, I'm sorry about that night. I wish it had never happened."

"But it did happen. Makes sense, though, that you're sorry *now*." Rage crackled around her, lifting strands of her hair as if she'd stuck her finger into a light socket. A moment passed while she calmed herself down, and her hair smoothed out. "I should have written myself inside the cell with you so I could torment you with my superhot bod, but I didn't want you to have access to my neck."

"So that's how you plan to punish me, is it? Magically transport me into a cell and make me horny? By all means, keep at it." He could imagine worse things.

"Oh, no. I plan to do much, much more than that." She licked her lips and perused him, gaze lingering on his stomach, between his legs. That gaze devoured him, eating him up one tasty bite at a time.

Clearly, she still wanted him.

His first thought: *Thank God.*

His second: *Holy shit, this is bad!*

"Don't look at me like that," he growled, not caring if she tried to punish him further. He could not allow this witch to desire him like that. Not when his resolve teetered so precariously. Look what had happened already. Any more . . . No. No way could he allow himself to have her.

Glory's eyes snapped to his, embarrassed hazel against furious violet. "I'll look at you however I want! You're my property right now. I own you."

"Stop this, Glory."

"Make me."

Very slowly, purposefully, he moved toward her.

Approaching her is dangerous, common sense said.

No other way, Little Fal replied.

Glory's mouth opened all the wider with every step he took, but no sound emerged from her. When he reached the bars, he whipped out his arms before she had a chance to stop him and clamped his fingers around her wrists.

"What are you doing?" Her tone lacked any heat, and she actually pressed herself into the bars until her body brushed his. "I didn't add this to the scene."

The contact, though light, sparked a jolt of pure fire in his bloodstream. Up close, she was even lovelier. Freckles were scattered across her nose. Her pale skin glowed with health and vitality.

"You want me to touch you? Is that what it's going to take to get you out of my life?" He anchored her arms behind her back with one hand and traced his other down the front of her robe. How he longed to linger over the small mound of her breasts, the hollow of her stomach . . . the waiting valley between her legs.

If she'd possessed her usual curves, he knew he would not have been able to resist. Her desire to be thin was actually a blessing. But even now, like this, his control wasn't what it should have been. He was trembling, for God's sake.

"Stop," she whispered. Her eyes said *more*.

All of his muscles bunched in reaction to that pleading tone, that needy expression, hardening, aching. He did not stop. He eagerly learned the length of her legs, her skin smooth and soft, like velvet. By the time he finished the full-body caresses, sweat beaded over his face and dripped in rivulets down his chest.

"More." She closed her eyes, all pretence of resistance gone.

He pinched several strands of her hair between his fingers, enjoying the silkiness. He brought the tendrils to his nose and sniffed. Nearly moaned. A fresh, blooming garden. That's what her hair smelled like. He could have breathed in the scent forever.

"If you want me to fuck you," he said, deliberately cruel, just as before, "you'll have to enter the cell." *For the best*. It was better to be punished than to cave, he decided.

"Wh-what?" Her eyes blinked open. He saw the need burning there, the want. Her nipples were hard, visible through her robe. The scent of awakened passion wafted from her, blending with the flowery fragrance of her hair.

"You heard me."

"No, I hate you." The words were spoken on a breathless sigh. Then she shook her head, eyes narrowing again, and backed away. "I'm going to make you want me, Falon. I'm going to make you crave me. But you are never going to have me. Do you understand? Never."

A moment later, she vanished. The prison shimmered before disappearing, too, and the next thing Falon knew, he was lying in his bed again. As the cool sheets met his clean, dry skin, he rolled from the mattress and stalked to his closet.

Fury, desire, and determination pounded through him. He strapped weapons all over his body, dressed, and stalked from his house. No way he'd allow Glory to use her powers against him. Not again.

He was going to find her. Whatever he had to do, he was going to stop her.

Three

Heart thundering in her chest, Glory kept her eyes squeezed shut and inhaled deeply. The first thing she noticed was how the air no longer smelled of decadent man, sweat, and dark spice. Now she caught the faint drift of powdered sugar and jasmine incense.

Who would've thought she'd mourn the loss of sweaty-man air?

Time to check out the rest. Slowly she blinked open her eyes. Her notebook came into view. Everything that had happened was right there, the words staring up at her. She quickly looked away, not wanting to be reminded of her near capitulation. All Falon had done was touch her, for love of the Goddess, and she'd forgotten her need for revenge. The feel of his hands on her body, exploring . . . the sound of his rough voice in her ear, whispering . . . the desire blazing in his eyes, beckoning . . .

Her stomach tightened, and the ache she'd experienced inside the prison renewed between her legs. *Keep looking.*

Her flat-screen computer came into view, followed by the wall of magazine pictures she used for references and her *Hunks of the Month* calendar. Trash and dirty clothes were scattered all over her carpet. She hadn't cleaned since that terrible night; she didn't know why.

"It worked," she said, just to break the silence. "It really worked."

She'd actually sent Falon to an ancient prison, *then* she'd actually followed him there. *Oh . . . my.* She sagged against the mattress and closed her eyes again. Falon's image filled her mind. His eyes, an exotic, come-to-me violet fringed by thick black lashes. His dark hair, a little long. The shadowy stubble that dusted his jaw. The bronzed skin and bodybuilder muscles she'd almost held.

The man had exuded a potent animal magnetism; it had oozed from his pores.

What was he doing right now? Cursing her to the heavens? She laughed, delighted by the thought. He might even be tugging on his clothes, determined to race over here and punish her.

She stopped laughing.

Having trouble catching her breath, Glory scrambled out of the bed. Her jeans and panties floated straight to her ankles. What the hell? Frowning in confusion, she grabbed them, jerked them up, and launched forward. Almost tripped as the clothes tumbled again. Growled. She needed to leave the house, like, now, and the wardrobe difficulties weren't helping. As she bent to retrieve her stuff, the notebook slid out of her fingers and onto the floor.

She released her clothes and reached out. Her eyes widened as she caught a glimpse of her hand. She was so . . . skinny. Her arm was slender, the bones fine. Her fingers were elegant. Wow. No wonder her jeans no longer fit.

Why hadn't her slenderness faded with the scene?

The answer hit her, and she grinned. She'd written it a little later. For the next few minutes, she'd be a total babe.

Seriously, she'd never looked hotter. Maybe she should wait here. Maybe she should allow Falon inside. Maybe, as she'd hoped, he would be overcome with lust for her and the real revenge could begin. He would beg her to sleep with him, and she would say, "Hell, no."

And what if you plump up right before his eyes, huh? What then?

Shit! Glory's heart jolted into hyperdrive, and she raced throughout her room, kicking off the too-big jeans and panties and jerking on a nightgown. The silky pink material bagged on her, but it was the only thing that would cover her *and* stay put.

Why was she so nervous, anyway? There was nothing Falon could do to her. Not while she owned the pen. *Uh, he could steal it and use it against you.*

A knock sounded at the front of the house.

Her mouth fell open, and she straightened. No way. No damn way he'd made it here so quickly. She looked at her bedroom door, turned, and craned her neck to see out the room's only window. A black SUV sat in the driveway. Damn! He had.

"Glory, Falon's here to see you," Godiva called a moment later, only sounding the slightest bit confused.

"Tell him I'm not here." Glory propelled herself over her bed and to the window. She shoved the glass up and out of the way, never letting go of the pen. Cool air wafted inside, ruffling the thin, gaping gown against her skin as she climbed out. The grass was soft against her bare feet.

Maybe she'd go to Candy Cox's, she thought, racing through the night. No, no. Candy's sister was in town or due to arrive in town, and rumor was the woman negated powers of every kind. Worse, Candy's shape-shifting werewolf boyfriend would be there, which meant more sickening PDA.

She could go to Pastor Harmony's. Ugh, no, she decided next. Harmony was now a mother. The Desdaine triplets, then? No. The brats were likely to welcome her inside and secretly call Falon and alert him. So where did that leave her?

"Oh, no you don't," a male voice boomed behind her.

She gasped, panic infusing her every cell. Goose bumps broke out over her skin. One backward glance—*Shit!* He'd jumped out her window and was now moving toward her, menacing purpose in his every step. His eyes were narrowed on her.

The forest was a hundred feet in front of her. If she could just—a rock cut into her bare foot, and she fell. Grass padded her landing, but the hard impact still managed to shove the oxygen from her lungs.

"Glory," he said, sounding concerned.

"Go home." She grabbed a long, thin stick as she jumped to her feet. Ouch, ouch, ouch. Might come in handy. She jetted forward, taking stock. Heart: still beating. Pen and stick: still in hand. Legs: workable. Aching, but workable. Twigs and rocks continued to scrape into her feet. *Worry about the pain later*. She just needed to get far enough away from Falon to write him into chains. If not . . .

"I called Hunter," Falon shouted, closer to her.

She yelped but didn't allow herself to look back. Already, his masculine scent wafted around her. *Faster, woman!*

"I want that pen, Glory."

Shit! He was even closer now. There was no time to hide. As she ran, branches slapping at her, stinging, she began writing on her arm. *Twigs reached out and grasped at Falon*. The words were barely legible.

Behind her, Falon growled. The rustle of trees echoed through the night.

Was it working?

Several of those twigs caught him and jerked him to a stop.

An animalistic snarl erupted. "Glory!" This time, Falon's voice carried on the wind. He sounded a good distance behind her. "Stop."

Glory slowed her steps. Panting, she tossed a look over her shoulder. Her eyes widened, and she ground to an abrupt halt. Limbs had indeed caught Falon. They were wound around him like bands of indestructible silk, anchoring him to the base of a tree. His lips peeled back from his teeth, and he scowled over at her.

"Come here," he shouted. "Now."

Despite her wheezing, she was feeling very smug. She turned away from him. One push of her fingers, and she broke the stick she'd grabbed when she'd fallen in two.

"What are you doing? Get over here!"

She gripped the hem of her nightgown and tied the pen inside it. Hopefully, if Falon managed to escape, he would confiscate the stick, thinking it was the pen. That done, she turned back to him and approached, waving the stick smugly.

Her muscles were sore from that run, and as she walked, her arms, legs, and waist began to fill out, the weight returning. Her breasts swelled, stretching the fabric of the nightgown. At least the pen stayed in place.

Still, some of her smugness disappeared. She didn't want Falon to see her like this, but she wasn't going to waste any ink making herself skinny again. Not now, at least. Right now he was too furious to experience desire, no matter what she looked like.

When she reached him, she hid her arms behind her back, as if keeping "the pen" out of his reach. Strands of her red hair blustered forward, stroking his face.

His pupils dilated, black swallowing violet. "You can escape tonight, but I *will* find you. And when I do, I'm going to take that goddamn pen and make you wish you'd never met me."

She leaned forward, as though she planned to reveal a big secret. "I already do wish I'd never met you." His warm breath fanned her cheek, a tender caress, and she had to jerk away from him before she did something stupid. Like suck on his earlobe.

Their gazes locked together, a tangle of emotions.

"Look at you," she said and *tsked* under her tongue. "At my mercy."

He raised his chin. "It won't always be this way."

"Like I want to keep you in my life that long. *Always*. Please." She snorted. "A few weeks should do it."

"You think I'll pretend it never happened? Leave you alone afterward?"

"Well, yeah." She arched a brow. "Unless you want more of me."

His eyes narrowed to tiny slits. His features were calm, but the pulse at the base of his neck hammered wildly. "More of you . . . interesting choice of words." Wind danced between them as his gaze perused her.

Her nipples hardened, and she barely restrained herself from covering them with her hands. Instead, she raised her chin and dared him to say something about her weight. She was surprised when he bit his lower lip, as though he was imagining her taste in his mouth—and liked it.

"Witches should have a code of honor, preventing them from hurting others," he said softly.

"Here's an idea. I'll draft up a witches' code of honor, and you draft up a how to reject a woman nicely code of conduct. Sound good?"

Shame colored his cheeks.

Gold star for me. Now drive the point deeper. "Let me tell you a little something about me, Falon. I have never had much self-esteem. My sisters are tall and slender, and men have always drooled over them. But not me. Not chubby Glor." She laughed bitterly. She loved her sisters more than anything on this earth, but they were so perfect, so pretty, that she, who was already vapor, became *nothing* in comparison. "In the span of five minutes, you managed to destroy what tiny bit of feminine pride I had."

His shoulders flattened against the trunk, his eyes closed, and he drew in a breath. "I admit it. I handled the situation wrong."

"Yes, you did. You didn't have to laugh at me. You could have simply said, 'No, thank you.'"

"I wasn't laughing at you. Not really. I just wanted to ensure you never came back. Wait. That sounds just as bad. Look, the truth is, sending you away had nothing to do with your appearance."

"Oh, please."

"It didn't." His lids popped open, and he was suddenly staring at her with such intensity she had trouble breathing. "You're a witch."

There was so much hatred in his voice, she stumbled back. "Yeah. So?"

"So, let's just say I'm not very fond of witches."

She snorted, refusing to believe him. "You've always been nice to Godiva and Genevieve."

"I wasn't . . . attracted to them." The admission was snarled, more an accusation than anything.

"That's—" Wait. What? He was attracted to her? Pleasure zoomed through her with such potency she almost fell to her knees. But the sensation lasted only five seconds before common sense reared its ugly head. *He'll say anything to soften you. Even a humiliating lie.* Pleasure morphed into searing fury.

Why, that . . . that . . . bastard! Her fingers tightened around the stick, and she had to fight the urge to grab the pen and write a hungry lion into the scene. "So you were attracted to me, were you?" she asked as calmly as she was able.

"What do you think?" he muttered, motioning to his dick with his chin.

She dropped her gaze, staring between his legs with wonder. Okay.

Maybe he hadn't been lying. He was hard, his erection straining against his jeans. "Th-that's not because of me." Was it?

"Your nipples are hard, and I can see the outline of fine red hair between your legs. Obviously, you're not wearing any panties. So yeah, it's because of you."

Her mouth floundered open and closed. "Only because I'm the only woman present and you're probably in heat." Warmth bloomed in her face as she finally covered her breasts with one arm and between her legs with the other. "So you can just look away!"

"Make me."

"I'll take away your sight. Just see if I won't."

Finally his gaze snapped back up to her face. "Are you truly that cruel?"

Damn him! He'd zapped her anger with those words, making her feel like the wicked witch Evie had teased her about being. "No. I won't go that far," she whispered, as shamed as he'd been a moment ago.

"How far *are* you going to take it, then?"

She peered down at her bare feet—*Ick, time for a pedicure*—and kicked a rock with the tip of her toe. "I honestly don't know."

Falon clenched his jaw, cutting off any words that might try to escape his mouth. A mouth currently watering for a taste of the woman in front of him. Her curves were a thing of beauty. And with ribbons of moonlight seeping from the canopy of treetops, paying her flawless skin absolute tribute, with that flame red hair dancing like naughty nymphs around her shoulders and her lips glistening from the sting of her teeth, his beast wanted to tame her beauty.

Except, she now appeared defeated.

He hated seeing her like that almost as much as he hated being bound. Almost. Right now, however, he was too primed to feel anything more than desire. He wanted her to reach out, to touch him, kiss him. Suck him.

He was hard as a damn rock and needed to come.

"The night you came to my house in that trench coat," he said.

Her attention suddenly locked on him and the fire blazing inside him. "The night you screwed that fairy hooker? *That* night?"

Surprisingly enough, her waspish tone delighted him. "Jealous?"

"As if!"

He hadn't invited the fairy, whatever her name was, to his house. He'd met her in town earlier that day, had talked and laughed with her, but hadn't meant to take it further. She was married, for God's sake. Had Glory not been standing in front of him, he would have sent the fairy away. He liked sex, yes, but he'd never allowed a woman inside his home. They tended to linger, and he liked to do the deed and move on.

In fact, the moment Glory had taken off, he'd sent the pink-skinned fairy packing. Despite the fact that she had offered him apples—off of her body. He hadn't even touched her. Had just stood at the window, peeking out the blinds like a criminal, hoping for and dreading a reappearance from Glory.

He'd been hard then, too, so maybe he should have slept with the fairy. But it had been flame red hair his hands had wanted to tangle in, hazel eyes he'd wanted to stare into, and a soft, plush body he'd wanted to penetrate.

No one else would have done.

Maybe that was why he hadn't been able to have sex these past few months. He felt guilty for how he'd hurt Glory, so his body would no longer allow him to respond to other women. Maybe he needed to sleep with her once—or twice—and build up her self-esteem. She'd feel better about herself, he'd stop feeling guilty for the way he'd treated her, and they could both go on with their lives.

Are you kidding? Are you so hard up you've got to bed a witch? Think of the consequences, idiot! She's nuts now, so how much worse will she be after you've slept with her? What if she didn't want things to end after the sex was over? What if she tried to punish him again?

"Uh, hello?" she said, exasperated.

"What?" he asked more harshly than he'd intended.

She crossed her arms over her chest, drawing the material of her gown tight over her breasts. And nipples. Which were still hard. She was killing him. He could make out the edge of the pen between her fingers, but he couldn't make himself care.

"You mentioned the incident," she said. "Well, what about it?"

He'd had a point, hadn't he? Oh, yeah. "You were aroused when you came to me."

A huffy gasp left her. "No, I was not! I was going to give you a *chance* to arouse me. That's all."

"Please. You flashed me, and baby, you were already glistening."

Her cheeks heated to the same shade as her hair, making her all the lovelier. "You are very close to losing your favorite appendage." Scowling, peering at him hotly, she jerked the hand holding the pen forward and poised it just below his nose.

"Wait, wait, wait," he rushed out. Damn her and her powers! He lost his erection as every reason he hated witches flashed through his mind. "I'm sorry." *But not as sorry as you'll soon be.* "You were cold as ice that night." *You nearly singed me.* "You weren't turned on at all." *The scent of your desire is still imprinted on my brain.*

Slowly, she lowered her arm, expression mollified.

The limbs binding him began to loosen their grip, and he blinked in surprise. Was it possible? With a twist of his wrist, he was free. That easy, that simple, as if he'd never been bound. *He* had to hold on to the limbs to keep them upright. He blinked again, doing his best to hide his elation.

Glory was going to pay. Oh, was she going to pay. First, he had to claim that fucking pen!

"Com'ere," he said as gently as he was able. "Please. I want to tell you a secret."

She shook her head, red curls flinging in every direction. "What kind of secret?" Suspicion danced in her eyes.

He tried to look troubled.

"Tell me like this. No one can hear us."

"I don't want to say it aloud. It's . . . embarrassing."

Several moments ticked by, and she remained in place. Then she sighed and stalked to him, hands fisted on her hips. She was so sure of her prowess—and his weakness. She'd learn . . .

"What?" she said.

Her feminine fragrance wafted to his nostrils, the same aroma she'd emitted that night on his porch. In the cell. She still desired him. He took a moment to simply enjoy. Savor. Crickets chirped a lazy song, and locusts rattled an accompanying, faster rhythm. In the distance, a dog barked. Around them, pink flower petals floated through the air, warm and sweet, each laced with a strong aphrodisiac. He'd heard that Glory had cast a love spell over the entire town, and since that day the petals had fallen from the sky like summer snow.

"What?" she demanded again.

"This." He grinned, and snapped his arms closed around her waist. She yelped.

"Got ya," he said.

Four

Shock coursed through Glory, and it was mixed with an insidious thread of desire. Falon had her locked against his hard, hot body so tightly she could feel the frantic beat of his heart. Or maybe that was *her* heartbeat. Her breasts were mashed into his chest, her nipples like hard little points, and every time she breathed, she sucked in the scent of strength and soap and dark spice.

"Nothing to say?" Falon asked smugly.

"Let me go. Now." Trying not to panic, she attempted to lift her arms, attempted to flatten her palms against his chest and push him away from her, but her arms were glued to her sides.

"None of that," he said, latching onto her wrists with one hand and shoving them behind her. With his free hand, he grabbed the stick. Clearly, he assumed it was the pen, because his grin widened.

"Mine now," he said, and stuffed it into his pants pocket.

Do not smile. "Give it back."

"Make me."

Not knowing how to respond, she ran her tongue over her teeth. His gaze followed the movement, his pupils dilating.

"What are you going to do with me?" she demanded. Or rather, meant to demand. Her voice was breathless. Again. Her body was trembling—and not with fury. How did he do this to her? Make her want him despite everything that had happened between them?

"I don't know," he answered honestly. "I need to think about it, consider my options. Because I can't allow you to run wild, using your powers against everyone who pricks your anger."

"Yeah, well, before you, I didn't use my powers for bad things."

"So I'm just special?"

"Of course you'd think so." Good. Her voice had substance now. "But the real answer is that you're simply the most irritating person I've ever met." *Kiss me. Let it be a terrible experience so that I never crave it again.*

He leaned down and traced the tip of his nose along the curve of her cheek, leaving a trail of decadent fire. Glory tried not to arch her hips and rub against his erection, but she did and, oh, Goddess, was he ever erect. Long and thick, hard and smoldering.

He groaned, his eyelids fluttering closed. "Again," he commanded. *Stop. Don't do this. Don't travel down this road. A kiss is one thing. But this. . .* Ceasing her gyrations was the most difficult thing Glory had ever done, but she did it.

And suddenly he was eyeing her again, lashes casting menacing shadows over his cheeks and electric gaze piercing her soul. "I'm going to kiss you." It was a promise. "And you're going to kiss me back." It was a rough demand.

"No, you're not." *Please, please, please.* "And no, I'm not." *Impossible.*

"Yes, we are. We have to do something to end the madness."

"Fine. Whatever. Do what you want."

"This doesn't change anything."

"I'm glad you understand that."

"Try to take the pen, and you'll regret it."

"I'll regret it anyway."

He arched a brow. "Do you always have to have the last word?"

"Why, yes, I—"

His lips smashed into hers. Her mouth opened automatically, welcoming him inside. He thrust deep, and his flavor filled her mouth. Drugging, addicting. White-hot. A tingling ache sparked to life in her stomach, then spread to her chest, her limbs. She melted into him.

The iron lock on her wrists loosened. Rather than shove him, she wrapped her arms around him, pulling him closer. Her fingers tangled in his silky hair. His hands were free now, too, and they fastened on her waist, urging her forward and backward, mimicking the motions of sex.

Waves of pleasure constantly speared her. This was what she'd dreamed of since going to him that night, so long ago. His mouth on her, his hands all over her, his body straining against hers.

"More?" he whispered.

She nibbled on his bottom lip. "More."

He reached between them and palmed one of her breasts. His fingers plucked at the hardened nipple. "So perfect."

Moaning, she arched her hips. Exquisite contact. Her head dropped backward, and her long tresses tickled her overheated skin. Had Falon not been holding her up with that arm around her waist, she would have fallen.

No, wait. She was gripping spikes of his hair, tugging them. Hard. A few had already ripped from his scalp and were wrapped around her fingers.

He didn't complain.

She eased closer to him, relaxing her clasp. Her mouth found his neck, and she licked. His skin was a little abrasive, but perfect.

"You're so hot," he said.

"On fire," she agreed. She licked the seam of his lips.

He captured the tip of her tongue and sucked. The hand on her waist slid down . . . down . . . and cupped her ass. As he'd correctly guessed earlier, she wasn't wearing any underwear, and the tops of his fingers teased her most feminine core. She was so wet, she practically dripped between her legs.

"Shit. You're killing me." One of his fingers stroked her clitoris.

A tremor rocked her. *Shouldn't be this good. Not with him.*

Before the thought finished whispering through her mind, her entire world spun. Then cool bark was pressing into her back, and Falon was searing her front. He pinned her arms over her head with one hand and palmed her breast with the other.

"I knew you'd be this good," he growled, not sounding the least bit happy about it.

"Wh-what?" Trying to find her common sense, she blinked open her eyes. When had she closed them? Falon loomed over her. His features were harsh, lined with tension, his gaze a swirling sea of blues, purples, and pinks. How odd. They'd never looked that way before.

His shoulders were so wide, his body seemed to engulf her. Sweat beaded over his sun-kissed skin. He was like an animal whose stomach was rumbling—and he'd just spotted his prey. "Knew it," he finished. "Feared it."

What was he talking about? Feared what? And why wasn't he kissing her? "Falon, I—"

"I want this nipple in my mouth."

"Yes." Please, yes. That still qualified as kissing. "Hurry."

He ripped her nightgown down, revealing both mounds of her breasts. They were large. Overflowing. The nipples were pink, the hardened tips desperate. For a long while, he simply stared down at her.

Glory's cheeks began to heat, and not with desire. Did he like what he saw? He was used to slender women, had once turned Glory away because she wasn't his type. How could she have forgotten?

Embarrassed to her soul, she jerked at his hold, meaning to slide the nightgown back in place. He held strong.

His lips curled in a frown. "What are you doing?"

"Ending this," she said, unable to look at him.

"Be still."

"No."

He increased the death grip on her wrists, and his other hand cupped her chin, forcing her to face him. "Why do you want to end it?"

"Because." Like she'd say it aloud. But maybe that's what he wanted. Maybe that's how he meant to punish her.

Punishment. Of course. How could she have forgotten?

You brought this on yourself. Tears burned her eyes, and her chin trembled.

"What's wrong? You look ready to cry."

"Let me go," she commanded brokenly, focusing on his nose so that she wouldn't have to see those amazing eyes of his and whatever emotion was now banked there.

A moment passed in silence.

"Glory," he said.

Do it; look at him. Get it over with. See his disgust and start to hate him again. Slowly, her gaze lifted. When their eyes met, she gasped. There was a fire raging there. Tension still branched his mouth, and sweat still trickled down his temples. He looked on edge, aroused to the point of pain.

"I think you are the most beautiful creature I've ever beheld. And, like I said, I want your nipple in my mouth, and I think you want it there, too."

She gulped, unable to speak past the sudden lump in her throat.

"I'm going to release your arms. You can push me away or you can urge me closer. The choice is yours."

And just like that, she was free. Her arms fell to her sides. She gripped the tree, and jagged bits of bark cut past her skin. The sting did nothing to dampen her desire. He was so hard and hot against her he was like a brand. The pulse in his neck galloped fiercely. His lips were red and glistening from the kiss.

His chest had stopped moving, she realized. He was holding his breath. Waiting. The knowledge . . . softened her. Was he afraid she'd leave him?

With a shaky hand, she reached out and palmed his erection.

He hissed in a breath.

The tip of his penis had risen well above the waist of his jeans. Actually, the material was so strained, the button had snapped open on its own.

"Trying to torture me?" he croaked. "'Cause it's working."

Was it? She moistened her lips and released him. Was bereft without him in her hand.

Now he moaned.

Despite the warnings trying to slither into her mind, she cupped her breasts and lifted them. "Touch me."

His eyes widened in surprised delight. A moment later, he dipped down and flicked his tongue against one pearled nipple, then the other.

She'd experienced pleasure before, but that had been nothing compared to this. There was an invisible cord from each of her nipples that lead straight to her core, as if he were actually thrumming her clitoris while he licked her. This was Falon, the man she'd fantasized about for years. The man's whose strength and heat and raw intensity destroyed her defenses and made her crave . . .

Soon she was writhing, couldn't have remained still if the plan had been to pretend she felt nothing for him to undermine his confidence and try to convince him he was lacking. He was not lacking.

He scraped her with his teeth, and she groaned. His fingers caressed a path down her stomach. Her muscles quivered when he paused. Glory felt as though she stood on a precipice, waiting to be pushed over. Would he delve lower, like before, only . . . deeper?

"How did I ever find the strength to send you away?" he asked hoarsely.

Some of the flames inside her dwindled to a crackle, and she almost screamed in frustration. If he kept talking, kept reminding her of their painful history, she might lose her pleasure buzz. "No more talking. You'll ruin it."

A soft chuckle rumbled from him. The tip of one finger traced a circle around her navel, then dipped again, lower this time. Dabbling at the small triangle of hair, tickling. "Nothing could ruin this. You're perfection."

Her? Perfection? Entranced, she parted her legs, giving him all the access he could possibly need.

Through the material of the nightgown, he circled her clitoris next. Again. Finally. He pressed.

"Oh, bright lightning," she gasped.

"Like that?"

"Yes. More."

He didn't give it to her but continued to play with her, revving her to that sense of uncontrollable desire again. "You're so wet," he praised. "For me."

"Yes. You." She tried to arch into his touch, tried to force his fingers to press harder. "Falon."

"Oh, but I like the sound of my name on your lips." His tongue glided up to her collarbone, his teeth nipping along the way. She turned her head aside, and he sucked at her pulse.

"I want to get on my knees. I want to taste between your legs. Say yes." He gripped the hem of her nightgown, slowly lifting.

"Ye—" *Red alert!* blared inside her mind, shoving past her need to scream *yes*. If he touched the knot in her gown, he would discover the pen. He would realize he'd taken a stick from her instead.

His knuckles brushed her thigh, and her knees almost buckled. "All you have to do is say *yes*, and my tongue will be inside you . . ."

His dark head, buried between her legs . . . one of her knees, draped over his shoulder . . . his tongue, stroking her to orgasm . . . She yearned for it so badly she had tears in her eyes. But she forced herself to say, "No," and at last to shove him away.

The action was puny, really, but he released her. He was panting, eyes narrowed. She was panting, eyes still burning.

"Things have already gone too far," she managed to get out. *Do I sound as breathless to him as I do to myself?* "This ends now."

He scrubbed a hand over his mouth, his gaze never leaving her face. "Oh, I get it. Punishment received."

He turned and stalked from her, and she wanted to shout that this hadn't been a punishment, not for him, but the words congealed in her throat, and then it was too late, anyway, because he disappeared from view.

Five

Falon fumed for the next three days. For three reasons. (Three must be his new lucky number.) One, Glory had outsmarted him, leaving him with a magicless stick rather than the revenge pen. Two, he hadn't gotten nearly enough of her and had thought about her constantly. And three, she was now ignoring him, as if he didn't fucking matter to her.

He should be happy about that last one.

He wasn't. Damn it, he wasn't!

Motions clipped, he paced through his living room, trying to decide what to do. Like his lack of happiness, this *should* have been a no-brainer: stay out of her life. Never antagonize her again. She'd had her revenge. She'd made him burn, desperate for her, and then had rejected him. They were even. There was no reason they had to deal with each other again. Most likely, bad, magical things would happen if they did.

"As well as hot and sweaty," he muttered. Her passion had been a thing of beauty. She'd writhed against him, her lush body flushed, her hazel eyes blazing. Her breasts had overflowed in his hands. Her skin had been the softest he'd ever caressed. Her long red hair had tumbled down her shoulders and arms, the perfect frame for her exquisite loveliness.

What would have happened if she'd have let him strip her? What would have happened if he'd spread her legs and pounded inside her?

"Heaven, that's what." *But what about afterward?* Would she have wanted more from him or been done with him? Would she have used her naughty magic against him again?

Falon scrubbed a hand over his scalp, nails raking. He was—or rather, had been—crown prince of the Fae. Women had thrown themselves at him, hoping to be queen. None had captured his interest.

Then he'd meet Frederica, the witch, and had been entranced. Now he thought, perhaps, she'd used a love spell on him and there at the end it had worn off. But even still, he hadn't hungered for her the way he hungered for Glory. Glory challenged him in every way imaginable.

"Not hard, nowadays," he muttered.

To serve Penelope for the required year in order to gain his freedom from Frederica's impotence curse, he'd had to relinquish his crown. His brother, Falk, had then taken over. Falk was a good king, respected, admired, and loved. Falon didn't have the heart to take it from him when the year ended. *What kind of king would I make, anyway?* Not a good one, that was for sure. He'd always been too wild.

Besides, over the years he'd managed to carve out a decent life for himself. He didn't need money, but he worked with Hunter at the bar. Amusements abounded, and there was never a dull moment. Brawls, seductions. Plus, it was a hub of information. When people were drinking, they tended to spill their deepest secrets. A few months ago, Falon had overheard three female fairies planning to poison Falk. He'd passed the information on, and the women had been captured in the act, Falk saved.

Falon sighed, his gaze traveling through his home. To thank him, Falk had sent him gifts. Lots and lots of gifts. From plush crimson couches to thick obsidian rugs. From jeweled goblets to a tiered chandelier. While the outside of his modest house might look ordinary, the inside was like a sultan's palace. White lace even hung from each of the doorways. Not his doing. Falk had also sent a decorator.

Falon stopped in front of the velvet sapphire lounge. He pictured Glory splayed across it, naked, her little pink nipples hard. The lamp resting on the marble table beside the seat would be lit, and she would be bathed in a golden glow. She would nibble on her bottom lip, her eyes closed, lashes casting shadows on her cheeks, hand delving down her soft stomach, fingers sinking into the red curls between her legs.

Just like that, he was rock hard. Again.

"Damn it!"

He needed to bed her. Just once. Otherwise, he'd never be able to get her out of his head.

Growling low in his throat, he stalked to the emerald-studded phone. He'd kind of liked his old one, plain and tan, but oh, well. He dialed Glory's number. *This is dumb, this is so damned dumb.* His blood heated at the thought of hearing her sultry voice. What would she say to him?

One of the Tawdry sisters answered on the third ring. "Yeah, hello." She sounded breathless.

"I need to speak with Glory."

"Falon? Is that you?"

"Yes, who's this?"

"This is Genevieve."

"Hey, Evie. I really need to speak to Glory." Before he came to his senses and took matters into his own hands. Literally.

"Is something wrong?"

He closed his eyes and prayed for patience. "Look, is she around?"

"Well, yeah, but I don't think she'll want to chat with you, and maybe that's for the best. She's in a mood."

Evie sounded like that was newsworthy. When *wasn't* Glory in a mood? "Is something wrong with her? Is she okay?"

"Meaning, did someone physically hurt her? No. You know they'd be dead by my magic if they did."

A warning? "Emotionally, then."

"I don't know. You tell me. Did you kiss her?" Evie asked.

"Who you talking to, baby?" Falon heard in the background.

"Let me speak with Hunter," Falon said.

Crackling static, and then his best friend was saying, "What's going on?"

"Glory okay?"

"Oh, man. She's been stomping around the house for three days, muttering about a stupid kiss, a stupid man, and stupid revenge. She write you into another scene or something?"

"No." But she could do so at any moment, which made him all kinds of an idiot for making this call. And why was she angry? *She'd* rejected *him*. He'd done nothing but try to pleasure her.

"My advice, bro, is to just leave her alone. She'll calm down, and then she'll forget all about you."

That was the problem. Falon didn't want her to forget him. Shit. *He* seriously needed to forget *her*.

"Uh-oh. Here she is," Hunter muttered.

"I'm going for a run," Falon heard her grumble.

"You? Run?" Shock dripped from Evie's voice.

"Well, no one in this household can seem to master magical weight loss, so I'm running the pounds off. You got a problem with that?"

"You don't need to lose weight," he wanted to shout. Then he thought, *She'll be out of the house. It'll be the perfect time to search her room and snatch that pen.* Once the pen was out of her possession, seduction wouldn't be so dumb. A lie, but he didn't care. "Talk to you later, Hunter," he blurted. "Don't tell her I called." He hung up, grabbed his car keys, and stalked into the waiting daylight.

Glory ran until her lungs felt like they'd caught fire. She ran until her body was shaking from exertion. She ran until her mind was mush. Sadly, none of those things shoved Falon from her mind.

Him and his too-soft lips, his decadent, drugging taste. His hardness, his sweet hands. His final request to taste her. She'd stayed away from him, hadn't even tried to punish him again.

Sweat poured from her as she stumbled up the porch steps and into her house. Cool air kissed her skin. She propped herself against the nearest living room wall and hunched over, trying to catch her breath. It had taken her a few hours after leaving him in the forest to deduce exactly how he'd convinced her, even for a second, that he truly desired her.

Good thing she'd stopped him. Only two other outcomes had been possible: *he* would have stopped before actual penetration, leaving her gasping and desperate, or, if they'd actually gone all the way, he would have told her how bad she was afterward. He might have laughed at her again.

Her teeth ground together as she straightened. He'd told her she would regret using the pen against him. Now she did. She needed a distraction.

The living room was empty. "Evie," she called. "Godiva."

No reply.

Had they left, or were they in their rooms, getting it on? Glory rolled her eyes and pretended there wasn't an ache in her chest. Probably the latter, the disgusting witches. Did they ever take a break? Legs screaming in protest, she lumbered forward, using the wall as a prop.

Down the hall she maneuvered. When she reached her bedroom door, she waved her hand over the knob, magically unlocking it. The door creaked open, and she stumbled inside, forced to kick past the clothes and food wrappers still scattered across the floor.

"Hello, Glory," a strong, male voice said.

She gasped, frozen in place, gaze searching. Her heart pounded in her chest, nearly cracking her ribs when she spotted the intruder. Falon was splayed out on her bed. His dark head rested on her pillow, his arms propped behind his neck.

He wore a clinging black T-shirt that veed at the neck and jeans that showed off the muscles in his thighs.

"Wh-what are you doing here? And how did you get in?" No. No! He'd seen the national disaster state of her bedroom. Seriously, a bra hung from the lamp beside her bed. Sadly, she looked worse. "Don't look at me," she said, wanting to turn away as his eyes drank her in.

"Why? You're beautiful. I *like* looking at you. Just as you are," he added.

She rubbed her damp palms against her thighs. "What are you doing here?" she repeated, because she didn't know how else to react to his praise. The pleasure she felt was unacceptable.

"I would have pegged you for a neat freak," he said, ignoring her question. Again.

At least he didn't sound disgusted. "So?"

"Where's the pen?" he asked conversationally.

She raised her chin. "Like I'll tell you."

"You haven't used it against me since our . . . the . . . our time in the forest." Had he just stammered? Had his voice dropped with desire?

"Maybe I just haven't thought of the appropriate punishment yet."

One of his brows arched, and he sat up slowly. "Punishment for what? Making you feel good?" Now his voice was dry. "Or not taking you all the way?"

"Just get out." She pointed to the hallway.

He flattened his palms at his sides, his gaze roving over her. That white-hot gaze lingered at her breasts, between her legs, reminding her of everywhere he'd touched—and everywhere he'd wanted to touch. She gulped. She was wearing a white tank top and sweat shorts, and sweat still poured down her flushed skin. She probably looked ridiculous and frumpy.

"Your skin is glistening," he said, and there was enough heat in his eyes to keep her warm all winter. If Mysteria ever got cold, that is.

"Sweat does that to a girl."

"I wish I had been the one to make you sweat."

Now her heart skipped a beat. "What do you want from me, Falon? An apology? Well, you're not going to get one. We're even. I'm done with you."

His eyes sharpened. "You're not done with me. Not until you destroy the pen in front of me."

"No. There's ink left."

"So you plan to use it against me again? You just said we're even."

"We're even *now*. I destroy it, and you're free to torment me for the rest of your life."

He leaned forward, and she caught the scent of soap and dark spices. Shivered—then shuddered. What did *she* smell like?

"I'll swear not to hurt you," he said.

"And I'm sure you'll mean it. Today. What about tomorrow?"

Growling, he fell back into the mattress and scoured a hand down his face. She noticed he did that a lot when he was frustrated. "I came here to find the pen, but do you know what I really wanted to do?" He didn't wait for her to reply. "I wanted to follow you on your run, make sure you were safe."

Really? How . . . sweet. Some of the ice around her heart melted. *Don't believe him, stupid!*

"I wanted—want—to strip you, make love to you. Finish what we started. I can't get you out of my mind. You're the last person I should want." Now he seemed to be talking to himself. "But want you I do. Maybe if I have you, I can stop thinking about you."

Oh, how she wished. He'd consumed every corridor of her mind since their kiss. Always she craved him. Always she dreamed of him, hungered. Sometimes she was even willing to toss caution aside and go to him, beg him to take her. But . . .

What would happen afterward?

She had several strikes against her. She was a witch, and he hated witches. He was perfection, and she was the epitome of *im*perfection. She'd spent the last week torturing him.

Three strikes. You're out, girl. Glory sighed. She was afraid she'd already fallen for him, though. He was strength, and he was courage. He hadn't backed down from her once, even though her powers were considerable, and she could do major damage to him. His kisses were the best thing to have ever happened to her. His touch, electric. Finally she'd gotten a glimpse of what Evie and Hunter, Godiva and Romeo must experience every night. And different hours through the day. She'd liked it, wanted more.

Wanted him.

"No response?" he said, cutting through the silence.

She shook her head in hopes of clearing it. "You're willing to have me now?"

"I was willing before. I just fought against it."

"But you're not fighting now?"

"No. I can't." He rolled to his side and stared over at her. "I'm helpless. Did you cast a love spell on me?"

"No!"

"I didn't think so," he muttered. "Hoped, but didn't think."

"Why not?"

"Because a witch did it once, and this isn't the same."

Her shoulders sagged. No love for her, he meant.

"It's more intense," he grumbled, surprising her.

Her legs began shaking more forcefully, and any moment she feared she would collapse. Somehow she managed to stumble to the chair in the corner and plop atop the many T-shirts heaped there. Falon's gaze never left her. She felt it boring past her skin and straight into her soul.

"You want me, too," he said. Hard, flat. "Don't try to deny it."

As if she could. "Who tried to deny it?"

His lips formed a thin line. Almost a smile, but not quite.

"Look, I came to you once offering the same thing. One night. You rejected me."

"Yes, and it was the biggest mistake of my life."

"Because you were made to suffer for it," she said. A statement rather than a question.

"No. Because I crave you."

Truth or lie? She dared not hope. "Now you're out to protect yourself from me, and that's perfectly understandable, but—"

"I don't need protection from you," he snapped.

"Falon, we'll never be able to trust each other. We'll always suspect each other's motives."

"We can call a truce. I'm not asking for a lifetime. I'm asking for a night. And when you came to me that night, that's all you wanted, too."

"I—I—" *Wanted to say yes,* she realized. Wanted it more than anything. After his kiss, though, she couldn't delude herself and hope the sex would be so bad she'd never desire him again. The sex would be great. At least for her. She *would* want more than a night; she knew that now. He . . . affected her. "I can't," she finally said.

"Damn it. Why?" He shot up again, glaring at her.

If he approached her, if he touched her . . . Tremors racked her, part of her wishing he'd do it. Force her hand. "We bring out the worst in each other."

Surprisingly, that mollified him somewhat. "I don't know. I thought we brought out the best in each other while in the forest."

"That was a mistake."

"My favorite mistake, then."

Goddess, if he kept saying things like that, she'd cave. Already her defenses were cracked. Really, what would one time hurt? Sure, she might fall for him even more than she already had. Sure, she might crave more from him. Sure, he might compare her to every girl he'd ever been with, and she would definitely come out lacking. Sure, this might be a scheme on his part to castigate her for using that pen against him. But she'd have an orgasm, so what did those things matter?

And what if . . . what if he truly desired her? What if he enjoyed being with her?

What if: the most dangerous words known to man.

"I just can't," she forced herself to say. Her voice cracked, just like her defenses. She had to swallow a sudden lump in her throat. "My answer is and will always be *no*. Find someone else."

"You want me to sleep with another woman?" he gasped out, incredulous.

"Yes?" she replied, a question she'd meant as a statement.

"You won't care?"

"No." Her hands curled into fists as rage swam through her bloodstream. She'd destroy anyone he touched. Obliterate anyone he— *What are you doing? Stop thinking like that!* "I can give you a love potion for the woman if you think it'd help." *Idiot! What are you saying?*

I thought I was supposed to push him—oh, never mind. Damage done.

Scowling, he jackknifed to his feet. "You want me to be with someone else, I'll be with someone else. I don't need a fucking love potion to do it, either. See you around, Glory."

Glory watched him stride from her bedroom, heard the front door slam. Her shoulders sagged against the chair, and she covered her mouth with a shaky hand. What the hell had she just done?

Six

He'd made the boast to see another woman. Now he had to see it through. *Shit,* Falon thought. But if he had to prod Glory's temper until she snapped and used that stupid pen, he'd do it. Do *anything* to have her in his arms again. *What's happened to me?* He'd gone from hating her powers to craving them. He just flat-out refused to be ignored by her any longer.

"I'll give you a love potion," he mocked. He'd seen the jealousy flare in her gorgeous eyes when they'd talked about him dating another woman. Glory hadn't wanted him to sleep with someone else; she just hadn't wanted to admit she desired him for herself. So he'd *make* her do it. Because he had to get his hands on her breasts, had to rub himself between her legs. Had to have her taste in his mouth and her pleasure moans in his ears. *Then* he could hate her magic again. Then he would go back to being a rational male who didn't need anyone in particular.

He massaged the back of his neck. Hopefully, if he worked this just right, he wouldn't earn himself another year of impotence. Hopefully, Glory would write the two of them into a sensual scene, and he would be able to finally, blessedly seduce her.

Who would have guessed he'd be reduced to seducing a witch? Not him, definitely. Yet here he was, at home again and picking up the phone to dial an old lover who was still a friend.

When she answered, he said, "I need a favor. And before you say yes, you should know we'll be dealing with a very powerful and somewhat insane witch."

And then, when he hung up with Kayla, he called Hunter. His best friend answered, and he said, "Look, I need a favor, and you owe me, so don't even think about saying no."

*   *   *

"Hurry, up, Glor!"

"I'm hurrying, swear." The moment Glory had sailed through the front door of their home, her sisters had rushed her into the shower. They'd thrown a tight black dress and lacy lingerie at her when she'd emerged.

Now she was in the process of fitting her body into the sheer clothing. She should use the pen to make herself slender again but didn't want to waste the ink for some silly dinner.

Hunter was taking them to the Love Nest, a five-star restaurant that catered to the affairs of the heart. Gag. She'd rather vomit than go, but Godiva had batted those sweet hazel eyes at her, and she'd found herself agreeing.

Unfortunately, the shower had failed to wash away the trials of the day. Glory had spent six hours in town, hawking her love potions for a little extra spending money. A few times, she'd wondered what she would do if one of the women who'd purchased a vial of Number Nine used it on Falon. Then she'd thought, *If he truly loves someone, no potion will sway his heart.* Then she'd thought, *If he doesn't love anyone, he's fair game.* Which basically meant Falon was fair game.

The knowledge had settled uneasily inside her, made her twitchy. She'd always considered her powers a blessing. For her, for others. Perhaps Falon was right, though. Perhaps she was a danger to everyone around her. But it wasn't like she could forsake her powers. They were a part of her.

"We're going to be late," Evie said, drawing her from her musings.

"So? I think the restaurant will survive."

"So Hunter is a vampire and only has a limited amount of time to play. Hurry."

Glory sighed. "You're right. I'm sorry. Maybe I should stay home. I'm in a terrible mood. Besides, I should be working. I have a book due in a few months, and I haven't written a word."

Now *Evie* batted hazel eyes at her. "You can put it off for another night. Please. For me."

She had no willpower when it came to pleasing her sisters. "Fine. I'll go. What are we celebrating, anyway?"

"The anniversary of the first time Hunter said he loved me."

Trying not to grimace, Glory spun and faced her sister. "Are you freaking kidding me?"

Clueless, Evie shook her dark head. "No."

The two lovebirds celebrated everything! The anniversary of the first time they had laid eyes on each other. The anniversary of the first time they had made love. The anniversary of Hunter's change from human to vampire. It was truly sickening. "Isn't that something the two of you should celebrate alone?"

"We will." Evie's lips curled slowly, suggestively. "Later."

Godiva peeked her pale head around the door. "Ready, sister dear? Oh, my." Her body rounded the rest of the corner, and then she was walking forward, expression warm. "You look gorgeous."

There wasn't a single malicious cell in her oldest sister. The woman was pure gentleness and had always been that way. "I feel silly," she admitted. She faced the full-length mirror.

The black dress flowed gracefully over her hips, gossamer, like a butterfly's wing. But with her arms stretched down at her sides, the hem did not even reach her fingertips. Thin straps held the material in place on her shoulders. A beaded empire waist cinched everything in just under her breasts, before flaring and floating free.

Overall, the dress was a naughty version of a Grecian toga. On her feet, she wore strappy black sandals. Her toenails were painted a vivid shade of emerald.

"You've always been the most beautiful of us," Godiva said.

"Hey." Evie frowned at their oldest sister. "I'm standing right here. What am I, dog food?"

Godiva waved a hand in dismissal. "You've always been the firecracker."

"You've always been the peacemaker," Glory said, "and let's be real. I've always been the—"

"Nope," Godiva interjected, gripping her shoulders and spinning her. "I'm not going to allow you to put yourself down. You are an amazing woman, and it's time you realized that."

Fighting tears, Glory kissed her sister softly on the cheek. "I love you."

"Love you, too."

Evie threw her arms around them with such force, they gasped. "I love you guys, too. Now let's haul ass! And, Glory, bring your pen. You know, just in case."

Everything inside of her froze with dread. "Just in case what?" Each word was punctuated with warning. Had Evie done something?

"Who knows? It's a beautiful night. Anything can happen."

"I never thought I'd see you like this."

Falon eyed Kayla Smith from across their candlelit table. She was a beautiful woman with pale hair, bright blue eyes, and legs that went on forever. Sadly, she did nothing for him. Not anymore.

She was cousin to Candy Cox, the infamous high school teacher now dating a werewolf; was fully human; and had lived in Mysteria so long she found nothing unusual about vampires, goblins, fairies, or witches. They'd dated on and off for a few months, realized they were working themselves into a relationship, and had backed off. Neither of them had wanted to be tied down. He'd always liked that about her. She was fun and playful and never took anything too seriously. Even men.

But he found himself wondering how Glory had been with past boyfriends. Fun and playful, which he decided he no longer liked? Hopefully, Glory had been miserable with other men. Or had she been serious, which for some reason he liked even less. Fine. He just didn't like the thought of Glory with another man, period.

More, he found that he didn't like the fact that he didn't know everything about her. Suddenly he yearned to know what she ate for breakfast, what her favorite song was, what she dreamed for her life, if she liked to snuggle and watch movies in bed. And if so, were they romantic comedies or action adventure? Probably slashers.

"Are you listening to me?" Kayla asked him.

No. What the hell had she just said? Oh, yeah. She'd never seen him like this. "Yes, of course I was listening. What way do you think you see me?" he asked, his gaze immediately straying back to the restaurant's front door. Where was Glory?

"On edge for a specific woman." There was laughter in her voice. "By the way, you missed a very scintillating conversation I just had with, apparently, myself about a hot tub."

He waved the hot tub away with a dismissive hand. Although, Glory, wet and naked . . . "I'll get her out of my system." He hoped. "Don't worry." With every minute that passed, he just wanted her more.

How would she react when she saw him with Kayla?

Hopefully—how many things was he hopeful about now?—her sisters had convinced her to bring the pen. Hopefully, she would write them into a bedroom. Maybe chain him to the headboard. Yes, chains could definitely come in handy.

The front door to the restaurant opened. He stiffened, poised on the edge of his seat.

Godiva strolled inside, directly behind her was her boyfriend, Romeo, tall and muscled and very wolfish. Falon's stomach rolled into a thousand different knots. Evie walked in, saying something over her shoulder. A moment later, Glory came into his sights. Finally!

Breath congealed in his throat. Dear God. She was . . . magnificent. Like the goddess she worshipped. Her long red curls tumbled down her back, and the sheer fabric of her dress swayed over her lush hips and thighs.

Hunter stepped in behind her and approached the hostess. The group was led to a table directly across from Falon's. The closer she came, the hotter his blood flowed. *See me. Want me.*

It was as Glory was helped into her seat that she spied him.

Her hazel eyes widened with shock then narrowed with fury. Or arousal. She licked her lips. Spotted Kayla. Gripped the edge of the table so tightly he feared it would snap in half.

"Wow," Kayla said. "I don't have to ask which one is yours."

His. He liked the sound of that.

"She's the one shooting daggers at us. Or rather, me."

"Right."

He should take Kayla's hand, perhaps kiss it. But he couldn't bring himself to do it. The only skin he wanted to kiss was Glory's.

Her sisters took their places at her sides, and he heard her bark, "Did you know about this?"

Both women nodded guiltily.

"Traitors! Why not ask him and his date to join us, then. I couldn't possibly feel any more uncomfortable."

"Hey, Falon," Hunter called. "Glory would really love it if you and your date joined us."

Glory's mouth fell open. "I was joking. I didn't—"

"We'd love to." He was on his feet a second later, jerking Kayla to hers.

Kayla chuckled softly.

Deep down, he didn't think Glory would turn the heat of her anger on the other woman. After he'd foolishly turned her away that night, she hadn't gone after the fairy he'd allowed inside. Only him. Clearly, she was a smart woman and knew where to properly lay the blame.

A waiter dragged two extra chairs to the table, positioning him and Kayla directly across from Glory. He wanted to be closer but would settle for simply looking at her.

You have it bad, man. You've gone from hating witches to being desperate for one in less than a week.

Strangely, he didn't care anymore. Not while he was soaking her in.

"Since the big guy isn't going to introduce me," Kayla said, breaking the silence, "I'll introduce myself. I'm Kayla Smith."

Everyone introduced themselves. Except for Glory. When it was her turn, she motioned the waiter over and ordered a glass of flaming fairy. Falon nearly choked on his sip of water.

"You know I'm of the Fae. How?" he asked her. Not many people did. He was too big, too much a warrior compared to the usually party-loving race.

Her eyes widened. "You're Fae?"

Okay, so she hadn't guessed. He didn't mind that she now knew; he wanted her to know everything about him. "Yes."

"Why didn't you tell me?" Hunter asked, incredulous.

"No one's business."

Awkward silence followed.

"Well, this is fun," Evie said, probably to break the tension.

"A blast," Kayla agreed. She tossed her hair over one shoulder, revealing sun-kissed skin.

Glory saw the action and popped her jaw.

"I've always had low self-esteem," she'd once told him. Oh . . . shit. Bad move, bringing the ex, he realized. He didn't want Glory to feel bad about herself or think he found Kayla more attractive. "You're the prettiest woman here, Glory," he said honestly.

Her drink arrived, saving her from replying. But her eyes had met his over the candlelight, soft and luminous. Her lashes cast dark shadows over her cheeks. Shadows he wanted to trace with his fingertips.

Menus were thrust at them. Falon didn't bother opening his. He didn't care about the food. He continued to watch Glory, couldn't stop himself. He was entranced. She opened her menu, though she didn't read it. She still watched him, too.

Her cheeks flushed to a rosy pink. She was clearly having trouble drawing in a breath, her chest rising too quickly and too shallowly.

"Hungry?" he asked her in a low, raspy voice.

Her gaze dipped to his lips. "A little."

"I'm starved."

"Why do I get the feeling they're not talking about food?" Evie muttered.

"Because they're not," Hunter told her, "so hush."

The table fell quiet, all eyes glued to Glory and Falon.

Get your pen, he mentally willed. *Write us away from here.* But she didn't. She finally looked away.

His teeth ground together. He'd just have to push her harder, then. *God, I'm pathetic.*

"I decided to take your advice," he said.

Fury curtained her features a split second before she blanked her expression. What thoughts tumbled through her mind? "Is that right?" The words were precisely uttered, as though shoved through the crack in a steel wall and ironed out.

"That's right."

The waiter came to take their order, but Kayla shooed him away. Hunter, Evie, Godiva, and Romeo propped their elbows on the table, unabashed by their staring.

"Funny that it wasn't too long ago you *protested* taking my advice," Glory said.

"Isn't it?"

"It is. I'd like to say I'm surprised, but I can't." She tapped a nail against her glass, and the red liquid swished. "Not if I'm being honest."

His lips pursed. Did she truly think so poorly of him? Of course she did, he thought in the next instant. He'd once told her that he hated witches. He'd once told her that he would pay her back for all she'd done to him.

Worry about that later. When she's naked and under you. Or over you. Right now, you have to push her. "I'm thinking about showing Kayla my favorite . . . gladiator costume. Does *that* surprise you?"

Hunter choked on his water. Romeo nodded encouragingly. Evie, Godiva, and Kayla leaned forward, obviously intrigued.

Glory gasped at the reminder of the night she'd written him into a slave's cell, splattered with blood and fresh from battle.

"I'm learning things about you I wish you'd kept hidden," Hunter muttered.

"Shut it," Falon told him.

"Why don't you show her your jackass costume?" Glory asked through clenched teeth. "Oh, wait. You're already wearing it."

Okay, he'd walked into that one. Had she been talking about anyone else, he would have laughed. He loved her wit. And she must love warriors. Why else would she have written him into such a situation?

He racked his brain for things he knew about ancient Rome. Not much. Everything he knew, he knew because of Russell Crowe. "For the woman I desire, I would be willing to do anything." The words were dare, a challenge.

"A few flicks of my wrist, and I can make you prove those words. Violently."

Do it. "Please." He snorted. "You've run out of ink, and we both know it."

She leaned forward, curls spilling onto the table. God, she was lovely. "Do you *want* to die?"

"Yes. Of pleasure."

Her pupils dilated, and her nostrils flared. Just then, she was like a living flame, fury crackling over her skin. *I'm close. So close. Just a little more.*

"Maybe you'd like to visit a village of Vikings? Or maybe you'd like to come face-to-face with a Highland chieftain and his sword?"

"If that turned you—her on, then yes."

Glory ran her tongue over her teeth. Every muscle in his body jerked at the sight of that pink tongue. Oh, to have it on *him*.

"It would," Kayla said. "It really would. What do I have to do to get in on this action? I'd prefer a Viking over a chieftain, but will graciously accept whichever you give me."

Slowly, Glory eased back in her seat. Slowly, she grinned, though the expression lacked any type of humor. "I think something can be arranged. For you," she added, eyeing Falon, "not her."

"Please," Kayla said at the same time he said, "Fine. I understand." He was thinking, *Finally!*

As she reached inside her purse, Falon added, "Oh, and Glory?"

"Yes?" Grin feral, she lifted the pen and tapped it against her chin—to taunt him, he wouldn't doubt. Fire still raged in her eyes.

Are you really going to do this? He peered at her heaving chest, her dilated pupils, her lush, red lips. *Hell, yes.* "Since I'm doubting you have the courage to write yourself into the scene, I guess I'll see you when I get back."

Her eyelids narrowed, and she lost her grin.

He barely stopped himself from laughing. *See you there, baby.*

Seven

He wanted her to write them both into a scene, an oddity on its own. He hadn't seemed to mind the thought of his precious Kayla being given to another man; he had seemed more interested in Glory. Glory knew all of those shocking things, but she didn't understand them.

Why had he fought for magic to be used against him? Why had he antagonized her?

Did the reason matter? she thought next. She was at home, alone in her room, and she was going to use the pen. Not to punish Falon— though she wanted to do so. He'd taken another woman to dinner. A beautiful, slender woman. No, Glory was doing this to be with him, to have him to herself. She'd simply used punishment and anger as an excuse.

When will I learn?

She'd tried to stay away from him. She'd ignored his phone calls, hadn't ventured near his house. She'd even walked out of a room any-time he had been mentioned. She feared falling so deeply in love with him, she'd never recover. As she'd once told him, they could never trust each other. But she was still going to do this. She craved him, and the craving wasn't going away.

Despite all of her reasons for avoiding him before, she couldn't stop herself now. She needed to shove him from her thoughts and dreams, and nothing else had worked. Why not give this a shot and experience another dose of that heady pleasure while she was at it? She'd do her best to guard her heart. Oh, oh. Maybe she could take an antilove potion.

She was nodding as she popped to her feet. Antilove. Of course! There was nothing she could do about the emotions she harbored now.

Once there, they were immune to magic. But she *could* prevent herself from falling for Falon completely.

Clothes and trash soared through the air as she crouched on the floor and rooted through them. Every vial she found, she set aside. Love potion Number Nine. Love potion Number Thirteen.

A magic suppressor. A magic unleasher. Ah, finally.

Straightening, she raised a tiny bottle of swirling, azure liquid. There was a warning label in the center.

"Take with food," she read. "May cause dizziness. If you become sick, consult your nearest witch."

She'd given the potion to hundreds of women but had never sampled the goods herself. There'd been no need. The recipe had been designed by her great-grandmother and was now used in every spell book she'd ever encountered. It had to work. No one had ever complained.

"Here goes nothing." Glory popped the cork and drained the contents. Tasteless but smooth. A minute passed. Nothing happened. Another minute. Still nothing. She tossed the empty bottle over her shoulder. Maybe she wasn't supposed to feel anything.

Frowning, she swiped up the pen and a notebook and plopped onto the side of her bed. What was Falon doing right now? Was he at home with Kayla? Waiting for Glory to act?

What was the couple doing to pass the time?

"Grr!"

Unable to wait any longer, Glory began writing: *Falon is alone in his house, unable to leave.* That took care of Kayla. Glory's frown faded. She wouldn't make him battle anyone like he'd suggested. That would make her admire him more. Even the image was dangerous. Falon. With a sword. Her mouth watered.

She'd get straight to the sex. Do him and forget him. *His clothing suddenly disappears, leaving him naked.* As the ink stained the paper, she had trouble drawing in a breath. Her hand was shaking.

Glory appears—

No. She scratched out those two words. Falon was now alone and naked. She couldn't just appear in front of him looking like this.

Glory weighs one hundred and fifteen pounds and is wearing a lacy, emerald green bra and panty set.

One moment she was draped in the black dress her sister had given her, the next, cool air was kissing her bare skin. Glory looked down. Sure enough, her *small*, perky breasts were pushed up by emerald lace. Her stomach and legs were thin and glorious. She grinned and kept writing.

Falon is chained to his bed, and Glory suddenly appears in front of him, pen and notebook in hand.

Glory's messy bedroom faded to black, and then Glory was lying against cool, silky sheets. Cold metal anchored her wrists and ankles in place, her pen and notebook gone. A white chiffon flowed overhead, like a cloud descending from heaven.

"What the hell?" She tugged at her arms. The chains rattled but didn't budge.

Suddenly Falon approached the side of the bed, the pen and notebook in his hands. He looked at Glory, and his eyes widened. He looked at the contraband he was holding, and he grinned.

"It worked," he said, shocked. "It really worked."

Her struggles increased. "What worked? What happened? What did you do to me?" What the hell was going on?

He was naked, and his tanned body was magnificent. Rope after rope of muscle, traceable sinew, and a long, hard erection. A glittering necklace hung from his neck.

She looked away from the sheer majesty of him, struggled some more.

"Be still," he said.

"Go to hell!" The metal began to cut into her skin, drawing warm beads of blood.

Falon *tsked* under his tongue. He strode out of the bedroom, leaving her alone.

"Falon!" she cried. Panic infused every corridor of her body. "Don't leave me like this! Come back."

He returned a moment later, the pen and notebook gone. In their place were strips of cloth. "Be still," he ordered again, sharply this time.

She obeyed. She was panting, skin overly hot. At least he'd covered himself with a robe, blocking all that male deliciousness from her view. "What's going on? How did you do this? You don't have any powers."

He eased beside her, and the mattress jiggled. She tried to scoot away, but the chains didn't allow her to go very far. "No, I don't have powers. But I do have a friend who is dating a witch who wants her sister happy."

Her jaw went slack. "*Evie* helped you?"

Leaning forward and wafting the scent of man and dark spice to her nose, Falon began wrapping the cloth underneath the chains, protecting her skin. *Do not soften.* She'd taken the antilove potion. She shouldn't have to warn herself to remain distant, but the potion wasn't freaking working.

"Hunter questioned Evie about the pen," he finally explained. "Apparently, Evie failed to tell you that she had a charm to counteract the effects of it."

"I don't understand." *Come closer, keep touching me.* She had to bite her lip to keep the words inside.

"Anything negative you wrote about the person wearing the charm would be done to *you* instead."

Shock sliced through her, as hot as he was. "That's—that's—"

"What happened. Hunter also emptied out your potions and replaced them with colored water. Just in case you tried to feed me one."

So that was why . . . "That little jackass!" No wonder the antilove potion hadn't worked. Now she was helpless, on her own. The knowledge should have panicked her all the more. Instead, she found herself praying his robe would split, and she would be able to see his nipples. Maybe lick them.

"I had wondered what kind of scene you would write, and must admit I'm surprised by what you chose. I expected hungry lions or a raging, bloody battle and thought I would have to pluck you from its midst. I'd even draped myself in armor, just in case. Then that armor disappeared and I began to hope . . ."

Her cheeks flamed; they were probably glowing bright red. She tried to cover her embarrassment by snapping, "Why didn't my clothing disappear instead? Since you have the charm and all."

"The removal of clothing isn't negative." His head tilted to the side, and his gaze roved over her. He frowned. "Why do you write yourself like that?"

"Like what?"

"So . . . thin."

"Because," was all she said. *Because I want to be pretty for you.*

"I like you better the other way."

"Liar. Now write me out of this scene!"

He shook his head. "Hell, no. I've got you right where I've always wanted you. And I'm not a liar. In fact, I refuse to touch you while you're like this. When you're back to normal, *then* the loving can begin."

A tremor rocked her. She didn't dare hope . . . "The chains will disappear by then, too, and if you think I'm staying here, you're crazy."

"You can be rechained."

Good point. "The pleasuring will never begin, because I've decided I don't want you."

"Now who's lying?" He pulled a plush lounge next to the bed and sat, gaze never leaving her. "I'll make a pact with you. I won't lie to you, if you won't lie to me. From now on, we'll be completely honest with each other. Okay?"

"Whatever you say," she said in a sugar-sweet tone.

"So what do you think of my bedroom?"

"It's—" She'd been about to say something mean, but then her sights snagged on the crystal chandelier, dripping with thousands of teardrops. On the intricately carved dresser, orchids spilling from vases. A bejeweled tray provided the centerpiece. "Unexpected," she finally finished.

"Everything inside the house was a gift from my brother."

Her head snapped toward him. "I didn't know you had a brother."

Falon nodded, his hair dancing over his cheeks. "There's a lot you don't know about me, but that's going to change. We're going to get to know each other, Glory."

"No." That would defeat the purpose of loving and leaving. If he continued this, she would leave, but she would not be unscathed.

"Oh, yes," he insisted. "And every time you reveal a fact about yourself, you'll earn a reward."

Goose bumps spread over her skin. "And if I remain quiet?"

Slowly, he grinned. "You'll earn a punishment. I have the pen, after all."

This is not fun. This is not exciting. I am not turned on. "Fine. Tell me how many women you've had in here." There. That should deepen—dampen—her terrible—wonderful—mood.

"You are the first."

She flashed him a scowl. "I thought we weren't going to lie to each other anymore."

"I spoke true. You are the first woman I've ever allowed inside this bedroom."

"What about the fairy? That night—"

He held up a hand for silence. "I sent her home the moment you were out of sight."

Seriously? Glory didn't know whether or not to believe him, but she adored the idea of his claim. "What about Kayla?"

"Sent her home, too. I didn't want her; I wanted you. As you might have guessed, I used her to get your attention."

"Well, you got it," she grumbled, then cringed at the admission.

"I noticed you the first day I moved into town, you know," he said.

He'd noticed her? In a good way? She shivered, feeling as if his hands were already on her, caressing, stoking her desire.

"Cold?" he asked.

She nodded, because she didn't want to admit his words had ignited a storm of desire inside her.

He rose, grabbed the black silk comforter, and tugged it over her. The material was cool against her skin, but damn it, it didn't dampen her need. No, it increased it. Every nerve ending she possessed cried for him.

Falon placed a soft kiss on her lips. Automatically she opened her mouth to take it deeper. He pulled away.

A moan slipped from her.

"Soon," he said as he reclaimed his seat. His voice was tense. "Now, back to the first time I saw you. You were outside with your sisters and selling your potions. At the time, I didn't know they were potions. I just saw a beautiful woman with rosy skin and hair like flame."

She gulped, couldn't speak.

"I wanted you so badly." As he spoke, his fingertip caressed her thigh. "I was making my way toward you when I heard the words 'potion' and 'witch,' and then I couldn't get away from you fast enough."

Maybe he *was* telling the truth about his desire for her. Maybe he did like her just the way she was. Maybe . . .

"I never tortured anyone until I met you," she admitted softly.

His head tilted to the side, and he studied her intently, violet eyes blazing. "Why me?"

"Because," was all she said.

"Glory."

Just tell him. She sighed. "Because I wanted you, and I knew I couldn't have you."

"You wanted me?" he asked huskily.

"You know I did." She watched him from the corner of her eye. He leaned back and stretched his legs out and up, the robe falling away and revealing his strong calves. There were calluses on the bottoms of his feet, as if he often ran through the forest without shoes on. Made her wonder if he wore any clothes at all. Her stomach quivered with the thought.

"Tell me about the first time you noticed me. Please."

Like she could deny him anything now. She thought back to that fateful day, and the quiver in her stomach became a needy ache. Well, another needy ache. She was consumed with them. He'd been moving boxes into this very house. She and her sisters had walked here to welcome him to town. When he spotted them, he'd frozen. Introductions had been made, and he'd smiled coolly but politely at Evie and Godiva. Glory, he'd simply nodded at before looking hastily away.

"I thought you were the most beautiful man I'd ever seen. The sun was shining over you lovingly, and you were sweating. Glistening. You'd taken off your shirt, and dirt smudged your chest."

His lips twitched. "I've noticed you have a thing for manly sweat."

"I do not."

"You placed me in a gladiator cell straight from battle, woman. You like men who do physical labor. Admit it."

"So what! There's nothing wrong with that."

"No, there isn't. It's cute." He didn't give her time to respond. "So why did you want to place me in chains tonight?"

She fought for breath. "You know why."

"Tell me. Say the words aloud."

"I—I'd decided to be with you. Just once. You know, to purge myself of you like you suggested before."

"And you thought you needed chains for that?"

"No. I just . . . I wanted to be in control of everything."

"I don't think so," he said with a shake of his head. "In the forest, you almost came when I pinned your wrists over your head and took control *away* from you. Right now, your nipples are hard, and your skin is besieged by goose bumps. You like where you are."

Her mouth dried as the realization settled inside her. He was right. She loved where she was. She loved that he could do anything he wanted with her, and she couldn't stop him. Didn't want to stop him.

Would one night be enough? She couldn't possibly learn all there was to know about his body, his pleasure . . . her own.

Oh, damn. Already she was doing what she'd sworn she wouldn't: falling deeper, wanting more. Fear dug sharp claws inside her. "Maybe this isn't a good idea," she said, squirming. "Maybe we should stop here and now and part. As friends. I won't hurt you again. You have my word. And you even can keep the pen."

"Oh, I'm keeping the pen," he said darkly, "but I'm not letting you go." He pushed to his feet. He was scowling.

"You're angry. Why? I'm setting you free from our war."

"I hate the thought of you walking out of this house—ever—and I don't understand it." The robe fell from his shoulders and onto the floor, pooling at his feet. She sucked in a breath and simply drank in his magnificence. He was harder than before, his erection so long it stretched higher than his navel.

He grabbed the pen and notebook and started writing. Before she could ask what he was doing, the chains fell away from her. Tentative, she eased up. But she didn't leave; she couldn't make herself, though common sense was screaming that she do so inside her mind. This was what she'd asked for.

"Thank you."

Fight for *me*. Wait. What? No.

"Not yet." He continued writing.

Quick as a snap, her weight returned, her bra and panty set nearly unraveling from the sudden excess. She gasped. Falon finally paused, his electric violet eyes all over her, eating her up.

Never taking his gaze from her, he locked the pen and paper inside a drawer on the nightstand, and then he was on the bed, crawling his way toward her.

Eight

Falon had never wanted a woman the way he wanted Glory.

What was it about her that kept him coming back for more, despite her origins? Despite her actions and her words? She was exquisite, yes. Lush and soft, panting with arousal. She smelled of jasmine and magic, which was a feast to his senses. She was vulnerable yet courageous, daring and volatile. She had never and would never bow to him. She would fight him if he wronged her and always demand the very best from him.

He liked that. Liked who he was when he was with her. She made him be a better person. Honest and giving. Hopeful. And now that he thought about it, everything she'd done to him with that pen hadn't been malicious, it had been . . . foreplay.

His skin was nearly too tight for his bones as he stopped, his palms flattened beside Glory's knees. "Still want to leave?"

"No," she said breathlessly. She leaned back, propping her weight on her elbows. The plump mounds of her breasts strained beyond the bra. God, her curves were lovely.

"Want me?" He barely managed to work the words past the lump in his throat.

"Yes." No hesitation. "Maybe I'm crazy, but yes."

"Good, because I want you. All of you, this time." Fingers sliding under her knee, he lifted. His lips met the inside of her thigh, the cool stone of his necklace brushing against her, and she gasped.

He kissed again, his tongue stroking closer . . . closer . . .

Another gasp from her, followed by a shiver. "Hot," she said, trembling.

"Good?"

"Very."

"Hunter told me you write romance novels."

"Sometimes. Kiss again."

Grinning, he obeyed, running his tongue to the edge of her emerald panties.

"Oh, Goddess." She fisted the sheets. He wanted those hands in his hair, holding on, holding forever.

She was perfect for this bed—his bed—he thought, staring down at her. A bright flame against black silk. "Have you ever thought of me when writing a love scene?"

"Yes." As though she'd read his mind, she gripped his head and pulled him down for another intimate kiss.

His cock throbbed at the thought, at the sight of her, at the taste of her, and he bit the inside of his cheek. Never had a woman appealed to so many of his senses. "What did you fantasize? What did I do to you?"

"Consumed every inch of me," she said, back arching, silently begging for more.

The best kind of answer.

Then she added, "We have one night together. I want everything I fantasized about."

One night. A muscle twitched underneath his eye. He didn't like the time limitation reminder but let it pass. For now. "Did it turn you on, what you wrote? Did you touch yourself?"

"Yes." Reaching up, she thrummed her nipples. "Like this."

"No. Between your legs. Show me."

She lifted her head, her eyes wide and focused on him. Her hands ceased moving on her breasts. "Wh-what?"

"Show me." Desperate for another taste of her, he kissed the center of her panties. They were wonderfully damp. He groaned, his mouth watered. "I want to see what *I've* been imagining."

"Oh." Slowly, so slowly, her hand slid down her stomach. "Like this?"

Licking around the seam of her panties, he fisted his cock. "More."

Slowly, so slowly, her hand circled the apex of her thighs, teasing. "Better?"

Down, he stroked. Up, squeezing tight. "Not yet."

He straightened; their gazes met again and held. "How about this?" Her fingers delved under the emerald lace. Her knees fell apart, and her lashes lowered. She cried out, hips undulating.

Shit. She *looked* like magic just then. Magic he craved. Down and up he continued to work himself, the sight of her so erotic he knew it was branded into his mind for eternity. *Touch her. Learn her*. He'd never wanted anything more.

"Stop," he commanded.

She stilled. Her eyes opened.

He released himself and latched onto her wrist, drawing her hand away from her body. She moaned, bit her bottom lip. "My turn." Leaning down, he lifted her fingers to his mouth and sucked one, then another inside. Her taste coated his tongue. "Like honey." And he needed more.

He laved his tongue inside her navel, gripping her panties and urging them from her legs. He thought she must have kicked them aside, because the bed bounced as he straightened.

"I've wanted to do this for a long time," he said, fingers parting her wet folds. The thin patch of curls shielding her femininity were as bright a red as the hair on her head. Beautiful.

"Do it. *Please*."

The desperation in her voice mirrored what he felt. He pressed her legs farther apart, spreading . . . spreading . . . God, so pretty. Pink and glistening. He lowered his head and stroked his tongue up the center.

"Falon," she cried.

He circled her clitoris as he sank a finger deep inside.

Her hands fisted in his hair just as he liked. "More."

Another finger joined the first, stretching her. All the while, he sucked and nipped at her. Had he ever tasted anyone so sweet? So addicting? Having her once wouldn't be enough, he realized. He'd need her over and over again. In every way imaginable. He just had to make *her* crave more.

As he licked her, he told her everything he wanted to do to her, how beautiful she was, how he needed her. Soon she was writhing, her head thrashing from side to side. He wanted to see her come. Had to see it, would die if he didn't. And then she was. Her inner walls clamped down on his tongue as she gasped and cried and even screamed.

He pulled from her, his gaze devouring her. Her eyes were closed, her teeth chewing on her bottom lip. Her skin was flushed. So quickly her chest rose and fell, lifting those rosy nipples like berries offered to a god.

A long while passed before she stilled. When she did, her eyelids cracked open.

He stayed just where he was, kneeling between her legs, cock rising proudly. "Like?"

"Like." She reached out and circled it with her fingers. "More."

A moan burst from his lips. "Glory."

"My turn," she said, squeezing him tighter. "I want to taste *you*."

He shook his head. "I don't want to come that way this first time, and if your mouth gets anywhere near my cock, I'll come."

She urged him forward, and he was helpless to do anything but follow wherever she led. "I'll stop before you come."

He found himself on his side. "No, you won't."

She grinned slowly, wickedly and rolled him to his back. Like a sea siren, she rose above him. "Okay, I won't. But you can try to force me to stop like the he-man you are."

God, the thought of her mouth on his shaft, hot and wet . . . her hair spilling over his thighs . . . His head fell back onto the pillow. "All right. But only because you insist."

She chuckled. "Such a martyr."

His cock twitched against her leg, her laughter as arousing as her touch.

Now she gasped. "Mmm, what was that for?"

"I like the sound of your laugh," he admitted. He wanted to hear it. In the morning when he woke up, at lunch, at dinner. Just before bed.

"Sometimes you're as sweet as candy." She crawled down his body until her lips were poised over him. Just like he'd feared, his already intense sense of pleasure revved to a new level. "Probably taste like it, too."

He hoped so. He wanted her to like him, this.

"Tell me what you've fantasized about." Her warm breath stroked him, teased him.

He had to grip the sheets or he would soon be fisting her hair, and then there would be no stopping himself from coming in her mouth. "You. Doing this."

"What else?" She licked the tip, lapping up the glistening moisture already beaded there. "Mmm."

Shit. "Me, inside you."

Her teeth scraped the head, and he groaned at the delicious sensation. "What else?" she demanded. "Tell the truth, and you'll be rewarded. Isn't that how you like to work?"

"Pounding, hot, hard, wild, screaming, you bent over, me taking you from behind. My fingers on your clit, working it. You coming over and over."

As he spoke, she sucked him down, up, down. Taking him all the way to the back of her throat. He barely managed to get the words out, but he kept talking. Anything to continue that delicious pressure. One of her hands kneaded his balls, the other glided up his chest and flicked his nipple.

He felt attacked at every pleasure point, and he loved it. He was bucking, unable to slow his movements, close to the edge. If she kept this up, he really would—*Shit, shit, shit.* Falon grabbed her shoulders and jerked her up. Her lips were swollen and wet, she was panting, her desire clearly renewed.

She moaned in disappointment. "I wasn't done."

"Condom," he said, the word more a snarl. "Now."

Her pupils were dilated, her cheeks flushed as she gazed around wildly. "Where are they?"

Damn, where had he placed them? He searched, saw two silver packets resting on the floor. He'd thought ahead, thank God. He reached out, way out, grabbed one and ripped it open with his teeth. Motions jerky, he straightened and worked it over his length.

His hands settled on Glory's thighs and spread them as wide as they would go. Her wet, needy core was poised over his cock, just like her mouth had been. "Ride me."

"I thought—you said behind."

"Next time," he said, and then she was pressing, he was arching, and he was all the way inside her, surging deep, taking all of her that he could get.

Her head fell back, her hair tickling his legs. Her breasts arched forward, and he cupped the small of her back, jerking her forward. When those hardened buds abraded his chest, he growled out a, "Fuck yes."

"Feels so good."

"Kiss."

"Please."

He pounded in and out of her as their lips met. His tongue thrust inside, and she eagerly welcomed it, rolling it with her own. Their teeth clashed together once, twice, but that didn't douse the intensity.

Every other woman he'd ever been with faded to the back of his mind as if they'd never existed. There was only Glory. There was only here and now. Eternity—with her.

"Falon," she gasped, and he knew she was close.

He reached between them and thrummed her clitoris. That was all she'd needed. She came in a rush, squeezing at his cock, crying his name again and again, nails raking his chest.

He, too, fell over the edge. And when he came, it was the strongest of his life. Every muscle he possessed locked and released, spasming. Blood rushed through his veins, so hot it blistered everything it touched.

"Glory," he chanted, and it was a prayer for more. More of her, more of this.

Now I've gone and done it, Glory thought. She was snuggled into Falon's side, warm and sated—more so than she'd ever been before. He was asleep, his breathing smooth. Even in slumber, his hand traced up and down her spine as though he couldn't stop touching her.

I love him.

There, she'd admitted it. She did. She loved him. Would have liked to spend forever with him. Making love, talking, laughing. Impossible.

She was a witch, and there was nothing she could do about that. She possessed magic powers. That wasn't something she could switch off. Not for long, anyway. And Falon would always fear her because of it, no matter what he claimed.

All these months, she'd gagged every time she'd seen her sisters with their boyfriends. Her chest had ached, and she'd assumed the ache was from disgust not love. Now she was experiencing the emotion for herself. The ache for what could not be.

Her eyes filled with tears. She loved Falon, but she couldn't have him. Even though he thought he wanted more from her. He'd said as much before falling asleep. She hadn't answered, hadn't known what to say. But she could just imagine him cringing during their first fight, suspecting her of evildoing. She could just imagine the accusations he'd hurl at her every time something went wrong in his life.

That would destroy her. Better to walk away now, as planned. It was the only way her heart could survive.

Gingerly, Glory slipped from his body, from the bed. Her legs were so shaky she almost fell. Since she'd written herself here without any real clothes, she borrowed a pair of sweats and a T-shirt from Falon.

Before she put them on, she held them to her nose and inhaled deeply. They smelled of him, like soap, dark spices, and strength. A tear fell. Once dressed, she walked to the edge of the bed. Still he slept

soundly. Must not have gotten any rest these past few days. He'd probably feared she'd attack with her pen at any moment.

What if things could be different? What if there was a chance they
could make it work?

He looked so peaceful. His dark hair was in disarray against the
pillow. His face was flushed with lingering pleasure. The sheet had
fallen, revealing the entire expanse of his mouthwatering chest.

Who are you trying to fool? Make it work? Please. Those silly
tears began falling in earnest. She was going to miss him. Taunting
him, being with him, sparring with him, had been fun. He was witty,
and he was warm. He was wild and protective and a lover who cared
more about her pleasure than his own.

His fingers flexed over the part of the mattress she'd occupied.

Her heart stopped beating. One step, two, she backed away from
the bed. Any moment, he would probably wake up. What would he
say to her? What would he do?

Doesn't matter.

Glory pivoted on her heel and stalked quietly from his house. They
only lived a mile apart, and she'd traveled the forest many times before, so she entered the night without hesitation.

She left her heart with Falon.

Nine

When Falon woke up alone, he was not happy.

When he rushed to Glory's house and discovered she had packed
a bag and taken off, telling no one where she planned to stay, he was
angry.

When he drove around town, asking if anyone had seen her and
found that no one had, he was beyond furious!

Why had she left him?

To punish him? He didn't think so. They were past that point now, he knew it, and she wasn't the type to do so without gloating—something he loved about her. Loved. Yes. He loved her. She was his woman, the other piece of him. He knew that now, and so there would be no more denying it. The fact that she was a witch didn't matter anymore. He'd rather have her and her powers than be without her.

Had she left because she was . . . scared?

Yes, he thought. *Yes.* Well, he was scared, too. New relationships were always scary, but this one more so than most. They'd been at odds for a while. But they'd also just had the best sex of his life. Addictive sex. He'd just have to prove they could be together, that he wouldn't hurt her, wouldn't stop loving her. But how?

You still have the pen.

The thought slammed into him with the force of a jackhammer, and he grinned. He rushed back home.

Glory was inside her Ford Taurus one moment and back home the next. Brow puckered in confusion, she gazed around. "What the hell?"

Her sisters were sitting in the living room, reading *Witch Weekly.* They glanced up at the sound of her voice.

"Oh, there you are," Godiva said.

"Where have you been?" Evie asked. "Falon's been desperate to find you."

She gulped. Rubbed her stomach. Falon. The pen. Damn it! He was using the pen. Why, why, why? She'd almost made a clean getaway. Had almost given them a clean break. Clean. Yeah, right.

A knock sounded at the door.

She whipped around, eyes wide. Oh, Great Goddess. Was it Falon? Another knock, this one harder.

"Well, aren't you going to answer it?" Godiva asked.

"Open up, Glory. I know you're in there. I made sure of it."

Falon's deep, dark voice filled her head, and she almost fainted. He'd truly come here. Why? He could have written her anywhere, but he'd written her inside her own home and knocked on her door.

"Glory!" Evie laughed. "Don't just stand there."

If he was going to ask—again—for more from her than one night, she wouldn't be able to turn him down. She'd sobbed like a baby the entire drive away from town. In fact, her face was probably swollen and red even now. Where she'd been headed, she hadn't known. She'd just needed to put distance between them, or she would have forgotten all the reasons to stay away and gone to him.

"Please," he said, and he sounded tortured. She could very easily imagine his hands resting on the door, his forehead pressing into the wood.

Shaky legs walked her to the entrance. Her palm was sweating so she had trouble twisting the knob. What was she going to find? Slowly, she pulled open the only thing blocking the man she loved from her view.

Falon stood there, wearing a trench coat and nothing else. Not even shoes. She blinked in surprise. *So* not what she had expected.

"What are you doing here?" she managed to get out.

Her sisters crowded behind her.

"Looking good, Falon," Evie said.

"Nice," Godiva said.

His cheeks bloomed bright red, but his attention remained focused on Glory. "I want you in my life."

Her stomach twisted painfully. "That wouldn't be smart. We'd fight, you'd hate me, fear my powers."

As she spoke, he was shaking his head. "You're different from the other witches I knew, I know that deep down. Even though you had every right to be angry with me, you were never malicious."

"You think so now, but what about tomorrow? Or the next day?"

Again he shook his head. "Not gonna happen."

"You can't guarantee that."

"But I *can* guarantee that I love you."

Her eyes nearly bugged out, his words echoing inside her brain. "Wh-what?"

"I love you."

Godiva gasped. "Oh my Goddess. Did you hear that, Evie?"

"I'm standing right here. Of course I heard. Glory, what do you have to say to him?"

"Give me a chance," he begged. "I don't deserve it, I know I don't, but I'll do anything to get it. I need you in my life."

She covered her mouth with a shaky hand. This was too much, too good to believe.

He forged ahead. "You once came to my door, wanting a night with me. Now I've come to your door, wanting an eternity with you. I'm here, just as you were, in nothing but a coat. My heart is yours."

Okay, now the trench made sense. Dear Goddess, that meant he was naked underneath. Her blood heated with the knowledge.

"Please don't send me away. I need you. You're a witch, yes, but I don't fear your powers. After last night, I'm grateful for them."

"Oh, Glory!" Godiva brushed away her tears. "This is the most romantic thing I've ever seen. Don't send him away!"

"If you don't take him," Evie said, "I will."

"Hunter," was all Glory managed to get out.

"He's only good for the night. Maybe I'm looking for a day man."

Glory elbowed her sister in the stomach.

Evie backed off, taking Godiva with her. "Come on. Let's give the lovebirds their privacy and listen from the kitchen where Glory can't assault us." Footsteps echoed.

"I love you, Glory." He dropped to his knees. "Please, say something to me. Anything."

Could he truly love her? Her? Could he live with a witch and not fear for his life? She studied his face. Lines of tension edged his eyes and mouth. His lips were drawn tight. He was pale. His hair looked as if he'd plowed his hands through it for hours.

He really was worried she'd say no.

"Last night wasn't enough," he rushed on. "Forever probably won't be enough. You're all I can think about, all I crave. I'm addicted to you. I know you're scared, but I vow to you, here and now, to protect you, cherish you, trust you. I know you aren't evil. That's something you don't have to fear. I know you're good and pure and—"

"I love you, too," she finally said. Making a leap, trusting him like he was trusting her.

He was on his feet in the next instant, jerking her into his arms. "Thank God. I would have had to write you into another scene if you'd rejected me." He placed little kisses all over her face. "Not that I would have minded."

She laughed as she wound her arms around his neck. "Are you sure about this?"

"I've never been surer about anything in my life. You're *my* witch, and I love you. I can't believe I was stupid enough to ever push you away." Grinning, he spun her around.

Her head fell back, hair flying, and she laughed again, joyful, content.

He stopped, peered down at her, his grin melting away, burned as it was by desire. "Okay, now I'm turned on. That laugh of yours . . ."

"Come on," she said, leading him to her bedroom and earning winks from her sisters, who stood in the kitchen entry. "I have the perfect spell for that." She shut the door, then proceeded to work her magic all over his body.

IT'S IN HIS KISS . . .

(Title hummed to the tune of Cher
singing "The Shoop Shoop Song")

P. C. Cast

To Gyna Snowater
with love from P. C. Castwater.
We rock when we team up, baby!

One

"All right, we're going to start a new unit, so get out your folders and get ready to take notes," Summer said in what she liked to hope was her best Teacher Voice.

"What's the new unit, Miss S.?" called a male voice from the rear of the class.

Summer frowned. Was it disrespectful to call her Miss S.? Oh, Goddess! Another question she'd have to ask her sister on the phone tonight. She cleared her throat and tried to look severe and ten years older. "Shakespeare's *Romeo and Juliet*."

The girls in the class sighed and looked dreamy. The boys groaned.

"Hey, I hear there's sex in that play," came the same voice from the rear of the class.

"Well, yes. Actually it's a play about star-crossed lovers whose families won't let them be together," said Summer.

The girls smiled. The boys rolled their eyes.

"So that means there's sex in it. Lots, actually," Summer said before her mind caught up with her mouth.

"Cool!"

"Of course, it's all written in Elizabethan English," she hastily amended, reconnecting with the excellent control she usually had over everything she said or did.

"Sucks fairy butt," said a surly voice from the other side of the room.

"So we won't get it?" asked a cute blonde in the front row who wore a short, pink cheerleading uniform with FIGHTING FAIRIES emblazoned across her perky bosom.

"Don't worry. I'll make sure you get it," Summer said.

"Awesome!" chorused several annoying male voices, accompanied by giggles from the girls.

"Hey, Miss Smith, can we watch the movie?" asked the cheerleader.

"The one that shows Juliet's boobs!" called the irritating male voice. Which kid was that, anyway? Maybe she should move him up closer. (As if she wanted the annoying child *closer* to her? Ugh.)

"I'll think about the movie," Summer said firmly. "What we *are* going to see is an art exhibit of Pre-Raphaelite paintings that features Ford Madox Brown's famous *Romeo and Juliet* balcony scene."

The classroom went dead silent. Finally a pleasantly plump redheaded girl who sat smack in the center of the class smiled up at Summer through extra-thick glasses and a face full of unfortunate zits and said, "You mean we're taking a field trip?"

"Yes, we're taking a field trip. Tomorrow."

There was a general class-wide sigh of relief and several high fives accompanied by murmurs of "Dude! That means no class tomorrow!"

"Okay, don't forget to work on the Shakespearian vocab I gave you at the beginning of class. It's due the day after tomorrow, and then we'll begin—" Summer was saying when—thank the blessed Goddess—the bell rang that signaled the end of the period as well as the end of the school day.

"High school sucks," Summer muttered to herself as the last pubescent boy filed out of her classroom, almost running into the door frame as he tried to keep his eyes on her cleavage as long as humanly possible. When the coast was clear, she dropped her head to her desk, and with a satisfying thud began to bang it not so softly. "I'm not a fool for teaching high school. I'm not a fool for teaching high school . . ." she spoke the litany in time to her head banging.

"Oh, honey. Just give up. We're all fools. That's one of the things that makes a truly great teacher: foolishness. The second thing starts with a *W*."

Summer looked up to see a tall, slender woman dressed all in black. Her acorn-colored hair was shoulder length and wavy in a disarrayed I'm-so-naughty style. She offered her hand to Summer with a smile just as the door to her classroom opened again.

"What?" The tall, slender woman whipped around, skewering the hapless teenage boy with her amber eyes.

The boy's eyes flitted from the scowling woman to Summer, and back to the scowler again.

"Mr. Rom? Isn't that your name?" asked the slender woman in a no-nonsense voice.

The boy nodded nervously.

"And what is it you wished to bother Miss Smith with?"

The boy's mouth opened, closed, and then opened again. "I have my journals to turn in. The ones that were due yesterday," he finally blurted.

The amber-eyed woman glanced down at Summer. "Do you take late work, Miss Smith?"

Summer swallowed. "No. I mean, isn't that the English Department's policy?"

"Of course it is." The slender woman raised one arched brow at the boy and trapped him with her sharp gaze. "No. Late. Work. Means no late work. Now, go away, child, before you truly anger me."

"Y-yes ma'am!" the boy's voice broke as he backed hastily from the room and then scampered away.

"How in the world did you do that?" Summer said, gaping at the tall, young woman.

She smiled and held out her hand. "I'm Jenny Sullivan, your across-the-hall neighbor and fellow English teacher, as well as a Certified Discipline Nymph. Sorry, I would have introduced myself last week at the beginning of the semester, but I was on that delicious staff development trip to Santa Fe." Summer blinked blankly at her, so Jenny hurried on. "You know, Discipline in the Desert 101. Goddess! There are just so many applications for desert discipline in the high school classroom." She shook herself. "Anyhoodles, just got back today and heard that you'd taken your sister, Candy Cox's, place on our staff, and thought I better welcome you." She paused and glanced at the closing door after the student. "I see I arrived just in time."

"What's the thing that starts with a *W*?" Summer asked.

"Whips?" Jenny said hopefully.

"Whips? We can use whips here? Candy never told me that."

"Wait—wait. I think we're having a communication difficulty. You asked me for a W word and, naturally, I thought of whips."

"Okay, no. Let's start over. You said foolishness and something that starts with a W make us great teachers."

"Oh!" Jenny brightened. "Sadly, the answer to that is not *whips*, though it should be," she finished under her breath.

"Then it's . . ." Summer prompted.

"Whatever."

"Pardon?"

"The other thing. It's the Whatever Factor. Honey, I can already tell that your problem is you give a shit too much about what the hormones and germs are thinking."

"The hormones and germs?"

"Aka teenagers."

"Oh."

"Darling Summer, you need to understand that teenagers rarely think." Jenny patted her arm. "Come on, let's lock up, and then I'll treat you to a drink at Knight Caps."

Summer started to grab her keys and her purse, then her eyes flitted to the clock on the wall. "Uh, Jenny. It's barely three. Isn't that too early to drink?"

Jenny hooked her arm through Summer's and pulled her toward the door. "When you teach high school, it's never too early to drink. Plus, rumor has it you ate lunch in the vomitorium. You'll need a good healthy dose of martini to cleanse your system of those toxins."

"Vomitorium?" Summer asked as Jenny took her hand and led her toward the door.

"Just another word for the cafeteria. And, yes. You should be afraid. Very afraid."

"Wow. Teaching is so not like I imaged when I was in college."

"Darling, nothing is like you imaged in college. This is the real world," Jenny paused and then snorted. "Okay, well, Mysteria isn't actually part of the real world in the *real*ity sense, but you know what I mean. College is college. Work is work. Teaching is work."

Summer sipped her sour apple martini contemplatively. "Teenagers are a lot more disgusting than I thought they'd be."

"Preaching to the choir here," Jenny said.

"I mean, Candy told me to change my major to anything that didn't involve teaching, and I just thought she was, well . . ." she trailed off, obviously not wanting to speak badly about her sister.

"Here, let me help you. You thought Candy was just old, burned-out, and disgruntled. And that you, being twenty-some-odd years younger and ready to take on the world, would have an altogether different experience with *touching the future*." Jenny said the last three words with exaggerated drama while she clutched her bosom (with the hand that wasn't clutching her martini).

"Yeah, sadly, that's almost exactly what I thought."

"Until your first day of real teaching?"

"Yep."

"And now you want to run shrieking for the hills?"

"Yep again."

Jenny laughed. "Don't worry. A few short lessons in discipline from an expert—that would be *moi*, by the by—and another martini or two, mixed with one of Hunter's excellent five-meat pizzas, which I'll split with you, will fix you right up."

"Okay, except I never have more than one martini, and, well, I'm a vegetarian."

"One martini? Sounds like you're a little tightly wrapped, girl-friend."

"I like to think of it as maintaining a healthy control."

Jenny rolled her amber eyes. "In my professional Discipline Nymph opinion, I might mention that 'healthy control' is often an oxymoron. And you're a vegetarian? Really?"

Summer chose to ignore Jenny's comment about control and said, "I'm really a vegetarian. I don't eat anything that had a face. Makes me want to throw up a little in the back of my throat even to think about it. So get my half with cheese and veggies."

"Cheese and veggies on your half it is." She motioned for one of the fairies to come take their order and then frowned when the pink-haired, scantily clad waitress ignored her and instead giggled musically at something a werewolf at the bar had said. Jenny lifted one perfectly manicured finger and started swirling it around in the air. "Looks like girlfriend over there needs a little discipline lesson. She needs to learn it's best not to ignore me when I—"

Summer grabbed Jenny's finger. "Do. Not. Use. Magic!"

Jenny yelped in surprise and put her finger away. "What gives?"

"Did Candy never mention what kind of, ur, *magic* I have?"

Jenny's frown deepened. "Well, no. Candy didn't have any magic, or at least she didn't until she hooked up with that handsome werewolf of hers. I think she felt kinda weird that everyone else had some sort of magic, so she didn't talk much about it. Plus, you know school's supposed to be a Magic Free Zone. There was no need to go into it much. Why? What's your magic?"

"Opposite."

"Huh?"

Summer sighed. "My magic is opposite magic. Any spell worked around me instantly turns opposite, or at the very least becomes totally messed-up and twisted around. That's another reason I decided to teach."

"To really fuck with the teenage mind by screwing up all the furtive little magics they attempt at school?"

"No, though that does sound like it might be a fun by-product. The truth is that I wanted to get a job back home in Mysteria. I really like it here. While I was in college, I missed . . ." She hesitated, trying to decide how much to say. "Ur, I uh, missed the people who live here," she finally decided on. And it was true. She had missed the people—some of them more than others. Actually, one of them more than others. "Anyway, I wanted to live in Mysteria, but I didn't want to constantly be messing up people's magic."

Jenny's expression said she knew there was more to the "Ur, I uh, missed the people who live here" nonsense, but the only comment she made was, "Oh, I get it. So working in the high school, a Magic Free Zone, sounded perfect."

"In theory," Summer said, mournfully sipping her martini.

"Hey, cheer up. It could be worse."

"How?"

"You could be teaching at the grade school. At that age they touch you *and* pee in their pants." Jenny shuddered. "Yeesh!"

Summer sighed. "This might fall under Emergency Procedures and require one more drink."

"Of course it does, and of course you do. I'll get it and order our pizza." Jenny slid her lithe body from their booth. "I'll go to the counter and order it. Although I do wonder what would happen if my kick-the-flirting-waitress-fairy-in-her-lazy-ass spell went opposite."

"You don't want to know. It's always a true mess and—"

A gale of giggles and the door opening caused Summer to lose her train of thought and glance over her shoulder at the entrance to the bar. Then she sucked air. Her face blanched white and then flushed a bright, painful pink.

"Oh, Goddess!" Summer whispered. "It's Kenneth."

Two

"Yeah, it's Kenny the Fairy. So? What's the big deal?" Jenny was saying when the gaze of the tall, blond, male fairy in the middle of the new group of laughing girl fairies lighted on Summer and, smiling, he hurried over to their table.

"Hey, Summer! You're back!"

"Hi, Ken," Summer said, managing to stiffly return his hug. "Yeah. That's me. Back. For a week." And she blushed an even hotter shade of pink.

"Come on Kenny-benny! You promised to buy us mushroom pizza and those fizzy blue hypnotic drinks," pouted a pair of identical twin silver-haired, gold-winged fairies.

Kenny gave Summer an apologetic smile. "Sorry, gotta go. I'll call you later, okay? Is your number still the same?"

"Yeah. The same. Still." Summer tried to smile, but her face ended up looking more like an enthusiastic grimace.

"Oh, no no no. This is so damn sad. You have a crush on Fairy Kenny," Jenny said when they were alone again.

"Shhh!" Summer hushed her. "He might hear you."

"Oh, please. He's too busy with the slut sisters and their trampy friends. Hang on." Jenny turned, faced the counter, and nailed the giggling pink waitress with her stern gaze. Her voice carried easily across the bar, slicing through the chattering fairies like a saber through a butterfly-infested flower garden. "Esmeralda, we need another round of martinis and a veggie pizza. Now. And do not make me repeat myself." The waitress gulped, nodded, and scampered off to place their order. Jenny briskly brushed her hands against one another, as if pleased at a job well done, then she sat back in the booth, turning her full attention on Summer. "Okay, give. Why did you turn into the Incredible Cardboard Woman the instant Kenny-benny spoke to you?"

"I like him," Summer whispered, upending her martini and patting on the stem as she tried to coax the last of the liquid from the glass.

"Yeah, so? That doesn't explain the stiffness."

Summer sighed. "He and I grew up together. We were best friends, or at least we were until we hit puberty and I realized how gorgeous and perfect he is. Since then things have been kinda awkward between us."

"Kenny's been through puberty? Who knew?"

"Stop it! He's cute beyond belief. Don't you think he looks just like Legolas?" she said, shooting furtive glances at Ken.

"I guess so, only gayer. If that's possible." Jenny shrugged. "But whatever floats your boat."

"He definitely floats my boat," Summer said.

"Does he know that?"

"Huh?"

"You said you guys grew up together, and then things changed when you started crushing on him. Maybe you should let him know why things changed."

"Oh, I don't know about that. I'm not very good at—"

"Here are your drinks, ladies. Your pizza should be right out," gushed the waitress as she sloshed their new martinis down on the table in front of them.

"Thank you, Esmeralda. How kind of you to finally show us special attention."

"I—I just didn't realize it was you, Jenny," the fairy said. "Discipline Nymphs always get special attention at Knight Caps."

"As well they should," Jenny said smoothly, bowing her head in gracious acknowledgment of the fairy's apology.

The waitress hurried away, and Jenny turned her gaze back to Summer. "So, you need to let Kenny know you have the hots for him."

"Ack!" Summer sputtered, mid–martini sip. She swallowed, coughed, and said, "Jenny, like I was saying, I'm not good at, well, the guy-girl thing. It's just so—I don't know—unpredictable."

"Oh, please. Kenny-benny isn't a guy. He's a fairy. And they're really predictable. They frolic—they flirt—they scamper."

"I happen to think there's more to Kenny than that, but as I said, I'm not good at the social interaction thing."

"You have issues with guys."

"No, just with guys I like."

"Okay, fine. Just with guys you like. What are you going to do about it?"

"Huh?"

Jenny snorted. "Darling, you're definitely old enough to take the bull by the horns. Figuratively and literally."

Summer took another drink of her martini. "You're right. I know you're right. But knowing and doing are two different things."

"Look, you don't seem especially tongue-tied right now. Actually, you've been rather amusing, so you're definitely not conversationally impaired. Just talk to the fairy."

"I'm only conversationally impaired when I have to talk to someone I want to sleep with. I like you, and you're attractive and all, but I definitely don't want to sleep with you."

Jenny preened. "Nice of you to notice I'm attractive." Then her arched brows went up. "Hang on—you want to have hot, nasty sex with fairy boy?"

"No, I'd like him to make tender, slow, amazing love to me," Summer said, blushing again.

"Are you sure?" Jenny studied her carefully. "I'm getting the need-to-have-it-uncontrolled-and-hot-and-hard vibe from you, and I'm rarely wrong about my vibes."

"Jeesh, I'm sure. I don't do uncontrolled. Enough already."

"Okay, okay. You two are friends, right?"

"We were."

"You can still play off that. Hey, aren't you living in your sister's cabin at the edge of the woods?"

"Yeah."

"So, invite fairy boy over for dinner. You know," she winked, "for old time's sake. Then jump his bones," Jenny paused, rolled her eyes, and added, "slowly and tenderly."

Summer chewed her lip. "I don't know . . ."

"Take it from me. When dealing with men, fairy or otherwise, it's always best to be in charge and direct. Plus, you like control, and you'll definitely be in control if the date's on your turf."

"I'll think about it," Summer said, her eyes moving back to where Ken was perched in the middle of the group of fawning fairies at the bar.

"What you should think about is taking another gulp of that martini, putting on some of this nasty red lipstick, fluffing your hair, and marching yourself right over to that bar and extending the big invite to fairy boy." Jenny fished in her purse until she pulled out a tube of lipstick called Roaring Red and tossed it to Summer. Then she gave the giggling fairies a contemptuous glance. "You're cuter than those pastel pansies; don't let them intimidate you. Female fairies would lust after a snake if you put jeans on it and called it Bob. Everyone knows how easy they are, and no one takes them seriously."

"I guess I could." Summer gnawed her lip again. "I mean, we are old friends."

"Exactly."

She took a big drink of her martini, letting the alcohol burn through her body. Another gale of giggles erupted from the fairies, and Summer seemed to shrink in on herself. "I can't. I just can't. It's so . . . I don't know . . . *unplanned.*"

"Girlfriend, life is unplanned. Get used to it. Okay, how about this deal: if you ask Kenny-benny over for dinner, I'll take my class on the field trip to the gallery with you tomorrow and be sure the hormones and germs act right."

Summer sat up straighter. "You'll come with me?"

Jenny shrugged. "I'm getting ready to start *Romeo and Juliet* with my freshmen, so I might as well. Plus, your students will probably behave dreadfully and need an ever-so-firm disciplinary hand," she finished with a gleeful smile.

"Promise?"

"That I'll jump squarely into your students' shit? Absolutely."

"Not that. Do you promise you'll come with me if I ask Ken out?"

"Yep."

"Even if he says no?"

"Don't put that negative energy out there. Of course he'll say yes, and of course, regardless of the fairy, I'll go with you tomorrow. Now gird yourself and go ask him out."

"Fine. Okay. I can do this." Summer gulped the last of the martini, ran her fingers through her curly blond hair, and in two quick swipes of Jenny's lipstick completed the transformation from Nice New Teacher into tipsy Discipline Nymph Trainee.

Just before she stood up, Jenny motioned for her to lean across the table. "Here, this will help." She deftly unbuttoned the top two buttons of Summer's blouse. "That's better. I'd do a quick make-your-nipples-hard spell, but what with your opposite magic, I'm afraid of what would happen."

"Don't even think about it," Summer said. She stood up and tossed back her hair.

"You are beautiful and powerful and desirable. Just keep telling yourself that."

"Okay. Okay. Okay." Nodding woodenly, Summer made her way to the bar.

"Kenny-benny, sweetie-weetie! You have a glob of cheese on your lip. Want me to get that for you, baby?" One of the twin fairies cooed.

"No, let me!" said her sister, using a tip of her wing to push her sibling out of her way so she could angle her lithe body closer to Ken.

"Girls, girls—settle! I can wipe my lip myself," Ken said, laughing.

"We know you can, honey-bunny!" said one twin.

"But it's so much more fun if we help you!" trilled the other twin.

None of them noticed Summer. At all. So she drew a deep breath, closed her eyes, and told herself, *When I speak, I'm going to pretend to be Jenny.* She opened her eyes, lowered her voice, and said, "Excuse me, I need a word with Ken." Summer almost jumped at the strong, stern tone she had (somehow) used. All of the fairies, including the ditzy waitress who was carrying their veggie pizza from the oven, turned to stare at her. *I'm Jenny . . . a Certified Discipline Nymph . . . beautiful . . . powerful . . . desirable . . .*

"Hi, Summer," Ken grinned at her. "Do you want me?"

"Y-yes, I do," Summer stumbled briefly, but then she straightened her spine and lifted her chin. "Could I speak with you? Privately?" She didn't let herself look at the scantily clad, beautiful fairies.

"Okeydokey!" Ken said. "Hang on, girls. I'll be right back." He took Summer's elbow and moved her to an unoccupied spot down the counter. "What's up?"

"Ken, I'd like to . . . um . . ." She swallowed the lump that had suddenly risen in her throat and made another attempt. "What I mean is would you want to—" Thankfully, a fit of ridiculously loud coughing from Jenny interrupted Summer's babble and gave her a chance to pull herself together. "Ken, would you like to come over tomorrow night and have dinner with me?" she finally managed to say.

"Yeah, sounds cool. Are you living at your sister's cabin?"

"My sister's cabin. Yes."

"Great. So, I'll see you about eight?"

"About eight. Yes."

"Want me to bring something to drink?"

"Something to drink. Yes."

"Okay, see you tomorrow at eight!" He smiled again and went back to his seat at the bar.

"Okay. Yes. Yes. Okay," she told the air as she moved back to their table.

"Here, have the rest of my martini. You look shell-shocked. Are you okay? What did he say? How did it go?"

"Yes. He said yes." Summer said and then gulped Jenny's martini.

Three

"Hangover. Ugh, I sooo have a hangover." Summer shakily sipped the sludge that almost passed for coffee she'd gotten from the teachers' lounge.

"I'm usually not a big proponent of control, but three martinis was probably one and a half too many," Jenny said. She studied Summer with a critical eye. "Good thing you're young. Only the very young can still look as good as you do this morning *and* deal with a wicked hangover."

"You keep talking like you're so much older than me, but you can't be over thirty," Summer said irritably.

"Oh, girlfriend, don't be silly. I'm two hundred and thirty-five. And a half."

Summer choked on her coffee.

"Discipline Nymphs are some of the most long-lived of the nymphs. It's because discipline is good for body and soul."

"I had no idea," Summer said.

"Well, girlfriend, you do now."

"Hey, speaking of stuff I'm confused about, would you please explain to me why a Certified Discipline Nymph is so roll-your-eyes about my control issues? Isn't control pretty much just another word for discipline?"

"Oh, my poor, deluded young friend. Let Ms. Sullivan help you. Discipline is what you have to be good at so you can release control. Girlfriend, you're too tightly wrapped. Flex those discipline muscles, relax that snoreable übercontrol you carry around with you, and you'll be amazed at the results."

"I dunno . . ." Summer said doubtfully. "But I can tell you I never thought of discipline as the antithesis of control before."

"Gives you a whole new outlook on discipline, doesn't it?"

"You're right about that. I can tell you that I'm going to start flexing my discipline muscles with the hormones and germs in my class. Like you said last night, I'm only going to call them by their last names, miss or mister whoever. It's much more formal; much more *disciplined*."

"Well done, you!" Jenny smiled encouragement. "I knew you'd be a quick study. Speaking of the germs and hormones, let's round them up. I do believe I see the field trip bus waiting for us out there." As they herded the students onto the bus, Jenny called, "You did clear this with Barnabas, the gallery owner, didn't you?"

"I sent him an e-mail saying that I'd be bringing a busload of kids to view the exhibit today. I got a reply saying that would be fine."

"Good. I was worried for a second, because I thought I heard that Barnabas had left for a vacation to France. The nymph gossip said that the poor gay vampire took off to France because he was inconsolable about Hunter Knight falling for Evie Tawdry instead of him."

"But Hunter's not gay," Summer said as they followed the last student on the bus and took their seats near the front.

"Moxie, we've got them all," Jenny called to the short, squat, green-haired bus driver.

"Moving out, Ms. Sullivan," Moxie growled, let loose the emergency brake, and pulled the bus out onto the street.

"What is she?" Summer whispered. Eyes focused on the back of Moxie's green hair, she was sure she saw one of the thick strands move of its own accord.

"Mox? She's a troll. They make the best bus drivers. They don't put up with shit." And then, as if she literally had eyes in the back of her head, Moxie's head turned almost all the way around and she barked, "Sam Wheeler! Get your big, nasty boots off my bus seat. You are not at home. Put them up there again, and I'll take those feet off at the ankles. I'd much rather clean up blood than pig crap."

"Yes ma'am," Sam said sheepishly.

"See? Trolls know their discipline. Anyway, where were we? Oh yeah. No, Hunter's definitely *not* gay, as everyone, including Barnabas, knows. But I feel kinda sorry for the poor gay vamp anyway; unrequited love gets me right here." Jenny fisted her hand over her heart.

"Really? I wouldn't have pegged you for the sentimental type, Ms. Discipline."

"I'm not sentimental. I'm romantic."

"A discipline romantic?"

"Girlfriend, you have so much to learn. Romance is best with a healthy touch of discipline. Especially if it involves whips and handcuffs. And since we're on the romance subject, what's on the menu tonight with Kenny-benny?"

"I really wish you wouldn't call him that."

"Sorry. I'll be good. Promise."

Summer noted that Jenny's sparkly eyes said she was the opposite of sorry, but she decided not to say anything. Plus, she really did want to go over what she was going to cook for Ken. *She was going to cook for Ken!* Just the thought had her stomach rolling with nerves. She cleared her throat. "Okay, I thought I'd make a nice salad, with lots of lovely greens, and then have spaghetti with tofu and, of course, garlic bread, and maybe finish up with a big slice of peach cobbler. What do you think?"

"I think I was asking about your lingerie and not about dinner."

"But you asked me what was on the menu tonight."

"Yes, and I expected you to say something like, 'Why, Jenny, me and my lovely black panty and bra set are definitely the first three courses.'" At Summer's blank look, Jenny's eyes got big and round. "Oh, Goddess! When you asked him over for dinner, you *really* meant dinner."

Summer frowned. "Of course I did."

"Oh, um. Okay, well, tofu spaghetti sounds just dandy then."

Summer seemed not to have heard her. "Ohmygoddess! Do you think Ken thinks *I'm* on the menu, too?"

"Let's hope so," Jenny said.

"No!" Summer gasped. "That's not what—I mean, I wasn't thinking that. Exactly. Or at least not on our *first* date. That's isn't in accordance with my plan. We weren't going to have sex until the third date." She chewed her bottom lip. "Jenny, have I messed up?"

"Are you kidding? Kenny-ben—ur—I mean, Kenny isn't exactly Mr. Forceful. If he comes on to you, and you don't want to do him, just say no."

"I might want to do him," Summer whispered.

"Okay, then just say no nicely."

"But that wasn't what I was planning."

"Oh, please! Would you loosen up? If you want to have sex, then boink the fairy. If you don't, then wait until the third or even the thirtieth date. Whatever."

Summer fanned herself. "I'm never going to be able to do this."

Jenny peered down her nose at her as if she were an unusual specimen under a magnifying glass. "Darling, didn't you date at all in college?"

Summer's cheeks flushed pink. "Yeah, of course I did."

"And?"

"And nothing. If I liked the guy, I decided when we'd, well, *do it*, and then we did it."

"Always according to your well-controlled plan," Jenny supplied.

"Always."

"Oh my Goddess! You've really never been swept off your feet by hot, sticky, steamy, raunchy sex."

When a couple of the kids sitting closest to the front of the bus gasped and laughed, Jenny turned her narrowed eyes on them, instantly quieting their tittering.

Summer frowned and lowered her voice. "No, and I don't think I'd like what you just described. It sounds so . . . so . . ."

"So out-of-control?"

"Yes. Exactly. And I'm not particularly good with out-of-control."

"That is shameful," Jenny said.

"Well, it's the way I am. And there's nothing wrong with the way I am," Summer said, more than a little defensively.

"Oh, girlfriend, I don't mean to make you feel bad about yourself. It's just that you're missing so much."

Summer shrugged. "I don't know. I had fun in college."

"I don't mean frat banging and one-night stands. I mean love."

"Huh?"

"Girlfriend, don't you know that love can't be controlled and planned and prepackaged or hermetically sealed to be taken out when it fits into your schedule?"

Summer chewed her lip and thought about Ken. When she spoke, her voice was so soft that Jenny had to tilt her head toward her to hear her. "I was kinda thinking that Ken would be the guy I let myself fall in love with. You know, college is over. He's here in my hometown. He's literally the boy next door."

"I don't know. It just sounds so clinical. And love is definitely not clinical." Jenny shook her head. "No. This will never do." She tapped a long, manicured red fingernail against her skintight black slacks. "What if I did a spell on you—one that I meant to be the opposite of what I really cast?" Before Summer could protest, she hurried on. "I could cast a control spell on you. That should get zapped by your opposite magic and allow you to relax with him tonight. Then what happens between you can at least happen naturally. Right?"

"Jenny, you can't ever, *ever* cast any kind of spell on me. It won't work like you expect. I guess the opposite magic isn't exactly the right way to describe what I have. It's more like opposite squared. It doesn't *just* make the spell reverse; it also makes it wacky."

"Define wacky."

"Okay, here's the perfect example. When I was in high school, Glory Tawdry thought she would help me out. It was right before our senior homecoming dance, and I didn't actually have a date with Ken, but I'd told him that I'd meet him there and would save all the best dances for him."

Jenny shook her head. "This has been going on between you two for years, hasn't it?"

"This?"

"Waffling. Unfulfilled romance. Missed opportunities. All because of your insane need for control."

"Yes. And my need for control is not insane. Anyway, as per usual for my high school days, overnight I grew the biggest, nastiest zit right in the middle of my forehead. No amount of makeup would cover it. It was like I had a third eye."

"Yuck."

"Yeah. So I asked Glory to cast a zit spell on me."

"Goddess! There's such a thing as a zit spell?"

Summer nodded. "She got the spell from her sister, Evie. You know she's a vengeance witch."

"Oh, that's right. Okay, go on."

"Well, it should have been simple enough. I wanted the zit gone. I have opposite magic. Glory casts a spell to fill my face with zits, which should have totally *cleared* my face of zits."

"It does sound simple enough."

"It didn't work out that way."

"What happened?"

"It cleared my face. Of everything."

"Everything?"

"Absolutely everything. I had no gigantic zit, but I also had no eyes, nose, or mouth."

"Shit! What did you do?"

"Freaked out. I knew it was bad, because I couldn't see anything, but when Glory started screaming, 'Oh great Goddess help! Her face is gone,' I lost it. I tried to scream with her, couldn't, so I did what any normal girl would do when scared shitless and utterly blind."

"You ran?"

"Yep. And promptly fell over my cool fuchsia beanbag chair, smacking my head on the corner of my very large and very metallic stereo cabinet, which negated the spell. Thank the Goddess."

"So your face came back?"

Summer nodded. "Along with the Cyclops zit. See, that's what happens when I think I'm smart, take a chance, and let my opposite magic do its thing. It never works exactly opposite. It's more like sideways, around-the-corner, upside-down magic. And the spell only goes away if something major happens to me."

"Like smacking your head."

"Like smacking my head."

"Okay, I get that that was bad, and your control issues are making more and more sense, but have you ever tried to control your *magic* instead of controlling yourself?"

"Huh?"

"Think about it. You have weird magic, fine. Besides that, you have strong weird magic. How you've dealt with it is to clamp down major control over everything else in your life, but maybe all you have to do is to take control of your magic—you know, show it who's boss—and make it act right."

Summer shook her head. "You're nuts."

"I'm just sayin' discipline can be a good thing."

"Sure, for someone who is comfortable with it," Summer said.

"So get comfortable with it."

"Easier said than done."

"Maybe you just need the right incentive," Jenny said. "Want me to give you a quick dominatrix lesson or twelve? It'd be fun."

"Thanks, but no thanks. I think I'll just bumble along as I am, which means no 'helpful' magic spells from you or anyone else. Okay?"

Jenny held up her hand like she was taking an oath. "Promise." Then she added, "Guess it looks like you're going to have to get a handle on your übercontrol issues and your bizarre magic."

Summer sighed. "Sadly, it looks like it."

"Well, never fear. You have a Certified Discipline Nymph on your side. Plus, Kenny-benny may surprise both of us and take forceful control of your date tonight and ravish you properly." Jenny giggled and then, at Summer's frown, cleared her throat and sobered up. The bus lurched to an awkward halt in front of Dark Shadows, Mysteria's only art gallery. "But before anyone gets ravished, we will edify and educate the masses." She winked at Summer, stood up, smoothed her hair, and faced the bus full of teenagers. "Touch *anything* and you will have to deal with me—before school in the boy's restroom with a toothbrush, a can of Comet, and a collection of Shakespearian sonnets."

"What're the poems for?" whispered a voice from the silent, staring students.

"To clean your minds out while your hands—your *gloveless* hands—clean out the urinals," Jenny said sweetly. She turned around and, to a chorus of gagging sounds from the students, grinned at Summer. "Let's go, shall we?" Jenny sashayed from the bus, leading the way into the gallery with Summer and the well-disciplined students following close behind her.

Summer thought entering the gallery was like leaving one world for another. Inside the spacious building it was cool and dark. Even from the foyer she could see that instead of the usual plain white expanse of gallery walls, Dark Shadows had been painted in unyielding black, broken only by spotlights trained on each painting so that the entire exhibit gave the impression of floating dreams poised on the surface of a dark, sleeping sea.

"Wow, it's been years since I've been here, and I'd forgotten how dramatic the black walls make this place," Summer told Jenny in a hushed voice.

"Yeah, Barnabas told me that he hadn't planned the effect. He'd painted everything black only because it's easier on his vampire senses. The weirdness of it was just a happy by-product."

"Well, vampires gross me out with their definitely non-vegan diet, but there's something about this place that I like, even if it is a little creepy and—"

"Ladies, how may I help you?"

At the sound of the deep voice, Summer jumped guiltily and looked up . . . and up . . . and up into the face of a god of a man. He was standing just inside the shadowy entrance of the gallery, and even though it was dark and cool within, he was wearing mirrored sunglasses. As she blinked at her own reflection in those glasses, the man slowly reached up and removed them, revealing eyes so dark they looked black. His gaze locked with hers. *Gorgeous, dark, dangerous* were the descriptive words that flitted through her mind. "You're not Barnabas," she said abruptly.

One black brow lifted. "Astute observation, ma'am."

"Oooh, you must be Colin, Barnabas's older brother. Tell me I'm right, handsome," Jenny demanded, flipping her hair coquettishly.

"You're right." His eyes sparkled playfully when he turned to Jenny. "And you must be a Certified Discipline Nymph."

"Smart and handsome—my second-favorite combination," Jenny said.

"Your first favorite?" Colin asked with a sexy smile.

"Smart, handsome, and bound by the wrists," Jenny said.

Summer felt the urge to roll her eyes. Instead, she cleared her throat and said, "High school field trip—students—right behind us. Remember?"

Jenny shrugged, barely glancing at the wide-eyed students. "I'm just being friendly. But you're right. We should get down to business." The purr in her voice said that she'd rather go down on Colin than get down to any other business.

Summer frowned at Jenny and then stuck her hand out to Colin. "Hello, I'm Miss Smith. I sent the e-mail several days ago reserving the gallery for the field trip this morning. I'm assuming that's still okay, even though your brother isn't here?"

Colin took her hand in his, and Summer had to force herself not to gasp. His grip was strong, but she'd expected that. He was, after all, a *very* big man who had *very* big hands. It was the temperature of his skin that shocked her. Being touched by him was like being touched by an awakened statue. His hand was smooth, hard, and cool. Their eyes met again, and Summer was jolted by the dark intensity with which he was studying her—as if she was, at that moment, the most important thing in his universe. She'd only known of one species of Mysteria's creatures who could spear someone with such intensity and whose skin felt like molded marble . . .

"You're a vampire!" she blurted, pulling her hand free of his firm grip.

His smile was slow and knowing, not in the least bit ruffled by her statement. "I am. Both of my brothers and I are vampires. It runs in the family, you know," he said smoothly.

"Does it?" Summer made herself not wipe her tingling palm down the side of her slacks.

"It does when you're all bitten by the same master vampire," he said.

Summer noticed that when he spoke to her, the playful sparkle that Jenny seemed to automatically evoke in his eyes changed . . . darkened, and even though he was no longer touching her, he was still studying her with that uncomfortable intensity. Feeling weirdly light-headed, Summer spoke more briskly than she'd intended. "That's interesting. Maybe we can talk about it later. Right now I think we should start our field trip. If that's okay with you—or your brother. Is Barnabas really not here?"

Colin cocked his head and looked down at her, a small curve of amusement shadowing his full lips. "Barnabas is in Paris drowning himself in wine and young Frenchmen so that he can forget being jilted by Hunter Knight." The vampire shrugged one of his broad shoulders. "Foolish of him to become so obsessed with a straight guy. I tried to tell Barnabas that Hunter's as gay as I am."

"Which is to say not at all," Jenny chimed in.

Colin's grin was almost a leer. He answered Jenny, but his eyes stayed on Summer. "Yes, ma'am. You're right about that."

"So, does that mean the field trip is off?" Summer said, wondering why Jenny's flirting with Colin should annoy her.

"Not at all. The reason I moved to town temporarily from my ranch is because Barnabas asked me to babysit this special exhibit. The field trip is definitely on. Besides, you just got here, Miss Smith. I'd hate for you to leave until we've gotten to know each other better." Colin's dark eyes trapped her gaze, and she felt her breathing deepen.

Is he making me dizzy? Is he working a vampire mojo on me? Summer mentally shook herself. She was being ridiculous. Magic didn't work on her. Or if it did, it went way wrong. Her overactive imagination and hormones were the only things working on her. What was probably happening was she was displacing her excitement about the impending dream date with Ken. No way was she interested in this vampire! He definitely didn't fit in with her well-thought-out plan for her future. "Excellent. Let's get started. The students have really been looking forward to this field trip," she lied.

"I hadn't been thinking much about this field trip at all." Colin lowered his voice so that it seemed to brush against Summer's skin. "At least not until I saw who was leading it. Now I do believe it's going to be a very interesting experience. It is good to meet you, Miss Smith." He tipped an imaginary hat to her in a cowboylike move that appeared to be second nature to him. Then he raised his voice so that the waiting students could hear. "Come on in and check out the art. And, yes, there are some nudes."

There were spontaneous high fives given in response as the students filed into the gallery.

"Ladies, if you'll follow me, I'll give you a more personal tour," Colin said. Though he spoke to both women, his eyes rested on Summer's face hungrily. He strode into the main gallery, giving Summer plenty of time to take in the faded jeans that snuggled his firm ass and the broad shoulders that strained the fabric of the black, long-sleeved shirt he wore. And were those cowboy boots? On a vampire? Sweet Goddess, gay Barnabas's brother was a sexy cowboy vampire!

"Damn, Summer! Are you secreting some kind of come-fuck-me! hormone? Tall, dark, and vampire is clearly hitting on you."

Summer pulled her eyes from Colin's muscular body and managed to scoff. "Oh, please. I'm so not interested in him."

"Really? That's not what your nipples are saying. Better check your control, girlfriend."

Horrified, Summer glanced down to see the outline of her very obviously aroused nipples pressing against her cream-colored blouse. Hastily she crossed her arms over her chest and muttered, "It's just cold in here," as she hurried into the gallery with Jenny's knowing laughter following her.

Four

"All right! Move away from the nude, and no one gets hurt!" Jenny snapped, and the group of gawking teenage boys shuffled reluctantly away from the full frontal nudity of George Wilson's *The Spring Witch*.

Colin waited until the three of them were alone before saying, "Wilson was a big fan of Dante and William Blake, so he liked the poetic and romantic subject here."

Summer blinked in surprise up at Colin. The tall vampire actually seemed to know something about art.

"Huh!" Jenny snorted a little testily. "I don't see anything terribly romantic about witches. Sexy—maybe. Wanton—for sure. Romantic? Nah."

"The subject isn't a witch as we know them in Mysteria," Colin explained, his eyes on the nude painting. "It's actually Persephone as she emerges from the underworld. See the pomegranate in her hand?"

"Oh, well, that makes more sense. Goddesses are definitely romantic," Jenny admitted.

"What do you think of her, Miss Smith?"

Colin's question, as well as the intense gaze he shifted from the painting to her, caught Summer unaware, and she automatically said what was foremost in her mind. "I think I like her body better than most of the other women in the exhibit. They look too manly."

Colin's brows lifted. "I agree with you, Miss Smith. The Pre-Raphaelites tended to give their female models masculine characteristics. I like my woman to look like a woman, and not like a man in drag."

"As if that matters to the germs and hormones," Jenny said, eyes lighting on a group of laughing, jostling teenage boys clustered around the huge, colorful, and seminude painting of *Toilette of a Roman Lady*. "Excuse me for a sec. I'm going to kick some boy butt."

As she hurried toward the students, Summer called, "Herd them back into the main gallery in front of the Romeo and Juliet painting. I'm going to give them their topic for the essay assignment."

Jenny's teeth flashed white as she grinned over her shoulder. "Oh, good. They'll hate that."

And, just like that, Summer and Colin were left completely alone for the first time.

She didn't have to look up at him to know his eyes were on her. Again. She could feel his gaze—against her skin, inside her blood. It heated her body, arousing her nipples and making her inner thighs tingle, and her woman's core became hot and wet and needy . . . needy for his touch, which wouldn't be sweet and gentle and loving, as she'd fantasized about Ken's touch being. Colin's touch would be like his body: hard and strong and sexy. No, Colin was nothing like Ken.

"What are you thinking about?"

His deep voice came from very close to her. *When had he stepped into her personal space?* She looked up at him. *Those eyes! They're so intense—so sexy.* He was close enough that his scent came to her, and it, too, was a surprise. Instead of smelling like the grave or worse, like a carnivorous, bloodsucking monster, Colin smelled as sexy as he looked. His scent was man mixed with something spicy, like cinnamon or even more exotic, like cloves and darkness and cool nighttime breezes sifting over love-dampened skin.

She stared at him and breathed the unique scent that was Colin distilled by his own skin. *Nothing like Ken, who smells like lemons and laughter, and who I'm supposed to be having a dream date with tonight!* "My date tonight," Summer finally managed to answer.

Colin's dark eyes narrowed dangerously. "You shouldn't lie to me. You know vampires can smell lies."

Summer took a step back and put up her chin. She was damn sure not going to let this overbearing, way-too-masculine creature intimidate her, no matter how yummy he smelled. She was a college graduate and a professional teacher!

"Then you should sniff again. I was definitely thinking about Ken," Summer said with finality.

"Ken?" his dark-chocolate voice was heavy with amusement. "As in Barbie's boyfriend?"

"No. Ken, as in *my* boyfriend."

With a movement too fast to follow with her eyes, Colin grabbed both of her arms and lifted her so that he only had to bend a little to fit his face into the soft slope of her neck. He inhaled deeply and then let his breath out slowly, caressingly, so that it brushed against her sensitive skin and caused her to shiver.

"You may have been thinking, *briefly*, of him. But you do not have a boyfriend."

"What makes you say that?" she asked breathlessly.

"If you belonged to a man, I could scent him on you, and you smell only of yourself: sunlight and honey and woman."

He let her go as abruptly as he had grabbed her, and Summer stumbled back a couple of steps.

Her head was spinning, and her breath was coming short and

hard. It was like he'd filled her mind with the white noise of the inside of seashells. All she could think to say was, "I smell like sunlight and honey?"

"Yes." Colin ran one cool finger down her heated cheek and the side of her neck. "Warm honey on a golden summer's day. You draw me to you like a field of lavender draws bees. Will you let me taste you?"

"Hey, Miss Smith! Miss Sullivan says we're all waiting for you, and we need you now. Uh, you better come, 'cause she seems kinda pissed."

Colin's hand fell away from her face, and Summer turned to see the little blond cheerleader standing in the doorway to the main gallery.

"Y-yes. Okay. I'm coming. Now." Without looking back at Colin, Summer hurried from the room.

She could feel him following her. She thought it was like having a dangerous but darkly beautiful panther stalking her. He wanted to taste her! Summer shivered and crossed her arms concealingly over her breasts. Again.

"There you are, Miss Smith. The students are ready for their essay assignment." Jenny told her, then her eyes snapped over the group of milling students. "I said get your notebooks out. Now."

Book bags exploded as kids hurried to do her bidding. Summer could only watch in awe. How the hell did Jenny do that? She hadn't even raised her voice. Soon the entire room (which included one dark and brooding vampire) was looking expectantly up at her.

Summer cleared her throat. "The topic of your essay is this: a Pre-Raphaelite art critic wrote that this painting of Romeo and Juliet by Ford Madox Brown was 'splendid in expression and fullness of tone, and the whole picture is gorgeous in color.' I want you to be a modern art critic and tell me in your essay what you learned about Romeo and Juliet from Mr. Brown's painting." Summer paused, narrowed her eyes, and did what she hoped was a believable impression of Jenny's firmness, then added, "No, that does *not* mean that I want you to tell me Romeo is wearing a gay-looking red outfit, and Juliet's boobs are showing. What I want you to tell me is what this painting says about them as a couple. Questions?" She didn't give them time to ask any but hurried on. "Good. I'll let you have about fifteen more minutes here in front of the painting to take notes and start getting your ideas on paper."

A hand went up. It was one of Jenny's students, so she said, "What is it, Mr. Purdom?"

"Does your class have to write the essay, too?"

"Yes. I suggest you get busy," Jenny said smoothly.

There were a few muffled groans, but most of the kids settled down to studying the painting and taking notes.

"I'm going to go tell Moxie to bring the bus around. Do you think you can handle *it* by yourself?" Jenny's tone made the pronoun semi-suggestive. The sultry glance she sent Colin made it fully suggestive.

"Yes, definitely. No worries here," Summer said.

Jenny met her eyes before she left the room and blinked a couple times in surprise before her face practically exploded in a smile. "You like him!"

Summer felt her cheeks warm. "I don't like him. I don't even know him," she whispered.

"Okay, maybe I should have said you're hot for him. Well, go ahead, girlfriend. He's clearly more interested in you than me." She winked at Summer and disappeared out the front door.

Summer sighed and turned back to the room of sullenly writing students. Thankfully, Colin was on the far side of the room standing close to the painting. She could see that he was busy answering questions about it for some of the students. Good. That should keep him occupied. It also gave her an opportunity to study him. Goddess, he was handsome, but not in a typical fashion. What was he like? He reminded her of someone, and she couldn't quite—

Then, with a little jolt she did remember who he brought to mind. Her favorite fictional hero, Mr. Rochester from *Jane Eyre*. Yes, that dark, powerfully masculine look of Colin's would definitely fit in as master of Thornfield. *You know you think Rochester is the sexiest of all fictional heroes, as well as your favorite,* her mind whispered. *No,* she told herself sternly, *Ken is really my type—all blond and sweet and gentle. He's what I planned for my future. The Rochester type needs to stay where he belongs—in the pages of fiction.*

But she was still staring when Colin looked up from the student he'd been helping and met her eyes.

Come to me . . . The words filled her—mind, body, and soul. Before she realized what she was doing, she was making her way around the group of students and heading for the vampire.

Summer was only a few feet from him when she stopped and shook her head, breaking the stare that had locked their eyes together and getting control of herself. Oh, hell no! What was she doing? Imagining his voice in her head and then obeying that imagining? Had she lost it? Had the stress of trying to teach teenagers cracked her already?

And then, not far behind her, she felt a too-familiar prickle up her spine. She knew even before she heard the whispered singsong words of the quickly uttered spell that one of the asshole teenage sorcerers-to-be had thought he'd be clever and whip up a little magic to see if he and his girlfriend could skip out of the assignment. Summer whirled around in time to hear the last stanza of the incantation. She opened her mouth to yell, *No! Stop!* Backing as quickly as she could away from the kids—and right into an impossibly hard, cold body she knew had to be Colin. She wanted to warn him. She wanted to do something—anything. But instead, the magic was already grabbing her, robbing her of speech.

Me and my bitch get in the picture, yo!
Somewhere our teacher can't go!
Where school and stupid essays ain't no mo'!
And it's cool to get with your ho!

Completely helpless, she did the only thing she could do. Summer closed her eyes, wrapped her arms around the pillar of strength that was Colin, and held her breath as she felt their bodies being wrenched, lifted, and tossed.

When everything was still again and the nauseating sensation of wobbly, opposite magic lifted, Summer slowly opened her eyes.

And looked straight into Colin's dark gaze.

"What the—" he began, and then his eyes widened in sudden fear.

"The sunlight! I have to get out of . . ." The vampire's words trailed off as he realized he wasn't bursting into flame. Completely confused, Colin gazed down at Summer. "What's happened to us? It's day. I'm outside in the sunlight, and my skin is not burning."

"It's, well, because of my magic and that kid casting a spell. If I'm close enough to magic, it always messes up, and—" she began, and then her words broke off as what her eyes were seeing caught up with her mind. They were, indeed, outside. Actually, it wasn't full daylight, just a lovely morning dawning in the east. They were on a balcony, surrounded by a perfumed profusion of flowering rose vines. Colin was there with her, but he wasn't dressed in his jeans, black shirt, and cowboy boots. Here he was wearing an amazing crimson-colored outfit, rich as a king, or maybe even a god. She glanced down at her own clothes and gasped. She had changed, too, and was wearing only a soft, transparent chemise, which was cut low to expose her breasts to the nipples. She could feel Colin's eyes on those nipples as she looked up at him. "Uh-oh," she said. "I think we're inside the Romeo and Juliet painting,"

Five

"By the Goddess, I think you're right! How could this have happened?" Colin said, gazing around them while he shook his head in disbelief.

"It's me," Summer said miserably. "It's because of me that we're here."

His dark eyes rested on her. "How could this possibly be because of you?"

"It's my magic. Or maybe my nonmagic would be a better way to explain it." Summer sighed. "One of the students cast a spell in the

gallery—something about getting inside the Romeo and Juliet painting so that he and his *ho*," she wrinkled her nose in distaste at the
word, "could get out of the essay assignment."

"But what does that have to do with you? Other than it being your
assignment?"

"I was close enough to the stupid teenager when he cast the spell to
have my own magic work on it. And my own magic is opposite magic—
kind of. Actually, it's more like sideways, opposite, totally screwed-up
magic. The bottom line is that my magic messes up all other magic
around me. So here"—she made a sweeping gesture, taking in the balcony and the pearly morning—"we are."

"In the Romeo and Juliet painting."

She nodded. "In the Romeo and Juliet painting." Summer smiled
sheepishly. "Sorry."

Colin shook his head in amazement and lifted his hand so that the
red velvet sleeve slid back to reveal his muscular arm all the way to
mid-bicep. The morning light gilded his skin so that for that moment
he looked tan and unexpectedly young.

"Incredible!" he said. Then he bared his other arm to the morning
light, threw back his head, and laughed. "Do you know how long it's
been since I've felt the sun on my skin?"

Summer couldn't answer him. She could only watch as he transformed from intense and brooding to vibrant and amazing. He laughed
again and, with one swift motion, ripped open the buttons on his linen
undershirt. Colin faced the rising sun, arms spread, face open. He'd
been handsome before—all Rochester-like and mysterious. But here
he'd transformed into a man whose beauty went beyond his height
and hair and bone structure. This new Colin was so incredibly full of
life that he seemed to vibrate with it.

"You did this?"

He turned the force of his full smile on her, and Summer thought
that the heat he radiated would melt her. She nodded a little weakly
and managed a "Yes."

With another laugh, he lifted her in his arms and spun her around
the balcony. "I knew you were special from the moment I touched you."

"It's just my weird magic. I've been wishing I could figure out how to get rid of it or control it for years," Summer said a little breathlessly as he finally released her.

"Get rid of it? No way! And, take it from me, control is overrated. No! You're perfect just as you are—and so is your magic." He took her hand in his and, with dark eyes sparkling mischievously, he bent gallantly over it. "Thank you, my lady, for granting me a reprieve from unrelenting night and bringing me sunshine again."

Colin kissed her hand. As his lips met her skin, Summer felt a jolt of sensation that rushed through her body. His lips weren't the cool marble of a vampire! They were warm and soft and very, very much alive. She gasped, "You've really been changed. You're not a vampire here."

He didn't release her hand. Instead, he lifted it and slid it inside the open front of his shirt so that it rested over his heart. Summer could feel the beating of that heart under the warm, pliant skin of his chest.

"I don't know how long this magic will last, but I'm going to enjoy every moment of it."

"You're . . . you're so different here," Summer said, having difficulty concentrating on words with her hand pressed against his bare chest.

"Different?" Colin smiled and shrugged. "I suppose right now I am more like I used to be." He looked from her to the morning sky. "I think I've lived so long in darkness that I'd forgotten what it is to feel really alive." His eyes met hers again. They were full of the emotion reflected in the deepening of his voice. "You brought me the sun."

"On accident," Summer whispered. "I didn't really mean to."

"I smelled it on you when we met. Remember? I said you reminded me of sunlight and honey."

"I remember," Summer said softly, completely lost in his gaze.

"You drew me to you even then." He touched her cheek caressingly. "What is your first name?"

"Summer."

His smile was brilliant. "Summer! Perfect. Let me taste you, Summer. Let me breathe in your sunlight . . ."

Summer knew she shouldn't. She should step away from him and take control of this ridiculous situation and then fall on her head or whatever it took to break the spell. Instead, she felt her face tilt up to him as he bent to her lips. But he didn't kiss her—not at first. Instead, his mouth stopped just short of hers. She could feel his warm breath as he seemed to inhale her. Colin nuzzled her cheek and whispered into her parted lips, "You are sunlight and honey, *my* sunlight and honey."

Summer shivered. One of his hands still pressed hers against his chest. The other slid down her back, holding her close to him. She molded to him; only the transparent material of the thin chemise separated them, and she could clearly feel every part of his hard body.

"Do you want me to kiss you, Summer? Do you want me to taste you?" He breathed the words against her lips as he inhaled her scent.

"Yes," she whispered back. "Yes."

"Summer," he moaned, and then he claimed her mouth. His kiss wasn't gentle. It was rough and demanding. He possessed her lips, plundered her mouth, tantalized her tongue. His kiss engulfed her. It was the kind of kiss she'd always imagined she wouldn't like. It would be too filled with unbridled lust, too overwhelming and uncontrolled. So it was with a sense of utter surprise that Summer felt herself responding, body and soul, to Colin. She wrapped her arms around him and met his passion with her own. White-hot lust speared through her as the kiss deepened even more, as she gave herself completely over to him and—

—And Summer fell so hard on her butt that the wind was knocked out of her and she saw little speckles of light dance in front of her eyes.

"Thank the Goddess! You're back!" Jenny's hands were patting her as if she was checking for broken bones. "Are you okay? You had me so worried!"

Summer sucked air, blinked rapidly, and managed to nod.

"Is she hurt?" a deep voice asked.

"Colin? Oh, good. You're back, too," Jenny said briskly. "I think she's just had the wind knocked out of her. Here, help me get her to her feet."

Strong hands lifted her, and Summer realized that it felt familiar and somehow right that he was touching her again, even though his skin had lost the flush of sun-kissed warmth and was cool and marblelike again.

"Are you really all right?" Colin's voice came from close above her.

Summer looked up, finally blinking her vision clear. He was still holding one of her elbows, and he was watching her with the same dark intensity with which he'd studied her before they'd been magicked into the painting.

"I'm fine," Summer said. "At least I think I'm fine. I feel kinda—"

"Let's get you on the bus and back to school where the nurse can check you out," Jenny interrupted. "Colin, keep hold of her." And she marched off, leaving Colin to support Summer as they headed to the door.

Summer glanced up at the tall, silent vampire. He was Rochester again, with his broody expression and his dark intensity. Had it just been moments ago that he'd been laughing openly and so full of life and joy and passion? Especially passion.

"I'm sorry," she blurted, although she wasn't sure what it was she was apologizing for.

His gaze met hers as they came to the front door. "Don't apologize. I don't want to know you're sorry about what happened between us."

Summer frowned. Well, she was feeling dazed and confused, but she hadn't meant *that*. "No, I didn't mean—"

Jenny threw open the door, and a bright shaft of sunlight filled the entryway of the otherwise dark gallery. Colin dropped her arm and moved hastily back into the shadows, pulling his mirrored sunglasses from the pocket of his shirt and placing them on his nose so that he completed the metamorphosis from the charismatic man who had been seducing her on the balcony to the tall, silent vampire.

"Colin, I—"

"Come on. You still look terrible." Jenny's hand replaced Colin's on her arm, and the Discipline Nymph pulled her firmly from the gallery.

Over her shoulder, Summer could see Colin turning away as the door closed on the bright afternoon.

The kids were suspiciously quiet on the ride back to school. Jenny kept shooting them slit-eyed looks.

"Detention does not begin to describe what Mr. Purdom is going to be serving for a solid week," she muttered. Then her gaze shifted to Summer. "Do you think you're okay? You're still looking pale."

"I feel fine. I guess." She lowered her voice and tilted her head to Jenny's. "What did it look like to you?"

"Well, I was just coming back into the gallery when the girls were screaming bloody murder, saying you and Colin had disappeared. I was trying to figure out what had happened—by the by, Purdom and his buddy, McArter, were looking guilty as hell, so I knew the little turds had something to do with it—when that damn nosy girl . . . oh, what's her name? You know, blond, chubby, thinks she's way cuter than she is, and her mom's a witch with a *B*?"

"Whitney Hoge."

"Yeah, that's her."

"So Miss Hoge was pointing at the R and J painting with her mouth wide open, unattractively, mind you. I took one look at the picture, saw you two in place of the originals, and hustled the kids out of the room. I briefly chewed out Purdom's ass—will do a more thorough job of that later—and ran back into the gallery at about the time you landed on your butt in the middle of the floor."

"So no one watched us inside the painting?"

"Nope. No one was inside the gallery." Her brows went up. "Was there something to watch?"

"Sorta."

"Oooh! Nastiness?"

"Kinda."

"*Sorta* and *kinda* are not answers. They are especially not answers with details."

"I know," Summer said, and closed her mouth.

A sly expression made Jenny's face look decidedly nymph-like. "If I remember correctly, and I have an excellent memory—it's part of the whole discipline thing—anyway, if I remember correctly, you said that the way your opposite magic gets broken is by you being shocked. Right?"

"Right," Summer said reluctantly.

"Okay, then what shocked you so much the spell was broken?" Summer chewed her lip.

"Look, you can tell me. I'm a professional."

"A professional what?"

"Certified Discipline Nymph, of course. We wear many hats: class-room disciplinarian, workout disciplinarian—yes, I'm hell in the gym—and, most especially, *sexual* disciplinarian. So, give. Details, please."

"It was his kiss," Summer said.

Jenny blinked in surprise. "Colin's kiss shocked you so much that it broke the spell? Jeesh, was it that bad?"

"No," Summer said softly. "It was that good."

Six

"No, Summer, I don't have your purse. Sorry. I'll bet you dropped it when that kid zapped you into the painting," Jenny said.

"Ah, shoot. I must have left it at the gallery."

"Could that have been a Freudian slip? Perhaps something that would give you a reason to see Colin again? You know you could just cancel the date with Kenny-benny, and go back there tonight," Jenny said.

"First, stop calling him that. Second, no, I'm not canceling my date. I'll go get my purse tomorrow or whatever. As I already explained, this thing with Colin was just a fluke. He's not my type, and he doesn't fit into my plan." A vision of Colin on the balcony, arms outstretched, head flung back, laughing his full, infectious laugh flashed through Summer's mind, but she quickly squelched the memory. That wasn't really Colin. The *real* Colin was much more subdued and uncomfortably intense, not lighthearted, fun, and happy. "The whole Rochester thing doesn't work for me in the real world," Summer blurted.

"Huh? Who's Rochester?"

Summer sighed. "You know, Jane Eyre's Rochester."

"Oooh! He's yummy. What about him?"

"That's who Colin reminds me of, and he is definitely not my type."

"You, my friend, might be insane."

"There's nothing insane about wanting a guy who's lighthearted and happy and fun. And blond," she added.

"You forgot 'and easy to control,'" Jenny added, then she hurried on, talking over Summer's sputtering protestations. "Girlfriend, just because a man is intense doesn't mean he's not happy and even fun sometimes, too. Plus, you might want to consider that lighthearted could mean light-*headed*, as in the guy might not have enough sense to be serious," Jenny said. "And what the hell's wrong with tall, *dark*, and handsome?"

"Not believing you about the whole broody-could-equal-happy thing," Summer said stubbornly, completely ignoring the obvious reference to Ken's brains or lack thereof. "And I happen to prefer blonds, light*hearted* blonds in particular."

"Did you prefer them when Colin had you in a lip-lock?"

"Yes. I still preferred them. I was just surprised, that's all."

"Which brings us back to my main point. You were surprised because it was so damn good. If it's so damn good, you might want to consider revisiting the scene of the crime."

"You want me to get back in the painting?"

"No, I want you to get back on the vampire."

"Jenny, I am going to get ready for my date. With Ken. The guy I'm really attracted to. So I'm going now. Bye."

"All right, all right! I hope you have a good time, and I want all the details."

"Good-bye, Jenny."

"Jeesh you're grumpy when you're sexually confused. Bye."

"I'm not sexually confused," Summer told the dead phone. She glanced at the clock. "Shoot! I am late, though." Putting Colin out of her mind, Summer rushed into the kitchen and threw the tofu spaghetti sauce together to simmer.

She also put Colin out of her mind while she showered. The warm water running down her naked body did *not* remind her of the warmth of his hands through the ultrathin material of the chemise.

"His hands aren't even warm. Not really," she muttered as she put on just a hint of makeup.

And she definitely didn't think about him while she picked out the ever-so-cute peach lace bra and panties set and then slid on the breezy, buttercup-colored skirt and the creamy, V-neck pullover that made her look and feel like a fresh spring wildflower, basking in the sunlight, just waiting to be plucked by a tall, dark—

"No!" she told herself, and marched into the kitchen. Summer was stirring the pot of sauce when the jaunty *shave and a haircut, two bits* knock sounded against her front door. She patted her hair and hurried through the living room.

"Hey, Sum! I couldn't figure out what kind of wine to get, so I got, like, three colors. I figured the more the merrier." Ken grinned boyishly and presented the bag that, sure enough, held a bottle of cheap Cabernet, cheap Chardonnay, and cheap white Zinfandel.

Summer returned his smile and motioned for him to come in, squelching her disappointment that there wasn't a bottle of nice Chianti in the mix. It wasn't like Ken could have known they were having spaghetti and that she preferred Italian wine with it. She'd just let him know next time. "How about we open the red? It'll go great with the spaghetti," she said.

"You made spaghetti?" He took off his jacket and dropped it over the back of the couch before she could ask him for it.

"Yeah, I hope you like it."

"Spaghetti's awesome! Hope it's almost ready. I'm starving."

She opened her mouth to tell him all she'd have to do is to boil the pasta, but he didn't give her a chance to speak.

"Hey, want me to come to the kitchen with you and open the wine? A drink would be awesome."

"Sure, come on back," she said and then led him to the back of the cabin and her sister's spacious kitchen.

"Wow, this is a great kitchen," Ken said appreciatively.

"Yeah, Candice loves her gourmet cooking." She sent Ken a shy look as she handed him the corkscrew. "Hope you're not disappointed that she got most of the cooking genes in our family."

"Nah, as long as it's hot and full of meat, I'm cool with it."

"Uh, Ken, didn't you remember that I'm a vegetarian?"

He looked up from opening the wine. "Huh? A what?" Then he

glanced at the simmering pot on the stove. "Oh, you're worried I won't like your spaghetti." Grinning, he grabbed the big stirring spoon and ladled himself a generous taste test. "Yum! You don't have anything to be nervous about. This sauce is awesome!" he said through a full mouth.

"Oh, uh, good." Summer stirred the bubbling pasta. *What he doesn't know won't kill him,* she decided. Or at least she didn't think fairies were allergic to tofu.

While Summer put the finishing touches on their meal, Ken sat on her sister's pristine butcher block island, drank wine, and talked. And talked. And talked.

"Hey, Sum, so you actually made it through college."

"Yeah. It's funny—I didn't think I'd like the academic part of it, but once I got into my lit major I—"

"Man, I don't know how you stayed away from Mysteria for four whole years. No way would I want to do that. The mundane world is no place for fairies."

"Well, I did miss Mysteria, and, well, lots of the people here." She smiled and felt her cheeks get warm when she added, "Especially certain fairies. That's one of the reasons I came back."

"Of course you missed fairies. The world just isn't the same without them!" He jumped off the counter and bowed to her with a big flourish before pouring himself more wine.

He looked so boyish and carefree that she had to smile at him. "Then I should feed you so we can be sure you don't expire. I know how much fairies love food."

"That we do!" He hurried into the dining room where she had two places already set with intimate candles and her sister's beautiful china, leaving her to carry in the spaghetti and the sauce. He had thought to bring the bottle of wine with him, though.

So they ate, and Ken talked. And talked. And talked.

At first Summer just listened to him, commenting now and then (although his exuberant "conversation" really didn't require much participation on her part), and thinking about how cute he looked in the candlelight. His blond hair was thick and a little shaggy, but it looked good on him, and it glistened with a sparkle of fairy magic when the candlelight caught it just right. His blue eyes were big and expressive, his face completely animated. He really was a cute guy. And the direct opposite of dark and broody and intense and sexy . . .

No! Ken was sexy. She'd always thought he was sexy. After all, she'd had a major crush on him since they were teenagers. And she also—

"Sum, did you hear me? I said that you've really grown all up. It's kind of a surprise. Not that you don't look awesome," he hurried to add. "But it's a grown-up awesome. You've changed."

"Oh, uh, thanks. I think." Summer took a sip of wine. "You haven't changed at all," she said.

"Thanks, Sum! You know how fairies are—young for years. Good thing, too, 'cause the party planning and supply business isn't for the old and serious."

"So you're going into your family's business?"

"Of course! I love parties, and I especially love fireworks." He sat up straighter, clearly proud of himself. "You've been gone, so you probably don't know this, but I've been put in charge of the pyrotechnics for *Fairies 4 Fantastic Festivals, Inc.*"

"That's great, Ken. I'm really proud of you. Your dad must be—"

"Yeah, it's awesome! Just wait till you see what we're planning for Beltane this year. It's gonna be super cool with . . ."

Summer smiled and nodded while Ken talked. And talked. And talked. She also studied him. She hadn't been exaggerating. He really hadn't changed in the four years she'd been gone. He was wearing a T-shirt that said this way to the gun show with arrows pointing to his biceps. Summer had to stifle a giggle. His biceps were like the rest of his body, young and cute and lean. They were definitely not "guns," loaded or otherwise. And she definitely wasn't comparing them to Colin's muscular arms.

She mentally shook herself while Ken paused in his monologue to jog into the kitchen to snag the bottle of Chardonnay. He came back in the room, still talking about the plans for the "awesome" fireworks show that would be the climactic event of Mysteria's Beltane festival. She saw that his faded, baggy jeans were fashionably shredded over both knees, and he was wearing bright blue Skechers.

Nope, he definitely hadn't changed since high school.

It was about then that Summer began to wonder if dinner would ever end.

"Dang, Sum, sorry about your headache," Ken said as she handed him his jacket and walked him to the door.

"I guess I'm just tired from teaching all day."

He stopped at the door she'd opened and turned to face her. "It was great to see you again. I'm really glad you're back, Sum." Ken rested an arm over her shoulder nonchalantly as he slouched in the doorway. His blue eyes sparkled with another smile. "Dinner was totally—"

"Awesome?" She provided the word when he hesitated.

"Yeah, it really was. And you're awesome, too." Slowly, Ken bent to her. His kiss was sweet and questioning and very, very gentle. In other words, it was everything Summer believed she'd wanted in a kiss from the man she'd been fantasizing about for years.

She didn't feel a thing in response.

Give him a chance, she chided herself. *This is what you decided you want. He fits in the plan.* Summer leaned into Ken and put her arms around his neck, returning his questioning kiss with an exclamation mark.

She felt the surprise in his body, and then he parted his lips and followed her lead, kissing her deeper, longer. Summer thought he tasted, weirdly, like wine and lemonade. She wondered vaguely why he always reminded her of lemons—not the tart kind, but the supersweet Country Time Lemonade lemons, with lots of sugar. Lots.

Ken was still kissing her, softly and sweetly, while Summer's mind wandered. She was thinking about what she was supposed to teach her sophomores the next day as she absently looked over his shoulder at the dark edge of the forest. She thought she saw something move there, just inside the boundaries of her yard, and wondered what it was. The moon was high and insanely bright and almost about full. Could it be one of the town's many werewolves?

And then it hit her; she was thinking about school, and werewolves, and the moon while Ken was making out with her. That just couldn't be right. When Colin had kissed her, she hadn't been able to think of anything except him. His touch. His mouth. His taste. His kiss. Ken's kisses made her want to compile a shopping list or maybe fold some laundry.

No. This definitely was not going to work. Time to change the plan.

Instantly she pulled away from him. He gave her a sweet, boyish smile. "Sorry, Sum. Did I get carried away?"

"No, Ken, honey." Summer patted his cheek gently. "I got carried away. I think it's best if you and I stay good friends and don't mess that up with trying to be more than that. Do you know what I mean?"

Ken's smile didn't falter. "Sure, whatever. That's fine with me. Hey, do you think I could have some of that awesome spaghetti sauce to take with me so I could snack on it later?"

"Sure Kenny-benny," Summer said and, laughing, made him up a quick to-go package, patted him on his head, and said good night. Before she closed the door, she heard the distinctive giggles of several female fairies who had obviously been waiting to escort their Kenny-benny home. Or wherever.

She was still shaking her head at herself while she cleaned up the dinner dishes. "Jenny was right. I might be insane." Ken was so not the man for her. Actually, if she was being totally honest with herself, Kenny-benny was so not a man yet, and clearly, he might never be. Rinsing the dishes, she laughed out loud. She should be upset at having her fantasy of the Perfect Man blown to pieces and her future plan messed up, or at the very least she should have been disappointed, but she wasn't. She definitely wasn't.

Her hands slid through the warm, soapy water making her think of slick, naked skin sliding against slick, naked skin . . . of heat . . . and passion . . . and a kiss that could seem to stop the world . . .

No! She couldn't want the vampire.

And then, while washing Kenny-benny's very empty plate, she looked up at her reflection in the dark window above the sink. Her face was flushed, and her eyes were big and dark with desire.

"Am I absolutely positive that I can't want the vampire?" she asked herself.

Yes, you're absolutely positive, her reflection seemed to reply.

"But his kiss was—"

Reason one you can't want him, her refection interrupted, *is that he is a carnivore, and that makes you want to throw up a little in the back of your throat.*

"I don't have to eat what he eats. Oh, Goddess, I don't, do I?" Did one share one's blood with a vampire, or did one's vampire eat solo?

Reason two, her reflection continued, *his flesh is cold, dead, hard . . .*

"Well, what's wrong with hard?" she argued with herself. "Plus, he touched me before we were in the painting, and it really wasn't that bad."

Reason three, he's not your type!

"Okay, look," she told herself sternly. "Up until about ten minutes ago, I thought Kenny was my type. Maybe I need to change my type!"

Reason four—her conscience ignored her—*he makes you feel out of control, and you don't like feeling out of control.*

"Well, that's because he was unexpected. He's expected now, so I won't have a control problem. I left my purse at his gallery." Silently she thanked the Goddess for that slip, Freudian or not. "I have to see him one more time."

"Yeah, so, tomorrow I'll just swing by the gallery after school and pick up my purse," she talked around her toothbrush to her reflection in the bathroom mirror. "No big deal. No enormous ulterior motive," she lied. "Just getting my purse, saying a quick hello, then coming home. There won't be any more kissing. None at all. It wouldn't even be appropriate. Really."

Summer crawled into bed, thinking about the difference between Ken's kisses and Colin's kisses. *What a difference . . .*

Why had she ever thought passion and heat were bad things? Okay, she knew the answer to that, even if she didn't like to admit it. She was scared of too much passion, that it would cause her to lose control, and if she lost control, she'd get burned. Summer had learned that lesson well with her stupid out-of-control magic. Maybe it was smart of her to be scared. Was playing with a vampire like playing with fire? Or ice?

Fire, she decided as her body heated the cool sheets. Colin's passion had been exactly like fire. Her hands touched her lips, remembering Colin's caress, and then slid slowly down her body, pausing to cup her breasts. Her nipples ached. Summer squeezed them, gently at first, and then she craved more, and her touch got rougher as she teased her ultrasensitive nipples. She moaned. Almost as if she couldn't stop the impulse, one of her hands moved down between her legs. Summer gasped at the slick heat she found there. She was liquid with desire. She closed her eyes and stroked herself. As her orgasm built, Summer imagined hands on her body and lips against her skin, and when her release came, it was Colin's intensity that she was thinking of and his touch she yearned for.

Seven

Colin had never felt like such an utter fool. What in all the levels of the underworld was he doing walking through the moonlit forest carrying a purse? *I know exactly what I'm doing. I'm being a gentleman,* he thought. *I may be dead, but chivalry isn't. Summer left her purse at the gallery, and I'm returning it.* A woman's purse was a sacred thing. Goddess knows what all was kept in one; Colin would almost rather take a long walk outside at noon than actually look in the damned thing. Thankfully, it was zipped closed, but he still held it gingerly, like it might explode if he handed it too roughly. There wasn't much he could do except return it. The sooner the better. Sure, he could hang on to it and wait for Summer to realize where she left it and then come claim it. But she'd been through a lot. It might take her a day or two, hell, even three, to get around to it. Until then, what about all that important stuff inside the purse? The only thing he could do with a clear conscience, was to return it to her right away. Or at least that's how he rationalized his overwhelming need to see her again—immediately.

The package carefully wrapped in the gallery's chic, black, hand-pressed paper was a damn sight tougher to rationalize away.

Or maybe not. Colin shrugged his broad shoulders. Why hide behind rationalizations? He was courting a woman. That was nothing to feel foolish about, even if it meant carrying her purse through the woods while pink love petals fell from the sky and fairies giggled annoyingly as they played naked hide-and-seek among the trees. Goddess, fairies were irritating!

Colin glared at a silver-winged, pink-haired fairy who had frolicked close to him and given the vampire a coquettish smile that was a clear come-hither invitation.

"Not interested," he said firmly, giving the naked creature a dark look.

Not at all offended, she shrugged her smooth shoulders and scampered off.

Colin scowled after her. Fairies had never interested him. Actually, now that he was thinking about it, it had been a long time since any woman had caught his interest. Were he completely honest with himself, he would admit that no woman had affected him as this one had. And it wasn't simply because she was beautiful and interesting. Summer had brought him sunlight!

Summer . . . Colin felt the urge to laugh aloud. The name fit her perfectly. Sure, he knew she'd said the whole sunlight thing had been because of how her magic worked on spells, but she'd been wrong. He'd smelled sunlight on her, felt it in her touch, since the moment he'd taken her hand.

After living in darkness for so long, there was one thing he definitely recognized, and that was the touch of the sun. He had to have more of that touch. So he was going to woo her until he won her.

"*You're so different here,*" she'd said of him on the balcony, and she'd seemed to like the difference. Colin had been different. He'd been himself again—or at least his prevampire self. Unending night had worn on him until he'd become as dark as his surroundings. Even his ranch had become a black place for him. He'd never been able to go out on his land, work his horses, or care for the cattle in the daylight. He hired hands to do that for him. But for decades he'd found solace in roaming his land at night—in chasing the last rays of sunlight as day reluctantly gave way to night, and then, in turn, giving way to the sun as it inevitably reclaimed the sky. Not so recently. Recently his life had seemed nothing but unending darkness, his beloved ranch not freedom and open space, but just another gilded cage where night continued to imprison him.

Living a life of shadows had worn on him and darkened Colin's personality as well. But that wasn't really *him*. It was what this damn vampire curse had turned him into. Summer could change that; Summer could change everything, and he wanted her to. He wanted to be the Colin who laughed and lived and loved again.

So he'd put in an overseas call to his brother who was still sleeping his way around gay Paris, and Barnabas had told him Summer was staying in her sister, Candice's, cabin, which sat in a clearing at the southern edge of the pine forest surrounding Mysteria. Which is why he had just trekked through said forest with Summer's purse and a gift for her and why he was now standing just inside the edge of trees facing the brightly lit little cabin with its homey, wraparound porch.

Colin drew a deep breath. Sunlight and honey—he could scent her from there. She had to be home. He started forward, telling himself that the jittery feeling in his stomach wasn't nerves, it was just anticipation. Which was only natural; it had been decades since he'd been interested enough to actually consider courting a lady. He just needed to remember that he used to be good with the ladies. Charming— that's how they used to describe him. Out of practice he may be, but he'd dig deep and put back on that old charm, and Summer would see that—

The door to her cabin opened, and Colin came to an abrupt halt when a man's body was silhouetted clearly in the doorway. Summer joined the guy, and Colin's gaze focused on her, blocking out the man and the night and everything but this amazing woman who was, to him, a waking dream.

He loved what she was wearing. The skirt was soft and feminine, and coupled with the creamy yellow of her shirt and the gold of her hair, she looked just like she smelled: like a vision of sunlight and sweetness. He wanted to take her in his arms and mold her softness to his body and inhale her fragrance until he had to fight with himself not to explode.

Then the guy moved, blocking his view of Summer. With a growing sense of horror, Colin watched the jerk nonchalantly drape an arm over her shoulder. Another scent came to him then: one of lemons and laughter and . . . and . . . fairies?

The asshole who was trying to steal his sunshine was a fairy? His jaw tightened, and it felt like someone had slammed a sledgehammer into his gut when the Goddess-be-damned fairy bent and began gently kissing Summer. For a moment Colin stood, rooted into place. Then, with a small sound of disgust, he turned and melted back into the darkness of the forest.

Just beyond vision of the cabin, Colin paced . . . and paced . . . and paced. He had the urge to throw her purse into the branches of the nearest pine and break the carefully wrapped package into a million little pieces, but he managed to control himself, although just barely.

Summer had said she had a boyfriend, but he'd scented her then and hadn't smelled even a hint of another male on her. He had most definitely *not* smelled that fucking blond lemon drop! Yet the fairy had been there—in her home—with his lips all over her.

All right. Fine. He should have expected a woman as attractive as Summer to have other suitors. He would just have to step up his game. He was more than a match for the lemon drop. Fairies, even the wingless male variety, were all fickle sluts. Didn't Summer know that? Maybe she didn't. His brother had said she'd just moved back after being away for most of her four years of college. Maybe she didn't have much experience with adult male fairies. Colin's jaw clenched again, and his hands fisted. He'd crush that damn lemon drop into a little yellow speck if he did anything to hurt her.

By the time he'd paced off his temper and returned to Summer's cabin, the lights had been turned out. The scent of lemon fairy had also been extinguished, which helped to calm him. The damn lemon drop hadn't stayed the night. Colin left his offering on the porch just before dawn.

* * *

The morning was gorgeous. It was weird how getting rid of an old crush had cleared her vision. Her plan had been flawed, but that didn't mean she shouldn't get busy on a new one . . . a new one that might just be tall and dark and handsome. She really shouldn't obsess so much about being in perfect control. And, anyway, she could handle the vampire. She'd certainly handled the fairy. She was definitely interested in Colin, or at least she thought she might be interested in him. Well, she was going to stop by the gallery on her way home from school to get her purse. She'd see then if there really was any attraction going on with the vamp and take it from there.

Summer felt amazingly alive and happy as she slathered black raspberry jam on a piece of toast and munched on it hurrying out of the cabin on her way to school—and almost tripped and fell face-first over the heap of stuff in front of her door.

"What the—" Summer rubbed the knee she'd landed on, looking back at the pile of . . . "My purse," she murmured. Sure enough, her purse was there. Right in front of the door. Sitting next to it was a package wrapped in expensive black tissue paper. There was a simple ivory card taped to it that just said *For Summer* in an old-fashioned-looking cursive script. Intrigued, she fingered the card and then opened the package carefully, so she didn't mess up the beautiful paper.

Summer gasped and oohed in pleasure. It was a copy of the Romeo and Juliet painting, reproduced in oil on canvas and framed in an exquisite gold-painted wood frame.

"Colin," she whispered and felt a thrill of pleasure thrum through her at the sound of his name.

"That might be the most romantic thing I've ever heard," Jenny said over the barely edible lunch they'd bought from the vomitorium, aka the school cafeteria.

"It has to have come from him. Right?"

Jenny rolled her eyes. "Of course it came from him. Hello! He brought back your purse, and—now, correct me if I'm wrong, but I do believe he's the only vampire you got zapped into the R and J painting with."

"Definitely the only one."

"The vamp is wooing you," Jenny said smugly.

"Wooing? Is that even still a word?"

"Yes. And that's what he's doing. So prepare yourself."

"For what?"

Jenny shook her head sadly. "Oh, you poor child. I would imagine that a rough ballpark on your vampire's age is probably at least two hundred."

Summer blinked. "He's not my vampire."

"Yet," Jenny said.

"Two hundred," Summer said as if she hadn't spoken. "As in years old?"

"Yep."

"Wow."

"And as that very tasteful, expensive, and sexy gift shows, men used to know how to do some wooing."

"Wow." Summer considered Jenny's words as she tried to chew her soyburger. "I'm going over there," she said decisively.

"To the gallery?"

"Yes. I'm going to thank him for the painting. And for returning my purse. Plus, uh, I'd, well, like to make sure there's no misunderstanding about anything he might have accidentally seen last night."

"You lost me on that one."

"Ken kissed me good night last night."

"So? You said you decided you're totally not interested in him."

"I did, and it was his kiss that sealed my decision. But first I thought I should give him a chance, which meant I kissed him back."

"Again, so?"

"Well, I was kissing him and looking over his shoulder and thinking about the moon and lesson plans and stuff, and I thought I saw something—or someone—outside by the edge of the woods. Then the next morning I found my purse and the painting on my front porch."

"Wait, back up. Kenny was kissing you, and you were thinking about lesson plans and crap like that?"

Summer nodded.

"That's a damn shame. I don't know what the hell's wrong with fairies these days. Kenny-benny doesn't ring my bell, but damn! He's a *fairy*, a fey being who practically has sex and frolics for a living. He should be able to hold a woman's attention with a kiss."

"Don't be so hard on him. I'd just been kissed by Colin, and the comparison was not good for Kenny."

Jenny rolled her eyes. "Yet you were going on and on about how you weren't interested in the vamp and how he wasn't your type and how he didn't fit into your control-freak plan."

"I'm not a control freak, or at least not all the time. Anyway, Colin might not be exactly what I've thought of as my type, but he's definitely a better kisser than Ken."

"Big surprise there," Jenny said.

"Be nice," Summer said.

Jenny rolled her eyes again.

"Like I said, I'm going to swing by the gallery after school. This time it'll be just me and not a busload of germs and hormones. Maybe sparks will fly again between us, maybe not. But I'm going to give him a shot."

"Good idea. And speaking of germs and hormones, I'm not done deciding on that damn Purdom kid's detention for that bullshit spell he cast yesterday. I'm still looking into the he-had-an-accomplice angle."

"You might want to interrogate McArter; they're buds. Oh, and remember, don't tell him about my magic," Summer added quickly.

"I got it the first hundred times you told me to keep quiet about it. Don't worry; I think it's hilarious that they don't know about your magic. Makes them think their magic is totally screwed up, which serves them right. They shouldn't be using magic at school or at a school event. Brats," Jenny said, eyes flashing.

The bell rang, and both women sighed. "Back into the fray," Jenny said.

"Do you think it's possible to Shakespeare freshmen to death?" Summer asked.

"One can only hope," Jenny said.

Eight

Summer checked her lipstick in her car's rearview mirror and smoothed her hair, feeling insanely thankful that the day was bright and clear and humidity-free, which meant she was having a good hair day. She glanced at the front of *Dark Shadows*. There were no other cars parked close by, and she mentally crossed her fingers that three o'clock was too early for evening visitors and too late for lunchtime visitors, so it would be empty. Well, except for Colin, that is.

She could do this. She could go inside and smile and thank him for returning her purse and leaving such a great gift. She could figure out a way to let him know that Kenny was history. And maybe, just maybe, she could see if that amazing sizzle that sparked between them yesterday was more than just a magical fluke. Then she could consider revising her future plan to include him.

Before she could chicken out, Summer forced herself to get out of the car and enter the dark, cool gallery.

Her first thought was that her hunch had been right; the gallery appeared deserted. Her second thought was that it was very uncomfortable to be standing there all by herself with only the feeling of being watched to keep her company.

The feeling of being watched?

Definitely. She definitely could feel eyes on her: dark, hungry, intense eyes. Almost as if he drew her gaze, she turned her head and looked deeper into the shadows of the gallery. Sure enough, Colin was standing there, his gaze locked on her.

"Good afternoon, Summer," he said.

His voice reminded her of dark chocolate and wine and sex.

"Hi," she blurted, hating how nervous she sounded. Then she

cleared her throat and got control of herself. "I hope you don't mind me just dropping in like this."

His lips tilted up slightly. "It's a gallery. The idea is for people to drop in."

"Then I'm glad I have the right idea," she said, tilting her own lips up.

"And I'm glad you came by. I wanted to see you again. Would you like to come back to my office?"

"Yes, yes, I would."

Summer's smile increased as she followed Colin, getting another excellent view of his tight butt as he led her through the room with the Romeo and Juliet painting, back to an inconspicuous door that opened to an ornate, fussily decorated office.

"This is definitely not you," she said, running her finger down the back of a gilded Louis the Something-or-Other chair. Then her gaze flew up to him as she tried to gauge if she'd just offended him.

He simply shrugged and said, "You're right. This is Barnabas's office, and it's definitely him. He likes pomp and circumstance and lots of gold."

"And what do you like?" Summer heard her voice asking the question that had flitted automatically through her mind. She clamped her mouth shut. She usually had more control than speaking her thoughts aloud, but she found herself being temporarily glad of her lack of control when his gaze went dark and intense as he answered her.

"If you mean what kind of decoration, I like it more masculine, although I don't think a house is really a home without a woman's touch." The vampire blinked, obviously surprised at his response, and then he smiled almost shyly at Summer. "I think that's the first time I've admitted that to myself."

"Admitted that you like a woman's touch?" she asked softly.

His gaze trapped hers. "Admitted that I *need* a woman's touch," he said. "But I shouldn't be surprised. You affect me oddly, Summer."

"Is that a good or a bad thing?" she asked.

"For me, it is a very good thing," he said.

They stared at each other until Summer became uncomfortable

under the heat of his scrutiny. "Thank you for returning my purse to me," she said, trying to temper the electricity that was building between them with words. "And I absolutely love the Romeo and Juliet painting. Thank you for it."

"I'm glad you like it. I wanted to give you something that might make you remember what happened yesterday."

"It's been kinda hard for me to forget," Summer said.

"For me, too." Colin moved closer to her. "Yesterday meant a lot to me. I haven't felt the sun on my skin in many decades. It's not something I want to forget."

"You know I didn't do it on purpose. I can't bring you the sun again." Summer was finding it hard to think rationally with him so close, but her mind was working enough that she wanted to make it perfectly clear to him that she couldn't just zap them back into the picture; she couldn't make the sun shine for him.

Colin touched the side of her face. "You're wrong about that."

Summer shivered. His touch was cool, but her skin beneath his fingers came alive with heat.

You are my sunshine.

Summer jumped when his voice sounded inside her head.

"You heard that, didn't you?" he said.

"Yes," she whispered. "I also heard you call to me from across the room yesterday."

That dark intensity was back in his eyes, and he spoke with such emotion, such passion, that Summer's heartbeat quickened, and she felt her breathing deepen.

"You don't know me, and I don't know you, but there is something between us that I've not experienced until I touched you yesterday. You say you can't bring me sunshine again, yet to me your skin, your breath, your hair, even the summer-sky color of your eyes—all of you is light and shining to me. It is as if, somehow, magically, you are literally *my* summer, *my* sunlight."

"I—I don't know how that could be. I'm just me." Summer couldn't help leaning her cheek into his hand. His scent and touch were intoxicating, and she wanted nothing more at that instant than to get closer to him.

"I don't know how it could be either, but you are an unexpected gift that I plan to cherish. If you'll let me. Will you give me a chance, Summer?" Colin lifted her chin. "I realize I'm not what you're used to—not the kind of man you would consider a *boyfriend*." He ground the word out. "And yesterday you said you were already seeing someone."

"I'm not," she said.

"Not?"

"Not seeing anyone." She stared up into his dark eyes, utterly mesmerized by his closeness.

"But last night . . ."

"Was nothing. There's nothing between us. Ken isn't my boyfriend."

"I saw—" he began.

"You saw him kissing me. It was just, well, basically a test. I wanted to see if he could make me feel what you made me feel."

"And did he?"

"No," Summer said, staring into the vampire's eyes. "Not even maybe. That's one of the reasons I'm here. I had to see if it was still there," she said softly.

"It?"

"The sizzle between us."

Colin smiled. "It's still there. Let me taste you, sunshine, and I'll prove it to you."

"Yes," she whispered, already leaning into him.

Colin didn't claim her mouth right away. Instead, he drank in her scent and touch, mingling breath with breath. "I want you more than you can know." He spoke the words against her skin. "When I touch you I'm alive again. I can feel the sunlight on my face." He nuzzled her neck and then buried his hand in her thick blond hair and breathed in the scent of sunlight and honey that clung to her.

"Kiss me, Colin," she murmured.

With a strangled sound, his mouth finally met hers, easily erasing any lingering memory of Ken's soft, sweet, boring kisses. His skin didn't have the heat it had the day before, but it didn't matter. It was still *him*, and Summer craved his taste and touch like she'd never wanted anyone or anything before in her life.

When they finally broke apart, it was only to stare dazedly at each other. "What is it between us?" Summer said. "It's crazy. It's like you're my human version of catnip."

His smile took away what was left of her breath. "I'm your catnip; you're my sunshine. I think we make an excellent pair."

"But I don't even know you. You're practically a stranger."

Colin took her hand, threading his cool fingers through her warm ones. "Can you say we're strangers when we're touching?"

Summer looked down at their linked hands. His was so pale and large and strong, and hers was tan from working in her sister's flower beds. They seemed direct opposites. He was the opposite of everything she'd believed she wanted for so many years. Yet he was right; when they touched, something was there, and it was something that hadn't been there with any man before him.

"Colin, we have to slow down. I have to think about—"

The buzzer that signaled the opening of the front door of the gallery made both of them jump. Colin threw a dark look over his shoulder. "I'll get rid of them and close the gallery; then we can talk." Like an amazing old-time gentleman, he kissed her hand before he started out of the room, but he stopped in the doorway, glancing back at her. "You were right, Summer. You don't really know me, and I don't know you. But what I do know is there is something special between us. I've walked this earth longer than you—a couple hundred and some odd years longer." She gaped at him. Was everyone a zillion years older than her? Colin's smile was sad and his eyes haunted with loneliness as he continued. "I can promise you that in all the long years of my life I haven't ever felt what I do when I so much as breathe in the scent of your skin. If you feel even a fraction of what I feel, how can you not give us a chance?"

"What if this is all just because of my messed-up magic?" she asked.

"What if it isn't?" Colin said.

Then he turned and left the room.

Summer's knees felt wobbly, and she dropped down into the closest gilded chair. What was going on with them? One thing was sure;

the attraction between them was still there, in spades! She wiped a shaky hand over her brow. He was right. She'd never felt anything like what Colin made her feel just with the touch of his hand on her face, let alone his lips against hers. What would happen if their naked bodies pressed together? A thrill of anticipation sang through her. Could she handle such passion, and if she couldn't, what happened then? Was it worth taking a chance on? What was it the ancient Greek playwright, Euripides, said about too much passion . . . something about a lion loose in a cattle pen?

Plus, she really didn't want to be in love with a vampire. Besides the whole vegetarian/carnivore issue there was the day/night issue. She loved daylight and sunshine and all that went with it. Wouldn't she have to give that up to be with Colin?

Her head was starting to ache when the voices that had been drifting to her from the outer gallery began to register.

"Yeah, man, we didn't mean for nothin' bad to happen," said one male voice.

"For real. We were gonna come by today and say sorry, even if Ms. Sullivan hadn't made us," added another.

Summer snorted a little laugh. That had to be Purdom and one of his partners in crime. Jenny had been right. There was more power behind that spell than one kid could have conjured.

"That Ms. Sullivan is one mean woman," said the first voice.

Summer smiled. Yep, Jenny had definitely known it.

"Yeah, but she's so fiiine," said the second, she now recognized as her student and Purdom's bud, Blake McArter.

She heard Colin's deep voice answering them but couldn't quite make out what he was saying. She attempted to sit still for a minute more, then curiosity killed discretion, and she walked quietly to the doorway of the office.

"We thought we'd make up a little thang for ya," said Purdom.

"Like, to make up for what we did," said McArter. "Okay with you if we bust out with it?"

"Sounds fine with me," Colin said.

This time she could hear Colin's voice more clearly, and the good humor in his tone made her smile. Her feet seemed to move of their own accord as she continued walking soundlessly down the hall. After all, she'd been a victim of Purdom's magical stunt. He should apologize to her, too. Well, again, that is. Naturally, Jenny had made him grovel appropriately at school earlier that day. But still, more groveling never hurt, plus the other kid was here, too, this time. She crept slowly into the gallery until she came to the room that held the Romeo and Juliet painting, aka the scene of the crime. The two boys were standing in front of the painting with their backs to her. Colin was facing them, so he could have spotted her, but his attention was focused, with an amused lift of one of his dark brows, on the boys as they started making the ridiculous rap noises that always reminded Summer of a mixture of farts and messed-up engine sounds. As McArter did the sound effects, Purdon rapped their song.

> We come to apologize 'bout the other day.
> See, we didn't know you and Miss S. would go away.
> We was just tryin' to get in some play.
> We sorry you had ta dress all gay.
> And then Miss S. and you almost went all the way.

Those brats! They did know Colin and I had been in the painting! At that point there was a "musical" interlude in the rap, and both boys mouth farted and popped around looking silly and semicharming at the same time. Summer had just decided she'd been entertained enough and had started forward again when her eyes went to Colin, and she froze in place. He was watching the boys and laughing with the youthful joy of a man filled with light and promise. And Summer once again saw the happy, open man who had shared the painting, and his passion, with her.

He was completely and utterly captivating.

It was then that the question of whether she should risk getting entangled in a life of passion and darkness became moot. She *was* entangled with him already. Somehow within this dark, brooding vampire there lay the man she'd fantasized about and longed for all these years. It wasn't a question of fitting him into her future. Colin was her future.

Summer must have made an involuntary sound, because Colin's gaze instantly went from the boys to her. The smile didn't leave his face; on the contrary, when their eyes met, his joy seemed to blaze from him to her.

"So we be here to make yestaday okay," rapped Purdom.

"Yea, we got to give you somethin' 'cause Sullivan says we got to pay," intoned McArter.

"And she's scary—even though I'd like to tap that play."

The fart noises came to a crescendo, then Purdom went into the closing lines of the rap.

"We thought 'bout what we could do that would stay.

And come up with a magic spell to melt our dissin' ya away."

Magic spell? Those words broke through the smoldering look she was sharing with Colin at the same time she noticed that the little shivers going up and down her spine weren't just because she was hot for the vampire. *The rap was really a spell the boys were casting!* Then four things happened simultaneously.

Summer opened her mouth to scream at the kids to stop.

Colin moved toward her with an inhuman speed that blurred his body.

Purdom finished the rap/spell with the line, "Dude, we give you a future bright as the sun's ray!"

And as the vampire's body slammed into Summer, she realized the magic catastrophe was unavoidable, so she closed her eyes and braced herself, sending out one concentrated desire: *This will not mess up Colin and me.* Then the area around her exploded with light.

Nine

When Summer opened her eyes, she was in a strange bed in a room she didn't recognize. It was nice—she noticed that right away. Actually, it was freakishly like her dream room: huge, antique iron bed piled with rich linens in soft blues and yellows. The furniture was simply carved oak, well made and expensive but not fussy. The floor was glossy pine wood, dotted here and there with thick butter-colored area rugs. The walls told her she was in a log cabin—a damn big one at that. There was a fireplace along one wall. The others held several incredible original watercolor paintings of landscapes that all had one thing in common: they were bright and beautiful and painted in the full flush of summer days.

Then her eyes caught something on top of the long, low dresser. Was that her jewelry box? She climbed down from the mountain of a bed and realized two things: One, she was wearing her favorite style of pajamas: men's boxer shorts and a little matching tank top. Two, it was, indeed, her jewelry box sitting on top of the dresser. Actually, as she looked around the room more carefully, she saw that the jewelry box was just one of several items that belonged to her. Over the ornate beveled mirror hung one of her favorite scarves. The Kresley Cole book she'd been reading was on the nightstand beside the bed, as was her favorite honeydew-scented candle. Feeling surreal and very *Twilight Zone*–ish she opened the top drawer of the nearest dresser and, sure enough, inside was a neat row of her bras and panties.

"What the hell is going on?" She cried, and then, wondering how she could have been stupid enough to forget, memory flashed back to her, and she recalled the two boys and their rap that had become a spell and the terrible light that exploded just as Colin had grabbed her.

Light? Colin?

Light! Colin! The two definitely didn't mix. Where was she, and where was Colin? Summer hurried to the window and peeked out. The sun was setting into the mountains, painting the lovely landscape around the cabin in hues of evening. She was definitely in a cabin, out in the woods. But it wasn't her sister's cabin. She tried to calm her freaked-out mind. *Think—I have to think! The kids' spell finished with something about Colin having a bright future. Goddess! Did that mean he was trapped in the dark somewhere? And if so, why was she here in this pretty cabin?* It didn't make one bit of sense.

"Okay. Okay. You're a college graduate. You can figure this out," she told herself. "This room looks like it could belong to you, so . . ." With sudden inspiration, Summer went back to the bedside table and, sure enough, plugged into the charger, just as it was in the bedroom in her sister's cabin, was Summer's cell phone. She grabbed it and dialed the first number that came to mind.

"Summer! Where are you? Are you okay?" Jenny's voice was uncharacteristically frantic.

"I'm fine, I think, and I don't know where the hell I am. Where's Colin? Is he okay?"

"Other than having lost his damn mind worrying about you, your vamp's fine. And what do you mean you don't know where you are?"

"What do you mean he's lost his mind?" Summer and Jenny spoke their questions together.

"I can't tell—" Summer began.

"He's freaked completely—" Jenny said.

Both women paused. "You start," Jenny said. "Why don't you know where you are?"

"'Cause I've never been here before. I'm at a gorgeous cabin and, weirdly enough, it's not just decorated exactly how I would have decorated it, but a bunch of my stuff's here. Now tell me what's up with Colin."

There was some unintelligible noise in the background and then Jenny said, "I'll do better than that. I'll let Colin tell you himself."

Summer could hear her passing off the phone, and then Colin's deep voice was in her ear. "Summer? Are you hurt? Where are you?"

"Colin! Are you okay? What happened?"

"I'm fine; don't worry about me. Are you okay?" he said.

"Other than not understanding what happened, I'm fine. Especially now that I know you're okay."

"I am okay, sunshine." She could hear the smile in his voice. "Now that I'm not scared into my second death. Don't ever disappear like that on me again."

"Disappear? Is that what happened? All I remember is a bright light. Are you sure you're okay? I know the whole light thing isn't good for you."

"I didn't see a light. The kid finished the spell just as I grabbed you, and then an instant later my arms were empty, and you were nowhere." His voice lowered. "I don't like my arms being empty of you."

His words made warm, fluttering things happen in the pit of her stomach. "Yeah, I know," she said.

"Where are you? The sun's setting. I'll come to you."

"I wish you could. I don't have any idea where I am. I woke up in this beautiful iron bed in an amazing room that, weirdly, has a bunch of my stuff in it." Summer walked to the bedroom door while she kept talking. "I peeked out the window, and I'm somewhere in the mountains—great view, by the by—in a big cabin. You should see this place. Your brother would definitely appreciate the quality of the watercolors on the walls, and they're all of summer landscapes. I haven't gone out into the rest of the house yet, though."

"Does the bedroom have a large, wood burning fireplace in it?"

Summer nodded. "Yeah, it does."

"Go out into the rest of the cabin, and tell me what you see." His voice had a strangely excited tone to it.

"What's going on, Colin?"

"I have a hunch. Just leave the bedroom, and I'll know if I'm right."

She took a deep breath and opened the door. "Okay, this is definitely my dream home," Summer said.

"Describe it to me, Sunshine," Colin said.

"I'm on a landing looking down at an incredible living room. The furniture is all leather, but it's not too testosteroney because it's mixed with antique end tables and thick, furry rugs. Oh, Goddess! I hope it's fake fur."

Colin's deep laugh was in her ear. "I'll bet it is now."

"Now? What do you mean?"

"First, go down the stairs and into the living room and describe to me the painting over the fireplace."

"Okay, it's kinda freaking me out that you know this place."

"Don't be scared, Sunshine. Trust me. All will be well."

She loved the tone of happy excitement that filled his voice and hurried down the stairs. Sure enough, there was a huge painting over the fireplace, and when Summer realized what it was, she laughed aloud. "It's the Romeo and Juliet! Goddess, it looks like it's the original."

"It is, sweet Sunshine. Stay right where you are; I will come to you."

"You know where I am?"

"I do, indeed. You're home, Summer."

"You're home, Summer" was all that Colin would say before he hung up. What did that mean? But she didn't have time to worry and wonder, because all of a sudden a dark mist began to spill into the room. Wordlessly, Summer watched it surround her and thicken and then change, elongate, and solidify until Colin was standing in front of her.

He looked around them, and his handsome face blazed with a triumphant smile. "I knew it! Makes me really glad I didn't eviscerate those boys."

"Colin, would you please explain to me what's happened?"

"*We've* happened," he said, still smiling. "This"—he swept his arm around them in a smooth motion—"is my home. Only it's been changed. A woman's touch has been added. *You've* been added to my home, Summer."

Summer stared around her in amazement. "This is your home?"

"It is."

"How did this happen?"

"The boy said that he was giving me a bright future. His spell, mixed with your magic, has gifted me with you." Colin closed the space between them and took her in his arms, inhaling her scent and touch. "Let me show you how much we belong together."

"Colin." She spoke his name like a prayer and reached up to touch his face. The instant her hand met his cheek, the vampire gasped and jerked as if she'd zapped him with a jolt of electricity. Summer pulled back, afraid she'd hurt him, but what was reflected in his dark eyes wasn't pain, but wonder.

"Touch me again, Summer."

Before she could respond, Colin took her hand and pressed it back against his cheek, and this time Summer saw the glow of light that came from her hand and felt what was happening beneath her palm. The vampire's cool flesh shivered and then flushed and warmed.

"What's happened?" she whispered.

"You're bringing light to me again, my darling. Only this time your magic is calling alive my flesh." He turned his face so that his lips pressed against the palm of her hand. She felt a tingle of heat pass through her hand, and then his lips were on hers. They were warm and insistent and very much alive. Speaking only her name, Colin lifted her into his arms and strode from the living room up the stairs, kicking open the bedroom door and gently placing her on the bed.

When he bent to kiss her again, she pressed him gently away from her. "Wait, I have to see . . . I have to touch you and know . . ." she murmured.

Slowly, carefully, she unbuttoned his shirt, pulling it apart so his muscular chest was bared to her. Then she lifted her hands and, pressing her palms against his skin, began at his shoulders, sliding her hands down his chest in a slow, thorough caress that spread light down his body. Against her glowing skin his flesh warmed, and she watched in awe as his carved marble skin and muscles shivered and then, as long as she touched him, flushed with health and life. When her hand reached the place over his heart, Colin moaned—a sound part pain, part pleasure—and he pressed his hand over hers, stilling her caress.

"Ah, Goddess!" Colin said. "My heart beats again!"

"I can feel it. Oh, Colin! I can feel it beating."

"Don't stop touching me, Summer. Don't ever stop touching me."

Light-headed with the swirling emotions of passion and awe and desire, Summer looked into Colin's dark eyes and saw love and life and her future there. And then she closed her eyes and bowed her head, breathing deeply while she tried to calm her turbulent emotions. *I will not lose control and cause this to end! I will not!*

Ten

"Summer, what is it?" Colin's voice was filled with worry.

She opened her eyes and met his gaze. "I'll never stop touching you, Colin. I promise, but you have to let me be with you on my own terms."

His expression only became more confused, and mixed with that confusion Summer saw hurt and withdrawal. "I know that my being a vampire is hard for you. I understand you might not want to bind yourself to someone like me."

"No, no I didn't mean that," she explained quickly. "It has to do with my magic. I have to maintain control of my emotions, because if they surge too much and I lose control, the spell will be broken and the messed-up magic, along with all of this, will end."

"Sunshine, *this* isn't as simple as a spell or magic. What's happening between us is real."

"I hope so," she said. And then she drew her hand down his arm again, watching as the glow under her palm warmed his cool flesh. "But *this* is definitely magic, and I don't want this to end for you."

"As long as I have you, I'll have sunlight—magic or no."

"You have me, Colin," she said, but still Summer controlled her breathing and kept a firm hold on her emotions as, never taking her hands from his skin, she undressed him. First she pushed off his shirt, skimming her hands down his arms until she threaded her fingers through his, staring into his eyes as her touch brought his skin alive.

"Summer," he moaned her name. "I never imagined I could feel like this again."

"How do you feel, Colin?" Summer asked breathlessly as her mouth moved down his naked chest.

"Like a man, Sunshine. You make me feel like a man again."

His words sent a thrill through her body. Summer caressed Colin's waist, reveling in her ability to give him such pleasure. She unzipped his jeans, and he stepped out of them. She stared at his naked body and imaged that she knew what Pygmalion felt as his sculpture of Galatea came to life.

Calm and slow, Summer reminded herself as she pulled him down beside her on the bed. *Focus on giving him pleasure.* When his eager hands reached for her, she allowed Colin to pull her into his arms. Her mouth met his as she pressed her body against his nakedness. Separated by only the thin cotton of her boxers and tank, it was an exquisite sensation to feel her heat warming him, her flesh bringing him alive.

His hardness pressed low and insistent against the softness of her stomach, and while their tongues met her hips shifted, bringing him fully against her core. He moaned against her mouth as she thrust against him, sliding him the length of her wetness.

When her head started to spin, she broke the kiss. Concentrating on controlling her breathing and trying to find calmness within her again, she rolled over on top of Colin and held his wrists, stilling his roving hands, which had been kneading her aching breasts. "Let *me* touch *you*," she said, regaining her breath. When he started to protest, she stilled his words with a kiss, then whispered against his mouth, "I don't want the magic to go away, Colin. Help me keep the magic."

"Sunshine, I've been trying to tell you that you *are* the magic." His voice was deep and rich with desire.

"Humor me," Summer said with a smile and then began to move down his body, kissing and caressing. When she reached his cock, she took him in both of her hands, loving the textures of him, the hardness sheathed in such soft skin. Still stroking him, she glanced up and met his gaze. "You're wrong, Colin. It's you who's magic." And then she bent and let her tongue flick out around the engorged head of his cock. He moaned her name as she licked the length of his shaft, discovering how exciting it was to be able to bring him such intense pleasure so easily.

"Do you want me to take you in my mouth?" she asked huskily.

"Oh, Goddess, yes!" he gasped.

Summer swallowed him. He was too large for her to take all of him in her mouth, but she stroked his shaft with her hand, squeezing while she tasted him, loving how his cock heated and pulsed beneath her touch. She cupped his heavy testicles, and another moan was torn from his throat as his hips lifted to give her better access to him.

"Your body is so beautiful," she murmured against his skin, teasing the head of his cock with her tongue. "I never knew a man's body could be so beautiful."

Then she swallowed him again. "Summer!" Colin gasped her name, his voice rough with barely controlled lust. "I can't stand much more. If you don't stop, I'm going to come in your mouth."

Summer loved that *she* was evoking this response in him. She felt gorgeous and sexy and very much in control. "Then give in to it," she purred, imagining for the first time in her life that she was the Marilyn Monroe type, the kind of woman men dreamed about. "Give in to me." She laved his engorged head with her tongue while she ran her hands down his thighs, feeling his muscles tremble and warm under her hands.

Summer heard a ripping sound as his hands gripped the thick comforter while he struggled to maintain control, and then he moved with a vampire's preternatural swiftness, and suddenly his hands were lifting her, and she was on her back looking up at him.

"Colin, wait, I need to do this my way!"

"Sunshine, lovemaking is something best done together, rather than controlled by one. And I have to have my turn." She started to protest again, but the dark intensity of his gaze caught her. "Trust me, Summer. Trust that I'm telling you the truth when I say that what's happening between us is more than an accident of magic."

"I trust you," she said softly, *but I'm still going to stay in control,* she added silently to herself.

His smile had a sexy, feral glint as, with one flick of his powerful hands, he ripped the cotton tank off her. Colin cupped her breasts, running his thumb lightly over her already sensitized nipples. She gasped and bit her bottom lip.

"Since I saw these beautiful nipples, aroused and pressing against that sweet teacher's blouse you had on yesterday, I've thought about doing this over and over again. His head dipped down, and he took her nipple into his mouth, sucking and licking gently. She threaded her fingers through his thick, dark hair and pressed him more firmly against her. "Harder," she whispered, and then all her breath left her body in a rush as he went from gentle to forceful, pulling on the nipple with his teeth while he lifted his hard thigh between her legs so that her hips could lift and grind against him.

Control . . . control . . . she reminded herself frantically. Summer breathed deeply, letting the pleasure wash in waves over her but not allowing herself to drown in it.

Colin shifted his attention to her other breast, and she closed her eyes, feeling the desire that was building inside of her but keeping it banked just enough that it didn't engulf her.

Then his mouth followed the edge of her rib cage down to the soft indentation of her waist. He hooked his fingers in her shorts and quickly skimmed them down her body, leaving her naked before him. She felt a moment of embarrassment, but it passed when she saw the expression on his face and heard his husky, "Sunshine, you're even more exquisite than I dreamed you would be." He kissed her stomach reverently, gently, before letting his hands glide down her body to cup her buttocks. He positioned himself between her legs as he lifted her to his mouth.

Summer stopped breathing completely when his tongue parted her folds and dipped within.

"You taste just like you smell: like sunlight and honey," he murmured against her intimately.

When his tongue found her clit, her hips buckled against him. She squeezed her eyes closed, fighting against the cascade of pleasure. She wanted too badly to let loose, to allow him to make her come against his mouth. But what would happen then? How could she bear it if she was suddenly transported, midorgasm, back to her cabin—alone?

"Colin, come here to me," she said, reaching to pull him up to her. When he only intensified his caresses, she added, "I have to feel you inside me."

That got through to him, and he raised himself over her. She took him in her hand again, lifting her hips so that she could position the throbbing head of his cock against her wet opening. Summer was already getting her breathing back under control, and she'd keep that control while he spent himself inside her—at least she hoped she could. That Colin could turn her on was abundantly apparent, but being turned on and actually orgasming were two very different things.

This would be for Colin. She'd bring him light and life and love. She'd let him bring her to completion another time, when she was sure her emotions wouldn't cause their whole world to disappear. So her plan was to take him inside her and just maintain her sanity this once. She'd worry about next time the next time. Everything would work out in the future when she—

"Look at me, Summer."

His voice brought her attention back to the present. She looked up into his expressive, dark eyes.

"I want to look into your eyes while I love you, while I make you mine," he said. He thrust into her with one powerful plunge, filling her completely.

Summer gasped as the pleasure spiked through her. Her hips lifted to meet his as her legs wrapped around him. Colin braced himself on one arm, raising up so that he could continue to look into her eyes. The vampire impaled her. They moved together, slick and hot.

Summer felt her body gathering itself, and she fought against it, even though the pleasure was so intense that it bordered on pain. But she maintained control—she did it. Until Colin reached between them and began rubbing his thumb rhythmically against her swollen, slick clit.

"Colin!" she gasped. "Oh, Goddess, I can't—"

"Shhh," he whispered. "What we have is beyond magic. If you

trust me, give yourself completely to me. I can prove it to you. Will you trust me?"

"Yes," she said without hesitation. "I trust you, Colin."

"Then I make you mine, truly and completely." He bent his head to her neck. Summer felt his lips, his tongue, and finally his teeth. At first they just grazed her, then she felt him gather himself, and Colin bit her, puncturing through the soft skin above her pulsing vein.

The pleasure she felt at his claiming was as sharp as the bite, and she couldn't fight against her desire any longer. Summer felt the wave begin within her and knew it would utterly, completely overwhelm her. She grasped Colin's shoulders and, for once in her life, completely gave up control to a man, body and soul. As her body shuddered in orgasm, and he joined her in release, she felt the familiar tingle of her magic becoming active. This time instead of running, or bracing herself against it, or fighting it, Summer released her magic, instead choosing to hold on to Colin and his promise that there was more between them than smoke and mirrors.

The flash of light against her closed lids had Summer opening her eyes in surprise. Colin jerked back from her neck as if her blood suddenly burned. And then *he* was burning as the light that had been focused in Summer's hands surged from her into him.

"Colin!" Summer cried, trying to pull away from him, trying to stop the transfer of light.

"Trust me, sunshine," Colin ground the words out between teeth clenched in pain. "I accept any price I have to pay to be with you, and it will not separate us." At his words the light intensified until it bowed his body. The vampire screamed, and then he was knocked from the bed. He landed on the floor, limp and unconscious.

Summer was sobbing when she rushed to him, touching his face, calling his name, praying to the Goddess to please let him wake up . . . please, she'd do anything . . . just please . . . please . . .

Colin drew a deep breath and then exhaled, coughing painfully. Summer helped him sit up. "Colin! Goddess, are you okay?"

"I'm fine," his voice was raw, as if he hadn't spoken in centuries. "I'm fine," he repeated, after clearing his throat. He started to take her in his arms but suddenly froze. "Blessed Goddess!" He sounded utterly shocked.

"What is it? Maybe I should call someone. A vampire doctor?"

Then Colin completely surprised Summer by jumping to his feet, throwing back his head, and laughing with uninhibited joy.

Still on the floor, Summer looked up at him, utterly confused. "Colin?" Was he hysterical? Is this how vampires acted when they'd been mortally wounded?

"I don't need a vampire doctor, Summer, my sunshine, my dream, my love. Somehow, someway, you and your magic have made me human again!"

She stared at him, this time really seeing him. He was still a tall, handsome man, but the marble cast of his skin was gone. It had been replaced by the healthy flush of a living, breathing man.

And she wasn't touching him at all. He was truly alive.

"It'll go away," she whispered. "It won't last."

"I think you're wrong, Sunshine," he said, pulling her to her feet. "Have you ever given up trying to control your magic before tonight?"

"No," she said slowly. "I've always fought it or run from it. And it's not just my magic I gave up control of tonight, Colin. It's my life. When I trusted you, I had to give up being in total control of myself."

"I think there was something about your decision to trust me that drastically affected your magic." Colin cupped her face. "All these years you've believed your magic was flawed, messed up. I don't think it was. I think it was pure light—the pure energy of sunshine—and when you gave me your complete trust, when you relinquished control, you also gave your magic to me."

"It should have killed you. You're a vampire; you can't stand the light."

"Perhaps, but I've never loved the light until I loved you. I desired it, coveted it, yearned for it, but never really loved it until you."

"So my light didn't kill you."

"No, Sunshine. Your light burned away the darkness of my past and saved me."

"So now you think we can make love and I can orgasm without worrying about us being zapped apart."

"Over and over again, Sunshine," he said, smiling.

"Sounds like a perfect happily ever after to me."

"Me, too, Sunshine. Me, too."

Colin took her back to bed and, as the Certified Discipline Nymph Jenny would say, ravished her thoroughly for many passion-filled, out-of-control years.